KNIGHT TO KING 6

A Cold War Thriller # 1

GREGORY M. ACUÑA

Copyright © 2019 by Gregory M. Acuña

All rights reserved.

No part of this book may be reproduced in any form or by any electronic or mechanical means, including information storage and retrieval systems, without written permission from the author, except for the use of brief quotations in a book review.

Cover Design by: Jessica Bell

jessicabelldesign.com

❁ Created with Vellum

FREE BOOK

For A Limited Time

*As a reader of my book, Knight To King 6 you can get a FREE copy
of my second book, The Balkan Network.
Go to: http://gmacuna.com*

Author's Introduction

I can still remember those dates as if they were yesterday. The first was February 20, 1962, Anaheim, California. Despite several months of delays, the United States was finally ready to launch its first, manned, orbital space flight. Astronaut John Glenn boarded the Friendship 7, Mercury space capsule at 0747 Pacific Time.

I had just woken up to get ready for school but still had time to watch an episode of morning cartoons. However, there were no cartoons or children's shows being broadcast over any local networks on this day. To my surprise, my mother and older brother were already awake and had been watching the countdown live on television for the past two hours. I remember asking my mom why she was up so early. She told me she wanted to see the liftoff of the first US astronaut to orbit the Earth.

I plopped down on the floor in front of that old black-and-white television set, still in my pajamas, just in time to hear Scott Carpenter utter those famous words, "God-speed, John Glenn," and then the Atlas rocket took off from the launchpad at Cape Canaveral, Florida.

From that point on, John Glenn was a national hero for successfully orbiting the Earth, catching up with the Russians. Every boy over the age of five wanted to be an astronaut or spaceman, as we called them back then. I, too, was no exception. I even made a space helmet from an old Kentucky Fried Chicken bucket and spray painted it silver.

The second date was July 21, 1969, on a hot, summer afternoon in San Diego, California. This time, I sat in front of a color TV set and watched the grainy, black-and-white image of Astronaut Neil Armstrong take the first steps on the moon.

This was the beginning of my fascination with aviation,

aeronautics, and space travel, which ultimately led to me becoming a U.S. Air Force pilot and eventually an airline pilot.

However, the lingering and persistent question I kept asking myself over and over again during those early years of the US space program was: ***How did all this begin?***

The Beginning Of The Space Program

Prologue
BERLIN, GERMANY JANUARY 1939

She hung naked from a chain apparatus tethered from the ceiling. Her arms and legs were held apart by leather straps; her stomach and breasts pointed down toward the floor. She drifted in and out of consciousness after each lashing on her bare back and buttocks. Blood, sweat, and vomit dripped from her face. Despite the cold, dark, and damp conditions of the women's jail at Alexanderplatz, sweat radiated from every pore of her body.

The pain was excruciating, but the worst was yet to come. The twenty-nine-year-old SIS operative feared what was to happen next. For the previous hour, she had been severely beaten by a female Gestapo interrogator. The Gestapo woman used a rough, twelve-inch wooden stick and lashed out across the woman's back and rear.

The Gestapo woman grabbed her prisoner from her wet hair and shouted in German, "Tell me your name. We know it is not Hilda Bradt!"

The young woman could only mumble and responded in German, "I've told you my name . . . It's Hilda Bradt.

I'm not who you say I am . . . there must be some terrible, terrible mistake."

The jailer had no more patience. She grabbed the stick then raised a set of ropes that controlled the torture apparatus which pulled and spread the woman's legs apart even further. The Gestapo woman was about to lash out again when the heavy wooden door to the cell swung open unexpectedly. A young, uniformed SS officer entered. He was medium height and slender in build. His dark hair was neatly cropped, and he held a hat under his left armpit. In his other hand he held a white hospital gown. SS Obersturmführer Otto Krupke commanded, "That will be all, Stürmmann. You can return to your post upstairs."

"But I have her almost broken. All I need is another five minutes."

Krupke simply pointed his finger at the jailer.

"She's lying. She's a British spy."

With that, the female torturer dropped the wooden stick to the floor and exited the cell.

When the Stürmmann left the cell, Krupke encircled his prisoner. Each step of his heavy leather jackboots was deliberately placed down on the wet pavement, dramatizing what was to come. The woman continued to gasp and weep. She had withstood the torture for several hours, over seventy-two to be exact. She had done as she was trained back at Broadway Street. She had held out for as long as possible to enable her colleagues to escape or change safe houses and identities. It was time. She would accept her fate.

Surprisingly, Krupke didn't do anything. He continued encircling the twenty-nine-year-old woman. Had the woman been able to see him, she would have seen a man gazing upon her in lust, but despite her broken appearance, she was still an attractive, young woman with a lean, muscular figure, firm breasts, bright, blue eyes, and light, golden blond-hair.

Krupke finally broke his silence and spoke in German as he released the prisoner from the torture mechanism. She dropped to her hands and knees. "You have performed admirably, Fräulein. It is time to end this charade."

The woman crouched into a fetal position, trying to cover herself as Krupke continued to speak in German. "We had you under surveillance the whole time. We saw you coming and going from the meeting. The persons you met were British agents working for the Secret Service. Those men have been caught and will be executed for the crime of espionage. If you cooperate, I can spare your life."

She continued to weep and did not respond, clutching her naked body. Krupke continued his monologue. "I have the authority to offer you an accord. Just tell me your real name for starters. We know it's not Hilda Bradt, and this all ends!"

Krupke stopped in front of the woman, bent lower to her face, and dropped the hospital gown on the floor. He simply said four words, quietly in English, "Put the gown on."

The woman was about to reach for the garment, but something in the back of her mind told her to *stop*, *think*, and then respond. She realized the SS man had spoken perfect English with a perfect *American* accent. It was the first time in her incarceration that anyone had spoken in English. She made no move, for any movement to reach for the gown would prove to her executioner that she understood English and was, therefore, a British spy. No, there was something that wasn't quite right about this young, clever Nazi. He was trying to trick her. She froze and stiffened up even tighter.

Krupke watched and waited. His prisoner did not respond or move. He waited for another five minutes, still no movement from the young woman. "Go on. Take the gown," he said again in English. Nothing. He tried a different approach. Then he responded in very good, if not fluent, Polish, the young woman's native language. "I'm not going to hurt you," he said. "There is obviously some serious mistake. You can put the gown on."

The woman was astonished. She realized that hurting her was precisely what the man was trying to do, trick her into a false sense of security with his perfect composure, English, Polish, and mannerisms. She decided she had won a small victory over her adversary. Slowly, she reached for the gown.

"Please, let me help you," he said again in Polish. Krupke assisted her to her feet and helped place her bruised arms through the armholes. They were now face-to-face, his brown eyes to her blue eyes. She could smell his clean body and aftershave lotion. "Let me escort you back upstairs, where we can sort this out comfortably," he said.

The SIS woman's mind was as sharp as a dagger despite the pain and torture. She was already well ahead of her adversary. *He's no match for me*, she thought. The aftershave lotion gave her an idea. She decided to push her luck as she spoke in Polish. "First, I must have a bath."

Not surprisingly, Krupke responded, "Naturally. I'll escort you to the washroom where you can freshen up. Can you at least tell me your name? All I ask is just a simple name."

The woman responded calmly and quietly, "My name is Irina . . . *Irina Jankowski.*"

Krupke contemplated his response while he took in the name. It was the first time she had said that name during her interrogations; he had been listening and recorded her dialogs. The name Irina Jankowski had never come up. "You see, that wasn't difficult. You can have your bath now, but I must accompany you the entire way."

The two walked up five flights of stairs to the top of Alexanderplatz. Krupke helped her at every step and believed that it was impossible for anyone to escape from the facility, especially someone in this woman's condition.

As they came to the washroom, Krupke pointed to the door, and the two continued in Polish. "Go inside, I'll be waiting here. Take the gown off and leave it with me. You can have it back when you're finished. There's a towel inside."

The woman did as she was told, and dropped the gown to the floor. She said, "Close the door. I won't take long. Please, I'd like some privacy after my ordeal."

Krupke nodded. "I'm a gentleman. As you wish."

Once inside the bathroom, with the door closed and locked, the woman quickly surveyed her surroundings. She knew she didn't have much time. The washroom was basic. A toilet, sink, and tub; no mirror. There was, however, one tiny window with no bars, above the tub, not more than a foot square. She had to act quickly and decisively. She turned on the water to fill the tub. As the water was running, she grabbed the bar of soap and lathered her body. Next, she placed the wash towel between her teeth and stepped onto the tub and looked out the window. She could see daylight and early-morning sunshine. She guessed it was probably near six. A good time. Few people would be up and about at this hour.

Without thinking further, she opened the tiny window and squeezed her lathered body through the small opening. She mustered all the strength left in her broken body. Once her upper torso was outside the window, she wiped the soap from her hands with the washrag, then reached for the rain gutter. She pulled her body up and onto the roof. Once on top of the roof, she wiped the remaining soap from her hands, feet, and legs, then tiptoed along the entire length of the Alexanderplatz. She followed the gutter to the farthest downspout from the bathroom. Then, she climbed down the full five floors to the street level, holding on to the downspout. Once she had a firm footing on the ground, the young woman, who would later be known as Vivian Tate, darted onto the streets of Berlin, naked but free.

Chapter 1

CENTRAL LONDON, OCTOBER 17, 1945

At 6:55 p.m. on a Friday, after a busy workday, a twenty-five-year-old woman named, Bertha Cordes walked hurriedly through the Charing Cross tube station to catch a train. The station was extremely hectic this time of day as employees from Whitehall and Parliament had finished their long workweek. She wore a wool coat and dress underneath and clutched a handbag over her right shoulder. Her dark brown hair was neatly styled, and she had just a slight touch of makeup but did not stand out in the crowd. In fact, it was the opposite. She looked like all the other fifty or sixty women catching a train after work. Bertha Cordes did as she was told. She went upstairs to the British Rail, Charing Cross ticket booth and stood in line as if to buy a ticket. That's when the brush pass occurred.

He was an elderly man carrying a briefcase, wearing a long wool coat, bowler, and scarf around his neck. "Excuse me," he said as he slipped by Bertha and the man in front of her. He was very polite. It was a professional job; Bertha deduced. Her handler was right; there were still many German spies in the UK who had survived the war. She barely felt a thing. The man simply placed a luggage key in her left hand as he brushed by.

Cordes twirled the key between her fingers as she watched the man disappear into the crowd. She waited in line until she was almost at the front. Then, as instructed, she turned to her left and exited the line. She went downstairs to the luggage lockers. She glanced in her palm and noticed the number, eighty-four. She continued down the row of lockers until she found the correct number. She inserted the key and opened it. Inside, she found a single, small suitcase. She grabbed the bag and closed the locker, turned around and headed for the nearest toilet.

Once inside the stall, Bertha placed the suitcase on the toilet seat. The case was unlocked. She flipped the latches and opened it. Inside she saw a layer of men's work clothes and shoes. She moved them aside and saw the brown, eight-by- ten envelope. She opened the envelope, and a luggage key dropped into her hand. Inside the envelope was a written text in code, a small paperback novel, several pages of sheet music, followed by a map of Germany and Poland. A crumbled, worn ferry schedule to Baltic ports was stuffed to one side. She placed everything back inside the envelope and continued the search. Next was a layer of cash bundles in US dollars and a loaded 9-mm Walther PPK automatic pistol, plus several passports from multiple countries with a man's picture, whom she recognized intimately. She picked up each bundle of cash and thumbed through it, making sure they were all .US dollar bills and not sheets of paper. Finally, she placed everything back into the suitcase and locked it with the key. She was satisfied; everything was in order as described by her controller. Bertha exited the toilet and walked out onto Strand Street, where she continued on to Northumberland Avenue. She came back to the Hotel Victoria and entered the lobby.

Chapter 2

Miss Vivian Tate emerged from her small, modest flat at number Sixteen Lexham Gardens. As with her old job at Baker Street, Miss Tate was not known as an early riser, preferring to work alone and after hours instead of arriving at seven or eight in the morning. This day was no exception at the Student Foreign Exchange. She felt she could accomplish more, staying late, after hours when it was quiet, and everyone had gone home for the day.

The war years had taken their toll on the thirty-five-year-old bachelorette. Her dyed brown hair was now faded to a mousey brown. Her firm muscles were weak. When the war ended, Vivian Tate left her administrative post at the Inter-Services Research Bureau on Baker Street. There, she was the executive officer for the section responsible for infiltrating British agents into Nazi-occupied Europe. She longed for the excitement of special employment, His Majesty's government no longer needed skilled linguists or saboteurs. It was challenging to find a job anywhere with her credentials and experience. The only opportunity for her was with the Student Foreign Exchange service, and even that she had help acquiring. However, her knowledge and fluency of French, German, Italian, Spanish, Polish, Russian, Romanian, Hungarian, and Serbo-Croat paved the way.

It was a beautiful October morning. The sun was actually out, and the skies were clear. She could see a few contrails from airplanes overhead. Except, this time, these aircraft were civilian airliners flying to North America instead of on bombing missions. As she walked down the street of Lexham Garden, she realized there was someone following her. She had no reason to suspect any ill will, now that the war was over, but she was schooled in the art of surveillance and counter-surveillance. She could never be totally sure with the outcome of the war that someone from the opposition wasn't, indeed, after her.

She continued on toward the Earls Court tube station where she would catch a train for Euston station and the Student Exchange. As she crossed the street at Cromwell Road, she felt the presence beside her. He was not threatening, moved closer to Vivian, and said quietly, "Can I offer you a lift, Miss Tate?"

Vivian turned slightly and recognized the figure, Major-General Stanley Cameron of the War Department. Vivian remembered him from the war years. He had assisted her with aerial logistics for returning agents from the field on several occasions.

"General Stanley, (as she had called him in the past) this is a pleasant surprise."

General Cameron was not in uniform, which was one reason why Vivian had not recognized him as he tailed her from Lexham Gardens. Cameron was in his late fifties, tall, with gray hair, and a distinct look. He was anxious to get to wherever he was going because he quickly passed Vivian and motioned to a car and driver parked on the other side of the street. This was a welcome treat for Vivian because, during the war, she had had a car and driver who picked her up every day and took her to work. She never bothered to get a driving license. When the war ended, she still never got her license. Cameron whispered something into his driver's ear that Vivian couldn't hear. Then the two quickly entered the back seat of the sedan and sped away.

"It's the Student Exchange Office, isn't it?" asked Cameron.

Vivian nodded.

"How are they treating you?" he asked as he made two distinct taps on the glass partition signaling his driver to move on.

"Fine, could be more exciting."

"And you're happy about the pay?"

"Could be better, but one can't be too choosy these days."

Vivian was not naive. She realized this was no ordinary, casual coincidence from General Cameron. He had something on his mind, and she didn't wait or want him to probe. "You didn't come all this way for nothing. What's really on your mind, Stanley?"

"As usual, always right to the point, Miss Tate. Yes, there is something, but it's entirely up to you."

Cameron reached for a packet of cigarettes (Silver Service, Vivian's favorite during the war) from his breast pocket and offered one. Naturally, Vivian accepted without hesitation. She didn't smoke, especially Silver Service, as much as she did during the war years, and certain things were expensive, and she couldn't waste her meager earnings on too many vices. After the first puff, Cameron continued.

"I can get you back on at Broadway," Cameron inhaled

another puff of smoke and blew it over their heads and continued. "Naturally, it will require something from you. If you're not interested, it's perfectly all right. We understand these things. I'll have David, my driver, take you to the Student Exchange. The two of us simply had a coincidental encounter, and I offered you a lift, nothing more. If, on the other hand, you *are* interested, we continue for a short ride, and I'll explain more. Either way, you will not have to explain your absence or tardiness from the Student Exchange. We'll handle everything, and there will be no adverse marks on your employment. Are you interested?"

"That depends."

Cameron let out a chuckle. "I knew you'd have a response like that. How about a name, then?"

Vivian stamped out her half-smoked Silver Service in the door ashtray. She was at this point quite curious. "Okay, let me have it."

"Fair enough. I'll mention the name. Same rules apply. If you're still not interested in getting your job back at the Service, I'll let you off at the Student Exchange—"

Vivian interrupted, "Oh for heaven's sake, Stanley, you know me. Enough of this nonsense, just tell me the bloody name. Of course, I want my job back at MI-6!"

Cameron, gaining a small, rare victory over Tate, answered, "Otto Krupke."

"As in the number two man behind Hans Kammler at the former Reich Security office, Berlin?"

"That's the one. Do we have an agreement?"

Vivian answered promptly, "Yes, by all means. He and I have an old score to settle."

Vivian knew perfectly well who Otto Krupke was as Cameron tapped the glass partition three distinct times to signal his driver. Krupke had been the head of all SS counter-espionage and counter-sabotage operations against Allied intelligence agencies during the war. His responsibilities extended to include action against all parachutists dropped or infiltrated into German-occupied Europe, whether from the Soviet Union or the Western Allies. More importantly, he was responsible for her arrest and torture while she was a prisoner at Alexanderplatz before the war.

Cameron's car stopped just a short distance from where he had picked up Vivian. They were still in Kensington. To Vivian's surprise, they were not at the War Department but instead outside the Royal Geographical Society (RGS). David quickly opened the door for Vivian, indicating he wanted her to step out.

"Follow me, please. Not another word until we're inside," said Cameron as David handed him his briefcase.

The two walked to the side entrance of the Royal Geographical Society located on Exhibition Road. They climbed the short flight of stairs, to the second floor. Cameron rang a doorbell. After a lengthy delay, the door finally opened. A small, middle-aged woman wearing a tweed skirt, jumper, and large, round spectacles greeted them. "We've been expecting you, sir."

The woman said nothing further but turned and walked back inside the building. Cameron and Vivian followed. They were escorted to the second-floor map room and took the room with the number two marked on the door. After unlocking the door with a large skeleton key, and turning on the lights, the older woman said, "Everything is set up per your request. Please ring me if you need anything," as she pointed to a white telephone. "No one will disturb you." She handed Cameron the key, and closed the door.

Once inside the map room, Cameron motioned to a chair at the large map table. On the table were several maps and aerial photographs detailing Allied occupation zones in Europe. Vivian was now visibly intrigued by her surroundings. She was starting to feel back home again. Vivian took a seat as Cameron lowered a large relief map of the Continent and continued. "Before we go any further, Miss Tate, I must remind you of the Official Secrets Act and the fact that I'm privy to state secrets from your past." He opened his briefcase and fished through the stuffed case and pulled out a disclosure form. "Please sign and date, Miss Tate."

Vivian already knew the form. She had personally handed out this form and given the same spiel to several of her agents during the war. She signed the form and passed it across the table to Cameron. "Question?" Vivian asked, wanting more information on the whereabouts of Krupke.

"Not right now. Let me finish what I was about to tell you in the car."

"This suspense, or should I say, this *nonsense*, is killing me, Stanley."

"Miss Tate. Let me begin by answering your question with a question. Operation Backfire. Know about it?"

"Naturally, but only from what I've read in the papers. It was your empire if I'm not mistaken, General."

"Well done. Get comfortable, Miss Tate, this could take some time. Shall I request a teapot?"

"No, thanks, I'll be fine. Just get on with it."

"The classified version then. Here we go. An entirely British military operation conducted at Cuxhaven. Backfire was designed to completely evaluate the entire V-2 rocket system and operations, using captured German scientists, engineers, and SS firing units. In a nutshell, a complete, comprehensive, and thorough evaluation of the V-2 weapon system. Something never undertook before, not even by the Nazis. SS security was extremely tight during the war. They would not allow such extensive coverage, feeling that no single person should know more about the entire rocket system than the absolute minimum."

Vivian listened intensely as she lit another one of Cameron's, Silver Service cigarettes. She didn't need to take notes. Her mind was almost photographic. Cameron, using the relief map continued.

"In April of last year, advancing American troops of the Third Armored Division overran the Nordhausen-Mittlewerks complex. There they stumbled across thousands of V-2 rockets and assembly parts. A real Aladdin's cave. The US Army plundered everything they could get their hands on, mainly because Nordhausen was scheduled to be handed over to the Soviet zone of occupation, and the Americans didn't want the rockets in the hands of the Russians. So, they requisitioned them rather quickly. Some three hundred and forty boxcars left Nordhausen under US possession, destined for Fort Irwin, Texas. By prior treaty agreement, however, half the captured V-2s were to be turned over to us, but the Americans laughed in our faces. Naturally, we protested. I being the one most vocal.

"Eventually, US Army Chief of Staff Marshall gave in to our demands. Sort of a compromise. He allowed the entire captured von Braun team to be seconded to me, along with what little missile components were left on the Continent to conduct the Backfire tests with the former SS firing crews. We scoured the Continent from Antwerp to Warsaw and came up with enough missile components to fire, are you ready for this—eight complete V-2 rockets.

"Less than a fortnight ago, we concluded the Backfire test. Of the eight missiles, only three were launched and only *one* successfully. Listen carefully, Miss Tate, because you'll probably get a partial answer to your stirring question. The most elusive components to the missile system were the so-called flight hardware: 'gyros' and the 'dry batteries' to power them. We also discovered that the Americans were having the same difficulties back in the US with the von Braun team. They had plenty of rocket parts, but no gyros or batteries, despite plundering thousands of missile components out of Germany. These shortages of so-called, flight hardware and batteries will stall the von Braun team from conducting further tests in the US until they can get them."

Cameron took another cigarette drag and continued. "During the war, Bomber Command pummeled Peene-müde to oblivion. Herr Hitler was not happy. So, he redeployed key V-2 production units to Nordhausen, and the training and testing range outside Germany, to Blizna, Poland. This secondary launch complex in Eastern Poland was larger than the one at Peenemünde. The problem the Nazis had at Blizna was they had to hide not only the launch sites but also the scientists involved in the research and development of key rocket components, again the dry batteries and gyros. Reason, the Russian front was closing in on them. Would you care to venture a guess as to who oversaw this entire Blizna V-2 redeployment process?"

Vivian looked at the relief map and Berlin and noted the distance from there to Krakow. "I would say for certainty because it was a high, Third Reich-security issue, it would have definitely been Krupke or Kammler."

"Bravo, Miss Tate."

"Tell me you have Krupke in custody, and it would simply be a matter of interrogating him to find the elusive components and scientists."

"I wish that were the case. Kammler reportedly died three times. I wish I could do that." Cameron now took a seat at the map table alongside Tate, lit another cigarette, and continued. "Miss Tate, I know more about Krupke than you'll probably ever know. I know he was your jailer in Berlin and the one who issued the death warrant for one of your most beloved recruits, Penelope Walsh.

"Here is the most sensitive information I'll pass on to you today. Krupke was arrested along the Baltic coast near Swinoujscie by military police units back in May. He was brought to England and processed by MI-19 before being handed over to the War Crimes Tribunal. Shortly after that, MI-5 discovered his true identity and insisted they interrogate him further before transfer. He was quite cooperative. He even had his secretary/mistress, Bertha Cordes, with him to help with typing and dictation. She was arrested along with him at Swinoujscie.

"For two months, MI-5 grilled him extensively. It seems that Krupke had more responsibilities at the Reich security office than we originally believed. He ran a radio play-back ruse with the Soviets that dwarfed what the SD did in Holland and France. His unit penetrated the Soviet *Rote Kapelle* network working inside the Third Reich. This resulted in the capture of some five hundred and fifty-two Soviet agents who parachuted right into Krupke's hands. For his accomplishments he was rewarded quite well from the Nazi government. He has a lot of money, all paid out from Göring's slush fund.

"Krupke admitted under interrogation with MI-5 that his department conducted over one hundred radio play-back games with Moscow. His position also resulted in substantial knowledge of Soviet intelligence capabilities, not only about NKVD activities, but also the GRU. This information had to be kept from the Soviets, so MI-5 protected him by issuing a fake death certificate to keep the

Soviets, and I might add, War Crimes investigators, off his tail."

"Unbelievable, first Kammler, then Krupke." Vivian then asked, "Was his death staged?"

"I'm not sure of the particulars, but I was told he died of complications from pneumonia."

"Simple enough. Was he buried?"

"As a matter of fact, he was. Right here in London."

Vivian didn't like to be held in suspense. "What's all this got to do with rockets and guidance systems?"

Cameron rose and moved back to the relief map. This time he addressed the UK. "During his interviews, or should I say his interrogations, here in London, MI-5 kept Krupke on a short leash. Sort of a house arrest. They had him staying in luxury at the Victoria Hotel. He could come and go as he pleased. Even dining with his mistress, Bertha Cordes at London's finest restaurants. Less than a fortnight ago, he simply vanished. Flew the coop, as they say."

Vivian was beyond baffled. "You mean to tell me he just walked away from MI-5 custody? What about the mistress? Did you grill her?"

Cameron shook his head. "We didn't get anything out of her. She claims to have no knowledge of Krupke's escape motives or plans. She confessed to being nothing more than Krupke's lover and secretary."

"If it were my decision, I'd string her up like they did to me. See if she cracks."

"That's not necessary, nor would it have produced any actionable intelligence. Cordes is in custody at Camp 020 Latchmere House, South London, at the moment, awaiting a decision from War Crimes investigators."

Cameron changed the subject and moved on to Krupke. "Part of the agreement to let him speak openly about Soviet intelligence capabilities was freedom of movement. It was right after the Backfire tests, which were all public, by the way. He was not prohibited from reading the papers or watching the newsreels. He obviously saw his opportunity. We're not sure where he went, but during his interview, MI-5 discovered his knowledge about the V-2 missile system. They believe, and I'm in agreement, that Krupke fled back to former Third Reich territory to try and contact remnants of his network operating in parts of Poland. Tuchola was the last-known site where uncaptured V-2 technicians were hiding. There it is believed he will try and EXFIL former rocket scientists to the American sector and hopefully get a better offer than the British. Remember, he has the financial resources to fund this kind of operation, and I'm sure he wants to spend this money in the US instead of dangling from the end of a noose here at the Tower. He had over three-million Reich marks on him when captured, and Betha Cordes had over nine-hundred." Cameron stamped out his cigarette and lit another, shaking his head in disbelief. "All he had to do was get to Liverpool Street station and take a train to Harwich. From there, a ferry to the Baltics."

"This brings us back to me, General," Vivian asked, keeping Cameron focused.

Cameron came back and retook a seat next to Vivian. "Right, during the Backfire test, the Germans were very tight-lipped about the V-2 research. However, one of the Germans, General Dornberger himself, who was also the commanding officer at both Blizna and Peenemünde, inadvertently revealed to me during a drunken binge that there was a more accurate gyro/navigation system in the arsenal. And it makes sense. If you wanted to hit New York or Washington, you needed a more sophisticated guidance system. This system was also lighter weight and could be fixed on top of not only rockets but the actual warheads themselves. He called it an inertial guidance system. He told me that unfortunately, these systems were probably in Soviet hands, since everything was left behind in Poland."

Cameron blew cigarette smoke over their heads. "Miss Tate, I believe the new navigation systems are not in Soviet hands; that's why Krupke fled. He knows their whereabouts and Soviet GRU capabilities and knows where the scientists and or gyro systems are located. I think he's going after them so he can make a deal with the Americans. We want you to go after him and bring him back before he does."

"Is it really that simple, Stanley?"

Cameron spoke freely now. "You know better, Miss Tate. During interrogation, Krupke was asked if he knew anyone from the UK. His answer, surprisingly, Irina Jankowski. It would appear he hasn't forgotten about you. How he got this information, God only knows."

"Nor have I forgotten about him, but this does complicate things."

"Given the seriousness of the advanced V-2 gyros, this latest bit of human intelligence, sparked our interest in you. A short time ago, when you agreed to this inquiry, I had my driver signal War Department identities branch. There they just released a false, three-year background on Irina Jankowski, who now goes by the name of Janica Kijowski. You're the proprietor of an elegant hotel in Tarnow called the Hotel Bristol. The current proprietor is a Polish Home Army agent and woman about your age with similar physical characteristics. We'll temporarily move her out the same time you INFIL, so there'll be no lapses. We'll keep her close by to re-insert her back into her former role, just in case the Soviets are on to you. You, as the hotel proprietor, struggled during the war, but now you're quite prosperous. One of the few thriving. It should be because the Hotel Bristol was, and still is, a Home Army black site. You are also, and more importantly, a conductor on a ratline directly to the American sector. Hopefully, Krupke will get word of this through his sources and attempt contact with you to help him get across to the American lines."

"Clever, Stanley, I'm the bait."

"To put it bluntly, yes, you are the bait. Hopefully, Krupke won't bite but swallow the whole thing, hook, line, and sinker."

"Okay, so I agree to do this, but why? Why not just send in a SAS hit squad and eliminate him? Wouldn't that be easier?"

Cameron shook his head. "He knows too much about Soviet intelligence activities, information we vitally need now that the war is over. We want him back, so the Soviets don't kill him, *and* the Americans in particular, want the gyros to create a nuclear-tipped ballistic missile. The von Braun team can only back-engineer so much. You do this, Miss Tate, along with your record and prior contributions to Bletchley Park, and you'll have your job back at MI-6, and in a leadership position, I might add. Perhaps even on the fast track to 'C' itself."

Vivian sat in silence for several moments, which seemed like an eternity, thinking. There was nothing she wanted more in life than to work at MI-6 again. Acquiring a leadership position was the icing on the cake. "Have you told the Americans about any of this?"

Cameron shook his head. "No, two reasons: first, the Americans have no consolidated intelligence organization left. President Truman shut down the OSS October first. Second, and most importantly, there are those at HQ, me included, who strongly believe the Soviets infiltrated British intelligence at the highest levels, perhaps the top of MI-6 or MI-5. It could be anyone, even Menzies or Dansey. Also, the American OSS was believed to have been penetrated."

Vivian raised an eyebrow, something she frequently did if it was interesting.

"Here's the deal, Miss Tate. I want you to head this operation completely independently from MI-6, MI-5, or civilian- contracted agencies. This is why we're having this little discussion here, instead of at Whitehall. You'll have full access to the facilities and this." Cameron reached into his briefcase and passed a single sheet of paper across to Vivian. It was a simple directive, typewritten on a plain piece of white paper with original signatures. Vivian read the single paragraph, then turned white as the blood drained from her face.

10 Downing Street
London, England
To Whom It May Concern,
Greetings,

Please give Royal Air Force Squadron Leader Vivian Tate complete and total access to any and all resources needed in support of the acquisition of the former V-2 rocket system. This mission is the highest priority for the national security of the United Kingdom.

Signed
Clement Attlee
Prime Minister

Cameron then said, "The PM was briefed on the entire operation and Soviet penetrations; he and His Majesty share my belief. Please stand and raise your right hand."

Vivian didn't know what to do so she simply stood as

Cameron directed. He administered her oath of office and then said, "As of this moment, you are now a commissioned officer in His Majesty's Air Force, not the WAAF, but RAF, something unheard of for a woman in today's times. Congratulations, Squadron Leader Tate."

Chapter 3

Once the formalities were accomplished, General Cameron decided to take a break. He picked up the white phone and ordered some coffee along with a snack from the administration desk. Once the coffee and snacks were delivered, both Vivian and Stanley Cameron didn't speak. Instead, the two drank their coffee and ate the small sandwiches. When they were finished, Cameron picked up his briefing.

"These facilities at RGS are yours. Anything you need, simply pick up the white phone. I'll leave the planning phase to you. I know your background. You're quite capable. No need for me to interfere. All I ask is when you get Krupke, contact me directly, using the cutout in Wales, not a moment before. Otherwise, the whole operation could be compromised. Let me know when, how, and where you want to do the EXFIL."

Cameron finished with one final bit of information. "I will give you one recommendation. You'll need someone who speaks German and Polish. This person must be familiar with the EXFIL of personnel from the Soviet zones. This person must have the technical expertise to evaluate the gyro systems and scientists. Finally, the person must be an American. There is only one person who fits this bill, Major Antoni Franko. He's a 'Lusty' collector from Wright Field, Ohio. Good chap, West Point grad, one of the best the Americans had. He's an electrical engineer and a specialist in avionics. He was assigned to the Backfire operation with me and provided us useful information. He was also one of the first to discover the Nazi advanced aerospace technology and make a full assessment. You'll be happy to know, Miss Tate, a little-known fact about Major Franko. He flew as a crewmember on the Most III mission to Poland to recover the first, nearly intact V-2 rocket during the war. He's familiar with the landing field and resistance fighters at Motyl. He was also trained by the OSS. He's still working for CIOS in Frankfurt. Of course, you'll have the final say. It's just my recommendation. He's working for Eisenhower's G2 staff at IG Farben, now USFET Headquarters, until his separation orders come in. He'd rather stay on the Continent collecting rather than go back to the States. Personal reasons, he says. Something about his ex-wife. As of this moment, he's got nothing to do, now that the Backfire tests have concluded, and most of the von Braun scientists have been captured."

"He sounds promising. I'll take it into consideration."

Cameron reached into his briefcase and emptied the remaining contents onto the table before Vivian. She reached for and took possession of three large files.

"Getting Krupke back and the gyros are not the problem," added Cameron. "We're confident you can accomplish that. The problem is Soviet interference. If the Soviets get word of what we're doing, especially if there is a mole, they'll stop at nothing in their endeavor to acquire Krupke and the advanced gyros. You'll have both the GRU and NKVD on your tails. A dangerous situation. You see, Miss Tate, we're now fighting a new kind of war, a Cold War, with the Soviets, a big, gigantic chess match played out on the chessboard of Central Europe. It's a race to acquire as much of the Third Reich's advanced technology, in many cases twenty-five years ahead of anything we have, before they do. It's a dangerous game because it could erupt into an all-out shooting war at any time with the Soviets, especially now since the Americans have the atomic bomb."

Vivian, now sensing where this conversation was taking them, added, "With the double agents in place here and in Washington, what about movements in the occupied zones? Who'll handle air and ground ops without tipping off the mole?—I surmise everything must be kept away from MI-6 and MI-5."

"Precisely, that's why I need you. You have the letter. You'll figure out a way. Everything I know is in those files. They're now yours. I wish I could say I have more, but with the mole in place, I took what I could get. What's the saying? 'Beggars can't be too choosy.'"

Vivian began to inhale smoke from her cigarette, something she rarely did. "I told you I'd do it, but as of a short while ago, I was officially unemployed, and I'll need funds."

"We can't draw too much attention, thus your commission in the RAF. We can't advance any cash. You'll draw a regular salary for your rank, just like I do. The Allied Control Commission will fund your initial movement to the American sector, after that you'll have to come up with a way to move about the Continent."

"All right, I'll get it done." Vivian now moved on to another topic. "Stanley, I know how these things work. Once the mission is completed, I'll be put out to pasture just as before. No, I want more than a job at MI-6. I want a lifetime commission *and* pension."

Cameron smiled, showing off a toothy grin. "Agreed, I'll arrange everything once you complete the mission and secure employment back at Broadway Street."

Vivian stamped out her cigarette in the ashtray, then opened the first of the files on the table. "I'll take Franko; I could use his expertise. I'll need the latest maps of the occupied zones, Eastern Germany, and Poland. Aerial photos too if RGS has them. I'll need the Ministry's escape route out of the Continent. I'll need to meet with Mr. Bor today, and have the PM get me a meeting with General Eisenhower three days from now. I should be ready by then."

"Excellent, Miss Tate. I'll contact the PM today. Remember, it's imperative the services be kept out of the circle. They'll eventually find out in due time, but this delay could buy you precious time. As far as your escape route, get to the British sector in Berlin. We'll get you out from there."

"Oh, one last thing," replied Vivian. "I want to interrogate Bertha Cordes before I leave. I'm sure she knows something about Krupke's escape plans and motives. I promise I won't string her up."

"In that case, approved, but remember what I told you concerning the mole. Exercise extreme vigilance."

"Don't worry, I know just how and what to do."

Cameron got up, indicating his work was over. "Then, that's all I got. When you get Krupke and are ready for EXFIL, call me on the secure line with the news. I'm sure you still remember it. Not a moment before. Then, and only then, I'll coordinate for two means of transport. One flown by British crews, the other American. The flight hardware with go with the Americans, you and Krupke will go on British transport. Safe travels, Squad Leader Tate."

* * *

VIVIAN WRAPPED-UP her meeting with Cameron and left the Royal Geographical Society on Kensington Road, turned the corner on Exhibition, and walked two more blocks to number fifty-five, where she entered the *Ognisko Polskie* Club. She walked up to the receptionist and asked, "Is Mr. Bor in?"

The young woman was slightly taken aback with Vivian's request and slowly answered, "Did you say, Mr. Bor?"

"Yes, that's right. I'm looking for Mr. Bor. Tell him, Miss Tate is here, and I'd like to have dinner with him."

The young woman turned and disappeared into the kitchen area. A short time later, the young receptionist returned with another man in his late fifties. He extended his hand to Vivian.

"I'm Mr. Green, the club manager. I understand you'd like to meet with Mr. Bor. Do you have an appointment?"

Vivian did not extend her hand in response. She was not used to stalling tactics. She was very clear in her request. "Mr. Green, you said you were the club manager. Well, I don't have all night. I'm hungry, not to mention tired. I'll be in the lounge waiting. Again, your job is to tell Mr. Bor Miss Tate has come to have dinner with him."

"Very well. My apologies, we're just not used to such urgent requests these days. I'll inform Mr. Bor immediately. It could take a while since he wasn't expecting you. In the meantime, please be our guest in the lounge. Your beverages are on the house. If you'll excuse me, I must call Mr. Bor." He turned and left the reception area.

Mr. Bor, whose real name was Tadeusz Komorowski, commander of the Polish *Armia Krojowa* (Home Army) during the war, entered the Polish Club a short time later. He was rather short, in his late forties, and bald. The only hair on his head was a thick mustache. He was wearing a dark-blue suit and a freshly ironed white shirt. "Miss Tate, this is a pleasant surprise. Of course, I'd love to have dinner with you."

By now, Vivian was ravenous and stated, "Mr. Bor, you have not changed a bit. Can we dine somewhere private? I'd like to ask a big favor of you."

"Certainly."

For the next two hours over dinner, Vivian Tate detailed her new assignment to General Komorowski. When she was finished, Komorowski said, "You'd never know the war is over. The resistance is just as active now as it was during the war. The Soviets are tightening the vice. Communist elements are everywhere. We are no match for them. It's only a matter of time before the Communists take over the entire country. Anything I can do to help/or delay this process will be my pleasure.

"First things first, you'll need a team on the ground, in Tarnow. We call it AK-22 Ranger Battalion because it's made up of mostly forest rangers working in the area. The circuit was one of the best and extremely secure. I'll be in touch with their commander. Her name is Ana Zawacki, code name Jawor (Sycamore). She was trained by MI-6. The other, Isebel Glowinski, code named Morena (Brunette) trained by SOE. Get to know both. You'll be in good hands; they both speak excellent German and English."

"I'm sure they'll be just fine if you recommend them. Mr. Bor, if it's not too much trouble, I'd like you to get me the locations of all Home Army safe houses and black sites inside southern Poland to finalize my plan. You never know when we may need their assistance."

"I'll pass your request to Jawor. She'll have the latest information."

"One last thing. I'll need a secure cutout here in London, preferably accessed by telegram and telephone. I might need something in case I have to play a double game."

Mr. Bor laughed out loud. "I know just the thing. I'll coordinate everything you'll need. They'll never be able to trace anything back to us."

Chapter 4

The morning after her meeting with Mr. Bor, Vivian Tate left London via private motorcar for Latchmere House in South London, otherwise known as Camp 020. Originally built during the Victorian era as a private residence, it was now owned by the Ministry of Defense and used as a maximum-security prison. From the outside, the casual onlooker would never suspect anything other than a peaceful residence with a walled enclosure and lush foliage. She had to find out if it was true that Krupke was looking for her and why.

The maximum-security section was located in the basement. Here, the most notorious military prisoners were held in solitary confinement until shipment to other security services could be determined. The cell was small, with only a cot and wooden chair. There were no toilet facilities other than a honey bucket. The once beautiful and robust Bertha Cordes was lying on her bed. She was dressed in a dirty, gray pair of overalls. A single ceiling light, which was controlled from the outside of the cell, switched on. Vivian Tate stepped into the cell as Bertha rose from the cot.

Bertha was not fully awake because prisoners had no idea of the time in the dark, windowless cell. Cordes struggled to adjust her eyes only to see a Soviet female military officer wearing the rank of colonel in the Red Army. She held nothing in her hands, not even a notepad. The Soviet officer spoke in German.

"Greetings, Fräulein," she said, not introducing herself. "I'm from the Soviet War Crimes Tribunal. I'm here to arrange your transfer into Soviet custody, but I have a few questions for you first. Your answers will determine your fate. You will either stay here in British custody or accompany me back to the Soviet Union, where you will most likely be incarcerated for life, at a special labor camp, if you know what I mean. It will be safe to say that your life span will be concise at this particular camp. The choice is yours, Fräulein."

Bertha blinked several times and shook uncontrollably, obviously contemplating the seriousness of her predicament and, most importantly, the fluent German by the Russian officer.

"Can I have a cigarette?" Bertha finally asked.

Vivian reached into her tunic and pulled out a pack of Russian cigarettes and matches, then threw them on the cot. Bertha took notice of the pack, seeing they were Russian, not English. Cordes quickly snatched them up and lit a cigarette. Vivian noticed Bertha's attention to minute details and surmised she was professionally trained in tradecraft and not just Krupke's secretary— She definitely knew something. Vivian continued.

"Let me give it to you straight. It is foolish to think you and your lover will ever be reunited, regardless of what he may have told you. You will never see him again. Ever! It's over. He has betrayed you."

"I've told you, or should I say, I've told the British,

everything I know. You can read my depositions. I really don't know anything. You, of all people, should know this. I didn't have a need to know, so he didn't tell me everything. To protect me, he said."

Vivian reached for the Russian pack of cigarettes and lit one. She blew the smoke into Bertha's face. "Who do you think I am? I'm not some nitwit sent from Moscow. Your lover, Otto Krupke, was responsible for infiltrating our biggest intelligence operations during the war. He was directly responsible for the death of over one-hundred of our finest agents. You were his secretary and lover. He told you everything, and you helped with his escape from British custody. We want him back in Soviet custody so we can interrogate him on the whereabouts of all Soviet agents who did not return after the war. Tell me, Bertha, why did he flee to the Continent? Surely, he must have felt some safety here in the West. Like I said, we know you helped him escape, but the question is why. Why would he risk being caught or killed by Soviet security forces?"

Vivian sat in silence as she smoked the rest of the terrible-tasting, Russian-made cigarette, then stomped it out on the floor with her boot. She continued to say nothing, waiting for Bertha to make the first sound. Finally, when she was ready, Vivian reached into her tunic and pulled out a small note-pad. "Can I have your hat and shoe size?"

"What for?"

"Your new uniform? You're being transferred to a Soviet prison camp."

"Wait, wait, don't do that! I can share what little I do know."

"It's too late. I gave you a chance, your shoe size?"

Bertha started to cry.

Vivian appeared to have no patience for theatrics, but patience was all she had. "Will you quit this nonsense? I need your hat and shoe size so I can facilitate the transfer!" she said once again.

"I. . . I. . . can tell you, but it must be kept confidential. The room is bugged. The British are monitoring and recording all communications inside the cell. Do we have an agreement?"

"We have an agreement. I can tell you that I insisted that all emitters be turned off before I entered your cell. That was my condition upon interrogating you. You have nothing to worry about."

Bertha sat upright on her cot. "Then I can tell you, Krupke was after some secret weapons left behind."

Vivian folded her note-pad closed with a snap to dramatize the moment. "Go on."

"He planned the whole thing before the end of the war. He knew the gig was up as early as September 1944 and wanted to save his own neck. He said he was doing it for us."

"How?"

"He knows the whereabouts of secret weapons and wants to make a deal with the Americans. Similar to what von Braun did."

"And just what kind of secret weapons are you talking about? We already know about the A-4 rocket."

"Super rockets, called the A-9 and A-10, capable of hitting the US, advanced guidance systems and . . . anti-gravity devices."

Vivian noted the mention of antigravity devices and raised her curious eyebrow. This was the first time she had heard of that but kept it to herself for the moment. She knew from her job at Baker Street that the Nazis were working on such weapons. "And . . . ?"

"And, he's searching for an escape line to the West, via Poland. He has a source, he told me."

"Do you know the name of this source?"

"All he said was that it was a woman who could have several identities and aliases, and that was his biggest challenge. Determining that source's loyalty and credibility. He had to vet her out first, to be sure."

"Where in Poland?"

"Not sure, somewhere near the Eastern V-2 test launch site."

Vivian moved off topic slightly to keep Bertha challenged. "I don't suppose he mentioned to you where these so-called secret weapons are hidden?"

"I don't think he even knows. Everything was controlled by Hanns Kammler, but he's supposedly dead now. Otto said he must first make contact with remnants of his former network still operating in Poland. He's afraid the Communists will close in on the network eventually, finding the secret weapons before the Americans. This will, of course, dash his hopes for a successful escape to the United States."

"Why should I believe you?"

"That's up to you. But, if I were you, I'd try and find these so-called secret weapons before the Americans do."

Vivian stood up and pounded on the door, indicating her interview was over. Bertha finally said, "I've told you what I know. Please, please don't take me, Colonel."

Vivian turned and faced Bertha. "I never got your shoe or hat size." Then the door opened, and Vivian stepped out.

Once outside the cell and the door closed, Lieutenant Colonel R. Stephens, Camp 020 commander, was waiting. "Will there be anything else, Colonel?" he asked Vivian.

Vivian responded in heavily accented English, not her poised, British accent. "Nothing more, please have my driver meet me out front. And you can turn the recording devices back on."

Vivian had accomplished her objective by interviewing Cordes. She did discover that Cameron's information was correct concerning her identity, and Krupke was indeed looking for her.

Stephens nodded as Vivian marched away.

Later that morning, after Vivian left the facility, Lieutenant Colonel Stephens returned to his office on the first floor and closed the door. He picked up the telephone receiver and made a call to his superiors at MI-19. "Put me through to 'Calvin's' office."

After a long delay, Colonel Scott Alexander, MI-19 Deputy Operations Commander, answered, "Yes?"

"Per your orders, sir. I had a strange visitor today. A young woman officer. A Soviet Red Army colonel with all the proper authorization from the highest authority, Allied War Crimes Tribunal Inspector General signed personally. She wanted to interview Cordes. She insisted all recording devices be turned off."

"Hum . . . that is highly unusual. What did this Russian look like?"

"Short, light-brown hair, good-looking. Spoke good English with a heavy eastern European accent. More aplomb than all the other Allied officers who interviewed Cordes combined. There was one more thing."

"What's that?"

"She wore her skirt three inches higher than regulation, showing off her shapely legs."

"Thank you, Colonel. I'll forward your report. Good day."

* * *

KENSINGTON PALACE GARDENS is a street in Kensington, West-Central London, and home to some of the most expensive properties in the world. During and shortly after World War II, these magnificent residences, numbers six, seven, and eight, were home to one of the UK's most secret military establishments, the London office of the Combined Services Detailed Interrogation Centre, commonly known as the *London Cage* and home to MI-19.

The Cage was commanded by Colonel Scott Alexander, code name Calvin a tall, forceful man recruited into military service by the War Office at the ripe old age of fifty-seven because of his fluency in German and his previous service record during the First World War. Now sixty-three, he was in charge of interrogating all former Nazi war criminals held in British custody.

Shortly after receiving the report on the Soviet officer from Colonel Stephens, Calvin secured the telephone on the receiver. He had important business to attend to with his Soviet controller. Calvin was the Soviet deep penetration mole. He needed to inform Moscow about this latest information on Krupke's secretary, Bertha Cordes, and her interrogation by a Soviet officer. He got up from his desk and proceeded to the coatrack, where he retrieved his hat and coat. Then he left his office and told his secretary that he needed to go for a walk to collect his thoughts.

As Calvin walked toward Bayswater Road, he thought about his reports already sent back to Moscow Centre. He was the first to divulge to the Soviets that Otto Krupke had escaped British custody, his staged death, and that MI-6 would probably send in their best agent to recapture him. This latest development was highly unusual in that if any Soviet officers wanted to interrogate Cordes, the request would come through his office, not the Allied War Crimes Inspector General's office. No, there was something strange about this event. He had to initiate an urgent distress call to his Soviet controller whom he wished to contact.

Calvin turned right on the corner of Bayswater and Kensington Palace Gardens. He walked another block and made a small, red chalk mark on the bus stop, located at Palace Ct. He reversed direction and headed back to number eight Kensington Palace Gardens.

Later that day, just before sundown, Calvin was standing in front of the Peter Pan statue in Kensington Gardens. He had a folded *Times* under his left arm, indicating the meeting was safe. He stood holding a bag of stale breadcrumbs, throwing a few at a time into the Serpentine, feeding a flock of ducks. That's when the woman approached. She was in her late sixties, slim in stature, pushing a baby stroller. The woman stopped close to Calvin and watched the feeding frenzy. To anyone passing by, it would look perfectly harmless. Nothing more than an older couple going for a walk in the park. Then Calvin's Soviet controller spoke.

"What's so important you had to signal an emergency contact?"

The couple switched from English to German. Calvin spoke, "Something's come up. I received a report today that a Soviet officer interviewed Cordes at Camp 020. The officer had all the authorizations signed personally by Soviet War Crimes Inspector General. I do not have a name for this officer because my source was unable to come up with a name. I do have a physical description, though."

"Go on," said the Russian.

"Pretty, young, provocative, spoke English with a heavy Eastern European accent. The most interesting trait was she had more aplomb than all the Allied officers combined, and she wore her skirt three inches higher than regulation. She insisted all recording devices be turned off before interrogation. Do you have any War Crimes prosecutors in the country?"

The woman stood in silence for a while, then she began, "I can tell you we do not have any officers in the UK that fit that description. What about you? Does that description ring a bell?"

"That physical description can be anyone in any number of departments."

The woman reached into her childless stroller and pulled out a paper bag with more breadcrumbs inside. She handed the bag to Calvin. "Your orders: find out who this woman is and report back to the Centre immediately. She could be a very clever and capable agent."

"That will not be easy. I could be exposed during my inquiries. I'll have to contact several agencies and departments. I'll need more money, twenty thousand pounds."

"Out of the question. I can authorize ten, no more."

"How about fifteen?"

The old woman stared off into the Serpentine momentarily and then continued. "I'll authorize ten. That is, of course, *on top* of your regular salary. When you come up with a positive identity, you'll get five more. That's it."

"Agreed." Then Calvin threw the rest of the breadcrumbs into the water.

Chapter 5

Dimitri Pavel, Colonel NKVD, Third Directorate,
Counter-intelligence, Soviet occupied Germany, was
summoned to Soviet Administrative Headquarters in Karl-
shorst. It was after eleven at night when Dimitri received
word by courier. This meeting was extremely urgent
because it was with Ivan Serov, head of all NKVD operations in Germany. The courier drove Pavel directly to
number four Zwieseler Strasse, where the Soviet Red Army
occupied a former SS officer's mess hall. The building was
surrounded by temporary barbed wire and was lit despite
total darkness in the eastern zone of Berlin.

Serov had a small office located in the rear of the
building which at one time was the cook's quarters for the
officer's mess. Serov was seated at a small desk littered with
files and papers. A large bottle of vodka sat in front of him,
along with two, shot glasses. Serov poured two shots and
the two toasted, "Nostrovia."— Serov placed his glass
down and filled another.

"I have been alerted to an extremely urgent matter.
One that requires your skills and expertise."

Pavel knew something extraordinary was about to come his way. He was prepared to handle anything in support of the Motherland. He was a trained intelligence professional and the best spy catcher the Soviets had to offer in the occupied zones. Pavel smartly saluted his superior. "I am prepared to serve the Motherland, Comrade General. What is it that you want from me?"

Serov poured Pavel another glass and said, "Drink up, Colonel."

Pavel did as instructed. Serov rummaged through the mass of files on his desk and produced a single folder, passing it toward Pavel. "His name is Otto Krupke, the slime, and former head of RHSA Security, Berlin. Specifically, in charge of all counter-espionage activities of the Third Reich and responsible for the murder of over one-hundred of our best agents who were dropped into Germany. He was arrested by the British but supposedly died in captivity. Our 'highest sources' tell us otherwise, that he actually escaped British custody, fleeing to his former territories in the Eastern sector, seeking sanctuary to the American lines. Our highest sources believe he is trying to make a deal with the Americans, proffering his knowledge of our intelligence capabilities, possibly a contract with American intelligence organizations, which, at this moment, are nonexistent. If this information is leaked to the Americans, it will set us back decades, not to mention the compromise of our assets operating in London, Washington, and New York, as well as Eastern Europe. We cannot allow this to happen."

Serov showed Pavel a map of Eastern Germany and Poland. "We have a small window of opportunity. Portions of Western Poland are scheduled to be handed back to Polish control. But at the moment, the Red Army still has occupation control under liberation status. You speak

German and Polish fluently. We need you to go there, find him, collect what information you can, then *e*xecute him. It's that simple. You are authorized a full Third Department complement."

Pavel picked up Krupke's file and opened it. "Can you narrow my search?"

"The son of a bitch could be anywhere. His network was vast, and he's got the hard cash to get around. Diamonds, gold, US dollars, Swiss francs. All paid out by Göring's slush fund."

"Colonel, British Secret Service will also be after him. They will most likely send in their best spy catcher too. They've got to correct their mistakes. They'll have an equally high priority. MI-6 can send in any number of their best agents, but a little bit of luck has come our way. Our highest sources in London have given us a very capable individual. Unfortunately, our highest sources cannot deliver a name, probably because the agent uses several aliases. We do have a description, though."

Pavel interjected, "Sir, why is this British agent so important? I thought you were after Krupke?"

"The answer is simple, my young colleague. You find the agent, you find Krupke." Serov then handed Pavel a typed message. It read:

HIGHEST SOURCES INTELLIGENCE:

BE ON THE LOOKOUT FOR A FEMALE OPERA-
TIVE. AGE 35, PETITE IN STATURE, EXTREMELY
HAUGHTY IN NATURE, APLOMB, PROVOCATIVE.
SPEAKS RUSSIAN, UKRAINIAN, POLISH, ROMAN-
IAN, HUNGARIAN, AND GERMAN FLUENTLY
WITH NO NOTICEABLE OR DETECTABLE
ACCENT. POSSIBLY OTHER LANGUAGES AS

WELL. ABILITY TO MOVE FREELY ABOUT THE
CONTINENT.

"As you can see, she could be anyone and anywhere."

Serov issued his final instructions. "The railway line is
open all the way to Krakow. You'll have unrestricted movement. Find Krupke before the British do! Go now. A military train leaves for the Eastern territories in one hour. Be
on that train."

"Yes, Comrade General!" Pavol said as he saluted his
boss.

Chapter 6

FRANKFURT, GERMANY AMERICAN SECTOR

It was a cold morning in early November of 1945, five months after the Allied victory over Nazi Germany. RAF Squadron Leader, Vivian Tate stepped off a US Army bus. She was wearing her new RAF uniform and carrying a small suitcase on Furstenberger Strasse in front of the IG Farben building, now USFET Headquarters. She had arrived in Frankfurt the night before. Vivian had been able to use her new position and authority to catch a military flight directly to the U.S. Army Air Base at Rhein-Main, near Darmstadt, where she had spent the night in military quarters. Because she was not an early riser, Vivian missed her opportunity to use the base motor pool, which was depleted and thus had no choice but to ride the army bus to USFET Headquarters.

The bus traveled on mostly deserted streets, void of any civilian vehicles. Debris and rubble had been bull-dozed off the streets into considerable piles to make way for reconstruction. She walked the long distance to the main entrance on Norbert-Wolheim-Platz, entered the lobby, and secured her luggage at the check-in locker. She walked up the stairs to the first floor and General Eisenhower's office. She had an appointment at 11:00 a.m., but it was already past 11:30 a.m. As she entered the reception area, Eisenhower's secretary, a middle-aged German woman, was about to speak, but Vivian simply raised her finger and said, "I've had a rather grueling journey from London. It was a short night."

"Please have a seat, Squadron Leader. You're a little late, but I'll inform the general of your arrival."

Vivian sensed she was a local Frankfurter and replied in German, "I'd rather stand. I don't expect to be waiting long, despite my tardiness."

The woman, surprised by Vivian's fluent and commanding German, replied back in German, "I understand, ma'am, but I will have to announce your arrival."

Just then, the door to Eisenhower's office opened and the Commander of USFET emerged. "It's all right, Mildred, please come in, Miss Tate. Good to see you again," he added as he extended his hand. He was not expecting to see Miss Tate dressed in an RAF uniform with the equivalent rank of major.

Vivian hurriedly moved past Eisenhower's secretary and her desk. She stood at attention and saluted Eisenhower. "Good to see you too, sir. It's been, what, late 1944?"

Vivian remained standing in Eisenhower's offices as he returned her salute, then took a seat behind the desk. "Has it been that long?" He offered a cigarette, which Vivian accepted. "Your reputation proceeds you. Your department was instrumental in the overall Allied victory. I received an intriguing cable from the Prime Minister requesting an urgent meeting with you. So, what can I do for you?"

As she was taking her first few puffs, Vivian reached into her briefcase and handed him the letter from Prime

Minister Attlee. The general read in silence and then crushed out his cigarette.

Vivian broke the silence. "I'll be quite frank, you've read my letter from Attlee, and you already know what I'm about to tell you, General. The von Braun team is lacking key flight hardware, mainly the more accurate and reliable gyros. The Germans called them inertial guidance units. You need these components to make a truly guided missile. I can get you those components, but I need your help." Vivian recapped the entire story about Krupke's arrest, escape from British custody, Soviet penetrations, and the ruse of using her as the bait.

Once Vivian finished, Eisenhower responded, "I read the entire report from the Backfire tests. You're right, on all accounts. We need those components you mentioned, no matter what the costs, and you're a brave woman going into the fire like this. So, how can we help?"

"For starters, I'd like Major Antoni Franko on my team, which I'll assemble here at IG Farben."

"Is that all?"

"I want total and complete command of the operation under *American* jurisdiction. I've given it the code name Operation Checkmate. I'll get you the scientists and the flight hardware delivered to the American sector. You can do what you wish with them once they're in American hands. His Majesty's government and I keep Krupke."

Eisenhower sat in silence, thinking about what to say next. "So, you'd like us to fund the operation, so the Soviets aren't alerted, is that it?"

"Naturally, all His Majesty's government asks is that we get Krupke back, *alive*. You keep the gyros and the scientists. It's a win-win for the Americans, no matter how you slice it, and it's a bargain price if you take everything into consideration."

This was an unexpected breakthrough in the recovery of the former, Nazi Wonder Weapons. Eisenhower finished the last of another cigarette, reached for a pad of paper, and scratched out two memos. Next, he called his secretary on the intercom. "Mildred, get me Major Franko's personnel file, and I'd like you to type up two sets of orders." He started to rise but said, "Please have a seat, Miss Tate, and help yourself to another cigarette. I'll be right back." He left his office with the two sheets of paper.

Vivian sat in silence and smoked another one of Eisenhower's cigarettes. She wondered if she wasn't too stern in her requests. However, she needed support from the Americans. Otherwise, her plan could not be accomplished; she was satisfied.

Approximately ten minutes later, Eisenhower came back in. He handed Vivian a set of orders assigning RAF Squadron Leader Vivian Tate to USFET along with a similar letter to that of Prime Minister Attlee. The other set was for Major Antoni Franko. Vivian read the orders and the letter.

November 2, 1945

United States Forces European Theater
American Sector
Frankfurt, Germany

To Whom It May Concern,

Greetings,

Royal Air Force Squadron Leader, Vivian Tate is assigned to the acquisition of all former Third Reich weapons technology at any cost.

This mission, code name Operation Checkmate, is the highest priority to the national security of the United States.

Give Squadron Leader Tate any and all resources needed in support of this operation. Any questions to this directive must be addressed directly to this office.

Signed

Dwight D. Eisenhower, General
Commander
United States Forces European Theater

Now armed with the two letters and movement orders, she was in total control of Operation Checkmate.

Eisenhower spoke to finish up the meeting. "I've cut your orders for sixty days. You'll be assigned to CIOS with movement orders signed by the Allied Control Commission. I'm actually leaving USFET but am still officially in command until the end of November. I'd like this wrapped up before the change of command in December. Major Franko's office is located at G-2 School Annex, 743 Schwarzburg Strasse, Special Projects branch. You have his orders. He should be there this morning. Good luck to you, Squadron Leader. My secretary will give you our cable addresses."

Chapter 7

Vivian Tate found Major Franko's office thanks to a U.S.
Army Jeep and driver she managed to acquire with Eisenhower's letter. To her surprise, Major Franko's door was
wide open and the office vacant. At first, she thought that
maybe Franko had left to use the restroom. But as she
walked in, it was apparent that no one had been there for
some time. No butts or burning cigarettes in the ashtrays.
Walls were void; shelves, and bookcases empty. The
meager desk was clear and neat except for a desktop calendar. The only thing recognizable as a utilized office in the
one-time school classroom was a chalkboard with a rough
sketch of a V-2 rocket. It looked like something a school
child would draw. She wondered if she was too late,
thinking perhaps Franko had left for the day. She was
about to search elsewhere when she saw a green military
jacket with the rank of major on it hanging on a hook. He
was still there and in the building somewhere.

Vivian walked down the hall to the next office. The
door was marked G-2 Intelligence Staff, and she knocked
politely. A young Hispanic-looking army sergeant with a

name tag that read Sanchez was busy stuffing files into a cabinet. "Excuse me for interrupting, but can you tell me where I can find Major Franko? He's not in his office."

The young sergeant, upon seeing an attractive woman officer in an RAF uniform, answered, "Hello, ma'am, I'm Sergeant Sanchez. Major Franko's assistant." He looked up at the clock. "He's probably taking a break at the canteen. They serve coffee and sandwiches at this time. The canteen is downstairs, basement level. You can try there first. I know he doesn't eat very much during lunch. Look by the chess and pool tables. You might find him there. He usually plays every day."

"Thank you, Sergeant Sanchez," she said as she walked down the hall and downstairs toward the canteen.

Vivian Tate entered the canteen. It was beginning to fill up because by this time it was after 12:30 p.m. She saw uniforms from all branches of the military, including several Royal Navy and Air Force. She could not recognize anyone who looked like Major Antoni Franko, though she only had a picture to go by, so she checked by the pool tables. There, in a secluded corner away from the noise, she saw someone who could be Major Antoni Franko seated at a table with a young female Marine Corps lieutenant playing a game of chess.

Franko was a well-built man about six feet tall, with blond, short-cropped hair and blue eyes. He looked younger than his thirty years. Furthermore, a fact Cameron failed to mention, he was extremely handsome. A half-eaten mystery meat sandwich was placed beside him. He was busy in deep thought, looking over the chess pieces. Quietly, she approached. Neither the woman nor Franko moved or made eye contact to see who the stranger might be who approached. Vivian looked at the game board intensely then addressed the young woman. "You can get his king in four moves, you know."

Major Antoni Franko, now curious, looked up from his game of chess and saw a young, petite RAF officer. She was dressed in her Air Force uniform flawlessly. Her skirt was hemmed slightly higher than usual, showing off her shapely legs, giving off the appearance she was taller than she was. Her light-brown hair was neatly pulled back FANY style. She had on light blush and lipstick. "Major Franko?" she asked.

Antoni Franko stood and extended his hand. "That's me, and whom do I have the pleasure?"

Vivian offered her hand in exchange. "Squadron Leader Vivian Tate. You can call me Miss Tate."

Franko was slightly taken aback by her introduction and said, "Very well, Miss Tate it is. You can call me Tony."

"I'm sorry to interrupt. I tried your office, but you weren't in."

Franko looked at his watch. "It's time for lunch."

Vivian now addressed the young marine lieutenant, "Will you excuse us for a few minutes? I need some private words with Major Franko."

The young woman answered, "Yes, of course, ma'am, as you wish."

As she was getting up, Vivian reached down to the chess board and moved four pieces in four moves. "Knight to King Six, checkmate, Major Franko. Can't you see, young lady, he left his queen exposed?"

The woman, speechless, dropped her jaw, then left the two.

"Do you mind if we continue in your office? I'd like to ask you a few questions."

"Can you tell me what this is about?"

"The inertial guidance units." Vivian then handed Franko his orders assigning him to her unit and Operation Checkmate. He read in silence and noted the signature from General Eisenhower.

Franko didn't need her to say anything further. He simply grabbed his half-eaten mystery meat sandwich. "Let's go to my office."

Back in Franko's office, Vivian spent the next four hours telling him the entire story and the reason for getting the gyros. She went into detail on the overall mission, and Tony Franko was surprised Vivian Tate would risk her life to trap Krupke and acquire the missile technology. Franko finally had to get up from his desk and stretch his legs.

"Let me get this straight. You planned this entire mission within the last three to four days?"

"Most of it. We are under a time constraint. Every second counts at this point."

"Impressive, I'll give you that." Franko changed the subject. "I see you're a chess player?"

"I prefer bridge, but I do play a little." Vivian moved on to a more serious topic. "I did have some help with the final piece. Let's be frank, Major. Neither you nor I are field operatives. I needed professionals who can work with us handling the dirty work. You know, like putting a knife in a man's throat or putting a bullet between a man's eyeballs. I came up with a solution. Back in London, I made several trusted contacts during the war, one of whom was a former Polish officer. We worked together on many operations. He's living in London now. So, I recently made contact with him and expressed my requirements and the need for secrecy. He gave me the names of two individuals. Both were former Polish intelligence agents of the home army. As you know, Polish intelligence was decimated during the war. Most were liquidated by the Nazis. Some managed to escape the roundup and worked their way to the Polish resistance units, where they worked alongside us for the remainder of the war. Some were actually trained by SOE and SIS. Anyway, he gave me the names of two individuals, Ana Zawacki and Isebel Glowinski. I ran a thorough vetting process and have determined these two women fit the qualifications for the job. Above all, they are independent assets, sort of freelancers. I've contacted them and reached an agreement. I've already arranged their salary and first payments. They're not cheap. They'll join the team in Poland."

Franko, thinking ahead, asked, "Can we trust them? How do we know they won't go to the Soviets for a better offer?"

"You don't know what's truly going on in the Eastern zone, do you, now that the war's over?"

Franko shook his head, conceding ignorance. "No, I'm a tech guy, not political. My job was to go after technical intelligence. I was never in OSS or CIC. I was assigned to 'Lusty' and that's where I spent most of my war years."

Vivian continued, "One of the reasons why we want Krupke back in British custody is because of his vast knowledge of Communist activities in former areas of the Third Reich. He ran a huge network of double agents against Moscow. He infiltrated and played back the wireless radios for the entire Rote Kapelle network. This playback game dwarfed anything the *Sicherheitsdienst* accomplished in Belgium and France. Polish resistance also knows about these activities.

"Major Franko, the Soviets are in the process of slowly adopting Communism in all their occupied states. It's only a matter of time before Poland falls to Soviet doctrine, not to mention East Germany, Czechoslovakia, Romania, Hungary, Bulgaria, and Yugoslavia. These former agents won't get a job anywhere. They're trying to make as much money as they can now before the door closes. They both lost their husbands in the war. The prospects of working for the Soviets aren't any better. The NKVD would rather send them to the gulag than offer them a job with Soviet intelligence."

"I see your point. I think I've heard enough for one day, Miss Tate. Let's say we pick this up tomorrow. You've been busy these past few days. I'll arrange your quarters. It's the same location we gave to General Dornberger. You won't be disappointed. Miss Tate, let me finish by saying this. I agree, we need those gyros. You get your pal Krupke to fall for the trap and hand over the scientists; I can get them to the American zone."

Next, Franko called the billeting office to set up accommodations, then had a driver take Vivian to her quarters for the night. The two agreed to meet at ten the next morning. Once Vivian was gone for the day, Franko made a secure call to his personal assistant, Sergeant Hector Sanchez.

"Sergeant Sanchez, this is Major Franko."

Franko gave him the full details on Operation Checkmate and informed Sanchez that they were now both working for Squadron Leader Vivian Tate. He then assigned Sanchez support tasks. Franko then moved on to another topic. "I need you to do me a little favor, rather short notice. I want you to contact your sources at Whitehall and get me everything, and I mean *everything*, on an RAF Squadron Leader Vivian Tate. We're supposedly working for her now. She's a bit of a stiff shirt very British, doesn't reveal much, never smiles. Nice-looking though and. . . I need it pronto!"

* * *

FRANKO WAS at his desk early the next morning waiting for Sergeant Sanchez's report. He hadn't slept the night before as he was busy thinking about his next assignment and this mysterious woman known as Miss Tate. Plus, the fact he was not only working with her, he was working *for* her, according to General Eisenhower's orders. She seemed to know a lot about former Nazi intelligence capabilities but also current Soviet abilities. She was one of the most brilliant minds he'd come across during his time with Lusty and CIOS. Not to mention the fact he was beginning to like her.

At 8:30 a.m., Franko's thoughts were interrupted by a knock on his door.

"Major Franko, I've got the report you requested. I was at headquarters until late last night and early this morning. I demanded everything, but there's absolutely nothing on an RAF Squadron Leader Vivian Tate. I'm sorry to report, sir, this is all I've got." He handed Franko a file folder with one single sheet of paper in it. Franko opened it and read.

Miss Vivian Tate

Current: Part-time assistant, Student Foreign Exchange Services, London, England

Past: Administrative Assistant, Inter-Services Research Bureau, London, England

Franko lit a cigarette as he read. He was startled by this enigma known as Vivian Tate. Then he broke the silence as Sanchez stood at his desk. "That's it? No military records?"

"Afraid not, sir."

Franko put out his cigarette. "Very well. We'll have to

do this the hard way. In the meantime, keep trying. Try MI-6, search under any aliases she may have used during the war. I need something."

Franko did discover one inquisitive fact about Miss Tate. The Inter-Services Research Bureau was a code name for the British Special Operations Executive (SOE). He also deduced that Vivian Tate had probably been more than a mere administrative assistant.

Exactly two hours later, sometime around midmorning, Vivian Tate entered Franko's office and closed the door behind her. She didn't have her RAF uniform on, but instead was dressed in civilian attire: a lightweight wool suit with a matching jumper, felt hat, no makeup, with her hair untidy and unwashed. In fact, she looked to Franko as if she were another woman than the one he had met the day before. She didn't say a word but went straight to work. She used one of the large tables in the room and placed her worn, leather briefcase on top of it. Next, she proceeded to reach deep into the case and produced neatly folded maps, drawings, and aerial photos. There were several. In fact, as Franko watched intensely, he was beginning to wonder if the briefcase was magically bottomless. It looked as if this mysterious woman known as Vivian Tate was really some sort of a sorceress rather than an intelligence officer. She proceeded to spread the items across the table in preparation for the brief. Finally, she said, "Can I have a cup of tea, please? I'm sure there's some in the building."

Franko now seized the opportunity to break the ice with a little humor. "Would you care for a biscuit as well?"

Vivian never blinked. She continued about with her papers and simply said, "No, thank you. Tea, but I'll settle for a strong black coffee if there's no tea."

Franko left his office and came back a short time later

with a piping hot cup of tea. He placed the mug down on the table as Vivian was busy marking the maps with pens and colored pencils. "I've come up with a plan for insertion. I'd like to run it by you."

Franko placed both hands on the table and looked over the maps as Vivian proceeded.

"We'll go in by clandestine airdrop using the Motyl field secured by the AK 22 Ranger Battalion. You're familiar with this, aren't you?"

Franko couldn't stand it any longer. She was an enigma. There were only four people on Earth who knew anything about Motyl, not to mention the Ranger Battalion. "Let's get something straight right now before we go any further, Miss Tate. Just *who* are you, really? To my knowledge, there are only four people who know what and where Motyl is, not to mention knowing the exact location of the airfield."

Vivian picked up her tea and took a sip, contemplating her words. "In due time, I'll share details with you, many of which will become available as we proceed along on the mission. Security being the most important. All I can tell you, Major, is that I was selected because of my expertise in this field. I just happen to know things you don't."

Franko knew he wasn't going to get much further at this point. He would try a different, less direct approach that he would employ on his terms. "Very well. Have it your way. To answer your question, yes, I am familiar with the airfield."

Vivian returned to business. "Good, because you'll confirm the location to the aircrew before landing. Next, what air assets can we use for the landing?"

"CIOS has unmarked C-47s at their disposal. Crews are on alert at all times. All I need is twenty-four hours' notice. How many do you need?"

"Only one for insertion, two for EXFIL. Let's talk about backup plans just in case the landing field is too soggy, like it was during your Most III mission. I want an alternate airfield. What do you have?" Vivian referred to Franko's mission into Poland during the war to recover a nearly intact V-2 rocket. His EXFIL aircraft had been stuck in the mud upon landing.

Franko, now back to seriousness, looked at the maps and aerial photos. "Not much in the area that can be used as an alternate field. Definitely not one that can support a backup reception committee and a C-47. We'll have to jump. That's the only way. It's the most secure."

Vivian jotted some notes on her tablet. "Very well, the secondary plan is to jump. Hopefully, it won't be necessary."

"When was the last time you actually did a parachute drop?" Franko hoped to gain some information about her from idle talk. Vivian didn't bite. She ignored his question altogether, looking down on her maps.

Vivian continued, "Like I said, hopefully, we won't have to do it. It's only if Motyl is compromised. On this mission, we don't have the luxury of aborting and returning at a later date. The Russians will be there waiting for us on our return. Also, we are under a time constraint. We've got to get in place at key times for the plan to materialize."

Franko looked at the map and photos once again. "We can jump here," he said, as he pointed to an area just north of the town of Zaborow.

Vivian circled the position with a colored pencil and nodded in agreement. "That will work. If we jump, it's still close enough to reestablish contact with the secondary reception committee. Now that that's settled, let's move on. Your record states you ran a ratline to the American sector.

You got several scientists out in late May, right from under the Russians' noses. How did you do this?"

Franko was starting to realize there wasn't much Vivian Tate didn't know about him but answered her question anyway. "They were mostly aerospace physiology experts who worked on high-altitude experiments used in the making of life-support equipment, otherwise known as spacesuits. We ran them across Czechoslovakia into Bavaria using a series of courier lines to various safe houses and black sites."

Vivian jotted a lengthy note down on a pad, something she rarely did. "What was your escape route if the Russians closed in?"

"If the Russians closed in on us, and it was inevitable we'd be captured, our instructions were to get to the US station in Prague. They'd get us out from there." Vivian made a mental note comparing it to the British escape plan out of West Berlin.

Next, Vivian produced an aerial photo of southeastern Poland. "Our primary working area is here," she said as she pointed. "During the war, the Germans used this area between Tarnow and Rzeszow as their secondary testing and launch facility. Unfortunately, it's now under Soviet control.—NKVD and military intelligence units have moved into the area in massive force, hoping to acquire any V-2 technology left over. As of this moment, they're not having much luck. The Germans did a good job of hiding key components and personnel, either by destroying them or executing the personnel. You and I, once we INFIL, we'll establish a Forward Operating Base here, in Tarnow," she said as she pointed to the town on her map.

"Polish AK units will provide operational security under the command of Ana Zawacki, codename Jawor. My cover story has already been established. I'll move into the Hotel Bristol as the proprietor, using the name Janica Kijowski. You'll go in undercover with Jawor's group. She'll probably have a safe house close by to monitor the Hotel Bristol. You'll move in with them until I call for you. Remember, you're supposed to be somewhere on the Continent searching for key missile components and scientists as per my fake background on you. It's all part of the ruse to lure Krupke in. Now, let's talk about the missile system. What can you tell me about the guidance systems? I know you were assigned to the Backfire test at Cuxhaven."

Franko took a seat on one of the chairs and placed his feet on top on the table. "Is there anything you don't know about me?"

Again, Vivian did not reveal anything in Franko's desire to acquire more information from idle talk. "I know your wife divorced you just before the war broke out, but I don't know the reasons why." She prompted the conversation in a direction she wanted to go. "Were the guidance systems new versions or standard equipment on operational rockets?"

"You're amazing. You know stuff about me that I'd forgotten about but still sidestep my questions." Franko removed his feet from the table and sat upright.

"The von Braun team was ecstatic to have a full-blown R&D program with all parties present. During hostilities, von Braun could never determine the causes for failures in the rocket systems because of widespread sabotage during assembly and reassembly by forced labor. We carefully reassembled eight rockets in the hopes of correcting any sabotage acts on the components. We were not one-hundred percent successful. The systems were so intricate and complicated, it was nearly impossible. We launched three rockets, but only one got airborne successfully. The team could never determine if the rockets failed because of flight hardware malfunctions or from sabotage, but I can tell you that we used the standard guidance systems, comprised of two gyros and a primary analog computer. That's all we could find on the Continent."

Vivian re-phrased her original question, "I heard the operational rockets used a guidance system twenty-five years ahead of anything the West had. What can you tell me about those older V-2 gyros?"

"The current version of the V-2 was what we call a dumb bomb. In other words, it was not fully self-guided. The flight hardware controlled the flight controls and engine deflector, nozzles only. Despite this fact, the systems were, as you said, still twenty-five years ahead of anything in US technology. The rocket was only fueled with enough propellant to get it roughly sixty-five miles or so into outer space. Then the fuel ran out, the engine cut off, and the rocket plunged back to Earth. Unknown to us, the Germans gave this process a term called Circular Error Probable or CEP. We did squeeze that out of them. The flight hardware and computer made small corrections to keep the rocket from dipping too far below the horizon, thus on course to hit its target, London. Late in the war, the Germans experimented with a homing beacon to improve CEP, but from our interviews with the von Braun team, it was determined the Leitstrahl beacon was vastly inferior compared to newer, self-contained internal guidance units and not prone to external jamming."

"I was told the Germans were very closedmouthed with regards to the V-2 guidance system during Backfire. How did you squeeze this information out of them?" asked Vivian.

Franko nodded in agreement. "That's correct. They kept to their end of the bargain during Backfire, which was to test-fire only the *existing* systems. However, after the last Backfire test, and we actually got the one rocket airborne, we had a celebration. General Dornberger, in particular, got himself into a drunken stupor, which was all part of our plan, by the way. That's when he revealed to General Cameron and me the existence of the more sophisticated guidance system, which he called the Inertial Guidance System (IGS). When the von Braun team left for the US, we had a final out-brief, and the topic of the Inertial Guidance System was our top priority. All we could determine was the IGS would enable the V-2s to be truly self-guided and not a dumb bomb. If von Braun knew anything further about the IGS, he kept quiet about it."

"Krupke knows where they're at, I'm sure of it."

"And if we could get our hands on them before the Russians do, we could put our atomic bombs on the rockets and fire them anywhere in the world. This would strategically tip the balance of power heavily in our favor. The Russians may not ever catch up."

Chapter 8

His escape was actually quite easy, especially with help from Bertha Cordes. Otto Krupke left Harwich, England, on a Danish freighter working as a crewman. He arrived in Copenhagen two days later, where he switched to a Polish ship and made the overnight voyage to Gdansk harbor. From there it was a short walk to the train station.

Krupke's strategy was to keep moving, stopping only for brief periods. He had to make contact with his former network. He found a public telephone at the train station and placed a local call. After several rings, a man answered. He spoke Polish, "Yes."

Krupke answered in German, "It's been a long winter."

The anonymous voice responded back in German, "Then you must do a very long penance. Where are you?"

Correct code words now exchanged, Krupke was confident. "Main train station, Gdansk. I need to make a withdrawal."

"How soon?"

"I'll need it by the day-after-tomorrow. In the evening. . . and I need the file on the agent known as Hilda Bradt."

There was a short break in the conversation as the man on the other end was obviously contemplating a response from the information.

"There's a small ersatz coffee shop inside the station. Meet there the day-after-tomorrow at sixteen hundred hours. We'll make a brush pass then. That's all I have."

Krupke hung up the phone and proceeded to the ticket counter. Speaking in Polish, he asked the railway agent, "I need a one-way ticket to Tuchola."

The ticket agent looked at his station clock and then responded, "If you hurry, there's a train leaving in five minutes. If you miss this train, the next one for Tuchola is at six tonight."

"I'll take it, first class, please."

Krupke paid for his ticket in cash, then hurried to the platform. The train left three minutes later. Two hours later, he was standing in front of the old train station at Tuchola. The town was virtually deserted at eleven in the morning, with only an occasional pedestrian or horse-drawn cart passing by. Not much had changed from the sleepy town since the war. He walked the short distance to the Corpus Christi Church. He entered and found the confessional booths. He took the one on the left and dropped to his knees. A small sensor sent an electrical signal to the rectory that someone needed to hear confession. A short time later, Krupke listened to the sounds of footsteps heading to the back of the church. A priest entered the confessional booth from a rear entrance, took a seat, then opened the partition. Krupke heard the barrier go up but could not make out the face of the priest; it was too dark in his compartment. It didn't matter; he only needed to speak and hear the words. "Bless me, Father, for

I have sinned. It's been a very long winter since my last confession."

After a lengthy delay, obviously thinking over Krupke's statement, the priest responded, "Then you must do a very long penance. Only Father Kobas can hear your confession. Go to the back pew on the left. Wait there for Father Kobas." The priest closed the partition and exited the confessional booth from the rear. After a short delay, Krupke did as instructed, knelt down at the last row on the left, and waited.

It wasn't long. Again, Krupke heard the faint footsteps approaching the rear of the church. Krupke kept his hands folded and closed his eyes as if in sincere prayer. The man sat next to Krupke. He was dressed in a black cassock with a white collar. He was slender and had a narrow face and round spectacles. His hair was closely cropped with speckles of gray. His real name was Dr. Kurt Mangus, a Third Reich gyro expert and codeveloper for the updated V-2 guidance system. He spoke in German, almost in a whisper. "So, Father Polski tells me you've done a very long penance. I've been waiting for you. It's about time you showed up."

"It's time. I have a plan. We need to talk. Is there someplace we can go?"

Mangus, speaking in Polish, made a sign of the cross over Krupke's head and then stood up. "Wait five minutes, take the side door closest to the altar on the right. Go outside and to the back. There is a small courtyard. I'll be sitting beside the fountain."

Krupke did as instructed. He found Dr. Mangus seated on a small cement bench next to the fountain. Krupke sat next to him. "I can get you out as well as the rest of the avionics team. I have a direct line to the American sector. It's my ace in the hole. Do you still have the components?"

Mangus lowered his head and spoke softly, "Keep your voice down. Pretend you're in deep, sincere discussion with the Holy Father." Krupke nodded in agreement. Mangus continued, "How did you find me?"

"Remnants of my network are still in place. However, those sources are drying up rapidly. We have a small window of opportunity. The Communists are taking over the country. It could be days, perhaps weeks. One thing is certain, if we don't act now, the window will be closed forever. But to answer your question, my contact, in Gdansk."

"Are they trustworthy?"

"As long as they're alive."

"Good, then I can report to you that the components are carefully hidden, as your office instructed. The Red Army was advancing quickly and overran the Leba complex, but we were able to move key components before we abandoned the launch site. They're buried here in a local cemetery. Dr. Hoch is still hiding as far as I know near Pustkow, awaiting my orders. Also, I am happy to tell you that all technical aspects of the new avionics system are hidden on microdots in parish sheet music. There is no need to carry documents out, except those sheets of music, which will not arouse suspicion."

"Excellent, when we get to a safe area, I'll have my contacts make copies of your music and send them by post to the United States. We have a cutout in New York. There, we can recover them as a backup if necessary. The first order of business—we must secure those components. I can't bargain our safe passage without them. We'll need transportation too. What do you have?"

"One small lorry, which I have access to from the parish motor pool."

"Excellent. What about excavating equipment?" asked Krupke.

"A few picks and shovels. Nothing more. We buried the devices in a shallow grave. But we'll have to go under cover of darkness."

* * *

NOT MORE THAN a block away from the church, Krupke and Mangus found the small cemetery. They carried picks, shovels, and oil lanterns as they made their way to the grassy graveyard. Many of the tombstones were over-turned or damaged. Some were non-existent. The one they were looking for, in particular, was a wooden headstone. Mangus shined his lantern on what he thought was the right one. As he came closer, stooped down and looked on the inscriptions. He saw the markings. They were of a German officer killed in action nearby. "This is it. There's no mistake. I planted the headstone myself."

Krupke turned up his lantern and placed it near the grave. "Get the shovels out. Let's start digging."

Mangus grabbed a square, flat shovel. "There's no need to get physical. Let me show you."

Mangus scrapped the grass a few inches below the surface and immediately touched metal. He tapped the ground further, and both men could hear the sound of metal on metal. He scrapped further around the grave and exposed a rectangular, flat object. He looked up at Krupke and smiled. "See, I told you. Just as I left it."

Quickly, the two men dug around the object until it was fully exposed. Mangus reached to one side and found a handle. "There should be a handle on the other side. We'll have to work together to lift it out."

The two men struggled to lift and placed shovels under the object until it came out of the ground. It was a box about three by five feet and approximately two feet high. The men placed the metal box on the soft soil next to the grave.

Krupke was surprised the device was so compact. "Let's get it into the truck. We can inspect it later when we get back to the safe house. I don't want us to be exposed any longer than necessary." The two men picked up the metal case and brought it over to a utility truck. Once the box was safely secured inside the truck, the two men returned to the grave site and proceeded to cover it. Sooner or later, the local priest or groundskeeper would notice, but they probably wouldn't say or do anything because it was a German soldier.

The men drove the truck back to Tuchola. There, they drove into a small automotive garage, closed the door, and proceeded to unload their precious cargo. Mangus used the engine hoist to lift the device onto a small workbench. Mangus used a set of tools that were already in the garage and proceeded to unscrew the bolts holding the metal container together. Once that was complete, the two men lifted the cover and removed the packaging material. What they found was a V-2 guidance system, complete with three working gyros wired together. Mangus looked at the device further using a work light. "That's it! That's the latest one."

For the first time in almost two weeks, Krupke finally relaxed, knowing he had his prized possession in his grasp. "Can we power it up just to make sure?" he asked.

"The best way is to start the generator, hook it up, and use that instead of the local AC current and the dry batteries. The units are equipped with a small internal transformer-rectifier to convert AC power to DC and recharge the batteries," added Mangus.

Krupke nodded. "Get the generator going."

A few minutes later, Mangus had the generator running and hooked the connection to the external power receptacle for the navigation system. Immediately, the loud, humming sound of the gyros could be heard spinning to acceleration speed. The noise was deafening. Mangus flipped a switch on the control box, and several lights illuminated on the mechanism, indicating the batteries were charging. He was about to check the system further when Krupke shouted, "That's enough! We don't want to spoil the goods! Turn it off!"

It was all quiet in the garage now. Krupke finally broke out in laughter. "Do you realize what we can do now? The von Braun team will have their super-guidance systems to power their rockets, thanks to us! Pack a small suitcase. We'll spend the night here, then leave at first light. We need to get back to the Gdansk train station with the goods."

Events were moving quickly for Krupke. He and Mangus drove the lorry on secondary roads to avoid Soviet patrols on the main highways and only came across the occasional ox and cart, nothing more. They arrived at the Gdansk train station just after 3 p.m. "Stay here in the truck with the goods. I need to meet someone," was all Krupke said.

"How long will it take?"

Krupke detected a slight uneasiness from Mangus, mainly due to a large number of Soviet troops inside the station. Krupke made a quick glance at the young soldiers. "Don't worry. They're mostly Central Asian conscripts. Many of them can't even read or write, let alone speak their native language. Ignore them. Probably waiting for the next train to take them east."

Krupke got out of the truck and proceeded into a small coffee shop inside the terminal. There was only one.

Krupke ordered a cup of ersatz coffee, which was extremely weak, and took the beverage back to a standing table at the rear of the shop.

He waited, expecting to make contact with his source. Fortunately, he was on time and didn't wait long. At precisely 4:00 p.m., a man entered the coffee shop. He was medium-height, in his late thirties or early forties, wearing workman's coveralls and a cap. He had dirt and grime on his hands, as if he'd been working all day. He was carrying a large, military green duffel bag. He placed the bag on the floor as he ordered a cup of the weak coffee. Once he had his beverage, he moved closer to Krupke. The two men made eye contact. "You must be the one who had the long winter?"

Krupke replied, "That's me. And I did a very long penance." Nothing more was exchanged. The man gulped down his coffee, kicked the duffel bag closer to Krupke, then quickly exited the coffee shop. The pass was completed in seconds. Krupke sat for a few minutes more and finished his coffee. He then grabbed the duffel bag, exited the station and walked a block, then crossed the street toward a vacant building, making sure he was not followed. He continued to the side of the building, then proceeded to the rear. Looking around to make sure no one was around, Krupke lit a cigarette, took a few puffs, then dropped the duffel bag and opened it. Inside were bundles of cash, mostly in US dollars, a pistol, and a small package wrapped in wax paper. Krupke tore off the string and wax paper from the package and opened it. Inside was a brown eight-by-ten envelope folded in half, stuffed with documents and a slip of paper written in English. Krupke read:

. . .

TOMORROW MORNING, proceed to the freight docks. Look for a coal barge traveling south. There will be only one. You have passage all the way to Szczucin with your cargo. It's slow, plan on five days, but it's the safest way to avoid Soviet patrols. You need to change to a smaller barge in Warsaw. The crew will know what to do. When you get to Szczucin, there will a truck waiting to take you to Pustkow. Good luck.

Chapter 9

Vivian Tate stood in front of the window of the former elementary school in deep silence, smoking a cigarette. She looked down upon the open courtyard below, which at one time was the school playground.

Franko, still seated at the table, looked at Vivian from behind, gazing upon her perfectly tailored suit, which showed off her curvy figure and legs. "Penny for your thoughts," he finally said.

Vivian turned around and faced him, showing her eyes were glassed over. She was thinking about something or someone, but again she revealed nothing. "I need to know your COM/SEC procedures. How do you communicate with the home station from the field?"

Franko stood up and slowly moved to the coat rack, removing his and Vivian's coats. "I think we've had enough for the time being. You're not thinking about COM/SECs. We can pick this up later. Let me take you out for an early dinner. I know of a place here in town. It's not too far, in Sachsenhausen. We can't be seen together here in the neighborhood. This place is notorious for being loaded with Russian spies. They'll put a tag team on us for sure if they see us together."

Vivian took Franko up on his offer. She realized she hadn't eaten dinner for the two days while she was in Frankfurt. All she had was what was served at the officer's canteen at the school annex, which wasn't much.

By now, it was after four, the sun was already setting, and with the overcast skies of Frankfurt, darkness was fast approaching. The couple drove the Jeep to Franko's quarters, where he changed into civilian attire. Next, the couple left the Jeep and proceeded on foot. They split up and took separate trams to the central train station and from there the Ubahn to Sachsenhausen, again using different trains in case there was a Soviet surveillance team. Vivian had a scarf over her head, and Franko had his wool cap tucked tightly over his head, obscuring his face. Had there been any Russian spies, it would have been tough to recognize their faces or take photographs without a flashbulb.

The couple entered the Klaane-Scheshauser, a German-style restaurant. Vivian entered first, followed by Franko. He grabbed Vivian's arm and led her to a secluded section where they found a small table for two. The couple took off their coats, hats, and scarfs and then took a seat. Vivian spoke first in German, "Your work wasn't bad; there is room for improvement. You looked around too much at Willy-Brandt station. Next time keep your head down as if you're thinking about something."

Franko plopped himself down at the table, ignored her comments on security altogether, and signaled the waitress. "Two pilsners, please."

"I don't drink beer," said Vivian.

"I don't care. This is a beer joint, and you're drinking beer. Besides, I'm buying."

The couple ate and drank. Their meal was conducted

in near silence since both were very hungry at this point. Vivian actually seemed to enjoy the beer since she was on her second half-liter. Franko detected a slight easiness from the usually tense Vivian Tate as she finished her second beer.

"So, Miss Tate," Franko began, "I know they didn't call you that when you were a little girl. What did they call you?" Franko asked in Polish.

The couple spoke exclusively in Polish now. "Nice try."

"Come on, I'm just trying to get to know you better. Where are you from then, Kent, Bedfordshire . . . Scotland perhaps?"

Vivian blinked several times at Franko, thinking of a response, then said. "Actually, I was born and raised in Poland."

Franko had broken the ice. He cracked a smile. Vivian Tate was no more British than he was. "Poland? And what did your friends call you back in Poland?"

Vivian sat in silence for a while, then responded, "Don't think you can liquor me up with a few cheap beers and expect me to divulge my entire background. Remember, you work for me, and I'm Miss Tate to you. Besides, for security reasons, the less you know about me, the better. Let's leave it at that."

Franko raised his beer glass. "Touché, Miss Tate, no more inquiries."

Vivian tensed up once again, picked up a coaster, and held it in front of her mouth, just in case there was a Soviet surveillance team monitoring their conversations.

"Good, now that we've got that settled, alert the air base. I'd like to leave within forty-eight hours. I'll signal the welcoming committee of our arrival. You'll be responsible for the air movements. Make arrangements with your quartermaster. For starters, we'll need fifty-thousand US dollars. Each of us will be going in carrying twenty-five-thousand a-piece. We'll draw more once we're in-country with the US station in Krakow. In the meantime, I'm going back to my quarters and pack. I won't be in tomorrow. I'll call you for the next meeting. Plan on giving me all your COM/SECS then. Now, would you kindly take me back to my quarters, Major?"

* * *

LATER THAT NIGHT, after the couple returned to Frankfurt, Franko called Sergeant Sanchez. "I couldn't even get a name out of her, but she said she's Polish. Can you believe that? The haughty stiff shirt is Polish. See what you can come up with. Oh, by the way, I'll need it by tomorrow morning."

The next morning, Sergeant Sanchez gave Franko the details in person. "I used my contacts at British Intelligence. Luckily, we have an American detail attached, one of my fellow Mexicans from Los Angeles. I asked for anything they had on agents from Poland. Naturally, they knew nothing. Then I started thinking about what you said concerning aliases. I tried to figure out a code word. I could think of nothing, so I asked for any information on female agents from Poland. To my surprise, I received this," and he handed Franko a cable marked: TOP SECRET: AGENT JAN.

"It came across the secure teleprinter this morning. You can read what little there is; most details are still redacted, but it's far more than what we've had before. Your mysterious enigma is quite the super spy and sultry, if, in fact, it is her. AGENT JAN is actually a code name for a person by the name of Irina Jankowski. She went by the nom de guerre Hilda Bradt. Details on her missions are vague and still highly classified. She's Polish, as you said, now a naturalized British subject, recruited by SIS in 1939 to infiltrate Polish intelligence.

"Working out of Warsaw, she was evidently the mistress of some high-ranking Polish diplomat, name unknown. She uncovered crucial information through pillow talk on Polish motives before Germany's invasion. The guy must have fallen for her hook, line, and sinker because he spilled his guts out to her. He told her *everything*. Cunningly, she was able to acquire a considerable amount of information on German motives, which she composed weekly in reports and sent to London via diplomatic pouch.

"Next, she discovered from her lover that Polish mathematicians working at a classified site called the Black Chamber were able to crack early Enigma codes. It was called Bomba. Mostly a series of stolen Enigma machines networked together, which Polish intelligence was able to acquire over the years. These machines were actually able to decode early Enigma traffic. Naturally, British intelligence wanted more for their own code breakers at Bletchley Park, so she was tasked to steal one of the Bomba devices, which she did successfully. Details of this operation are also redacted, but we all know the outcome from those code breakers at Bletchley Park.

"Unfortunately, shortly after the Bomba operation, she and her entire SIS team were rounded up by the Gestapo and taken to Berlin for interrogation. There, Agent Jan was subjected to extremely harsh interrogations by her captors. Despite these horrendous acts, she amazingly held out for over seventy-two hours, allowing her remaining colleagues to flee. She somehow miraculously escaped from Gestapo custody and eventually worked her way back to England."

Franko tapped his fingers on the desk as he listened in awe. Sanchez continued.

"Because of the huge significance of the ULTRA traffic during hostilities, and injuries sustained from her captivity, Broadway Street couldn't risk keeping her at MI-6 for fear the Germans might discover what the Allies truly knew about the Enigma decoding efforts. She was released from MI-6, given a false background and identity, which, of course, could be Vivian Tate. This does explain why a mysterious and unfamiliar woman known as Vivian Tate was then able to get employment at the Inter-Services Research Bureau code name for SOE, as an administrative assistant to the section responsible for infiltrating agents into the Continent. Keeping secrets a secret, is that what they say, Major? Vivian Tate could very well be Irina Jankowski. I hope this helps."

It all made perfect sense to Franko and, more importantly, it was believable.

"Any information on this Hilda Bradt? Is there a possibility there could be a person by the name of Hilda Bradt who did these things?"

"No, not at all. Records indicate Hilda Bradt is a German national, killed in Berlin in 1939."

"A stolen identity, I'll be goddamned! If it is her, she truly is an enigma! Let's keep this to ourselves for the time being."

Chapter 10

Meanwhile, in the Germany Soviet Sector, Villa Franka was situated in the small town of Bleicherode, just outside the Nordhausen missile complex. This stately villa, located in a quiet neighborhood was once the home to Wernher von Braun. Now it was the headquarters for the Soviet Ballistic A-2 missile program and home of Boris Evseevich Chertok from the NII-1 research institute.

It was after eleven at night. Chertok had just finished dinner with three of his associates: Vasily Mishin, guidance and avionics expert; Sergei Korolev, believed by many to be von Braun's counterpart in the Soviet Union; and Major General Alexi Kuznetsov, chief of Soviet military intelligence (GRU). The men were discussing results from the recent British/American V-2 missile tests known as Backfire. Kuznetsov delivered the grim news to his associates of the enormous potential for the rocket and guidance system.

"Gentlemen," Kuznetsov continued, "I cannot overemphasize the importance of the system. The Americans have the atomic bomb. If they should get hold of sophisticated

Nazi missile technology, this will enable them to place their atomic bombs on top of these rockets and fire them directly at Moscow. We would be annihilated within ten minutes. Therefore, it is the top priority of this section to acquire this technology at all costs. We have our own captured A-4 rocket parts, but what we're missing are the key guidance and flight hardware."

Chertok spoke next. "What do you have in mind, Comrade General? If I'm not mistaken your military intelligence units overran then occupied the Blizna complex in August of 1944. They sent everything they could find back to Moscow."

Kuznetsov continued, "Our sources in state security informed us they are after an SS war criminal named Otto Krupke of the Reich Security Office, Berlin. He was responsible for hiding the missile technology from our advancing forces on the Eastern Front. They believe the advanced hardware was hidden near Leba. I want to put one of our best men in the field, Air Force Colonel Vladimir Sivan, to find that hardware. Here is his file."

Kuznetsov passed the file toward Chertok and Mishin and the two men thumbed through the material and read. Vladimir Sivan was the officer responsible for capturing A-4 components and recovering them to Moscow back in 1944.

"Is he here now, General?" asked Chertok.

Kuznetsov nodded, stood, went to the door, and opened it. "Come in, Colonel."

Vladimir Sivan entered the lavish dining room. He was young, at thirty-five, for a full colonel. He was tall with a lean build and blond hair. He gave a smart salute and addressed the men. "You wanted to see me, Comrade General?"

"You can relax, Colonel. This is an informal meeting,"

said Chertok. "Tell me something, Colonel, you're a military intelligence officer. You were the first on the scene at Blizna to recover the A-4 components. You've read the reports on the A-4 rockets and the guidance system. Is it possible some components are still hidden inside Poland?"

Sivan spoke with confidence. "Comrades, I was there from August 1944 until September 1944. There was not much left to recover. We shipped everything we could find back to Moscow. The components you're referring to are relatively small in nature, compared to other A-4 components. It is technically feasible some of the more sophisticated units are still hidden. It would be almost impossible to recover everything."

Kuznetsov nodded in agreement as he looked at Chertok. "Unless you have a lead, Colonel," said Chertok. "We have a job for you. We've just learned that the location of that unrecovered hardware is somewhere in Poland. State security divulged to us from our sources within that agency. The last-known site for the advanced hardware was at a testing site near Leba. We want you to deploy to Poland and recover that hardware."

Now it was Kuznetsov's turn to speak. "Have a seat, Colonel," he said as he poured a glass of vodka for Sivan.

"Let's talk about the Americans. As you know, President Truman disbanded the OSS on the first of October. They have no consolidated intelligence agency remaining. They only have scattered remnants left on the Continent, mostly working for General Eisenhower's G2 intelligence division out of Frankfurt. Our GRU personnel shadow these individuals to see what they're up to. It has recently been brought to our attention that one of their most experienced technical experts, Major Antoni Franko, has been showing suspicious activity recently. He's been receiving daily briefings from two female intelligence officers, one civilian, one military, identities unknown. We don't have photographs of the women. Their tradecraft is superb. Our agents have not been able to photograph any of these women, but we have a photo of Franko." He passed Sivan a picture of Antoni Franko in his US Army uniform. "If anyone is going after the elusive A-4 components, it will be Franko. Here is his file."

Kuznetsov passed Major Franko's file toward Sivan and continued. "As you can see, Major Antoni Franko was assigned to the British Backfire tests at Cuxhaven. He knows everything about the weapon system. We want you to look for him. Because if you find him, the elusive components will be close by him. Here are your movement orders authorizing you to travel anywhere in the Soviet sector." Kuznetsov shoved the orders toward Sivan.

Rocket expert Sergei Korolev finally interjected. "Comrade Colonel, do you know what would happen if the Americans put an atomic bomb on top of those rockets and fired them at the Motherland?"

"The results would be cataclysmic," replied Sivan.

"Precisely, Colonel," replied Korolev. "We'd be wiped off the face of the earth! The Nazis were never able to advance their A-4 rocket and guidance technology during the war to hit targets in the US or the Soviet Union. We know they had plans for more advanced guidance systems and super rockets capable of hitting the US mainland. Comrade Stalin has tasked me to develop our own Soviet-made rockets and put them into lower Earth orbit to thwart the US-von Braun advantage, but I need those guidance systems to do it, Colonel! This is a matter of survival!"

After the dinner meeting, Colonel Sivan returned to his quarters in Nordhausen. In November 1945, the Red Army completely occupied the city. Billeting was hard to come by. Most of the hotels still surviving the war were occupied by military leadership. Sivan was fortunate to be one of those individuals. He had a small room at a hotel just a short walk from the train station at Nordhausen.

General Kuznetsov directed all signals intelligence and correspondences related to missile technology be forwarded to Colonel Sivan. Sivan sat on the small bed in his quarters and went through his cable messages and the dossier on Major Antoni Franko; there was even a photograph provided by state security. Next, he read the cable from NKVD detailing a possible abandoned Nazi launch site near the small town of Leba, in northern Poland along the Baltic Sea. Sources indicated that a highly secure test site for the Rheinbote rocket was fired from this location. The site was now occupied by the Red Army. It's highly possible that the advance guidance system could have been tested at this facility. Sivan would make his first stop there. In particular, he wanted to interview a former SS officer being held captive at the one-time subcamp of Stuttof near the village of Nawcz, which was only a short distance from Leba. He was the last SS commander before Soviet forces overran the site.

Unlike state security, GRU did not have unlimited resources and petrol. They took what they could get and used what they could use. Sometimes it was horse and wagon. In Sivan's case, this meant using a military train to Gdansk and securing any transport to Nawcz and on to the coastal town of Leba. For the time being, he would conduct his investigation by himself. Only when he had definitive information would he call in his NII-1 support detail.

Chapter 11

Colonel Vladimir Sivan acquired a military vehicle from
the local Red Army motor pool at Gdansk. It was an
American Ford station wagon, painted green with the
windows painted over in the same color as the rest of the
vehicle. It looked more like a green hearse than anything
else. It was also in desperate need of a new muffler and
was firing only on two cylinders, but it got the job done.
Luckily, he had a driver who knew the local area and was
able to quickly get on the road leading to the outskirts of
the city.

When they reached the village of Nawcz, it was
already dark, and the young Russian driver had difficulty
finding the one-time sub-facility of the Stuttof concentration camp. There was not much left of the facility because
the Nazis had destroyed most of the camp during their
retreat from the Red Army. What was left were a few
administrative buildings. Now these facilities were used as
detention centers for Nazi war criminals, mostly SS
officers.

Sivan was anxious to interview a former SS officer

named Franz Starke. His records indicated he had worked at the nearby Leba launch site used for testing the Rheintochter and Rheinbote sounding rockets. Sivan was particularly interested in finding out if it was possible the Germans were working on the advanced guidance system for the V-2 there. At the moment, Starke was being held captive and was awaiting trial by Polish authories in connection with crimes against humanity and sadism.

Sivan wore his Soviet Air Force uniform. It was tailor-made to show off his full chest of medals and decorations. This was very much unlike the latest generation of Russian technical experts who were only recently conscripted into military service and wore new, loose-fitting Red Army uniforms devoid of any military decorations. Sivan was an impressive sight to the Polish lieutenant who escorted Sivan into the interrogation room. Sivan took a seat and waited for Starke to arrive.

A few minutes later the door opened, and the young Polish lieutenant ushered in Starke. To Sivan's surprise, Starke was a tiny figure, all of five-feet, at best. He still wore his military breaches and a white tee-shirt and looked nothing like a fearsome SS officer. He had nothing on his feet except a pair of green military-issue socks, showing his true height. Upon seeing a Soviet Air Force officer, Starke trembled, fearing he'd be sent to the gulag and because he hadn't been interrogated by the Soviets before, only Polish authorities.

Sivan said, "Take a seat," in German. Starke did as he was told. The Polish officer left the room, and Sivan didn't say anything for a few seconds. Finally, he pulled out a pack of American cigarettes, filterless Lucky Strikes, and handed one to Starke. Sivan allowed Starke to finish his cigarette before he continued with the interview. He spoke in fluent German, which surprised Starke.

"Tell me, Starke, for the record, what was your job in the SS?"

Starke recapped his duties with the SS for Sivan, then crushed-out his cigarette in the ashtray. It was nothing Sivan didn't already know. Sivan continued, "That was an eloquent description of your duties with the SS. It might have given War Crimes investigators a challenge. But I could care less about your duties and criminal activities concerning the labor camps. I'm not here to collect that kind of information. I want to know what you did at Leba, not Stuttof."

Starke, obviously surprised to hear this from the young Russian officer, sat back in his chair, contemplating a response. Finally, he asked, "Can I have another cigarette?"

"By all means, after you tell me what you did at Leba."

The little man fidgeted in his seat, then began. "As you probably are aware, Leba was the testing site for the Rheinbote and other sounding rockets used by our forces. The place was used for years as a test site due to its proximity to the Baltic Sea and distances away from Allied bombers. Then one afternoon I got an urgent request to go to Leba. This was unusual because the facility was historically run by the Wehrmacht, not the SS. When I got to the facility, I was met by the Wehrmacht commander, sorry, I can't remember his name."

"Don't worry, it's not important. Go on."

"The commandant then told me that I was his replacement and that the facility was now under the control of the SS, hence my transfer. I was to assume his duties as commander. I knew nothing about missiles or rockets."

Sivan knew that all productions, related to the V-1 and V-2 were under the direct control of the SS. He felt he might actually be getting somewhere. Sivan decided to play in. He offered the cigarette to Starke, which he snatched up quickly and began to smoke. Sivan continued his interrogation.

"What's so unusual about that? Enlighten me."

"There were a few scientists, specialists in guidance and engineering brought in from Southern Poland to get away from the Russian front. These specialists, I was told, were working on the V-2 guidance system. Hence the reason for the SS taking control of the facility. These specialists were there for some time. They arrived long before I got there."

"When was this?"

"I was there from September 1944. At the beginning of the month, I believe."

Sivan took out a notepad and began scribbling. "How did you know they worked on the V-2?"

"Because only the SS worked on those types of weapons."

"Did you ever see a V-2 launched from Leba?"

Starke shook his head. "No, none whatsoever. They launched only the sounding rockets and Pheinbote, occasionally a V-1, never a V-2."

"How long were you there at the launch facility?"

"Not long. Only a few months. I was transferred back to the SS camp at Stutthof in November 1944. The Leba facility was being outflanked by Soviet naval forces coming in from the Baltic. We had no choice but to leave quickly. In fact, I was one of the last Germans to leave the facility."

"What happened to the scientists and the testing?"

"They received orders from Berlin by teleprinter to go to Tuchola, to continue testing."

"Who issued the orders?"

"They came for RHSA and were signed by SS Sturmbannführer Otto Krupke."

Sivan annotated that name, then took out a map of

Poland and noted the locations on the map. He circled
Stutthof, near Sztutowo, Leba and Tuchola. He moved the
map toward Starke and said, "Tuchola is due south of
here. Why go there and not back the to Third Reich or
Czechoslovakia? Wouldn't that be a safer location? Away
from the Western or Russian Fronts?"

Starke sat in silence for a while, then spoke. "It had to
do with the launch site itself at Tuchola. You see, Tuchola
was a mobile test launch site, not a fixed site. The priority
at that time was firing the rockets from mobile launchers.
This was for obvious reasons—to get away from Allied
bombers."

Sivan was by now quite curious. "Did the scientists take
any equipment or components with them to Tuchola?"

"Certainly. I helped pack the devices myself."

Sivan was floored. "Can you describe anything to me?
What did they look like?"

"The equipment was not very big. In fact, I was
surprised when I saw the components for the first time.
They looked as if they were miniaturized: gyros, circuit
boards, lots of dials, and lights. The main thing I
remember is the small, compact size of the components.
Anyway, we loaded everything into a metal container
about three by five feet total."

"One last question. Can you tell me the names of these
scientists?"

"Why, yes, Dr. Hoch and Dr. Mangus."

Chapter 12

It was after ten at night when Sivan finished his interview with Starke. He wanted to make the trip to Tuchola as soon as possible to track down the elusive V-2 components and scientists. He and his driver secured a room for the night in Nawcz. It was the former officer's quarters at the one-time sub-labor camp of Nawcz. It was one of the few remaining buildings of the complex.

The next morning Sivan and his driver left Nawcz bright and early. The trip to Tuchola would take them most of the morning. Roads were unmarked, non-existent in this section of Poland, or had been destroyed by Russian tanks. They did stumble across a few peasants along the way who spoke some German and were able to give directions back on to major roads leading to Tuchola.

Sivan and his driver arrived in Tuchola by mid-day. Their first stop was the local police station, located just across the street from the train station. There, Sivan wanted to acquire the whereabouts of the former V-2 launch facility. He was told that the launch site was in a remote forested area northeast of town, and they couldn't access the site by vehicle. Sivan was told by the police chief that the local forest rangers had more knowledge of the area and that he should inquire with them. He gave Sivan the location of the ranger station located at Wieczorne (Woziwoda in Polish) and was told he could reach that station by vehicle.

A short time later, Sivan and his driver pulled up to the ranger station at Wieczorne. They were greeted by an elderly man in his sixties, who was the duty officer for the day. The man was not in the best of shape and overweight. He did not show signs of suffering during the war. It was hard to imagine him even getting out into the wilderness, but, nonetheless, Sivan pressed for information. It turned out the old man did know the location of the launch site, but that it could only be accessed on horseback. The old man escorted Sivan and the driver to the stables, where two younger forest rangers were busy cleaning out the stalls. The two younger rangers were more than happy to get a break from their chores and show the two Russians the location of the launch site.

Luckily, the site was not far from the stables, and in less than an hour, Sivan and his driver were walking among the abandoned SS structures. The two rangers showed Sivan the protected launch control room for firing the rockets. Next, the rangers showed them the roads and protected areas in the forest where the actual rockets were fired from. Sivan asked the rangers if they had recovered anything left behind by the Nazis. The rangers said there was nothing left, and that everything was either destroyed or relocated. Then they rode their horses further into the forest and came upon a large clearing deep in the woods. This was an airfield used for the launch facility. This was how the Nazis were able to move key components and hardware from the launch site in and out promptly. They also informed Sivan that the Red Army used the airfield for counter-attacks on German positions. Finally, Sivan asked the rangers if any Germans were left behind who would know more about the facility. To Sivan's surprise, he was told that several Germans had moved to the city of Tuchola and that the local Catholic church harbored those individuals for some time and kept them hidden from the advancing Red Army until after the war.

Sivan got back to Tuchola as quickly as he could and found the local Catholic church called Corpus Cristi. There he proceeded to interview the head monsignor, Father Polski.

Sivan sat in front of Father Polski and asked about Germans being hidden in the church. Father Polski told Sivan that two Germans, both baptized Roman Catholics, came to him asking for sanctuary and who were hiding from the Russians. He said one of the Germans was captured by the Russians, but the other stayed hidden in the facility for several months. His name was Kobas, but he had died from a severe infection caught from working at one of the camps.

Sivan asked, "What happened to the body?"

The priest said, "We gave him a Catholic funeral and buried him in the local cemetery."

Father Polski then showed Sivan the location of the cemetery on a map, which was only a short distance away and next to the railway tracks. "His grave is the only one marked as a German officer. I'm sorry, I can't remember the actual location."

It was getting dark, but Sivan had his driver take him to the cemetery. There, they got flashlights out and proceeded to look for tombstones marked for a German officer. It wasn't long before Sivan's driver shouted that he fhad ound something. Sivan came over to the grave, and they both shined their flashlights on the site and noticed it had recently been dug up.

Sivan took out a knife from his pocket and began poking around the site. That's when he noticed that the entire coffin had been recently removed. Also, he noticed the hole was smaller than normal. Then he remembered what Starke had said about the size of the box containing the components—a box about three by five feet. Sivan didn't have a tape measure, but he could judge by the opening that the grave was approximately dug to fit a container three by five.

Quickly, the two raced back to Corpus Christi church and the rectory. It was obvious Father Polski was not telling the whole truth. There they found the monsignor slumped over and his head buried on his desk. Sivan moved his head back to check for a pulse, but it was useless. From the foam coming from his mouth, it was apparent Father Polski had taken his own life with a cyanide capsule. Sivan cursed under his breath.

Chapter 13

The clock was ticking for Sivan. After Father Polski's death, he and his driver returned to Gdansk the next morning. There was not much more they could have done. Sivan would have to pursue a different lead. He needed to go back to the Tuchola forest and interrogate the local forest rangers. Up to this point, they seemed to have the best information. Perhaps one of them had seen something that could be useful.

Armed with movement orders signed directly by General Kuznetsov, Sivan took a whole garrison of Red Army soldiers. They drove to the ranger station at Tuchola forest with some twenty vehicles, including tanks armed with machine guns. They meant business.

When the Soviet military detachment arrived at the ranger station, Sivan had all the forest rangers summoned to headquarters at gunpoint. He grilled every one of them individually in the hopes of finding more information on the possible location of V-2 components. His persistence finally paid off. After more than three hours questioning the rangers, a young man about twenty-years-old came forward. His name was Cyrek Drozda. He told Sivan that there was an extremely active ranger battalion that had worked in the Resistance for the Home Army. The unit was called AK-22 or Ranger Battalion B, commanded by an officer known only as Jawor, and that they were working in the area around Tarnow. That unit worked specifically in the forest at the Blizna launch site.

This was all the information Sivan needed to know for now. He knew Tarnow was the largest city in the vicinity of the Pustkow labor camp. That camp was responsible for assembling key rocket components for the V-2. He had scoured the area earlier in the year but had come up empty-handed. There was nothing left at the Pustkow labor camp. However, armed with this new information, he would move his operations to Tarnow and look for rangers and the person known as Jawor.

* * *

KRUPKE AND MANGUS had no trouble finding the coal barge from Gdansk to Warsaw. They spent the night sleeping in the back of the truck. It was cold, but they couldn't take the chance of leaving the gyros exposed and unprotected. They paid their passage to the barge captain, loaded their precious cargo, and were instructed to stay below deck at all times. It was evident that this particular barge was used many times to smuggle people and goods along the river. It was probably a thriving business during the war.

The overnight trip to Warsaw was uneventful. In Warsaw they switched to a barge that could navigate the smaller waterways all the way to Szczucin. As was the standard procedure, the two were instructed once again to stay below deck at all times. However, the leg from Warsaw to

Szczucin was much longer due to the slower speed of the barge navigating the narrower waterways. This section would take another two nights. Krupke used this time to brief Mangus on the next phase. Most of the crew were either above deck or sleeping. It was a perfect time for Krupke to unwrap the envelope he'd been carrying in his duffel bag. He emptied the contents on the floor and proceeded to tell Mangus the next move.

"My ultimate objective is to establish contact with my source in Tarnow. She has access to a ratline directly to the American sector in Bavaria. I'm not totally sure how she does this. Intelligence is sketchy in this area. I'm assuming she must use a series of courier lines and safe houses across Poland and Czechoslovakia."—Krupke produced a mug shot of the woman from the pile. "This picture is all we've got to go by. It was taken before the war. She was held captive in Berlin for a while. Her file indicates she's an entrepreneur. She has no allegiance to any particular government or political ideology. She does everything, I'm told, for cold, hard cash and does quite well. She runs a very prosperous and successful hotel near the train station in Tarnow. We can't just show up and expect her to take us to the Americans, even with our credentials and goods, so we've got to find Dr. Hoch and bring him out too. The two of you developed the advanced gyros. Only then, when I have both you, Dr. Hoch, the batteries, and the gyros, can I bargain with her. She's not stupid either. I'm sure she has informants everywhere." Krupke removed a map of Poland from the pile, unfolded it, and dropped it to the floor. "So, show me where we can find Dr. Hoch."

"We staged his death to keep him away from advancing Soviet forces." Mangus adjusted his glasses and took a closer look at the map. "That's the part we may have difficulty with. As you know, Dr. Hoch worked directly for the head of the Pustkow labor camp. In particular, the Jewish camp. He went into deep cover to avoid War Crimes investigators. Last I heard, he got a job at a local bakery as a baker, but I can't be sure if that's still the case. This information was the latest on Dr. Hoch as of June of this year. The only way to know for sure is to actually make visual contact. He uses an alias, Adolf Ruf."

Krupke folded up his map. "The barge makes a final stop at Szczucin. We'll get off there and secure transportation to Pustkow."

* * *

IT WAS three in the morning and dark when the small river barge pulled into the dock outside of Szczucin. There, Krupke and Mangus hopped onto a small, white utility truck that was waiting for them as they arrived. This had been arranged by Krupke and the remnants of his circuit still operating in Poland, who operated through third-party resources. The driver was only told to pick up two passengers and take them to Pustkow, a forty-five-minute drive. It was an all-cash deal paid for by Krupke. "Let me know when we get to the outskirts of town," Krupke told the driver.

Forty-five minutes later, they entered the outskirts of Pustkow. It was still dark, and the small hamlet, had few lights or dwellings, for that matter. The town was basically deserted at this time of the morning. The lone light came from a small bakery next to the post office. The driver informed Krupke they'd reached Pustkow.

Krupke wiped the fog from the window with his coat jacket so he could take a look. He saw the light from the bakery. "Pull up next to the bakery. Wait here. I'll be right back," he told the driver as both he and Mangus jumped from the vehicle and went to the back of the small building. The two men could smell the aroma of the freshly baked goods and heard music playing softly over a phonograph.

"This is it," said Mangus. "His instructions were to hold up and wait here until someone came and gave the code words."

Krupke reached into his pocket, pulled out the pistol, cocked it, and handed the gun to Mangus. "He should authenticate within seconds. If there's a problem, and it's a Russian trap, go in and start shooting."

Mangus took the gun and nodded while Krupke slowly opened the back door and entered.

Initially, once inside, he couldn't see anyone he only heard the music from the phonograph. He didn't like going in without a weapon, but in case it was a trap and not having a gun, he could always talk his way out. He tiptoed through the baker's table and into the main area when he saw a figure of a man wearing white baker's clothing. Dr. Hoch was a tall, thin man in his middle fifties with a bald head. He wore a pair of gold spectacles and was humming the tunes on the phonograph. The two made eye contact. Dr. Hoch was not startled and rather calm, as if he was expecting someone, even at this early hour of the day. Krupke didn't wait any longer and clearly spoke the code words, "It's been a very long winter."

Dr. Hoch untied his apron and responded, "Then I must do a very long penance."

Correct code words having been exchanged, Krupke responded, "Quickly, we must go. We'll get you a change of clothes and a jacket. For now, come with me outside. I have a driver waiting. It's time we meet with the Amis."

Chapter 14

Colonel Dimitri Pavel arrived at the Soviet consulate in Krakow, where the NKVD had a regional headquarters set up. Pavel took over the former offices of the agricultural ministry. Now all assets allocated to that ministry were Pavel's. For the past week, his team had scoured the areas around Krakow and Tarnow looking for any leads that would take him to Krupke. Thus far he was unsuccessful. He even arrested several individuals who were known British spies and held them for extreme interrogation. None of the suspects had any information on the whereabouts of Krupke or the mysterious female British agent.

Pavel decided to try a different tactic and focused his efforts on signal intelligence coming in from London and Washington. He was specifically looking for any information on intelligence-gathering missions. In particular, anyone and anything related to missile technology. Of special interest on this day was an encrypted cable from the US military headquarters in Frankfurt. Thanks to NKVD efforts, the American ciphers were decoded. The cable stipulated an urgent request was made for airlift support. That request was for a single C-47 for a turn-around flight to an undisclosed location to the East. This in itself was not of interest except that the airlift request was for a passenger complement of two. That was the part that Pavel found interesting. *What would the US military be doing flying this deep into the Soviet sector with only two passengers?* he thought. Most airlift missions sent in from the West were War Crimes prosecutors with teams of investigators or members of the Allied Control Commission.

Pavel picked up the telephone on his desk and called NKVD regional support for Eastern Poland. He requested that the asset collection team that was responsible for squeezing Polish sources in Poland, be sent over to his office immediately. A short time later, two NKVD asset collection officers appeared before Pavel's desk. The two young men were career NKVD agents, recruited from Moscow's criminal desk. Pavel did not wait for formalities. He was more interested in results. "I've read your reports. You indicated you were unable to acquire information from your sources about British or American intelligence operations going on in the Eastern sector. Did you squeeze them for any information on logistics or mobility? Perhaps possible clandestine landing sites?"

The two young men looked at each other before making a response. The older one, probably the lead agent, in his late twenties, responded, "No, Comrade Colonel, we did as instructed. We focused our investigations on known British or American espionage activities. Our sources were unaware of such activities at the moment. Especially this far in the Soviet sector."

"The reason why I ask, gentlemen, is that I've recently come across information that a possible clandestine landing of enemy agents in our zone has been in the works. Perhaps I need to re-conduct the interviews and ask more specific questions. Who is your most trusted source?"

The younger one spoke this time. "We have many, Comrade Colonel, but the one who has been the most trustworthy goes by the code name Warlock and is actually a female. Specifically, she's the aging grandmother of a Polish ranger. Her grandson was active in the Resistance during the war. Unfortunately, she only speaks Polish. We can't communicate with her without an interpreter."

"That won't be a problem. I speak Polish. Take me to her immediately!"

One of the things Soviet NKVD had at this time was unlimited petrol and the use of vehicles. This enabled Dimitri Pavel to travel anywhere on a moment's notice and gave him a huge tactical advantage in time. He was able to cover large distances in a matter of minutes. In a very short time, Pavel and his two asset collection officers arrived at the small town of Zebolo, twenty-five kilometers to the north of Tarnow. Here was a small dairy farm with a farmhouse and a barn.

The older asset collection officer spoke. "This is where Warlock lives. During the war, the Home Army used this place as a safe house for the Resistance. Many meetings were planned at this facility. The barn was used as a briefing room. We developed this source fighting the Nazis. She helped and provided us with valuable information on troop movements in this area. After the war, naturally, we kept up the relationship, but this time, we asked if she could help us find German sympathizers. She agreed, but only if we promised not to seize her farm and animals. After all, this was her only source of income. We agreed. But, unbeknown to her, these German sympathizers were actually Polish resistance units resisting Soviet expansion. They would meet at her barn to plan their activities.

Slowly, we asked for small bits of information, dates, times, etc. Then we asked her to provide names. She did so willingly, again not knowing we were going after the people who she was harboring. Eventually, she would overhear a name, mostly German officers still in hiding or occasionally the name of a scientist. Naturally, we followed up, which eventually led to their capture. We actually got one German rocket scientist and immediately sent him to Moscow."

The large, green American sedan they were driving, pulled up to the farmhouse, and Pavel exited the second the car came to a stop. It was an intimidating sight. Three plainclothes Soviet officials wearing long overcoats and fur hats stormed to the front door of Warlock's small dwelling. Pavel immediately pounded his fist on the door.

"Open up! Soviet State Security!" There was nothing.

Pavel repeated the maneuver. This time the door opened slowly. A small, elderly woman opened the door. She was dressed in peasant attire complete with a scarf over her head and large leather boots. Her weatherworn face was wrinkled but pleasant. She must have been in her late eighties. "Please come in. What can I do for you?" she said in Polish.

Pavel removed his fur hat but kept his overcoat on. It was freezing inside the dwelling. "We are sorry to disturb you, but we need some information. Can we take a seat?" he asked in Polish.

The woman, obviously surprised one of the Soviets could speak in her native tongue, responded, "Yes, by all means, have a seat at the table." She led them to an old, worn, wooden table, and everyone took a seat. The old woman produced a small pouch from inside her garments and plopped it on the table. She then proceeded to roll a cigarette from the shredded home-grown tobacco she had in the pouch. She offered one to Pavel, but he shook his head. Then she placed it between her lips and lit it from a candle on the table.

Pavel continued his query as the old woman smoked her cigarette. "Let me introduce myself. My name is Dimitri Pavel. I work for Soviet Security."

"Yes, I know all about you people," the woman interrupted Pavel.

Pavel resumed his interrogation, using his fluent Polish. "This is just a friendly visit. I'm new to this area. I was recently transferred here late last week. I'm trying to familiarize myself with the various sources we have in the area."

The two exchanged pleasantries for several minutes, the older woman even divulging her real name, Maria Wasinski to Pavel. Finally, Pavel decided to take the conversation to a different course once he had acquired a certain amount of trust from the old woman. "You have a nice farm here. We will continue to abide by our agreement. You can have your farm and animals. We shall not interfere with your operation. Can I ask you one question, my dear lady?"

"Why, yes," she said.

Pavel continued. "Why is it you have so much land but only raise a few animals. You could easily pasture many, many more."

Without hesitation, the woman responded. "Mr. Pavel, you should know the answer, or at least your colleagues should have told you. But, as you said, you are new to the area. My barn is used as a meeting place for the Home Army. Occasionally, they ask if they can land airplanes in my fields. Naturally, when the conditions are just right, we land large airplanes right over there," she said, as she pointed out the small window to the open pasture.

Pavel sat in silence for a few seconds, not believing the words he had just heard. "How often do they come?"

Astonishingly, the woman said, "Not often, but coincidently, I was told to expect one tomorrow night."

Pavel acted like it was nothing and continued his small talk for another fifteen minutes. Then he said, "Again, I'm sorry to bother you on short notice. I must get back to my duties. These men have to take me to other sites. Have a good day, madam."

As they were driving away in the sedan, the older collection agent asked, "Why didn't we take her and question her further?"

"Are you nuts? If her accomplices found her missing or dead, the whole operation would be blown. They'd abort the mission. No, we come back tomorrow night. See who lands. Then we eliminate her."

Chapter 15

FRANKFURT, GERMANY G-2 SCHOOL
ANNEX

Later that morning, after Sanchez had delivered the new information about Vivian Tate, Major Franko went to USFET Headquarters and secured the money requested by Miss Tate. All fifty-thousand dollars were locked in a steel suitcase and stored at the quartermaster's office until departure. Then he made several phone calls to the American air base at Darmstadt to finalize flight arrangements and alert the crews for the flight to Poland. Once that was done, he decided to go for a walk and clear his head.

Frankfurt was still in ruins. Reconstruction crews were everywhere, and sometimes the noise was overwhelming. So he went to Gruneburg Park and Palmen Gardens. He walked around the pond several times to collect his thoughts. In retrospect, he was only three blocks away from Miss Tate's villa on Sophien Strasse. For a while, he contemplated walking up to her doorstep, but better judgment told him otherwise. She might not be happy with him appearing unannounced. For now, he would keep his emotional thoughts to himself and concentrate on the mission and recovering the V-2 guidance systems.

He returned to the School Annex, went to his office and pored over the details of the mission Miss Tate had laid out for them. She had a beginning, middle, and end, but crucial details were missing in between. Most of the mission relied on massive assistance from the Ranger Battalion. If there were any specifics, Miss Tate had purposely omitted that information from him, or it was non existent. Either way, he'd have to wait for Miss Tate to bring those details out on her terms. Franko actually lost track of time, and his thoughts were interrupted by a telephone ring. He was about to answer it when he looked at the clock. It was after 8:00 p.m. He decided to wait for several rings before he answered.

"Major Franko."

"So, one actually works late into the evening besides me." Franko heard Vivian's distinctly, British-accented voice. *Hard to believe she's actually Polish*, he thought.

"Are we on a secure line?"

"Of course."

"I tried your number at the BOQ, but there was no answer, so I thought I'd try the office. How was your day?"

Franko stuck to business. "I accomplished all of your tasks. Funds secured, air base alerted, and I have the COM/SECS waiting for you."

"All good, Major. Now, as far as tomorrow. This will be our last full day here in Frankfurt. We have a lot to discuss. I'll meet you at the School Annex at ten in the morning. Please have a driver pick me up at nine thirty. I've made contact with the reception committee. The landing is set for two in the morning, which means we need to take off by eleven thirty tomorrow night. Contact the air base tomorrow to set up the actual departure time with air ops."

Franko picked up a note-pad, and pencil and started scribbling. "Ok, what else?"

"Have you been followed? After all, you did say this town was loaded with Russian spies."

Franko was surprised to hear this bit of information, but the thought had crossed his mind, especially during his outing to Gruneburg Park. "Not as far as I know."

"So, you can't be totally sure, can you?"

"No, of course not."

"Why do you think my appearances and routines change daily? To throw off a Russian surveillance team. To make it look like I am not the same person." Vivian answered her own question. "Just to be on the safe side, we'll stage from my quarters on Sophien Strasse, eight o'clock tomorrow night. We'll go to the air base from there. A car and driver can use the back entrance to the residence. Now, as far as what to pack. One small suitcase and the clothes on your back, nothing more. Once we get there, you'll be issued all necessary clothing and accessories from the Home Army. The suitcase will contain your COM/SEC equipment only. That way, if we have to get rid of it, that won't be a problem. Understood?"

"Of course. What about the money? I have it," he asked.

"Bring it. I've made two money vests for us to use. We'll go in with it attached. I'm already packed. I've got one small suitcase as well and some warm clothing. You may want to consider doing the same. I checked the weather forecast. No snow, but the temperature is dropping to single digits."

"All right, I know just what to bring."

"Then that's it. Good night, Major. See you tomorrow morning."

* * *

THE NEXT MORNING, as per Vivian Tate's request, the two met at the School Annex at ten in the morning. Major Franko was already in his office when Vivian arrived. She came dressed not in civilian attire, as she had done the previous days, but instead came dressed in her RAF uniform. Except her hair was a mess, and she had no makeup. In fact, as she entered Franko's office, it appeared to him that she had rolled out of the sack. Her eyelids were heavy and her eyes bloodshot. He wondered if she had even brushed her teeth or slept for that matter. She had her bottomless, magician's, briefcase as usual and wasted no time digging in and emptying the contents onto the table.

Franko pulled out his pack of cigarettes, placed his feet on the table to make himself comfortable, then took a sip of his coffee. "Rough night?"

"Why do you say that?" she asked.

"Well, you don't seem as, crisp as I've seen you before."

Vivian didn't even bother to respond and started right in. "Your COMS, how do you plan on keeping in touch with Home Station?"

Franko took his feet off the table. "We use the Joan-Eleanor and homing beacon. SOP for these types of operations. I've coordinated the SCHED forty-eight hours after INFIL. Location, Lisia Gora, twenty-five klicks to the north of Tarnow. Time set for 0300 hours. As per your request, Joan is packed away in my only suitcase. Once in the field, I use the M-209 for encryption and decryption, followed by standard telegraphy. I've also come up with a codename for you and Krupke. I'll be Redstone, you Agena, and Krupke, King Six."

"Perfect."

"Miss Tate, can I ask you something?"

"Yes, by all means."

"I've gone over your plan extensively, at least what

you've shared with me, but it appears many details are lacking or missing. You have a beginning, middle, and end, but nothing between. I think it's time you shared more details with me if we're going to pull this off."

Vivian took a seat at the table next to Franko, grabbed one of his cigarettes, and placed it between her lips. Franko flicked his Zippo lighter and lit her cigarette as she contemplated a response. She took a puff inhaling, something she rarely did, then blew smoke out into the room.

"This is a different type of mission than what you're used to. For starters, we're not operating in US occupied territory. Second, we won't have an entire numbered army behind us in support. We'll be on our own, deep inside Soviet-occupied territory going after a high-value asset. NKVD, GRU, and most importantly, their sub-unit agents, will be everywhere. We can't trust anyone, not even our most trusted sources. Therefore, the planning has been purposely vague because it will probably change based on current situations. I've found over the years, doing these sorts of missions, that the best-made plans are always the first to become unraveled. It's the fog of war. With no alternate plans in place, the mission is doomed from the start. So, what we're going to do is modify and adopt the basic plan as we go along. That way, we're constantly moving forward toward our objective, which is, of course, capturing Krupke and securing the flight hardware."

Franko now seized an opportunity to acquire more information about Miss Tate. "Just what kind of experience do you have? Can you be more specific? After all, I'm entrusting my fate into your hands."

Vivian finished her cigarette, then stamped it out in the ashtray before she spoke. "Very well, I'll share a tiny piece of information with you. But that's it. That's all you're going to get out of me. Agreed?"

Franko nodded.

Vivian continued. "All right, during the war, it was my department that was responsible for sending agents into the field. It was my job to come up with the specific plans for each insertion. I planned everything down to the most minute detail: escape routes, false backgrounds, cover stories, etc., only to have those plans abolished the moment the agents set foot on enemy soil. The agents were left to fend for themselves. Most cases, they were captured or killed by the Gestapo. Had I given them several options at each phase of the operation, there was a good chance those missions would have been successful. Of course, I tried to pass this on to my superiors during the planning phase, but their ignorance and arrogance were against me. They were all a bunch of amateurs and had no business in the intelligence community. Toward the end of the war, we finally did plan such missions, but only after the tides turned, and it was a sure bet the Allies would be triumphant. That's it. That's all you're going to get from me."

Franko was now convinced through idle talk that Miss Tate was in all likelihood, Irina Jankowski. Her experience in the field was profoundly evident. Plus, she let it slip that she was not an amateur, unlike most of the imbeciles at SOE. This was in line with Sanchez's report. He would keep it to himself for now.

"How secure is this building? I mean, what are the chances the Russians can eavesdrop on our conversations?" asked Vivian.

"G-2 sweeps the building every day."

"That may not be good enough for what I'm about to tell you. Do you have a radio where we can pick up a musical station?"

"I'll be right back." Franko came back a short time

later with a large phonograph. "The local Armed Forces Radio Station is not totally up and running, but my assistant next door has this. I'm sorry, all he has is Mexican music."

"That will work."

Franko set up the phonograph and placed a record on the turntable. Mexican folk songs blared out into the room.

Vivian motioned Franko to come closer so she could speak. With the backdrop of Latino music, she began. "I interrogated Krupke's mistress, Bertha Cordes, before leaving England. She was being held at a maximum-security prison outside London. Anyway, I wanted to find out what Krupke knew about me, if anything. During the interview, Cordes told me that Krupke was after Wonder Weapons. She mentioned something I've never heard before. She said Krupke knew about, not only the advanced guidance systems for the V-2, but other devices. Especially anti-gravity devices used by the Nazis. Is that true? What did the Americans know about such devices?"

Franko was startled to hear this revelation but answered as best he could. "There was always the concern at Lusty that the Nazis were working on these so-called, Wonder Weapons, but, to my knowledge, it was nothing but hearsay. We knew back at Wright Field that they were working on some sort of high-tech devices, but what you're talking about is the work of science fiction. It's technically feasible from an engineering perspective, but way beyond the scope of our capabilities and existing technology."

"My thoughts also. There is one possible explanation why Cordes divulged that information to me."

"What's that?"

"During my interview, I could tell Cordes was professionally trained. She was more than Krupke's mistress. In fact, she's probably a full-blown Abwehr or Sicherheitsdi-

enst agent. It could be some sort of a blind or bluff security check to signal Krupke that we're on to him or in
control of Cordes. The mere fact we mention it in casual
discussions can signal Krupke that we interviewed Cordes
and thus we can be exposed."

Franko sat in silence, thinking about the possibilities.
Then he said, "Fascinating, that is something I would have
never considered, but it does make perfect sense." Then he
got up from the table and walked around the room, gathering his thoughts. "I think you're right. It could very well
be a security check. Krupke did outsmart the Russians in
his radio playback games. Let's keep this to ourselves for
the moment. We won't bring up the topic unless he initi-
ates it. Let's concentrate on the V-2 guidance systems. And
if he does bring it up, we'll play stupid."

"Fair enough, now, can you get rid of this ridiculous
music?"

For the next several hours, the two went back and
forth with various communications and security procedures, all of it finally approved by Squad Leader Tate. By
four o'clock in the afternoon, Vivian finished up her tasks
with Major Franko and gathered her belongings. Franko
called the motor pool to have a car and driver take Miss
Tate back to quarters. Franko walked her to the street
where her driver was waiting. She removed her RAF cap,
put on a large, dark pair of nonregulation sunglasses as
she took a seat in the Jeep, and said, "See you tonight at
eight."

* * *

THAT NIGHT, Franko took added security measures.
Rather than have a Jeep and driver drop him off at
Vivian's front door, he elected to have the driver drop him

off several blocks away near Gruneburg Park at the corner of Gruneburgweg and Siesmayer Strasses.

Civilian vehicular traffic was still nonexistent or extremely light in Frankfurt. Plus, one could hear the cars approaching well in advance due to the lack of spare or replacement mufflers. Franko only saw one small Italian sedan speed past his military Jeep with two occupants in the front. He was unable to get a good look at the occupants but could determine they were both males. What he couldn't determine was whether they were NKVD or GRU.

Franko wore casual, warm clothes with a light jacket and carried the single suitcase with the Joan-Eleanor and COMS per Vivian's request. He hopped off the Jeep, cut through Gruneburg Park, took the path around Boostsweiher Pond, then up the side of the hill and exited onto Zeppelinallee Strasse. It was here, he saw that same civilian sedan approaching from the south. The car was moving slowly, and with the damaged muffler, the noise gave Franko ample time to dart back into the shadows of Gruneburg Park. He crouched down below a bush as he watched the sedan slowly pass by. The two occupants both looked into the park shadows. *It has to be a surveillance team, no one else would look into a darkened park,* he thought. Franko ducked further below the bushes and waited, listening for the noisy muffler to pass further and further away. When he could not hear the loud sounds any longer, he exited from his hiding place and continued on Ludolfus Strasse and to Vivian's house, at number thirteen.

It was a beautiful three-story home set back from the street. Surprisingly, this section of town was spared bombing by the Allies. It was one of the few neighborhoods in town not flattened to the ground. There was a small hedge and fence covered by ample foliage surrounding the front. A gate led directly to the front door on the left side of the building. The gate was closed, but Franko pushed open the iron gate slowly so he wouldn't be noticed and continued. All the lights were bright on the first floor. He found what looked like a doorbell and pushed the mechanism. A short while later, Franko saw the face of Vivian Tate peek through the glass-partitioned door. She opened it slightly.

To Franko's surprise, she was elegantly dressed in a modest, long-sleeved, light-gray evening gown, showing off her shapely figure. Her hair was neatly styled. She wore a layer of freshly applied makeup and lipstick, making her stunningly beautiful. The most interesting fact was Vivian was completely barefoot, making her accurate height at five-feet-three inches tall. She had, in fact, looked shorter to him as he stepped into the foyer. Given Vivian's mysterious and enigmatic behavior, this did not come as a complete and total surprise to Franko. She was the complete opposite of the prude, British officer she had been just a few hours earlier. The reason for this behavior was still obviously not clear to him.

He could also detect a homey odor of stewed meats and vegetables permeating from the house. He was quite surprised at this because the entire time Vivian was in Frankfurt, she gave off the impression she had no desire to cook for herself, let alone for others. The most intriguing fact of the evening was that she was not dressed as if she were leaving on a clandestine mission in less than three hours. Vivian motioned with her open hand for Franko to enter. "Come in. You caught me slightly unprepared because I was expecting to hear a noisy Jeep out front announcing your arrival. Were you followed?"

Again, Franko was caught off guard by Vivian's intuition, "Possibly, but I cut through Gruneburg Park just to make sure. I did notice a small sedan with a noisy muffler and two men in the front seat. Could have been a surveillance team. No one saw me, though. How did you know?"

"Gut instinct, but not unexpected. Careless of them to not fix the muffler. As you said, this town is loaded with Russian spies." Vivian mentally noted his precautions to security and detail. "Good work of you though. By the way, why do you think I came to the School Annex looking as if I was a different person each day? A Soviet surveillance team could not determine if I was one and the same person. Thus, giving us a slight advantage."

"Well, that explains your enigmatic, eccentric behavior." Vivian ignored his remark.

Franko entered the foyer, removed his cap, and dropped his suitcase to the floor. This was his first time inside the elegant house, which was the one-time residence of a former high-ranking SS official now imprisoned for war crimes. The home was now the property of the US government and used as VIP quarters for USFET. "I trust your quarters have been adequate?" was all Franko could muster.

Vivian placed her hands on his shoulder to help him remove his jacket. "Oh, by all means, but much too large for me. There's something I want to share with you; come with me."

Vivian led Franko to the dining room, which already set for two. The table was beautifully set with candles and formal china, obviously left by the previous occupants. On the table was a platter of stewed meats and vegetables and the source of the comfortable aroma Franko smelled when he entered the house. To his surprise, Vivian backed up a chair for him, indicating it was time for him to have a seat and eat. Franko was now dumbfounded by her actions and behavior this night.

Vivian moved to her side of the table and took a seat. She then picked up the platter and passed it to Franko. "This was a tradition right before our agents left for the Continent. We gave them a large supper right before their flights. I'm continuing that tradition."

"Probably not as formal. I appreciate it. I'm starving."

The couple dished out their portions and ate, only occasionally speaking or asking for one another to pass a tray or platter. When supper ended, Vivian placed her elbows on the table, sunk her chin into her hands, looked Franko in the eyes, and asked, "Well, what did you think? I cooked the meal myself."

"I'm sorry, I don't know what to say, other than the dinner was fabulous, very Polish."

"It's part of my cover. I wanted to share it with you. If I'm to operate the Hotel Bristol and entertain my guests, then I must have some knowledge of food preparation and presentation. I'm glad you liked the meal. As far as my appearance, no, I won't be going in, like this. I wanted to show you what I'd look like in case we come across a situation where I have to invite you, a high ranking military official,—with ties to the US missile program and in a position to offer a former Nazi V-2 rocket scientist a contract to work in the US to supper. I don't want you to slip up or act dumbfounded like you just did or give the slightest indication that there is a collaboration. Understood?"

"As true to form, Miss Tate, very clever. I must admit, if I had seen you for the first time, dressed and acting like this with your pal Krupke, I'd be speechless. I could have aroused suspicion by my reaction. Tipped him off somehow. We can't have that. He is a trained counter-intelligence professional. And, I'll say, you look absolutely ravishing."

Vivian's relaxed mood and expressions disappeared as she continued. "Let's move on, Major. I need to discuss the landing. Listen carefully because I'm only going to say it once, understand?"

Franko nodded in agreement.

"I've made contact with our reception committee. They're expecting us. Motyl is still a secure landing site from my intelligence sources. They've changed procedures since the war. They say they don't need to land in total darkness, preferring to land at first daylight, which puts this at just after 0600 local time. However, I don't want to take the chance. I want to land in darkness. Gives us one more advantage. So, I've coordinated for a 0300 landing. They'll, of course, have to light lanterns to illuminate the runway. A slight exposure to them, but they'll manage. They do have blinders for the lanterns so the light will only be seen in the air by the flight crew. We'll depart Frankfurt so as to arrive by 0300. The reception committee already has the discreet UHF radio frequency. You and I will be in the cockpit to monitor arrival procedures. We'll attempt radio contact first. If we don't hear a response, the next action is the high illumination light. Authentication is Morse code for HORSE. Their response back will be WAGON. If we don't get the proper voice or Morse coded messages, we abort and proceed to the jump site. So, make sure our jump equipment is aboard before departure. As a final security check, you'll visually confirm the landing field, since you've been there before. Any questions? Comments?"

"No."

Vivian didn't say anything further. She placed her napkin on the table, indicating the meal and the conversation were over and cracked an ever so slight, seductive smile, the first time ever since she'd arrived in Frankfurt. This did not go unnoticed by Franko.

"I'm going upstairs to change now," she said. "Make yourself comfortable. We leave for the air base in one hour. Oh, by the way, *merde!*"

Chapter 16

Dimitri Pavel was not going to lose this opportunity. He left Krakow with a team of fifteen NKVD operatives backed up by twenty-five Red Army soldiers. He planned to have the Red Army soldiers surround the perimeter of the farm-house and secure the aerodrome. He and his NKVD team would then assault the house and arrest Maria Wasinski. If there were Home Army collaborators, then they too would be arrested or shot.

It was after one thirty in the morning when Pavel's green sedan and three Soviet troop carriers pulled up to Wasinski's dairy farm and came to a stop in a cloud of dust. The lights were out in the small dwelling. Pavel quietly ordered the Red Army team to disperse and surround the airfield. The remaining NKVD officers then went to the door. Pavel pounded his fist. "Soviet State Security. Open up!"

* * *

TWO ADVANCE TEAM scouts from AK-22 Ranger

Battalion sat in the shadows overlooking Warlock's farm. They arrived just before 1:00 a.m. to set up security and wait for the rest of the reception committee. Also, they would conduct a preliminary security assessment to make sure the airfield was still secure before the arrival of their aircraft. The two security scouts were none other than Jawor and Morena. If the airfield were still secure, they would meet the rest of the reception committee at Warlock's barn to begin preparations for the landing.

The Ranger Battalion was the most secure network in all of Poland. They survived the war by precise detail to security matters. They were using those same tactics on tonight's clandestine landing. If the airfield was still secure, members of the welcoming committee would look for the closed window at the top of the barn. That was the signal that it was safe, and they could all proceed inside the dwelling. Since members of the welcoming committee would probably all arrive at different times, this security check had worked well in the past. If on the other hand, it was determined that the airfield was unsafe or compromised, the small window would be open. As an added security measure, this window was always open. One had to reach the barn and physically close the window in a secure, safe condition. This measure was implemented by their commander, Jawor. It was the default security setting. That way if there were any problems reaching the farmhouse, it was already prepped for the abort. If it was a safe situation, one had to physically open the window to signal that everything was secure and they could proceed inside. As a final security measure, no landing equipment was stored inside the barn. Each member of the welcoming committee brought with them a lantern. That way, if they were stopped or questioned, it was easy to explain the necessity of possessing a lantern at night. Only Jawor or Morena would have the radio and signaling devices.

Everything was proceeding as planned. Why would the landing site be anything other than secure? The war was over. But Jawor was not worried about the Germans. Her focus was on the Russians. Her mission was to provide security for the operation that was set to begin on this night. However, the enemy this time was not the Gestapo but Soviet intelligence forces. It was this thought that interrupted this quiet night with the sound of large vehicles approaching. She turned to her, colleague. "That's highly unusual. That sounds like heavy vehicles, possibly trucks or troop carriers. We'd better move to a better vantage point."

Jawor and Morena moved up the hillside to a secluded area with a better view. Here Jawor took out a pair of binoculars and scanned the airfield below. All she could see were military vehicles with headlights full bright and personnel moving about taking up positions around the airfield. It was completely surrounded. "Take a look," she said, handing Morena the glasses.

Morena scanned the area with a slow sweep. "We've got no choice. The airfield is compromised. Those are Russian trucks and Red Army. We'll have to abort and move to the alternate location." She gave the binoculars back to Jawor.

"The reception committee will get the abort signal and reset to the alternate staging location. We've got to move now in order to be at the alternate site before daylight," Jawor continued. "Get to a telephone. Contact the Zabola asset and put them on alert that we've moved to the alternate site. I've got to stay here and take care of something. Hand me the rifle."

Morena unslung the rifle from her shoulder. The gun was simple to use. As with many Polish Home Army units, they used captured or abandoned German equipment. In this case, Jawor favored the Wather Gewehr 43 self-loading, semi-automatic sniper rifle equipped with an Af42 optical crosshair scope for precision shooting at long range. The optimum distance for the weapon was one hundred yards. However, she couldn't take the chance. She needed one shot and one shot only. She had to get within fifty yards for maximum efficiency and accuracy.

Jawor slung the rifle over her shoulder and proceeded down the hillside and made her way to close proximity of Warlock's house. She moved slowly, not wanting to give away her position. She stopped beside a large tree and took her binoculars out. She scanned the farmhouse in the darkness. What she saw was unbelievable. Security forces had already taken control of the residence and were probably squeezing Warlock for more information. She knew the Russian's strategy. They would be slow and deliberate. They would not be in a hurry. The NKVD preferred to torture their victims slowly. However, she could see that the Russians had made a fatal, tactical blunder. The Soviets had deployed all their forces to secure the airfield and left the farmhouse unprotected from the outside. This would be easier than she expected. She moved closer to the structure. She was now less than twenty-five yards from the farmhouse. This was as close as she dared to go. She needed the additional space for an escape route.

Jawor took out her rifle and used the optical scope to sight in on her target. She looked through the kitchen window and saw another fatal blunder. The Russians failed to place their victim away from the windows to conduct their interrogation, and it was totally illuminated in the kitchen. Every light inside the structure must have been on. She saw three men standing around the kitchen table talking to Warlock. Security of her cell was compromised, and the weak link was the old woman. She probably didn't even know what she was doing. The Soviets could be very good at extracting information unbeknown to their victims. Unfortunate for her. Jawor had to act quickly; otherwise, her opportunity would be squandered. She placed her finger on the trigger and took one large breath of air. Slowly, she let it out and squeezed the trigger. She watched through her scope as the side of Warlock's head blew open. The shot was clean. Quickly she got up from her position and raced back up the hillside and to her escape route.

PAVEL COULDN'T BELIEVE IT. One moment he was having a pleasant conversation with the old woman, and the next, the side of her head exploded. The shot was clean and professional. The NKVD security men quickly raced outside to return fire in the direction from the shot. Their small caliber pistols were completely ineffective.

"Hold your fire, you imbeciles. They're probably long gone by now!" shouted Pavel.

Just then, the men could hear the faint sounds of an aircraft approaching from the Northwest. It sounded as if the aircraft was circling overhead. Then, almost as suddenly as it began, the noise from the aircraft dissipated. If it was a landing aircraft, the landing was aborted.

Pavel now knew that he was dealing with a gang of very thorough professionals. This was not the work of a ragtag group of saboteurs or resistance fighters. This was the work of coordinated activities with Home Army units and British intelligence. He would go back to headquarters and inquire more information from Soviet 'highest sources' intelligence.

Chapter 17

The two-hour flight from Frankfurt to Poland was uneventful. It was a beautiful, cloudless night, and the moon was up illuminating the surface. As the C-47 dropped down to an altitude of 1200 feet above the ground, one could see the surface. There was a light dusting of snow over the countryside. The brutal cold of a Polish winter had not yet set in. In the cockpit of the C-47, Vivian Tate and Tony Franko sat with the crew. Both wore headsets to monitor communications traffic and to enabled them to talk directly to the pilot and copilot. As previously briefed, Tony Franko was seated on the jump seat while Vivian Tate stood in the doorway to oversee the entire landing operation. This was her mission, and she was the mission commander.

The C-47 pilot announced to Franko, "We're approaching the landing site from the northwest. This is a different approach than flights coming from Italy. You'll have to verify the landing zone. Can you confirm, sir?"

Since passengers were simply identified as "Joes" to the crew, they did not know the identity of their passengers. They were addressed in generic titles. Franko leaned forward as much as he could so he could get a better look at the landing site. He cross-checked it with a map on his lap.

"That's definitely it. I can make out the bend in the two small rivers, and I see the staging area in the trees."

Vivian ducked lower to confirm the site along with Franko. "Are you sure?"

"Positive."

Then she ordered the crew. "Go ahead, make radio contact."

The copilot dialed in the pre-set covert frequency on his radio and called the station using the tactical call sign. He waited for a reply, but nothing came. He tried again, but there was still no reply from the landing committee.

"Should I flash the signal, ma'am?" asked the copilot. "They could have problems with their radio. Happens all the time."

"No, not yet, keep trying."

The copilot did as he was told, but there was still no response from the ground. Vivian announced to the crew through her com mic. "This is highly unusual. No hostilities are going on. The reception committee was well briefed on primary and secondary authentication procedures. If the field is in control of the Russians, we don't want to compromise the ground assets."

Vivian had seconds to make a decision on continuing or proceeding to the alternate, which was the drop zone. Slowly, she thought of her options, but nothing was encouraging.

Franko asked as she was contemplating, "Should we circle overhead? Maybe they're not ready."

Vivian thought back to the war and all the agents she had sent into the field that never returned. Many of them never knew the dangers they were about to face. She made a decision. "I don't like the looks of this. Something tells me this isn't right. The reception committee should be there waiting for us. The only reason why they're not answering the radio is that the airfield is compromised. No, we'll jump. Proceed to the drop zone! NOW!"

Franko unstrapped from his seat, "I hope you know what you're doing!"

"I know what I'm doing; get back there and suit up."

Franko didn't argue. He got up and proceeded to the cabin where a crew member would help him into his jump gear.

"How much time do we have?" Vivian asked the pilot as he put the aircraft in a steep turn away from the landing zone.

"Ten minutes, maybe more. But no more than fifteen; otherwise, fuel is a consideration."

"Make the course adjustment. Every second counts if the field is compromised. They could have heard us or even gotten a visual. In the meantime, we'll suit up. Let us know when we're over the drop zone."

"Roger that, ma'am, I'll have the crew let you know."

Tony Franko and Vivian Tate made the final adjustments on their green jumpsuits and parachute harnesses. A crewman double-checked their equipment, then gave the thumbs-up signal. He shouted to the two of them, "All we have to do now is wait for the lights to flash. Get in position!"

Vivian and Franko proceeded to the rear door, attached their lanyards to the extraction cable, and waited for the signal. Franko looked at Vivian, wondering if she was even prepared for the landing and fall. All he saw was extreme confidence in her eyes. Then she shouted, "Don't worry, I'll go first!"

Two seconds later, the red light flashed. The jumpmaster opened the door as the super cold air rushed into the already frigid cabin interior. Vivian held on to her harness, waiting for the signal. Then a green light came on steady. The jumpmaster pushed Vivian out the door, followed by Franko, then their equipment canister.

The jumpmaster watched as the two fell to Earth. Seconds later, he saw three fully opened canopies, and the two Joes dropped safely to the surface. He announced to the pilot over his intercom, "Good canopies. Good jump. Let's go home."

It was all rather peaceful as Tony Franko fell from the sky. The visibility was excellent, with light snow covering the surface. The landing would not be difficult. He watched as Vivian touched down on the ground first, then rolled over on her side, her parachute drifting softly to the surface. There was no wind; a good sign. Seconds later, Franko hit the surface. Their supply canister landed just a few feet away. The ground was soft as he rolled to his side in a perfect parachute landing. He quickly unlatched his parachute and harness and gathered up the silk as he was trained. Once his and the supply parachute were crumpled in his arms, he ran to Vivian's position to assist her. As he got closer, he could see she was already standing and gathering her silk. She had safely made the landing.

"You all right, is anything broken?" he asked, unstrapping his Styrofoam helmet.

"Piece of cake. Help me out of this infernal thing so we can get out of here. I'm freezing!"

The two climbed out of their green jumpsuits and retrieved their supply canister. Franko removed the COM/SEC equipment and secured them inside a small backpack, which was also inside the canister. The then hid the chutes, jumpsuits, and supply canister in the bushes and proceeded with their next task, which was determining their position so they could find adequate shelter until daylight. Then they would attempt contact with the secondary reception committee. Franko pulled out a small compass from his pocket and pointed it east, cross-checking his position with the stars. Frost blew from his mouth as he spoke. "The temperature is around freezing, maybe even a few degrees below freezing. We only have light jackets and footwear. Luckily, the snow is thin, but we have to find shelter somewhere. What happened to your boots?" he asked, as he looked at Vivian's feet.

Vivian couldn't lie and keep this bit of information from him, so she told the truth. "I couldn't get into the jump boots with them on. They didn't fit right inside the over boots. I was afraid I wouldn't have a strong footing on landing and didn't want to risk breaking a leg or ankle, so I took them off and put on my pumps."

Franko didn't respond and moved on to more important tasks. Under the circumstances, it was probably the right choice. She could have easily broken a foot or ankle. "According to the imagery we saw of this site, there should be some shelter close by. Just to be on the safe side, let's make our way there," he added, as he pointed to a small creek bed. "We don't want to be visible in the fields or leave a contrast just in case someone heard the aircraft or saw the parachutes. Let's stay concealed as much as possible."

"Lead the way," she said. "Tony?" she said, placing a hand on his shoulder.

"Yes?"

"Thank you."

"Thank you for what, we both knew what we had to do."

"No, thank you for not making a big scene on the

airplane and agreeing with me. Trust me. It just didn't feel right. If it doesn't feel right, it probably isn't."

"You should know. You've got the experience."

The two made their way toward the lower creek bed. It was a small stream but with a steady flow of water. In the middle of winter, it would probably freeze over. Franko looked at Vivian. She had a dark green scarf wrapped over her head, and the frost was coming from her mouth as she breathed. She only had a lightweight coat, dress, and thin shoes not meant for walking long distances, over snow. "Be careful with your steps. Those shoes are not meant for walking in slippery conditions. There's no soles. Stay behind me and follow my steps. I'll make sure the footing is sound."

Vivian nodded. Her face was already turning pale from the cold.

"Let's move slowly. There's not much light in the shadows."

The couple made their way along the creek bed, following the current. Each step was carefully placed to avoid the slippery conditions. They were not making good time. Franko could tell that Vivian was not used to harsh conditions in the field. She was struggling. Too many years behind a desk and in the warm comfort of her London flat.

His thoughts were interrupted when he heard a screech, then a splash in the water. He turned around just in time to see Vivian slip below the surface of the water. She had obviously lost her footing and slipped. Even though the creek was small, the water was deep and swift in this area as Vivian was carried past him.

Tony didn't waste any time. He quickly followed the stream and Vivian until he could find a place to fish her out. He saw a slight bend in the water and used that to close the distance. There he saw an area where he could retrieve her. He stepped into the water, which was only knee-deep in this area, and reached for Vivian's coat collar. He grabbed on and tugged with all his might. It was dead weight. He had forgotten about one important item. The money vest she wore under her garments contained a lot of cash and therefore, excess weight, which was pulling her under. He tugged and tugged to overcome the swift currents of the stream. The weight of Vivian's clothing slowed him down. He secured his footing, went deeper into the water, up to his waist, and pulled harder. She began to come closer to him and to shallower water. He pulled and pulled with all his six-foot two-inch strength, and slowly she began to come out of the water. He pulled her safely to the shore.

He was sweating profusely from the effort, but Vivian, on the other hand, was far worse. She was completely stiff and unresponsive. Hypothermia was setting in. Her face was blue and her skin was like ice. "Miss Tate! Miss Tate!" he shouted, trying to get a response, but nothing. He dragged her body further up the embankment. He searched for a pulse and checked her breathing, but he couldn't tell if she was dead or alive. It was as if her body had completely shut down. He tried again, this time shaking her slightly. "Vivian! Vivian! Can you hear me?" Still nothing. Then he thought about something from his military training when pilots were unresponsive. He tried calling out a familiar name. He decided to take a chance. He was now desperate. "Irina! Irina! Can you hear me?" he said in Polish.

To his surprise, her eyes opened, and she responded slightly, speaking Polish, "I'm so . . . cold." He was relieved to hear her say something, anything.

"Yes, I know. I'm going to help you. Hang on, I'll get you warmed up," he said in English.

Franko pulled her up to the field level where the ground was flat. He could make out the outline of a farmhouse and lights. He heaved Vivian on his shoulders like a fireman would and carried her toward the cottage running as fast as he could. He pressed further and faster, each step a little closer to saving Vivian's life. He was sprinting now. That's when he saw the figure. At first, he thought it was only shadows, but as the distance closed, he could make out the figure of a heavy set man, frost puffing from his mouth, running toward them. The man waved his hands above his head, but he didn't say anything until they met up.

The man was in his late fifties with a strong, powerful build. He was dressed in dark clothing, including a dark cap. Speaking Polish, he said quietly, "Don't make a sound. There could be others out here. I'm from the receiving committee. I just got the word you moved to the alternate site. What happened?" he asked.

Franko stopped to catch his breath and spoke Polish, "I'm HORSE, who are you?"

"WAGON," the man replied.

Since the correct code words were given, Franko began, "She fell into the water. I think she's unconscious, suffering from hypothermia."

The man looked at Vivian still on top of Franko's back. He touched her face, then felt around for a pulse on her neck. "Lucky for you, I'm a doctor. We don't have much time. I'll help you carry her to the house. We've got to move quickly!"

The house was basic and looked like all the others in the area. It was white stucco with a red tile roof. The structure had a small, covered porch with an ample stockpile of wood. The chimney puffed white smoke into the night sky. As they came closer, a woman came out of the house to lend a hand.

"Hurry up, we need to get her into the back room and get these wet clothes off," shouted the stranger to the woman.

The man and woman carried Vivian into a side room, which was probably the single bedroom for the house. Exhausted, Franko dropped to the floor to catch his breath. He too was soaking wet from the waist down. He moved closer to the small fire to get some heat. The fireplace was also used for all cooking. Several large pots hung nearby, and a large kettle was hanging over the fire. The strange man stuck his head out from the bedroom door and barked out orders. "Get more wood on that fire! Put some water in that kettle and get it boiling! We'll need a lot of heat. She's not out of danger. Her body is going into shock. I'll be out in a few minutes to give you a hand." Then he went back into the bedroom to assist his wife.

Franko got up and proceeded to get some more wood from outside. As he passed by the door, he took a peek to see how Vivian was doing. As he did so, he just got a glimpse. Vivian was still limp, but the two had managed to get off her wet dress and underwear. She was sitting on the edge of the bed, completely naked. That's when he saw her back. It was covered with hideous scars several inches long, all over her back and buttocks. He shook his head in disbelief and went outside to gather the firewood as instructed. It was becoming clear now that, through misfortune, he was acquiring more and more information on the true identity of the woman known as Vivian Tate. First was her response to the name 'Irina.' Then the physical evidence from the whippings she had taken from the Gestapo. Next, it was her tradecraft and skills. There was

no mistake now. Miss Vivian Tate was Irina Jankowski—
Agent JAN. He focused on the next tasks, getting more
wood, getting himself warmed up, and . . . saving Vivian's
life.

Franko threw several logs on the fire and got it going,
producing a good amount of heat. Next, he filled the kettle
from a water pump in the other room and placed it over
the fire. He removed his wet boots and socks, then moved
closer to the fire. He slipped off his wet jacket and placed
his hands over the flames. That's when the man emerged
from the bedroom holding some extra blankets.

"She's going to be all right now. If it had been another
three minutes, we would have had a corpse in the other
room. Let me formally introduce myself. My name is Josef
Lupa, doctor of veterinary medicine. I'm the local veteri-
narian and ground security coordinator for the Urban
group. We'll talk operations later. In the meantime, I'll
make some tea. You need to get warmed up as well."

The two men sat in front of the fire, drinking tea to
warm themselves. Lupa picked up the conversation where
he had left off.

"It's a shame. A young, beautiful, blond woman
hideously maimed like that. I conducted a full medical
examination on her. She was brutalized beyond my
comprehension. I was almost sick to my stomach. I know
they did things at the camps but never like this. I've never
seen anything like that before in all my medical profession.
Not even on animals. Do you know how it happened?"

Franko spoke. "It wasn't me who did those things to
her. I'm an American officer. This is the first I've known
about *that*. How could I know? I wouldn't do such a thing.
She never spoke of it before, but no doubt, it was probably
the work of the Gestapo. I do know she was held a prisoner in Berlin before the war."

Just then, Lupa's wife emerged from the bedroom assisting Vivian who was now on her feet and walking on her own, slowly. She was wrapped in dry, warm blankets as the two women came towards the fire.

Lupa was relieved to see Vivian on her feet. "Come have a seat by the fire." he said to Vivian, in Polish. "We must warm you up slowly. Let me get you some hot tea to drink."

Lupa then fetched a cup and poured the tea. "I'll leave you two by the fire. Take those wet trousers off. Get some rest, both of you. Doctor's orders. We can talk ops later. I have a phone. We can make contact with the leaders then. You were both very lucky tonight. I was told the Russians took control of the airfield right before you landed."

Franko took off his wet shirt and trousers and hung them by the fire. Vivian slowly drank some of the hot tea then handed the cup to Franko. She didn't say anything, seeing Tony almost naked by her side. She just lay down next to the fire and closed her eyes. Tony placed another blanket over her, and within seconds she fell asleep.

She's suffering from both hypothermia and extreme exhaustion. She probably hasn't slept for days, Franko thought as he looked down upon Vivian. He could see that she was indeed an attractive woman despite her condition. He was beginning to not only like her but respect her. She had made the right call aborting the landing. She had an instinct that something wasn't right. According to Lupa's information, she was right. Tony placed his hand on the side of her face. She was a lot warmer now than she had been back at the drop zone. He slid down on the floor and lay close to her, under her blankets to maximize their body's heat. He covered them up with more blankets then placed his head down next to hers and the fire. In no time, he too, fell fast asleep.

* * *

A FEW HOURS LATER, Franko woke from his deep sleep with the crashing noise from the front door as it was closing. Lupa was probably up and gathering more wood for the fire. Franko could tell it was now daylight. Probably still early in the morning, though. Vivian started rustling in her blankets and finally opened her eyes. Franko looked at her face, then said in English, "Good morning."

Vivian placed a finger to her lips to indicate silence. "Speak Polish, *where are we?*"

Franko sat up. "We're at the Zabarow safe house. We made contact with the alternate receiving committee, Dr. Lupa and his wife."

Vivian, still only partially awake, half-shouted, "Where're my clothes? My money vest? What are you doing here next to me with your clothes off?"

"Hey, take it easy. You suffered from a case of extreme exhaustion and hypothermia. Dr. Lupa and his wife had to get your wet clothes off. They're drying next to the fire. My clothes were wet too and had to be dried. According to Dr. Lupa, I too was suffering from a case of mild hypothermia."

Vivian sat up, keeping the blankets wrapped around her naked body as she saw her clothes drying next to the fire. Her senses were starting to come back to her as she began inquiring, speaking in a normal tone of voice now. "I remember slipping into that frigid water and trying to get out. How *did* I get out?"

"I waded in after you. That water was deep in the area, and the current was swift. You traveled several meters before I plucked you out. Luckily we were not far from the safe house, and Dr. Lupa made contact and helped us here."

Just then the front door opened and Lupa entered, carrying another large bundle of firewood and dropped it to the floor. "I see you two are doing much better, after some rest. You slept for hours. It's after eight in the morning."

Lupa proceeded to recap the events to Vivian from the last few hours. "I have a telephone here and the number you can reach Home Army leadership. They will coordinate movements back to Tarnow. Security is extremely tight in our cell. They will probably not make the trip here to pick you up since the airfield was compromised. We'll have to make a rendezvous at another location nearby, then go into town from there. It's up to them."

Lupa's wife came into the sitting room and gathered Vivian's clothes from the fireplace. Lupa continued, "My wife will assist you with your clothes. You can change in the next room. In the meantime, I need your colleague to assist me with sanitizing the landing site. I'm sure you left your parachutes and overalls in the area. If the Russians come looking in this area, we don't want them finding anything. They'll come to each and every house making inquiries."

Franko and Lupa left the two women and proceeded to the drop zone and recovered the parachutes, supply canister, and overalls. Next, they returned back to the house and built a fire outside next to the house. They burned everything, leaving nothing, including the cords. When they returned back to the house, Vivian was already dressed and had resumed her leadership position. It was as if nothing had happened to her.

"I've made telephone contact with Morena. They'll meet us at a town called Koszyce. From there, they'll take us by vehicle to the Tarnow safe house. Do you have a car, Dr. Lupa?"

"Of course, I make all my rounds with a truck. Petrol is

expensive and scarce, but I can usually get a ration. What time is the rendezvous?"

"Eleven. We wait for half an hour. If no one shows up, we return here and make another attempt tomorrow, same time." Vivian reached into her money vest and pulled out the bundle of wet cash. While Lupa and Franko were away, she had gone through the money vest to make sure all the money was there. It was. She counted out several bills and handed it to Lupa. "For your troubles and petrol. Also, we'll have to take the supply canister with us. We don't want it left here in case the Russians come."

Franko helped Vivian re-pack her suitcase retrieved from the supply canister. "All good?" he asked Vivian, with concern.

"I'm fine."

A short time later at the rendezvous location, a Polish forest ranger driving a small utility truck met Franko and Vivian and took them into Tarnow.

* * *

PAVEL RETURNED to his regional headquarters in Krakow. Here he made a trip to the Soviet consulate and announced to the resident chief that he wished to make a secure call to Moscow. A short time later, Pavel was on the secure telephone line to Moscow Center speaking to his controller.

"I need the latest developments from your highest sources concerning my investigation." Pavel recapped to his controller what happened at the airfield. "We are dealing with professionals. The resistance had to have help from the West."

Pavel's controller at Moscow Center advised him that the highest sources intelligence information was coming in sporadically. The British had foreseen a possible leak in their system and had taken the proper security precautions. However, he was told that the Polish Home Army was receiving assistance from a woman agent. Positive identity was still unknown, but the woman agent was well connected in the city of Tarnow. This was all the information Pavel could acquire for the moment about his elusive British agent and the pathway to Krupke.

Pavel returned to his office in Krakow and asked for a report on the latest civic activities in the city of Tarnow. To his surprise, he received a report that a hotel, the Hotel Bristol was having a holiday celebration and all loyal guests and clients were invited. The proprietor of the hotel was a woman named Janica Kijowski. Pavel picked up his telephone and called his administrative assistant.

"I want to make travel arrangements for my team and me. We need to spend a few days in Tarnow. See to it that billeting and travel orders are set." Pavel hung up the phone and thought, *I need to find out if this woman, Janica Kijowski, speaks multiple languages and is helping former Nazis.*

Chapter 18

The safe house was located near the Hotel Bristol at Fifty-three Krokowska Boulevard. It was on the top, fourth-floor corner, facing the main railway station and the hotel. A forest ranger drove Vivian and Franko to the rear entrance of the safe house, and he carried their tattered suitcases as he escorted the two inside, then promptly left. Once inside the safe house, Jawor and Morena were waiting. Franko was amazed at the scene in front of him. The safe house looked more like a tactical situation room. Maps and drawings were taped on the walls, radios, listening devices, and coding machines were everywhere about the tables. Clothes, suitcases, and accessories were on the chairs. Guns, rifles, and machine guns were in abundance. Vivian, still all business, proceeded to remove her outer garments and took off the money vest. She counted out several bills in US dollars and handed them to Jawor. "The first install-ment, paid as we agreed," she said.

Vivian then addressed Franko. "These are our Home Army contacts and security assets. This is Major Ana

Zawacki, code name Jawor, circuit commander, and her assistant, Lieutenant Isebel Glowinski, code name Morena. Their circuit is called Urban. They will be working with us for the entire operation."

Franko tried to extend his hand out to greet the two, but Vivian interrupted. "No need for formalities here. These two are tasked with our safety and security. Ladies, this is Major Antoni Franko."

Jawor spoke next. She showed no emotions or expressions as Franko listened. "As your colleague just mentioned, I'm circuit commander for the AK-22 Ranger Battalion, code named Urban. The first order of business. I need to issue you your cover names and identities. Ma'am, as per your instructions, you've been issued the code name, Janica Kijowski. We have another suitcase already packed and ready to go. I have a new set of clothes for you. You can change in the other room."

Jawor continued, "We feared the worst for you two. The airfield was compromised shortly before your arrival. Russian security forces were there waiting. They've taken control of the airfield. At this point, we don't believe there was a security breach. The information was more than likely inadvertently revealed by one of our sources. That source has been eliminated, so there are no further security risks. We must, however, take security precautions seriously. We cannot afford another lapse. The Russians were careless and overconfident last night. They underestimated us. They will not make the same mistakes twice. I have the airfield under surveillance by my team. The Russians will probably move on after a few days, but to be on the safe side, you should come up with another location for future clandestine landings."

Vivian nodded. "Agreed, it's already factored into our plan."

Once preliminaries were exchanged, the team moved onto the mission. Jawor went into the bedroom and came out with a couple of dresses for Vivian and addressed her. "Pick out one and change. We must move to the Hotel Bristol this afternoon. But first, I have some appointments scheduled for you. The alternate landing put us slightly behind schedule, but we can make up the time. Franko will stay here until the next phase of the operation."

As soon as Vivian changed into the new set of clothes, both she and Jawor left the safe house. Vivian never looked at Franko or said goodbye as she left. She just turned and walked out of the room. Franko couldn't believe she left without saying anything to him.

As Vivian walked down the steps of the apartment, her face, however, told a different story. A face that Franko did not or could not see. It was a face of sorrow. She regretted not saying anything to him for saving her life. She had to stay in character. She was grateful he took the initiative to rescue her from the frigid water.

Morena stayed with Franko and briefed him further. "I'm your immediate contact and bodyguard. I will tail your every move. If we must leave the safe house, we go together, understood?"

Franko addressed her in Polish, "Of course."

"You look like you were hit by a truck, what happened?"

Franko recapped the story of what had happened the previous night.

"You're lucky. These things happen unexpectedly, but you managed to overcome your misfortune. By the way, your Polish is good. You'll have to practice, though. The Soviets will not recognize flaws in your speech; however, if they have local informants or agents working with them, they'll recognize you immediately. I can help you with phrases and common words in this region. Please don't take it as an insult. It may save your life."

"Question?" Franko asked in Polish. Morena simply looked at him from the top of her eyeballs as if she didn't have time for inquiries.

"Where are you taking her? I thought we were all staying together?"

Morena ignored his question. She walked over to the table and picked up a Colt .45 pistol from the pile of weapons. She handed the gun to him. All she said to him was, "Janica Kijowski is the proprietor for the Hotel Bristol, which of course, is a black-market hotel. That's it across the street. She has to make contact with her black-market sources."

Franko grabbed the gun and checked the chamber. "Shouldn't I be using a Russian or German one?"

"If that's what you prefer? Take your pick. They're on the table."

"No, I'll stick with the Colt." Franko put the gun in the shoulder holster, then slipped it over his shoulder.

Morena came back to a map on the table, motioning Franko over. "I was told you were one of the few Americans who appreciated our intelligence services during the war. The British were appreciative, but the Americans, not so. I also know you helped Urban safely EXFIL the first, nearly intact V-2 rocket to the West. You'll also be happy to know, we are the remnants of that group. Most were lost during the war."

Franko was surprised to hear this piece of information but remembered what Vivian had told him concerning the two women losing their husbands.

Morena continued. "Our human intelligence is still extremely effective." She picked up a file folder that was on the table and opened it. "This is your Russian counterpart. He's very good at what he does, which is looking for key former Nazi Wonder Weapons. Our sources tracked his movements near the Tuchola launch area. His name is Vladimir Sivan, an Air Force colonel assigned to GRU. Get familiar with his face. He could appear anytime. He has been aggressively looking for key V-2 missile components and scientists. Our sources have determined that, as of this moment, his team has not uncovered the sophisticated flight hardware. He will be on your tail."

Franko picked up the folder and looked through its contents and the picture of Colonel Sivan. Then he asked, "Can we trust your sources? How do I know they won't betray me?"

"Look, Major, let's get something straight right now. Our circuit survived the war because of our team. We are the most secure in all of Poland. We were picked to help you out because of that. You can rest assured that our sources will not betray you. If there is a betrayal, it will not come from Polish sources."

"What about Motyl? You said one of your sources betrayed you."

"That was unfortunate. The source was an old woman. She unknowingly compromised the airfield to Soviet agents due to the ruthless tactics of the NKVD. I am sorry to say she has been eliminated. She no longer is in control of that airfield."

Franko lightened up. "All right, fair enough. I was told that many of your sources are forest rangers working in the area. Is that still the case?'

Morena nodded. "They've been loyal even without pay. But as your colleague has brought funds for payment, that will make things easier. Just to let you know. The Nazis actually respected the forest rangers and their management of timber resources. The rangers were allowed a certain amount of freedom-of-movement near the missile sites, which were located deep in the forested countryside. The Soviets, on the other hand, do not value our natural resources. They may not have the same attitudes as the Germans. That is why timing is so important on this mission. The window can close at any time. This would tip the advantage toward the Soviets."

"How much do you actually know about our mission? What were you told?"

"We were told *everything*. We know about the SS war criminal you're after and the ruse to capture him." Morena rummaged through her pile and pulled out a picture of Dimitri Pavel. "This is your colleague's counterpart and the one who will give us the most challenge, Dimitri Pavel, NKVD. He is also after the SS war criminal. His unit is believed responsible for taking control of the Motyl airfield last night."

Franko swore under his breath. This was not going to be easy. Just as Vivian had told him, they were battling two enemies on two fronts: one political one technical. This was a massive chess game played out on a huge chess board. He now also realized why Vivian had withheld key information from him.

Morena moved on to another subject. "This is our working area," she said as she circled the region with her fingers. "We've had a development that came to our knowledge just recently. One of our rangers picked up a man near Blizna. A Polish Jew by the name of Leopold Waldorf. He goes by Poldi. He claims to have been a prisoner at the Pustkow labor camp. He survived deportation to Birkenau mainly because he was a skilled technician in the field of rocket assembly. Specifically, flight hardware. He worked his way back to Debica and was looking for work when our rangers found him. The first order of business. You and I need to make a trip to Debica and interview him before Sivan finds out about him. Time is on our side in this matter, but we must leave soon."

* * *

JAWOR TOOK Vivian to their first stop, which was a hairdresser. Here, Vivian had her hair dyed very blond. Next, the two women went to a butcher shop and entered from the rear. Jawor said a few words to the butcher who then produced a box which contained several cuts of meat. Vivian reached into her money belt and pulled out more bills and paid the butcher. Next, the two women made their way to the Hotel Bristol. They entered from the back entrance, which had utility access by the kitchen. They dropped off the meat for the cooks then proceeded into the main hotel and up to the second floor. There was an office located for the proprietor. Once inside the office, with the door closed, Jawor continued.

"This is our base of operations for the time being. I am your daytime hotel manager. The night shift is covered by one of our battalion chiefs. You have a room here in the hotel, and I will take the guest room just outside this office. I'll cover your every move. If we suspect someone is after you, I'll take the appropriate security measures for your safety. Just to be on the safe side, I want you to take this." Jawor reached into her blouse and produced a Russian Makarov pistol. "Keep this handy."

Vivian took the gun and placed it in the desk drawer.

Next, Jawor showed a calendar of the week's schedule. "This is our schedule for the week. It's imperative we stick to it. We have guests tonight that we're planning a dinner party for. That's why we needed to stop at the butcher shop."

Vivian then reached under her dress and pulled out the money belt and handed it to Jawor. "Funds for the operation. I trust you can keep it in a safe place."

Jawor nodded. "We have a safe in my office."

Chapter 19

Franko couldn't believe the form of transport for his trip to Debica. It was a captured German motorcycle with a sidecar. The vehicle actually ran well. Morena drove the bike while Franko sat in the very cramped sidecar. He wore a pair of goggles to keep the dust and dirt from getting into his eyes. After a few minutes on the road, Morena stopped off at a small tavern in the town of Pilzno. At the back of the tavern was a section used as a black market petrol stop. A young man came out from a structure with a small gas can and immediately filled the tank of the motorcycle sidecar. "Petrol is not cheap or in plentiful supplies in the region. He only accepts cash," said Morena.

Franko took his cue and counted out several US dollar bills. The attendant wanted more, so Franko gave him a total of forty dollars for the equivalent of two gallons of gas. Once the filling was complete, the two were on their way again, headed for Debica.

The town was actually located outside of Debica in a hamlet called Brzeznica. Here, Morena rode on the main highway and exited near a large church. She continued down a smaller road into a residential area with a few small dwellings. Morena pulled into the gravel driveway of an inconspicuous house and came to a stop in a cloud of dust. She took off her riding helmet and goggles and said, "Let's go inside; they should be waiting for us."

Franko followed Morena into the small structure and was greeted by two men from the nearby forest ranger battalion. They introduced the guest sitting at the kitchen table as Leopold "Poldi" Waldorf. Franko could not be sure of his age because he was thin and frail. If he had been a prisoner at the local concentration camp, then there was not much difference in his appearance now than it was back during the war. He had obviously not been well fed for several months. Morena dismissed the two rangers and told them to come back in a couple of hours. By then, they should have more information on what to do with their guest.

Morena said to the man in Polish, "This is Major Franko from the US military. He's come all the way from Frankfurt to ask you a few questions. Major Franko."

Franko pulled a chair next to Waldorf and produced a small note-pad from his pocket. "I understand you were a prisoner at Heidelager. For starters, state your name and tell me what you did at the camp?"

The man fidgeted in his chair and replied, "My name is Leopold Waldorf. You can call me, Poldi. I was known as a *Kapo*, or prisoner leader at the Pustkow labor camp, also known as Heidelager. I arrived at the camp in May 1944. By that time, the camp was already fully operational. What I mean by that is the camp was fully constructed and divided into skilled and unskilled sections. Also a Polish camp and Jewish camp. Of course, I worked in the Jewish camp. I'm an electrical engineer by trade. I was singled out immediately to work in the skilled section. Our job at this camp was the construction of navigation hardware for the V-2 rocket. The rockets were shipped-in by rail from Dora. Final assembly was done nearby at the Blizna complex. We did not put the actual rockets together. In fact, I never even saw a V-2 rocket the whole time I was at Heidelager. As far as I know, that job was done by actual SS firing crews. Our job at the camp was to put together the components for the guidance system."

FRANKO WAS STARTLED to receive this information. "Can you give me a general description of the system?"

Waldorf did as he was told, and it appeared from his descriptions he was telling the truth because there was too much accuracy in his description of the V-2 flight hardware.

"All right, let's move on," said Franko. "What can you tell me about the latest version of the guidance systems? I was told the Germans were working on a more sophisticated guidance system, one that would enable a rocket to hit New York or Philadelphia."

Poldi nodded in agreement. "It began, I was told, shortly after July 1944. By this time during the war, all V-2 launch testing was moved from Peenemünde to Blizna. Conditions were still extremely harsh at that time. People were dying every day because of these conditions. The Nazis were demanding more and more production because of the Allied landings in Normandy. However, they continued to have one rocket failure after another. In August of 1944, that camp commander was taken away and presumably shot. He was replaced by another SS officer by the name of Hoch. I don't know his first name or his SS rank. He was always in civilian clothes.

"Anyway, this new commander called a meeting with the head Kapos, I being one of them and he asked us for inputs on the situation. Since most of us were on starvation diets, the first thing we said was we needed more food. We told him that if we were fed better, we might be able to not only improve output but actually make improvements to the guidance system itself. Naturally, he agreed because he didn't want to go out the same way as his predecessor. Almost immediately, we received a breakfast of bread, butter, honey or jam, and coffee. Lunch was another piece of bread and a piece of canned meat, usually sausage. Supper was a thick soup and more bread. We then told Hoch that the missile failures were not because of the flight hardware but the actual rockets themselves.

"The system was so complicated that it was virtually impossible to correct all acts of sabotage from the assemblers back at Dora. This was when we moved on to developing a more accurate and reliable guidance system. We proposed that instead of using one system, we wired two in series. That way, if one failed during launch, the other would take over. So, we did. As far as I knew, several test launches with the dual guidance system took place at Blizna but again there were still failures after launch."

Franko lit up a cigarette and give it to Leopold, and he continued his discussion.

"Several engineers in my camp proposed putting three guidance systems in place. That way you'd have the capability to mix. If one failed, the other two would take over. Also, all three would integrate with each other and determine the more accurate system. This would also isolate mechanical malfunctions after launch and quickly rule out failures with the guidance system. The process was called mixing. This is what we were working on until the Russian Front started closing in on us."

Franko asked, "What was it about this mixing system that enabled the rockets to hit long-range targets, say, New York?"

Waldorf continued, "Operational V-2 rockets required a time-consuming and complicated alignment process to a fixed present position. This was usually accomplished by a ground site survey team, composed of SS civil engineers. Then the gyros were aligned to that position. On the new system, we fashioned a tumbler with numbers that provided the present position directly to the system. We attached a tumbler to each gyro, enabling the present position to be inserted into each of the two or three gyros independently. Since most of the operational rockets in the field were fired from mobile sites, this was a huge tactical improvement. Once the gyros were fixed to a present position, all movements of the rocket were then controlled via that present position. Most importantly, the rockets could be fired more quickly."

Franko couldn't take notes fast enough. He needed to ask more questions. "What happened to the mixing systems? Are they still here in Pustkow?"

"That, I do not know. There was talk of moving the testing to another site in Poland away from the Russian Front. And, I might add, testing the new system on smaller sounding rockets instead of the V-2, possibly a V-1."

"Do you know where that site was?"

"I do not know. It could have been anywhere. Especially if the Nazis were using smaller sounding rockets for the gyro testing. You see, the Blizna site was primarily a mobile launch test facility. All the rockets were fired from mobile launchers. The new facility would have also been a mobile-launch test site since this was the emphasis at that time. Unfortunately, we were relocated to Auschwitz-Birkenau just a few hours before the Russians overran the camp. That was in August 1944. One of the last assignments we had was to box up the new navigation devices and batteries in preparation for shipment. Hoch was the last one to leave Heidelager. If anyone knows, it would be him. He joined us at Auschwitz a few days later. In fact, when Hoch arrived at Birkenau, all of us Jewish prisoners from Heidelager were to be relocated for greater security. Hoch intervened and convinced Mengele of our importance to the Third Reich. The intervention worked, and we were given a reprieve. We were sent to Nordhausen. However, Hoch wasn't as fortunate. Instead of going to Nordhausen with us, he was ordered to stay at Birkenau to conduct further testing. Testing on what is a different matter, since there were no V-2 testing facilities at Birkenau."

"How did you survive the Dora missile complex? I understand the conditions were horrific."

"The train that transported us to the Dora complex was a military train, and we were attacked by Allied aircraft. The Nazis were cut to pieces. I managed to escape the mayhem. I went into hiding until the war ended."

"That's a fascinating story. Can you draw a description of the mixing system and the tumblers for me?"

Franko handed the man his notepad and within a few minutes had drawn a detailed sketch of the navigation systems, complete with electrical equations and mathematical formulas. As near as Franko could tell, Poldi was telling nothing other than the truth.

"Just out of curiosity, since this is all new to Western technology, how could you get three gyro systems installed in the nose cone of one rocket? Surely that is considerable weight and cumbersome."

"Simple, we miniaturized the components with solid-state materials instead of vacuum tubes, and we used smaller, lighter-weight dry batteries instead of heavy, lead-acid batteries."

Franko was astonished to hear this piece of information. "Is there anything else you can tell me about the guidance systems here at Blizna?"

Poldi finished off his cigarette and asked for another, which Franko complied. Then Waldorf continued. "It was right before the Red Army overran the camp and we were transported out. I was part of a labor group that would periodically make trips to a local gypsum quarry to mine gravel and sand used at the concentration camp. One night I was called out for this detail. It was highly unusual because most of the labor teams left during daylight hours so the SS guards could keep us under control. This detail was called just before supper. We went to the quarry at night and helped bury a device."

"What do you mean by a device?" asked Franko.

"It was actually a complete V-2 guidance system and battery. An operational one, of course, not the newer, triple-mix system. We were not sure the camp commandant wanted the device for himself or to hide it from the advancing Russian Front. Either way, we hid the device."

"Do you know where the device is buried?"

"Sure, I was on the detail that buried it."

"What about the men on the detail? What happened to them?"

"I was the only one who survived the war, other than the commander, Hoch. He was actually on the burial detail with me."

Franko then turned to Morena. "I want him in protective custody. When the rangers get back, have them go to the quarry and retrieve the device. Mr. Waldorf can show them the way. These new components he's talking about are something that haven't even been invented in the West;

fifty years ahead of U.S. technology. Make all the necessary arrangements. It's imperative we keep Mr. Waldorf away from the Russians. He must not fall into Russian hands. And . . . let's get the older guidance system in our hands. Those things are hard to come by as it is."

"I have one small request," interrupted Poldi. "I was told you can offer safe passage to the American sector. Do you think you could get me a job working with the rocket team back in the United States? My family is all gone. It is just me now."

"Mr. Waldorf, that is exactly my intention!"

Chapter 20

Later that night in Tarnow, Franko was anxious to get this latest information back to Vivian. He convinced Morena that he needed to meet her right away and give her the news personally. Plus, he *had* to see her. Morena told Franko that there was a way into the Hotel Bristol through the coal chute. This emptied directly into the cellar. She informed Franko that he must not go inside the hotel itself for fear of breaking his cover. There was always a chance that a guest or employee would recognize him at a later date. He would have to wait in the cellar for Tate to make an appearance. She gave him a total of one hour to make contact with Vivian. After which time, he would have to leave and head back to the safe house. She also insisted that she go with him and provide perimeter security and surveillance. Franko agreed.

It was actually quite simple. Tony Franko opened the door for the coal chute and slid down the slope until he reached the bottom. He stumbled over the coal pile and entered the cellar. By this time of night, it was after eight o'clock, the cellar was in total darkness. He fumbled around in the darkness until he found a light switch. He twisted the knob and a single light bulb illuminated. He could see that the Hotel Bristol had a well, stocked supply of food and wine. As the hotel proprietor, Vivian Tate would probably have to make a trip or two to the cellar before the night was over. Hopefully, she hadn't come already. The clock was ticking because Morena was waiting outside. Luckily, he didn't have to wait long. He heard a noise from the cellar door and the flight of stairs.

The door opened, and another light switched on, illuminating another row of lights over the stairway. He heard footsteps coming down the stairs. Franko did not want to startle anyone, so he hid behind a basket of fresh fruit. He watched as a blond woman came down the stairs holding two bottles of wine. The woman placed the bottles back inside a wine rack and picked out two more bottles. She started to go back up the stairs when Franko finally recognized her. At first, he wasn't sure who the woman was, but as she turned and climbed the stairs, he finally recognized the figure. Her shapely legs and figure were unmistakable. It was Vivian Tate with her hair dyed, very blond. Calmly he said in English, "Don't be afraid; it's only me."

Vivian stopped dead in her tracks, then backed down the stairs, keeping her face away from the voice. She obviously recognized Franko's voice. When she got to the bottom of the stairs, she placed the two wine bottles on the floor, reached into her dress and pulled out the Makarov pistol. She struggled to see where the voice came from.

Franko spoke again.

"It's safe. I used the coal chute to get in. I needed to talk with you . . . alone."

"You've got some balls coming in here like this, scaring me half to death. Your orders were to wait at the safe house until I called for you. I hope you didn't come by yourself. You could've been followed."

Franko emerged from the shadows. "A 9.2 millimeter Makarov? Impressive, but you won't need that tonight. I didn't come by myself. I was escorted by Morena. By the way, where did you get those things? She's more like a light fixture. You turn her on and turn her off. There's no inter-action at all."

"That's no way to talk about our close partners. They're professionals. Let's cut to the chase, shall we? What's so bloody important you had to make a trip to the hotel and scare the dickens out of me?"

"Well, for starters, I can honestly say you look lovely as a blond."

"That's kind of you. It's part of my new cover. To blend in with the locals."

Franko wasn't totally convinced. After all, she was a native Pole. *How much more could she blend in?* he thought. He took a seat on a wooden stool next to a storage shelf. "I was worried about you. You left so unexpectedly this morning, I never asked how you felt. My colleague didn't share a lot of details with me on your whereabouts or the next phase of the mission."

Vivian came over to Franko and stood next to him, taking in his comments. "I'm actually doing well, thank you. You'd never know I almost froze to death." Then Vivian changed the subject. "The hotel is a well-oiled machine. The transition to the new proprietor went smoothly, thanks to Jawor. She's also my day manager."

"I won't take up your time. I wanted to pass on some information about a source we met this afternoon in Brzeznica." Franko recapped the story told to him by Leopold Waldorf, the buried flight hardware, and his desire to work in the United States.

"This *is* interesting. Any chance it could be a trap by the Russians? Maybe a way of getting into our network, then double-crossing us as we make the jump to the West?" Vivian raised her curious eyebrow.

"I guess there's always that possibility. You know better. That's why I asked Morena to put him in protective custody. Maybe we can all make the crossing."

Vivian sat in silence, thinking about the situation. "All right, keep him in protective custody for now. We'll keep those older gyros hidden with Urban. Who knows, we may need them at a later date. I'll let you know when to bring Mr. Waldorf out for further interviews. We don't want him having free reign then going back to his Russian controllers if he is a double. First priority though is Krupke and the scientists. Once we get them in our possession, we'll revisit your asset and what to do with your newly acquired gyros."

"Fair enough. My arrival SCHED to Home Station is set for tonight. I'll inform them we've arrived safely and that I've made contact with this valuable source."

Moving on to another topic, Franko asked, "What more can you tell me about the mission? Where do we go from here? Remember, you're not sharing a lot of details."

Vivian rubbed her forehead with her hand thinking about a response. Then she said, "Our team is in place and waiting for Krupke to make his move. We've sent out an advertisement for our valued hotel clients. We're hosting a holiday celebration in a few days for them. Krupke should get notification of this through his sources and make his move on us if he's close by."

"Another dinner party? Looks like you're having a good time tonight," he said, as he pointed to the two bottles of expensive black market port on the floor.

"Part of the job." She looked into Franko's eyes. She felt a sense of guilt in not saying anything to him when she had left earlier in the day. Actually, she was very happy to see him. Then she let something slip out.

"We hosted a large dinner party tonight for our guests. We have a lot of food left over. Can I bring you something to eat? You must be hungry. It's no trouble, you know."

Franko glanced back into Vivian's eyes. Her bright, blue eyes radiated out with her newly dyed blond hair. He placed a hand on her shoulder and said, "I'd love to, but I've got Morena outside in the cold waiting for me. She only allotted me one hour. I've got to get back to the safe house."

"All right, I see your point. Go now before someone comes down here looking for me."

Franko picked out an apple from the fruit basket. "Do you mind if I take this?" he said as he scurried up the coal ramp.

Vivian nodded. "Off you go." Before she could think, she let out a response unexpectedly, "I do miss being with you, Tony."

Franko heard her and turned his head slightly but didn't want to face her or say anything. He simply left the hotel the way he came in. Vivian was now all alone in the cellar. She was there for a few moments, thinking. As usual, her mind was always going in different directions. Then she picked up the two bottles of port from the floor and climbed back up the staircase.

Chapter 21

It was after ten that night. Most of the hotel guests and staff were either sleeping or in the lounge having drinks. Vivian was all alone in the kitchen. Jawor returned to her quarters for the night, and the night manager was busy working at the front desk and lounge. Vivian was busy putting away serving dishes. She was still thinking about Franko's sudden appearance in the basement. She regretted not being more appreciative to Franko for saving her life. She was starting to actually like him but, sooner or later, he would inquire more about dying her hair blonde. Slowly and methodically, he was peeling off the layers to unmask her.

She went to the sink to rinse out a pot. That's when she saw a reflection in the window glass. For an instant, she thought it was Franko. She brushed the thought out of her mind. *What's happening to me? I'm always in control*, she thought. She was starting to fall for him. Something she hadn't done with *any* man in several years. Then, to her unexpected surprise, she heard an unanticipated voice— Franko's voice. It *was* him.

"I'm absolutely starving. Do you have anything left to eat?"

Vivian gasped, nearly dropping the pot, turned around and saw Tony Franko, in the flesh, standing in the kitchen. She didn't want to ask how he got in. He slowly stepped toward her.

Quietly she said, "You're not supposed to be here."

"Yes, I know."

The two didn't say anything to each other for what seemed like an eternity. The couple just looked at each other intimately. Vivian trembled slightly. Then Franko said, "I thought I had lost you."

Finally, Franko moved closer to Vivian. The next thing he knew, he had his lips pressed against her moist lips. She responded by slipping her tongue deep into his mouth and placed her arms around his broad shoulders. Franko placed his hand around her face and continued to kiss her neck and face. Vivian responded by lifting up her skirt. Franko picked her up from the back of the thighs and carried her to the kitchen counter, being careful not to touch her back or buttocks. He didn't want to spoil the moment in case she was self-conscious about her injuries.

Vivian spread her legs and wrapped them around Franko's waist. The two continued to kiss each other affectionately on the lips, acting like a couple of teenagers, as Vivian smeared her lipstick all over his face. She wrapped her legs tighter around Franko's waist, moaning softly. Then, as soon as it started, it ended. Franko backed off, and Vivian slid down from the counter and dropped her skirt.

"What the devil . . . just happened?" she gasped.

"I don't know! It just happened. I'm sorry. Please forgive me."

Vivian straightened up her dress and brushed her hair

back into place. "You silly fool, can't you see I was enjoying it?"

"I'm sorry, Miss Tate. I don't know what to say."

Franko stepped away from Vivian and took a seat at the small wooden table in the kitchen. He noticed Vivian was still trembling. Looking down at the table and not wanting to make eye contact, he said, "I came here because I was hungry. The apple didn't go very far. Morena went to bed and locked herself in the bedroom. There was nothing to eat in the apartment. Do you have anything left over?"

Vivian stopped trembling and chuckled ever so slightly, something she rarely did. "You're too late. I've already put everything away."

"That's a bummer."

Vivian perked-up. "I could make you some breakfast, though. It will only take a couple of minutes."

"That's fantastic, why not."

Vivian turned around, opened the icebox, and pulled out eggs, cream, and sliced, Polish sausages, and placed them on the counter. She then took a cold bottle of beer, opened it, and placed it in front of Franko. "I'm sure you'll like one of these." Next, she went over to the stove to prepare the scrambled eggs and Polish sausages.

Franko took a long swig from the cold bottle; he needed that, then placed the beer down on the table. He looked at Vivian from behind and saw her beautiful body and lovely blond hair. He couldn't help himself. He was definitely falling for her. Slowly, he got up and came over to Vivian, who was frying the sausage in a pan. She had her back to him busy working at the stove. Franko placed his face on the side of her cheek. Vivian jerked slightly, and then he whispered into her ear. "A woman truly after my heart. Breakfast, and a cold bottle of beer. I think I'm in heaven. Make it four eggs, love."

Vivian turned around and faced him again. Their faces were inches apart. "I *can* cook, you know."

Chapter 22

Franko came back to the safe house a short time later, after devouring his breakfast. He made sure he took a serendipitous route back to shake off any surveillance team. It turned out it wasn't necessary, and it took longer than expected. He inserted the key into the lock and entered. As he stepped into the apartment, he felt someone grab his arm. It was Morena. She yelled obscenities at him and continued to hit and kick him. She threw him to the floor in a judo maneuver and jumped on top of him. She was about to strike him in the face when she stopped and rolled off him.

"Don't you ever leave here by yourself again! You're going to get us all killed! All it takes is one sleepless hotel guest having a cigarette to see you enter the hotel. The next thing you know, the Russians will be all over us. Do you understand?"

Franko nodded.

"If you want to make a rendezvous with your lover, just let me know so I can go with you. This is not some game we're playing! One by one, resistance groups are falling to the communist. The Soviets have infiltrated their agents among us. We never know when one will betray us."

Franko surprised by Morena's sudden act of fast, skilled violence conceded. "I understand! It won't happen again, and . . . she's not my lover."

"Right, get up, and wipe that stupid look and lipstick off your face! Get some rest. Someone will be here shortly to take us to the S-phone site."

Franko did as Morena suggested. He went back to his bedroom and slept for a few hours. He was finally awakened by Morena's pounding on the door. She gave him a large brown package tied with string.

"This is your new set of clothes. We have more, but this will do for tonight. Get dressed and meet me in the kitchen in ten minutes."

Franko realized he was still wearing the same clothes he had on when he left Frankfurt. Inside the package were a pair of wool trousers, a long-sleeved work shirt and a jacket, which fit surprisingly well. Next, he recovered the backpack, which held his communications equipment, homing beacon, and headset, necessary to make the Joan-Eleanor call. He washed his face and got dressed in the new set of clothes Morena had given him, then went to the kitchen. There was a man about Franko's age sitting at the kitchen table drinking a cup of coffee. He was medium build with dark hair cut short. He wore the uniform of a Polish forest ranger.

Morena said, "This is our guide. He will escort us to the transmission site and provide security cover while you make the S-phone call."

The man didn't introduce himself because there was not a need to know, but he simply said, "I have a truck outside waiting to take us. Are you ready to go?"

It was after one in the morning when the three left

Tarnow. They traveled for about a half an hour outside the city limits to the countryside. This portion of Poland was mostly flat. There was very little high terrain. To make the JE call, you had to be in an area of line-of-sight transmission with the transmitting aircraft. Franko had coordinated this transmission to occur on this night at 0300 local time. An aircraft was scheduled to fly over Tarnow, flying north, in an attempt to make contact with Franko.

They actually used a church in the nearby town of Lisia Gora. Here, they climbed the steeple and set up the radio set and homing beacon and waited for the aircraft to fly overhead. Since the aircraft didn't have to fly directly over their station, they had to be on the lookout for the sight or sounds of the aircraft. The forest ranger already had his eyes and ears directed skyward, and it wasn't long before he nudged Franko and pointed to the sky. Franko immediately got on his headset and dialed in the preset frequency. He waited for several minutes, then began the transmission authentication.

"Alpha Foxtrot calling Home Station, do you read me?" He replied several times before he finally got a response. Franko read off his authentication. "This is Alpha-Foxtrot, authentication Juliet-Mike-Golf-Lima. I say again, authentication Juliet-Mike-Golf-Lima."

The radio operator responded, "Roger Alpha Foxtrot, authentication Sweet-Sweet. This is Sanchez."

Franko was surprised to hear his voice, but as soon as he mentioned his name, he immediately recognized the voice. As pre-arranged before he had left, this forty-eight-hour call was to inform home station of their safe arrival. However, because Sanchez was on the line, he decided to tell him about Waldorf and the recovered gyros. Sanchez recorded the information, then told Franko that a secure cutout had been established at the US consulate in

Krakow. He gave Franko the telephone number and the seven-letter cable address. For telephone contact, he was to use the code words, "How's the weather back home?" and the response would be, "Warm and sunny." He informed Franko that all COMS would be directed to Home Station via standard encrypted telegraph through the Krakow station. Sanchez also reminded Franko to use the correct codewords. Sanchez then added some closing remarks.

"I received a follow-on message from my original request to Whitehall. Are you ready?"

"Go ahead, my friend, I'm listening."

"It's an addendum on Squad Leader Tate. Whitehall says that toward the end of the war, while at the Inter-Services Research Bureau, Miss Vivian Tate almost suffered a nervous breakdown and took an extended time off. It appeared that one of her most beloved recruits, Penelope Walsh, was murdered by the SS at Jasenovac Concentration Camp, in Yugoslavia. Walsh's death warrant was issued from RSHA Office Berlin and signed personally by none other than Otto Krupke."

"That *is* interesting. So, she does have a soft spot. I'll add this tidbit to her profile. Thanks."

They secured the radio transmission, and the team headed back to Tarnow for the night.

* * *

IT WAS STILL early in the morning as Krupke's white utility truck, with the advanced V-2 gyros and the two top scientists who had worked on the project, safely on board, entered the deserted streets of Tarnow.

Not much had changed since the war. Vehicles were almost non-existent; there were mostly horse-drawn carts and the occasional motorcycle sidecar. All Krupke had was an address. It was in a former Jewish ghetto. Most of the occupants had either perished during the war or were still missing. Either way, the neighborhood was largely abandoned. This was a perfect setting for Krupke to establish a working base and formulate his plan to make contact with his agent. The driver was able to maneuver the vehicle into the protected courtyard of the one-time lavish residence, now reduced to a shell of its former luster. The vehicle was partially hidden from the street out front. It still could be seen if someone took a closer look, but the spot would do until they could secure the vehicle in a better location. Krupke jumped out of the van first, then took out several bills and paid the driver. "Go now, before someone sees you." The man took the money and quickly vanished into the deserted streets of Tarnow.

Krupke now addressed Hoch and Mangus. "First order of business. Let's get this vehicle into a garage or barn and away from the streets. I'm worried someone might steal it for a method of transportation. We'd all be screwed should that happen."

A short time later, the men had the van safely hidden in a horse stable adjacent to the residence. Then the men found the address to their safe house. It was more difficult than Krupke thought since the homes were void of numbered addresses. There were no locks on the front door. In fact, the door and hardware were completely missing. Once inside, the men pushed old, abandoned furniture against the opening for security. Most furnishings and wall coverings had been plundered. The kitchen was only a sink, no stove or oven; those had also been confiscated by the Nazis. The temperature was freezing inside, but they found a usable fireplace that could warm the place. The challenge was finding fuel to burn. It was obvious by looking at the surroundings that whoever had used the facility last had burned most of the furnishings for heat.

Krupke dropped his duffle bag on the floor, opened it, and gave Dr. Hoch an extra jacket to put on over his baker's clothing. "I'll find us some warmer clothes later today. There are still remnants of my network that can help. I will need to contact them."

In the meantime, Krupke pulled the brown-paper-wrapped package out for his bag and emptied the contents out on the floor, since there were no tables or chairs in the building. He proceeded to brief Hoch and Mangus on his plan.

"This is what I've come up with for our escape to the West. Listen carefully, gentlemen. My contact, who will get us safely to the American sector, is here in the city. RHSA gave this person the code name of Hilda Bradt. That, of course, is not her real name. She goes by several aliases. Here is a picture of her," he said as he passed the photo of Vivian Tate around to the men.

"She runs the very prosperous and successful Hotel Bristol located here in the city. It's also a Polish Home Army black site. That's where we'll make our move on her. The challenge is that we can't just walk in there and introduce ourselves," he said, pointing to their grimy clothes. "She or her security detail could call in the Russian security services, and it will be all over for us. So, we must proceed with this phase of the operation with caution. I have come up with a plan."

Krupke then pulled out a postcard of the Hotel Bristol taken some time before the war. "As you can see, it's a fairly upscale establishment. Only the elite or military officers can afford a room. However, there is a way for us. I've been told that the hotel will host a holiday celebration shortly to honor their valued guests and to kick off the holiday season, war free. The hotel has a ballroom, fancy dining room, and lounge. They'll have a full orchestra *and* piano music. The hotel should have one, if not more, pianos. These pianos probably have not been tuned since long before the war. Lucky for us, I know how to tune them. And with the sheet music in our possession, we should have no trouble convincing Hilda Bradt her pianos need tuning before the holiday festivities begin. This will be our moment to reveal ourselves. I have a way of doing that too." Krupke reached into the pile from his duffle bag and produced a simple calling card. He had had this card produced while he was still at RSHA Berlin, in case he needed it at a future time. That time was now; he showed the men the card. It read:

OTTO'S PIANO TUNING
ALEXANDER PLATZ, BERLIN

"The final piece is our attire. We can't go in looking like this. So, I'll secure work clothes and coveralls for us to add authenticity. All we need to do is wait for the right moment. I will conduct surveillance on the property and determine the best time to make a move. In the meantime, we wait here."

Chapter 23

A few days later, back in Tarnow after ten O'clock in the morning, an unmarked white van pulled into the back parking lot of the Hotel Bristol. Three men exited the van wearing gray coveralls, wool caps, and carrying small utility bags. One of the men knocked on the door of the back service entrance of the hotel. He had to knock several times before someone answered. It was Jawor.

"Yes, can I help you gentlemen today?"

Otto Krupke responded in Polish. "We are piano tuners. I come here to tune your pianos. Tell your proprietor that I did some work for her before the war." He handed the calling card to Jawor, written in German.

Jawor was stunned as she read the words. She was surprised the Germans had found Vivian Tate and made their move on the hotel so quickly. She was not expecting contact for at least three to five days henceforth. She held her emotions in check and stuck to business and was relieved the team was in the position to make the ruse.

"It's up to our proprietor, Janica Kijowski. She makes all the decisions with regards to the hotel furnishings and

169

equipment. She's busy at the moment, but I can announce your arrival, and in the meantime I can bring you a coffee. Please come with me to my office."

Jawor opened the door and allowed the three men to enter. She escorted them to the second floor and her office, which was located next to Vivian's. The four entered. "Have a seat while I order you a drink. Would any of you care for tea? Or just coffee?

Krupke answered for both men since they did not speak Polish. "We'll have coffee. Cream and sugar, please."

Jawor looked at Krupke, taking note of his very fluent Polish, then picked up the house phone and called the kitchen. "Please bring a pot of coffee for three, cream and sugar, please." Then she secured the receiver.

"Care to introduce me to your associates? I'm guessing they don't speak Polish."

Krupke answered, "Kurt and Franz; my name is Otto. They are obviously German. We are all German war veterans. The war is over. We all need to survive. My associates help me with the pianos, providing manpower and labor. Some of the pianos we work with are extremely heavy and hard to push around. You can understand our situation. We're trying to live off the land, making money as we go along, eventually working our way back home."

As soon as he finished his sentence, there was a knock on the door. Jawor opened it, and a man wheeled in a small trolley with the coffee. He closed the door behind him. Before Krupke and the other two men realized what was happening, the man quickly pulled out a pistol and began to frisk the Germans for weapons. Next, he told the men to open their utility bags. The three men complied as he went through the three bags. All he found were tools, instruments for tuning pianos, and sheet music. Krupke was smart enough to have left their pistols back in the truck.

"Nothing out of the ordinary, except a microscope," he told Jawor.

Krupke interrupted, "For extremely fine work."

"Leave the cart here. You can go now," Jawor said, and the man left the office.

Jawor responded, "You'll have to excuse me for the security precautions. We must take precautions. Some people would rather see us dead than succeed. I'm sorry if I offended you," she said as she poured three cups of coffee for the men. She let them help themselves to cream and sugar and let them have a few sips. Then she said, "We have three pianos in the hotel. A concert grand, baby grand, and an upright. I take it you can do all three?"

Krupke nodded. "Of course."

Jawor picked up her house phone and called Vivian's office. Krupke listened as she spoke. "I'm sorry to disturb you, ma'am, but we have some piano tuners here in my office. They've just arrived. Three men and one who claimed he did some work for you before the war, in Berlin. Shall I let them in?"

Obviously, Krupke could not hear Vivian Tate on the other end of the line, but he assumed she was at least curious because he heard Jawor respond into the receiver, "Very well, I'll let them in."

A few minutes later, Vivian Tate was seated at her desk, buried in sales receipts and invoices when the three men entered carrying their utility bags. She did not look up from her work, dramatizing the moment. Finally, she looked into the eyes of her former jailer and torturer. Krupke removed his cap so Vivian could get a good look at his face. There was no mistake. Each recognized the other.

"So, we meet again, Miss Jankowski," Krupke said in

German. "That was a very daring stunt you pulled on me. I see you are, in fact, who you said you are, a business-woman. My sources told me you're hosting a large festive celebration, and your pianos are in desperate need of tuning."

* * *

BY EARLY MORNING, Morena was back at the safe house, starting her daily routines. She got up and set up the communication equipment to begin monitoring transmissions from the Hotel Bristol. They had two listening posts wired. One was in Jawor's office, the other in Vivian's. She turned on the recording device and began listening. As Morena adjusted the dials and control switches, she picked up the distinct voice of a man speaking German. She isolated the location and determined it came from Vivian Tate using the office of Janica Kijowski. Next, she picked up the voice of Vivian Tate speaking in German to a man. She removed her headset and quickly rushed to Franko's bedroom door. He was still asleep. She pounded on the door. "Get up! I think we made contact with the Germans!"

Franko came out from his room wearing his underwear. "Can you be sure?"

"I don't know, but you'd better listen."

Franko came into the dining room where the listening post was established in the safe house. He put on the headset and began monitoring the communications. "Get me a pad of paper and something to write with. It's Krupke. Make sure all conversations are recorded." Morena flipped on a switch to record all voice transmissions.

* * *

VIVIAN DIDN'T EVEN FLINCH. Calmly, she pulled out her Makarov pistol and pointed it at Krupke's head. She spoke in German. "Why shouldn't I put a bullet through your bloody head right now? An SS war criminal and desk murderer who killed over five hundred Allied agents." She then stood up from her desk. "Put your hands up so I can see them. All of you!" All three men complied.

She switched to English, speaking with a very distinct, American tone. "You've got some fucking balls coming here like this. Who're the two gofers? No doubt some of your SS cutthroats," she said as she swung her pistol toward the two other men.

Krupke responded back in his perfect American English. "Well, well, well, your English is excellent. You speak as if you were from Ohio. Judging from your accent, you have obviously spoken English for quite some time. Well before 1939." Krupke lowered his hands. "I can explain, please put the gun down. I didn't come here to kill you. I want to do business with you. I was told you're very good at what you do. You can make a lot of money."

Vivian uncocked the pistol but still pointed it at Krupke. She switched back to Polish. "I know you're not armed. No one gets into my office without being searched. Keep talking," she said as she took a seat back at her desk. Then she asked, "What's so important you risked coming here to see me directly? I can just as easily pick up the phone and call the Russian Secret Police and tell them I'm holding SS war criminals."

Krupke replied back in Polish. "You're definitely not going to do that after I tell you what I'm offering."

"All right, you've got my attention. What is it?"

"This is Professor Hoch and Professor Mangus,

avionics specialist and gyro expert, respectively. Both worked at the Blizna missile complex nearby. We have in our possession, perfectly intact, the latest version of the advanced V-2 guidance system, as well as complete technical specifications and blueprints installed on microdots in the sheet music. I understand you have access to an escape network directly to the American lines. The offer is simple. Get us to the Americans along with the goods."

Vivian calmly placed the weapon down on her desk but still kept it visible. "What makes you think I can do that?"

"Come, come now, Fräulein. I have my sources. You've coordinated the escape of several of our leading scientists already. I know all about your ratline."

Vivian pretended to think about a response then she said in English, "It's too dangerous now. The Russians control the major routes to the West. Poland is doomed to fall to the Communist. You'll never get out. I'm sorry, it's too late."

Krupke, not surprised at Vivian's switch from Polish to German, English, and then back to Polish, responded in his version.

"But you have sources in high places that can help you. This I know for a fact because the Americans lack key components and flight hardware for their captured, or should I say *stolen* V-2s. American technical teams are still on the Continent looking for those devices."

"What's in it for me?"

"I can pay you. Direct wire transfer into your Zurich account. I know you have an account, several actually."

Vivian still playing the ruse, said, "As a former Nazi intelligence officer, you did your homework well. But I can't give you a price. I don't know if it's even possible. There are too many questions. I don't know if my sources are even capable of doing the job anymore. More importantly, how do I know you even have the merchandise or the money, for that matter?"

Krupke chuckled, then broke out in complete laughter. "We have the merchandise outside in our utility van. Care to take a look? We can even power it up for you if you like. As far as the money, we can get it. I don't carry that amount of cash on me."

"Show me the goods."

Vivian escorted the three men outside and to the parked van where Krupke showed Vivian the complete inertial guidance system for the V-2 rocket. Vivian pretended to be stunned. They secured the lorry inside the hotel garage and continued back to her office.

Vivian stared at her former adversary as if contemplating a response. She said nothing.

Krupke finally spoke. The two spoke exclusively in English from this point on. "Let me show you some collateral." He reached into his pocket and pulled out a small pouch. He emptied a few diamonds onto her desk. "Ten thousand carats worth." Next, he picked up a glass from Vivian's desk and scratched a mark onto it. "As you can see, they're real." Vivian could only imagine from who or which concentration camp he had gotten the diamonds from.

Next, Krupke reached into his utility bag and produced the microscope from a myriad of instruments, tools, and some sheet music. He nodded toward Dr. Mangus, and he then proceeded to set up the device on the table and placed the sheet music under the microscope. He adjusted the music until he found what he was looking for. He focused the lens and said in German, "Here, take a look; complete technical readouts on microdots of the latest version of the V-2 guidance system."

Vivian bent over and took a look through the microscope. She was not a technical expert, but as near as she could tell, the documents were authentic. She responded in German for everyone's sake, "All right, you've got my attention. As you mentioned, I have a source. He's an American officer from Wright Field, Ohio, a technical expert on these matters. He's already got several of your top scientists out. I helped him on several occasions. Specialists in aerospace physiology,—I believe. He works primarily here in Poland, mainly because he speaks Polish and German fluently. The problem is, I don't have direct communication access with him. It's all done by dead drops. It could take several days to make contact with him."

"We've got nothing but time."

Vivian now began to divulge details of her plan. "First, we have a room on the top floor that is secure. You'll be confined to that room until I make contact with my source. Trust me, you will all be taken care of quite comfortably here in my hotel. Finally, you must tune the pianos. If the Russians should ever come and query us about unexpected visitors, we can tell them you actually tuned the pianos. So, for your sake, I hope you know how to tune them."

Krupke spoke next in German. "We've come prepared; I can tune the pianos."

Vivian continued to sit in silence, acting as if contemplating her next move. She already had her next responses memorized. "There is a bench in the park across the street next to a lamppost, near the center. This bench supported by four small concrete blocks instead of resting on the ground. It's very easy to spot. That's my dead drop. All I have to do is leave a message that I wish to make contact by leaving a chalk mark on the lamppost. Someone will be by on the following Monday morning and sit at that bench, reach under the right front leg and the concrete block. There will be a message indicating I wish to make contact with the source. Most of the time, he calls me here at the hotel, and we agree on a time and place."

"Does this source have a name?" Krupke asked.

Vivian, still well ahead of her former adversary, said, "I'm sure he does, but I only know him by his American code name, Redstone. He only knows me by my American code name, Agena. I'll set the meeting. Naturally, you'll be present, and we can discuss your offer. Ultimately, it's up to him. He may want a physical inspection of the goods before he makes a decision. As far as you three are concerned, I have no control over assets turned over to the Americans. My job is conductor on the ratline, that's it. He may want more money or something else in return; perhaps information. Each situation is different."

"I can understand," replied Krupke.

"Good, with that, I'll have my manager show you up to your new quarters upstairs, and we'll secure the goods in your room with you. That way, you can keep an eye on them. Next, she'll show you to the pianos for tuning. When you're finished, you will go back upstairs to your quarters and wait. Someone will contact you when the time comes, and I've made contact with the American asset."

Chapter 24

That night, Franko wanted to make another trip to the
basement cellar of the Hotel Bristol using the coal chute.
This would be a more extended meeting that the first
night, and Morena had to coordinate with Jawor over the
telephone. She informed her that Franko wished to meet
Janica Kijowski and needed more time. The meeting was
planned once again after the evening meal for the hotel
guests.

Vivian came down the basement stairs where Franko
was already waiting. This time Vivian was dressed in
evening attire and not her work clothes. Her blond hair
was neatly styled, and she had on light, makeup and
lipstick. On the other hand, Franko wore the same clothes
he had worn all day and the previous night. Vivian turned
on a lamp as Franko approached her.

Franko spoke first. "I listened to the conversations on
the transmitter radio. I heard almost everything. How did
it go between you two?"

Vivian took a seat on a stool. "He arrived sooner than

we expected. His network sources are still in place and well informed. Luckily, our identities branch in London did their job. He had no trouble finding me and . . . he knew about you to a certain extent. That's a good sign."

Franko interrupted, "No, I mean, how did it *really* go with him?"

"I'm not following you?"

Franko pulled up another stool and sat next to her. "You need to be upfront with me now that the Germans have made contact. There's something I need to share with you. It happened back at the drop site shortly after I plucked you out of that frigid water."

Vivian moved her fingers through her blond hair and listened. "And . . . what's that?"

"First of all, I thought you were dead. You weren't responding. I couldn't find a pulse. I tried calling your name out. Several times, actually, but no response. Then I called out in Polish, *Irina*. You immediately responded and looked at me. That's not all. Back at Lupa's house, when he tried to revive you, in the other room, I saw your naked body. I saw your back and the scars."

"So what, lots of people have scars."

"No, Miss Tate, not like that, and there's more. It was something Lupa said to me. I didn't catch it at first. It was kind of an afterthought. He said he had conducted a full medical examination on you and said you were a beautiful, young, blond woman hideously maimed. He said that *before* you had your hair dyed in Tarnow. In other words, he saw your natural hair color, your pubic hairs. You're naturally blond, not brunette. You had your hair dyed for Krupke's sake because he knew you as a blond.

"Finally, I have my intelligence sources too. My security assistant, Sergeant Sanchez, back in Frankfurt, gave me a full dossier on a woman known as Agent JAN whose real name, is Irina Jankowski, a former MI-6 deep-penetration operative. I know all about you and Krupke and what he did to you back in Berlin. I know about the enigmas, the bomba operation, the Polish diplomat, and I know your name is not, Vivian Tate or Janica Kijowski. I also know Krupke issued the death warrant for one of your most beloved recruits, Penelope Walsh. Last but not least, you had low altitude parachute training similar to what secret agent go through at MI-6. You knew exactly what to do at the drop site. So, are you going to tell me how it *really* went with him?"

Vivian sat upright on her stool. She tried to hold back her emotions but finally broke. Tears began to trickle down her cheeks. She sniffed and sniffed until Franko finally pulled out his handkerchief and gave it to her.

"You don't know how difficult this has been all these years. I'm haunted by the nightmares of my ordeals. I have many. That's why I have trouble sleeping. My life is one enormous secret. It's difficult to keep track of all the lies. I can't talk to anybody about them. Everything is an official state secret."

She blotted her eyes with the handkerchief and continued to sniff. "Yes, my name is, Irina Jankowski, Hilda Bradt, Agent JAN, former SIS operative. Yes, the meeting with Krupke today was extremely and emotionally difficult. I almost killed the bloody bastard. I wanted to put a bullet between his eyes. I didn't have to tell him my real name. He already knew it. He called it out as soon as he walked into my office. For your information, Major, my ordeal in Berlin with him was horrific. I was tortured beyond belief by the most brutal, sadistic maniacs mankind has ever known. As you said yourself, my body was maimed. I can never have children after what they did to me. No man could ever want me. My body is in ruins."

Just then, Vivian began to remove her dress methodically. She dropped it to the floor of the basement. Next, she unstrapped her bra and let it fall as well. Finally, she slipped off her panties. She was standing completely naked in front of Franko. She turned around, slowly, kicking off her shoes and showing off her blond, pubic hairs. Franko got a good glimpse of her entire body. Then she said, "Look at me, Tony! This is what I endured in Berlin at the hands of Krupke! How could any man want me looking like this?"

Franko shook his head in utter disbelief. "No, Miss Tate, you're gravely mistaken." He took off his jacket and placed it around her naked body. "If I didn't care about you, Irina I wouldn't have pushed the issue. I know you kept this from me for security reasons, but all the more, I won't let anything happen to you, *ever*. In fact, I've admired you since the day I first met you, back at the canteen. Why do you think I came back here the other night? I had to see you. I wanted to be with you, and I don't care what your body looks like."

Vivian went off subject slightly. "Except for Krupke, no one has called me my real name in years but you."

He placed his arm around her shoulders. The couple embraced. Finally, he told her to get dressed. The unmasking of Vivian Tate was complete. "You're a brave woman to have gone forward with this mission. You could have stayed in your comfortable London flat, working for the Student Foreign Exchange. I know about that too. So, where do we go from here, Irina?"

Franko wanted to move on to operational details. "I heard you looked into a microscope over the transmitter. Tell me what you saw on the microdots?"

Once again, Vivian switched her emotions off like a light to discuss operations. "It was Dr. Mangus who adjusted the microscope for me. He appeared to be the expert on the technical drawings. A lot of complicated drawings, mathematical formulas. I believe they were genuine, but you'll have to authenticate."

"What about physical proof? Washington is going to want something."

"Yes, I know."

Vivian finished getting dressed and wiped away the tears with Franko's handkerchief, then handed it back to him. It was all business now. Vivian's emotions were a complete one-hundred-eighty-degree turn. She continued, "Yes, I think he's telling the truth about the gyros. He wouldn't have proceeded to this stage in the operation if he wasn't. As far as *my* story, I think he bought it. He has no choice but to believe it if he wants to get to the West alive. Give it a day or two. As you probably heard from the transmission radio, I have to make contact with you by dead drop. For security reasons, we'll have the meeting here, at the hotel. They're staying in the VIP suite. There is a dining room adequate in their room. We'll plan for a dinner meeting with all parties present. We're hosting a holiday celebration here at the hotel for our loyal guests. We'll schedule our meeting at the same time so as not to arouse suspicion. Naturally, Morena will have to come with you as your secretary/associate. That's when we'll make the proposal. I'll send over a script for you to memorize. Of course, you can't make a final offer until you see the goods."

"I agree." Franko now decided to debrief her on the schedule transmission. "I made contact with Home Station using the S-phone, as you Brits like to call it. They've set up a secure cutout for us in Tarnow. Anything we need will pass through this cutout." Franko gave her all the details. Then Franko asked, "Anything else for me?"

"It's time to go ahead and squeeze Mr. Waldorf. I'll coordinate with Jawor and the Ranger Battalion. It could help out with your meeting with Krupke and his scientists. I think we better move him into the safe house with you. Everywhere you go, he'll go. That way, we can keep an eye on him. The money? Do you still have it secured?"

"Yes, all of it minus a few dollars for petrol."

"I'll have Jawor come and retrieve it. We need to secure it here in the hotel safe. We don't want all that money in your possession in case the Germans find out about it. That would surely tip them off that something's amuck. There's one more thing."

"What's that?"

"If Krupke found me this quick, it's a sure bet the Russians will be right behind; be alert. We'll have state security *and* military intelligence on our tails, and, most importantly, their subagents."

Franko placed a finger and thumb under her chin and raised her head slightly. "Look at me, Irina."

"Please don't call me that. You need to be careful. You might slip up sometime." But Vivian complied. The couple looked at each other in the eyes.

Franko could see into her soul. The unmasking of the enigma known as Vivian Tate, was complete. "You're an amazing woman, you know that?"

* * *

FOR THE PAST SEVERAL DAYS, Colonel Scott Alexander of MI-19 codename, Calvin, the Soviet, deep penetration mole, worked feverishly to try and uncover the identity of the mysterious Soviet colonel. His first task was to reach out to Colonel Stephens at Camp 020, which he did almost immediately to see if he recalled the name of the Russian. Stephens apologized but said he was caught off guard when the Russian suddenly appeared out of nowhere and shoved authorization papers in his face. He did not query further but let her interview Cordes without emitters. His only recollection was the aplomb and haughtiness of the officer's behavior, and her skirt hemmed three inches higher than regulation. Not to mention her English was the best he'd ever heard from any Russians in all of his career. Alexander gave Stephens a formal reprimand and told him that he should have contacted his office the moment the Russian appeared, as opposed to after her appearance.

Next, Calvin tried the services. This inquiry was a lengthy process because he didn't want to show his sudden urgency. He inquired about military personnel who possessed the traits of the Russian female officer. He told the services, he needed help interrogating Russian-trained parachutists caught working for the Third Reich in order not to arouse suspicion. Unfortunately, the services had no females who matched those characteristics. Then he tried MI-6 and MI-5. Again, neither of those agencies had anyone with the traits described. He then put a call out to SOE. This wartime organization was scheduled to be disbanded, and thus, most of the personnel were transferred either out of the service or to other agencies. All that was left was a skeleton crew to close the organization down. The acting head of SOE did say that at one time SOE had employed a person in F-section with those characteristics requested. That person had left SOE and was now working at the Student Foreign Exchange Service. The person's name was Vivian Tate.

Calvin was at least getting somewhere. He contacted the Student Foreign Exchange and asked for Vivian Tate.

To Calvin's surprise, he was told that there was a person by that name working at the Student Exchange, but unfortunately, Miss Tate had taken an unexpected leave of absence. He was able to get an address and telephone number for Miss Tate. Calvin tried calling several times but no answer. He even tried calling at different times of the day and night, but the same result: no response. He then decided to make the trip to South Kensington and her Lexham Gardens flat, which was only a short distance from The Cage.

Colonel Alexander rang the doorbell at number fourteen Lexham Gardens, but there was no answer. He tried looking into the apartment, but a senior man walking by noticed him intruding.

"Can I help you with something?" the man asked.

Calvin replied, "Why yes, I'm a friend of Miss Tate's. We worked together during the war. I was trying to contact her, but she's not answering her phone or the doorbell. I was afraid there could be something wrong. It's not like her."

The passing man spoke. "I'm afraid Miss Tate has gone on a long, extended holiday. Somewhere to the coast, I believe. She didn't say. I don't know when she'll be back."

Calvin pretended it was nothing more than an unfortunate inconvenience and replied, "Not a problem. I was in the area and thought I would try her flat. I'm sure I'll run into Miss Tate sometime in the future. Thank you, sir." Then he left.

As he was walking back to The Cage, Calvin was convinced that the mysterious Russian officer was none other than Vivian Tate. He knew from her record that she spoke multiple languages. The most convincing element was that Miss Tate was known within SOE to show up at Baker Street, wearing her skirts hemmed higher than fashionable, even though she was a civilian. The question for him to decide before he sent his report off to Moscow was, why?

To find that answer, he had to interview Cordes himself.

Chapter 25

Back at the safe house, Franko decided to use the time delay in the operational plan to make contact with the secure cutout at the US consulate in Krakow and secure the safety of the first-generation gyros recovered by Poldi and the rangers. He would have Morena work on the gyros while he concentrated on coding his message from the M-209 coding device. As Franko and Morena were eating breakfast, there was a knock at the door.

"Were you expecting someone?" asked Franko.

"Not this early. If I don't recognize him, start firing. It could be the Russians." She got up from the table, took a pistol out from a drawer, and approached the door. The knocking continued, this time slightly harder and louder. Franko drew his Colt and stood ready too. Morena unlatched the safety chain and cracked the door open. A man in forest ranger uniform stood outside. "I have the package you requested," was all he said.

Morena recognized the man and said, "You're early. I wasn't expecting you till this afternoon."

"Operational reasons, as per my instructions, he's to stay here with you from now on," he said as he pushed the door open.

Mr. Leopold Waldorf was standing next to the forest ranger. He looked weaker than he'd looked before. His loose-fitting clothes hung from his frail body, probably because he still hadn't eaten a square meal in several days. He was holding a small, worn suitcase. Franko barely recognized the slender figure. Mr. Waldorf was ushered into the safe house as the ranger reversed direction, headed downstairs, and disappeared.

Morena offered Mr. Waldorf a seat at the kitchen table. "You probably haven't eaten. Let me fix you something to eat," she said, then she left to prepare something for their new guest.

Franko poured Poldi a cup of coffee and passed it to him and then offered a cigarette. Waldorf accepted both and took a puff from the cigarette. Franko took out a small note-pad from his pocket, flipped to a blank page, and started.

"I'd like to pick up where we left off the other day. Let me start by saying we've kept you in protection for your safety as well as ours. Naturally, we can't take the chance that you're working for the opposition, thus your seclusion."

"Fair enough. Your colleagues treated me kindly, but it has been lonely."

"Let's go back to the navigation system. We left off with the triple-mix system and installing those components in the nose cone of the rocket. We discussed the weight issue, and you said you used solid-state components. Can you elaborate on that?"

Poldi recapped the solid-state system again, using mathematical equations on Franko's notebook. Only a fully trained electrical engineer could make any sense of his details. It was a wonder Vivian Tate could understand what she was looking at on the microdots. Franko looked over Leopold's notes and couldn't believe what he was seeing. "What did you call these so-called solid-state components?"

"Hoch used the term transistors. I was told he came up with the name himself. They're micro-conductors made from inexpensive materials soldered to a circuit board. These circuit boards provided the continuity control instead of vacuum tubes."

"Fascinating, and you mentioned other lightweight materials used in the nose cone."

"We had to lighten the weight overall in preparation for bigger and bigger warheads. So, we used a new type of battery called a dry battery. This battery was not only lighter but more effective in that it doesn't trickle down. It holds a full charge of twenty-four volts up until the time the battery depletes. In our experimentation, none of the batteries failed, thus a fully charged battery, nearly one hundred percent of the time."

"What you're describing doesn't exist in today's technology."

"You are correct. It was all the mastermind of a French-German Nazi scientist. He used the term nickel-cadmium batteries. I only met him once, back when we first implemented the triple-mix system. Once we had an operational system, he was relocated to another test site. You see, the Nazis were so paranoid about security, they dispersed their key scientists to different locations. That way, if one was captured or killed by the enemy, the whole project would not be compromised. More importantly, this information could not be leaked out."

Waldorf's thoughts were interrupted as Morena placed

a plate of fried eggs, bread, and cold cuts in front of him, then she went back to the kitchen to clean up. Waldorf dove into his meal, sipping coffee in between mouthfuls of food. Franko wanted to move on to another topic, but before he could do that, he'd have to divulge more information about his own identity. He decided to get up from the table and talk on his feet.

"If you'll recall, I was introduced as a major from the US military. Specifically, I'm with the US Army G-2 staff, stationed at Frankfurt. I'm also an aeronautical engineer. My job is to go after any and all sophisticated former Third Reich technology left on the Continent before the Russians do, plain and simple. The United States can't afford to have these Wonder Weapons fall into the hands of the Soviets. Furthermore, I participated in the Backfire tests, which was a comprehensive testing and evaluation of the V-2 rocket system with the entire von Braun team and the SS firing crews.

"During my three weeks at Cuxhaven, the von Braun team was extremely tight-lipped with regards to their knowledge about advanced V-2 guidance systems. They only divulged information about the current operational system, which, as you know, was a dumb bomb, not a guided missile. We knew they knew more than they were willing to share, but it was a British operation. I was the only American on the team, and I could only squeeze them so much. I can tell you that the von Braun team is now in the United States. Thanks to the US Army, they have plenty of these older, operational V-2 rocket components. What they don't have are the advanced gyros or specialists who worked on these systems. Most importantly, these so-called dry batteries. You, my friend, are probably the last person left alive who knows anything about these advanced systems other than Dr. Hoch and Mangus."

Franko decided to divulge his knowledge of further Nazi Wonder Weapons through the interrogation of Bertha Cordes. "Let me ask you another question. While you were at any of the camps, did you ever come across other types of Wonder weapons?"

Poldi was candid in his response. "Why yes, but it was all hearsay."

Franko was shocked to hear this. "Go on, I'm all ears."

"It was on the ill-fated train to Dora. There were many skilled workers on that train, not just me, but several from other camps. To pass the time, naturally, we talked among ourselves. One man in particular, who was not from our camp, told me he came from an SS camp called Die Riese near the Wenceslaus mine. He said he worked on a project called Die Glocke. Some sort of a high-tech acceleration device. Naturally, that caught our attention, so I asked him what the device was used for. He told me it was a bell-shaped device covered in ceramic, which housed two rotating cylinders around a core axis. After connecting to high-voltage current, the cylinders spun in opposite directions, creating some sort of a way to master gravity vortex. He went on to say that the camp was being overrun by the Soviets, and anyone in connection with the Die Glocke was either killed or shipped off to a concentration camp to keep them away from the Russians."

"Fascinating. So, these devices do exist?"

"I don't know that for sure. It was all hearsay."

"Yes, but from what you're describing, from an engineering perspective, is technically feasible?"

Poldi nodded in agreement.

"Let's keep this to ourselves for the moment. If this information should get out, they'll think we're all a bunch of lunatics anyway. Can you show me where this Die Reise facility is located on a map?" Franko asked as he passed a map of Poland to Poldi. Poldi circled an area near the town of Ludwikowice.

Just then, Morena came back and sat at the table next to Waldorf. She had not overheard the conversation between the two men on Die Glocke. "Now you can see why we kept you in protective custody. We have a plan in place to get not only you but also any remaining flight components and scientists out of the Continent and to the United States. That plan calls for strict adherence to operational details. Major, tell Mr. Waldorf what we have in store."

"Mr. Waldorf, we need you just as much as you need us. You said you wanted to work in the US, is that right?"

Waldorf answered, "Yes, yes, by all means."

"We need something from you. I can tell you that we have Dr. Hoch and Dr. Mangus in protective custody as we speak. Can you verify the identities of both Dr. Hoch and Mangus?"

"Yes."

"Will they recognize you?"

"Yes, remember, I was a camp leader. They know me. I was the one who proposed the concept of feeding us properly in order to do the work. However, they were all SS. Surely, they are wanted by the War Crimes Tribunal. They slaughtered everyone except for me."

Franko looked at Morena to get her approval. She nodded. "That is why we must stay one step ahead of War Crimes investigators *and* the Soviets. All right, this is what we want you to do." Franko shared with Waldorf bits and pieces of the operational plan and the ruse to get Krupke, Hoch, and Mangus out of the country.

Franko continued, "As you can see, the plan is complex and can unravel at any time if either one of them suspects a ruse, especially if word gets out about other Wonder Weapons. You help us, and I'll personally guarantee you'll get EXFILED along with Hoch and Mangus. Understood?" Franko extended his hand. Waldorf extended his hand, and they shook in agreement.

"Now that we have an agreement, you'll stay with us here at the safe house in protective custody as part of our team. When the time comes, I'd like you to verify the components with me. Naturally, we can't take their word on face value. It's imperative we have the real deal; otherwise, it's a no deal."

Franko came back to the table and took a seat. He continued, "Thank you for helping the rangers recover the older gyros from the quarry. I can report to you that we have them hidden in a secure place. We may need that older system as a bargaining chip if the need should arise. But in any case, I want it because the von Braun team is still lacking key flight hardware back in the United States for their own testing, mainly the dry batteries. So, if we can get both the older gyro and the new triple-mix system that would be even better."

Just then there was another knock at the door. Again Morena got up, pistol in hand. The door opened, and Jawor entered. She was not surprised to see another person at the safe house as she came into the kitchen holding a large envelope. She handed it to Franko.

"I was told to give this to you, instructions. It's in clear text. Take all the normal precautions. I see the rangers didn't waste any time with the request to bring your asset. Events are moving quickly, and . . . Janica told me to get all the money you have in your possession. She told me that you two already discussed this. Trust me. It will be safe in my office."

Franko got up from the kitchen table to retrieve the money. "I'll be right back."

Franko returned and gave Jawor all the money in his possession, then went back to his bedroom, then closed the door. Next, he reached under his bed and pulled out the knapsack, which contained all his COM/SEC equipment. The M-209 mechanical cipher machine was compact and lightweight. It was stored in a small green carrying case along with the TM11-380 converter table booklet and message tablet. He already knew what message he would send to G-2 Frankfurt. All he had to do now was code it into the machine. He took out a blank piece of paper he had in his room then wrote his message free text. It read as follows:

TO:
GIANT KILLER
FROM:
REDSTONE
AUTHENTICATION 11071945 TIME 2345Z JSGW
CONTACT WITH KING SIX AND TWO
OVERCASTS
ONCE IN BAG WILL HEAD FOR RZ POINT
PROVIDE SCHED FOR NEXT JE
WILL PROVIDE DETAILS THEN
REDSTONE

Next, Franko set up the cipher machine and dialed in the appropriate codes assigned for the day. Then he began to type out his message, one character at a time. The message was simple. It would be transmitted to Frankfurt in minimal time. Russian intelligence would have a difficult time intercepting and decoding the message. Giant Killer was G-2 staff, Frankfurt. King Six was the code name for

Krupke. Overcasts were the code names for leading Nazi scientists. JE was short for the Joan-Eleanor call.

Once the message was coded, a small printer attached to the machine printed out the letters in code. He tore off the strip of paper, then transcribed those letters onto a blank message form from the tablet. The form also had a carbon copy for his records. If he were ever caught with this device and keypads, the results would be catastrophic. The Russians would be in control of his cipher machine. Therefore, he had to maintain a high-security awareness. Luckily, the device and pads were easy to destroy. He folded up the addressed message form and placed it in his pocket. He then pulled out his lighter and burnt the free text message on the blank sheet of paper and placed it in the ashtray. He then exited his bedroom. Jawor was still in the living room with Morena.

He addressed Jawor. "I need to get this message to Frankfurt." He reached into his pocket and pulled out the message form. "What's your standard transmission method?" he asked as he handed Jawor the folded message form. "Make sure it gets sent off by midnight tonight."

"During the war, we used radio transmissions. Now that the war is over, headquarters no longer has the staff for operators to maintain listening watch twenty-four seven. Now we just use tele-print or the telephone. The telephone has been the preferred method of transmission lately. We'll courier your message to one of the ranger battalion stations, then use their lines to transmit the message to the Krakow station. Krakow, in turn, will forward it to Frankfurt. All I need is your voice transmission authentication and time."

"It's all on the pad."

"Very well, I'll make sure this gets sent off."

What Franko and the rest of the team didn't know was

that by November 1945, Soviet signals intelligence agencies had already broken M-209 coded messages. It was, however, a lengthy process and could take the Soviets several days to actually decode Franko's message. This delay could still enable the Checkmate team to conclude their mission before the Soviets closed in on them.

Chapter 26

It was early-November 1945. The holiday party at the Hotel Bristol hosted by Janica Kijowski was exquisite. It was a formal attire event. All of the best and well-known clients were invited. The hotel was decorated with green and red accents in the main lobby. By 7:00 p.m., most of the guests had arrived and were ushered to the main dining room, where a lavish feast was waiting.

Around 7:30 p.m., a taxi pulled up to the hotel with a young couple. A man in his early thirties opened the door and assisted his companion from the back seat of the taxi. The man was dressed in a tuxedo, and the woman wore a formal, white evening gown. She had her hair styled in curls. Though the couple was dressed elegantly, they were not extravagant. The woman wore only a modest pair of earrings. The man's hair was cut neatly and combed back with hair cream, giving it a slight luster. The couple was escorted into the hotel by the doorman. They went directly to the hotel bar, where they ordered drinks from the bartender. They did not stand out but instead blended in with the crowd, which was by now fairly large.

The couple took a seat at a table. They briefly exchanged pleasantries with each other over their beverages, then a hotel clerk approached them, spoke a few words, and then the couple followed the clerk out from the bar. They ascended the elegant stairway to the second floor and the manager's office. The hotel clerk knocked politely and opened the door and motioned for the couple to enter. The man and woman entered as the hotel clerk closed the door. Antoni Franko and Isebel Glowinski entered Jawor's office. Ana Zawacki, code name Jawor, was standing and waiting. She had a clothes rack with casual attire hung on it. "Get out of those ridiculous outfits and get these on. We can't have the Germans suspecting anything. Good work. Our surveillance team didn't see anyone tailing you."

"Everything set as I requested?" asked Franko.

"All taken care of."

Franko and Morena then quickly changed clothes and put on something less formal. Once the couple finished changing, Jawor escorted them to a back staircase, which was used as the hotel service access to the upper floors. They exited the top floor and went to the suites. Jawor knocked three times, and the door was opened by Vivian Tate. "Please come in," is all she said.

As Franko entered the VIP suite, he noticed three men sitting around a table set for dinner. The three men were dressed in casual attire with unshaven faces. It was apparent the men hadn't used a razor probably because Vivian feared one of them could possibly use it as a weapon or kill themselves if events didn't go their way. Franko immediately recognized Krupke from the numerous photos he had seen of him, except this time his face was thinner, and he had deep, dark circles under his eyes, obviously from all the stress. Before he would say anything, he would let Vivian make all the introductions as per her scripted instructions.

The three men stood as Franko, Morena, and Jawor approached the table. Vivian then spoke in English, "Mr. Krupke, this is Redstone and his assistant, Miss Isebel, and my manager Miss Ana."

Franko did not extend his hand out to a former Nazi officer but instead placed his hand on the small in Morena's back and responded, "Mr. Krupke, this is my associate, she helps me get around the local area. Please to meet you both. I understand you have something of value to offer."

Vivian broke in. "Please have a seat, you two," she said as she moved chairs out for Franko and Morena.

Franko and Morena took a seat at the table, followed by Jawor, while Vivian immediately poured wine for all her guests, then took a seat. "Please enjoy before we discuss business, shall we? After all, we are celebrating the holidays." Immediately Vivian began dishing out ladles of soup for her guests.

As everyone was sipping their soup, Franko began acting on the script Vivian had given him earlier. Speaking English, he addressed Krupke. "Before we get started, let me formally introduce myself. My name is Major Antoni Franko, US Army. Our hostess here, Agena, doesn't even know my real name, so there you have it, for everyone's sake. I work for G-2 military intelligence, USFET Frankfurt. I've been sent here by General Eisenhower himself to collect any and all remaining former Third Reich missile technology left undiscovered by the Western Allies. Miss Agena here informed me recently that she came across your acquaintance and knowledge of missile works. She also informed me you have something in exchange for safe passage to the West. Is that true?"

Krupke spoke next. "For simplicity sake, since I know you speak German, can we stick to that so I will not have to translate for my associates, and there will be no misunderstandings due to language?"

Franko was impressed with Krupke's English. He had an American accent, not a guttural tone. He looked at Vivian and she gave a slight nod. Everyone spoke in German from that point on. "I see no problem with that," Franko replied in his fluent German. "Let me begin by saying this is not an interrogation. I have no authority in my position as a prosecutor for war crimes. I'm what is known as a technical collector. I collect technology, not evidence for trial. For the time being, none of you are going to trial. For the record, Mr. Krupke, please state your full name, and can you give me more information about your two associates and why they're so important to your overall objective?"

Krupke introduced himself as Sturmbanführer Otto Krupke, former head of RSHA Security Service, Berlin. Then he introduced both Dr. Hoch and Dr. Mangus and gave a brief description of their duties and responsibilities.

When he was finished, Franko asked, "Dr. Hoch, what was your specific responsibility with the V-2?"

Hoch repeated the information Franko already knew concerning the advanced gyros and his position as camp commandant for the Jewish camp at Pustkow. Then Franko said, "I'd like to bring in a guest to our conversation. Naturally, you can't expect me to believe who you said you are by face value. My superiors will want confirmation."

Franko nodded to Vivian as she got up from the table and went to the door. She came back with Leopold Waldorf. He was offered a seat at the table, then Franko asked, "Mr. Waldorf, can you tell me who these men are in front of us?"

Krupke showed a face of pure utter disbelief, but Hoch and Mangus obviously recognized the gaunt figure seated in front of them. "Why yes," he said in German and pointed to Hoch. "Hoch here was the camp commander for the Heidelager concentration camp. The other person I only know as Dr. Mangus, who was one of the scientists working on the dry batteries."

Leopold recapped his entire story of incarceration by the Nazis and verified to all present that he was treated with modest respect in exchange for working on the new guidance system.

Then Dr. Hoch added. "Major, what we did at Blizna was purely scientific in nature. We found that with these new guidance systems and a second-stage rocket, we could get the vehicle into the upper reaches of the atmosphere, which means we could actually put it into lower Earth orbit. Once that object is in orbit, we'd have the capability for human space travel. After this discovery, for weeks, von Braun and the rest of us were in a state of euphoria. Von Braun said to us, 'Now I know how Columbus must have felt.'"

Franko added sarcastically, "And you could have also hit New York or Washington with a warhead! Now that we've established credibility, let's begin." Franko recapped to the Germans what he already knew about the V-2. "Now, what is it you have to offer?"

Krupke spoke on behalf of all three men. "Simple, you get me, Dr. Hoch, and Dr. Mangus to the American lines, and I'll give you the latest version of the V-2 guidance system and flight hardware. Once we are safely in the American sector, I want immunity for any war crimes for my associates and me. Also, Dr. Hoch and Dr. Mangus would like their families ex-filed as soon as practical to the United States. Dr. Hoch and Dr. Mangus also want a contract to work in the United States with the von Braun team."

Franko interrupted, "That's a tall order. What about you? Why should I bring you out? What have you got to offer? After all, von Braun had thousands of V-2 rockets. My superiors are going to want something from you."

Krupke detailed his entire background and responsibilities within the Third Reich and his radio play-back game with the Soviets. Instead of a contract working for the US missile program, he wanted a contract to work with US intelligence, providing information on Soviet intelligence capabilities, operations, and cryptology. Specifically, knowledge of covert Soviet Communist activities in former Third Reich territories. And to everyone's astonishment, he would divulge his knowledge of other Nazi secret weapons hidden in Poland. But he would only reveal this information once safely in US custody as an added guarantee.

Now it was Vivian's turn to speak. "Let's not forget about me. I was the one who brokered this whole deal. I took certain risks too. I'm a businesswoman. I don't work for free. Plus, many sections on the ratline are closed or in Soviet control. Routing will be long and indirect. Sources will have to be paid for. What can you offer me, Mr. Krupke, monetarily?"

"She's got a point," added Franko still following Vivian's script. "If she can get us to a secure site, preferably close to the Czech border, I can have an aircraft waiting to take you and the hardware out. I don't have a financial stake. But I must have visual verification you have the real goods. My associate, Mr. Waldorf, will verify the authenticity of the components before I agree on any movements."

Krupke responded, "We anticipated such a response from the Americans." Krupke looked at Vivian addressing her in particular. "Shall we show the major what we have in store for him?"

Vivian nodded. "Let's finish our meal first," she said.

All the guests, including Poldi, suspended their technical inquiries and ate their meals. When dinner was finished and the plates cleared, Vivian said, "You may proceed now."

Dr. Hoch then got up from the table and proceeded to a corner of the room. He brought out the V-2 flight hardware which was concealed under a blanket. He addressed Franko. "A key step in the rocket's guidance system is to first align the gyros. To do that you need both AC and DC electrical power." Hoch connected the power cable to a room outlet which used the standard AC voltage from the hotel. Next, he attached the battery lead to the system. "This is the dry battery. We actually have three of these here in the hotel with us tonight. I do believe the Backfire team had the most trouble locating these devices."

Franko was stunned. Hoch was right. The batteries were the most difficult items to locate. The Backfire team had even contemplated recycling the batteries until they discovered four more hidden in Germany.

Hoch continued, "These nickel-cadmium or dry batteries were invented a long time ago. However, our scientist went further and developed a sealed unit. One that is more powerful and holds a charge longer. Here it is." He flipped a switch on the component, and the system began to hum to life. The hum of the gyros spinning to acceleration speed grew louder, and Hoch quickly turned off the device so the noise would not be heard below. "Before the gyros can align up to speed, the battery goes through a small, self-test. If the voltage on the battery is insufficient, the alignment process stops. Von Braun wanted a fully charged, twenty-four-volt battery upon alignment to begin the launch sequence, thus the battery self-test. If the test failed, we could quickly and easily swap a new battery and begin the re-alignment process."

Franko responded, "And the reason why he wanted a fully charged battery was so that the battery would power the guidance system in flight once the rocket was launched. The standard charge of twenty-four volts would last a minimum of thirty minutes. Enough time for the warhead to reach its target?"

"Precisely, you are indeed well aware of the capabilities of the V-2 rocket."

"Let me guess," said Franko. "The new flight hardware could navigate the warheads even further distances, like New York or Philadelphia, someplace that could be within thirty minutes of flying time."

"Yes, but you could also power a vehicle into Earth's orbit in that same length of time too."

"All right, I agree. Let's move on, shall we" added Franko. "Did you have or were you working on an alternate power source that could be used in flight? One that would also trickle-charge the battery or power the vehicle for longer periods of time?"

Hoch answered, "You can't actually put a conventional fuel-driven generator on a space vehicle and start it up like you can in an airplane. There is no oxygen in space. But the answer is yes. We were working on that up until the end of the war. But Himmler's office placed emphasis on the actual production vehicles for obvious reasons. They wanted to change the outcome of the war. Von Braun called this system fuel cells, or oxygen generators. Dr. Mangus knows more about that phase of the operation. You can ask him. But if you'd like more verification, why don't you have a look." Hoch pointed to the microscope and sheet music.

Vivian addressed Franko. "They have everything on microdots. It's all set up."

Franko moved over to the microscope and looked through the lens. He already knew most of the information, but it was a reassurance that the team had all the research material.

Everyone from the Checkmate team then got up and examined the flight hardware further. The triple-mix V-2 guidance system was verified authentic by Franko and Waldorf, and the team could proceed with the actual operation. Franko gave Vivian the okay to continue with her end of the mission. She cleared off the table and placed a lamp on it to provide more light in the dimly lit room. Next, she took out her maps and drawings for their escape route. Vivian spoke next, "I want fifty thousand Swiss franks deposited directly into my numbered account, along with the diamonds you have in your possession."

"Fifty thousand Swiss francs is a lot of money, Fräulein," responded Krupke. He turned to Franko. "How much do you actually know about our hostess? What did you call her, Agena?"

Franko looked at Vivian and stuck to script. "I don't know anything about her. That's the whole point. She coordinates the escape line for my assets. That's it."

"She has several aliases, Janica Kijowski, Hilda Bradt, to name a few."

"I'm sure she does. I would, too, if I was in her shoes."

"She could double-cross us all for money. She might even lead us directly to the Soviets."

"That's a possibility, but I'm willing to take the chance if that's what it takes to get the rocket technology."

Krupke came back, "For fifty-thousand Swiss francs and the diamonds, I need a guarantee."

Krupke now looked at Vivian, and there was a brief pause in the discussion. Then he looked at Franko.

"Her real name is Irina Jankowski. Remember, I was the former head of all counter-intelligence matters for the Third Reich, and I have my sources."

Vivian interrupted, steering Krupke toward a different topic. "You and I know I can't guarantee safe passage. There's always risks with these kinds of operations. Anything could happen."

Krupke sat back in his chair, then lit a cigarette, and blew smoke over everyone's heads. "How about this? I'll settle for a partial guarantee. I want Fräulein Agena, or whatever her name really is, to go with us, right up to the point we actually board the transport. Then and only then, I'll divulge the codes to release the funds from my Zurich account to her Zurich account. That way, I know she won't betray us to the Russians or anyone else along the way." The room fell silent. Obviously, no one had expected a response like this from Krupke.

Franko finally looked at Vivian. "Your thoughts. Can you escort us the entire way, Miss Jankowski?"

Vivian sat in silence for a while, acting as if contemplating a response, slightly moved by Franko's mention of her real name, which was not part of his script. Then she looked down at her maps and then at Jawor. "My assistant here, code name, Jawor, is also my associate on the ratline. That is why she is here tonight. She will give you more details on the actual escape line. Can we do it?" she asked Jawor.

Jawor, now revealing more details on her false identity, continued, "As you already mentioned, the ratline is closing. The Soviets are taking control of more and more sections of the country. Specialized NKVD units are actively assassinating former Home Army officers. We'll have to proceed away from the major cities, Krakow in particular. Also, it has recently come to our attention that one of our most secure airfields has been compromised to the Soviets. That means we'll have to use our secondary recovery site, located in Walbrzych." She pointed out the location out on the map for everyone to see. "Home Army also operates a black site here."

Vivian responded, "That's a long way away. It will be more difficult, but we can do it. How about you?" she asked Franko.

Again, acting on Vivian's script, Franko responded. "All right, I'll authorize Fräulein Jankowski here to proceed with the plan, and Mr. Waldorf goes with us too. We may need him once inside the American sector. Also, I must point out that my job is strictly technical. Once I get you to the American sector, it's ultimately up to CIOS or CIC to determine your fate, Mr. Krupke. They may hold you in custody or interrogate you further. Do we have an agreement?"

Everyone nodded. Then Franko raised his wine glass. "Then let's do it. To the future of space travel!"

Chapter 27

The VIP suite became a briefing room. Dinner plates, silverware, and used glasses were cleared from the room. All members of Operation Checkmate were present, which included, Vivian, Franko, Jawor, Morena, Waldorf, Krupke, Mangus, and Hoch. Vivian indicated that all members present would take part in the actual EXFIL to the American sector. Now it was time to turn to operational details. Franko, for one, took particular interest since Vivian had only revealed minute details and only on her terms. Vivian spoke first.

"For starters, we need to get the flight hardware out of the hotel and secured into a small truck, which we will use for transport out of the city and to Walbrzych by caravan. Next, we'll need two sedans. One for me and Jawor, which will lead the caravan. The other will take up the rear. Major Franko will take that vehicle along with his companions, Morena and Waldorf. This will also be the security detail protecting the element. The Germans will ride in the truck along with the goods. Ranger Battalion will supply the driver for this vehicle. For this configuration to work effectively, the Germans will have to go along as prisoners of war, wearing their actual German uniforms, stripped of rank of course. Thus, our cover will be transporting these high-value POWs back to Germany to face war crimes charges. This, of course, will not be the reality. This is the most secure option if we are stopped and questioned by Polish or Soviet forces; this will get us past any security checkpoints. We'll have forged authorization from the Allied Control Commission for movement in the Soviet sectors and orders from the War Crimes Tribunal." She looked at Morena. "Can your Home Army sources come up with petrol and the assets we need?"

Morena spoke from the script. "Ranger Battalion has two sedans and a requisitioned Soviet utility truck complete with military markings we can use. All vehicles are in excellent condition. Petrol is available to the rangers, but it will have to be paid with cash along the way."

"Excellent, we can pay for the fuel as we go along. Let's move on to the courier line."

Jawor now took her cue. She stood up and addressed the map of Poland, so everyone could see. "As I mentioned, up until a few days ago, our secure landing site was seized by the Soviets," she said as she pointed to the Motyl field. "The next secure site is at Walbrzych in the western region of Poland."

"As you can see, it is some distance from our present location. "Since the end of hostilities, Soviet troops are not on alert. Our sources tell us they billet for the night along the major rail line between Krakow and Gorlitz. So, all of our movements will be planned at night away from the major rail lines. We'll travel from midnight to four in the morning. This will, unfortunately, take approximately three nights to travel the distance to Walbrzych. We'll have three courier legs. One at Bielsko-Biala, the other at Nysa, and the final leg to Walbrzych. Each leg will be handed off to the next secure leg. We'll then go into hiding at a safe house during the day and wait until the cover of darkness to travel on to the next sector. When we get to Walbrzych, we wait at a secure site until transport can arrive from Major Franko's air assets."

Vivian looked at Franko and said, "Major Franko?"

Franko took the brief now, again sticking to Vivian's script. "Once we get to Walbrzych, I can use the safe houses to set up and transmit my coded message to USFET. I'll coordinate for transport then. It could take twenty-four to forty-eight hours for them to coordinate the airlift. In the meantime, we wait at the secure location until the aircraft arrive."

Krupke spoke next. "Your plan is simple in nature, and I'm sure your assets are trustworthy, but I have my sources as well." He turned to Franko. "Major Franko, my informants tell me Russian military units are on to you. Air Force Colonel Vladimir Sivan GRU, in particular. They know who you are and know why you're here. It's only a matter of time before someone betrays our location to those units."

Franko was surprised to hear this piece of information coming from Krupke, but, fortunately, he already knew of it thanks to Morena. He addressed Vivian, "How come I wasn't informed of this before?"

Krupke interrupted, "Probably because she didn't know either. She also has her adversaries. Dimitri Pavel, Colonel NKVD, Third Directorate is on her tail. He has an inkling on who she might be but doesn't have a positive identification yet."

Vivian was right, Soviet state security and military units were closing in on them. Franko decided to speak off script, given this new piece of information. "How does this

Colonel Pavel know about Agena, excuse me, Miss Jankowski?"

"He doesn't have specific information on her. He just knows a woman is collaborating with local units. If he can find her, he can find me."

Just then, there was an unexpected knock on the door. Vivian got up to open the door, and one of the hotel staff members handed her a written message. She acknowledged, then closed the door. She came back to the table and addressed Jawor. "Get downstairs and find out what they're up to."

She handed Jawor the note:

RUSSIAN OFFICERS AT THE FRONT DOOR

Vivian addressed the group. "It would appear Mr. Krupke is well informed. I just received word that Soviet officers are at the door. Don't worry, our security is extremely efficient. They'll be no match for them, and they'll never get up here."

Krupke spoke, "That would probably be Colonel Dimitri Pavel or someone from his section."

Chapter 28

Jawor left the room. The staff member was actually a Home Army security guard. Jawor took the normal security precautions. She would accompanied the security guard and made visual contact with the Russians to find out what they were up to. They proceeded downstairs to the kitchen, where Jawor changed into a service uniform. The two then grabbed a service cart and pushed it out onto the main dining room floor. Piano music played in the background.

The holiday party was in full swing. People were mingling about eating, drinking, and talking. As the two pushed the serving cart closer to the front door, they noticed three uniformed Soviet military officers. One was wearing the rank of colonel, the other two were non-commissioned officers. They had on the powder-blue, shoulder boards of the NKVD. Jawor took care, not wanting to be noticed by the three men, so she left her companion and headed to a secure location behind a service partition. There she got a good look at the three men. She then moved over to another service attendant and whispered a few words into her ear. The woman nodded, as if following directions, then disappeared into the crowd.

This was the signal for the Home Army security detail to photograph the three Russians. The film would be rushed to the developer and processed for Vivian Tate. In the meantime, Jawor's security agent proceeded to confront the three Soviets and asked them what they wanted. There was a brief exchange, then the three officers began looking about the guests. The security agent offered each man a glass of champagne. None of the Russians accepted.

Pavel spoke in Polish, "We're looking for war criminals, German officers."

The security agent responded. "We have no Germans here tonight. This is a private party for our loyal, local guests, all Polish residents."

"Can I speak to your hotel manager?"

"That is not possible tonight. She has many duties and responsibilities. At the moment, she is unavailable."

"Then I must see your hotel registry. I'd like to see your guest list for the past three days." This was not a request from Pavel.

The security agent paused, then nodded. "Very well, please come with me."

He escorted the three officers to the front desk and asked for the hotel registry. He then gave it to Pavel. Pavel opened the ledger and scanned the list, looking for any German names or a recognizable name. He went back several days but could not see any name he recognized. "What about nonpaying guests or other workers? Surely you must have had many in preparation for the festivities."

"You'll have to speak to the proprietor. Her name is Janice Kijowski. She will be available tomorrow."

Pavel snapped the ledger closed. "Then I will take this

until we meet tomorrow. Please tell your proprietor I will be back then." Pavel then nodded, indicating to his two men that it was time to leave. The Russians then left the hotel.

Jawor returned to the VIP suite and resumed her position at the table, still dressed in her service uniform. "They were Soviet state security. They have left the hotel for the time being. The three men were not schooled in fieldwork. Probably desk agents. We had them photographed as they did their investigative work without their knowledge. The leader was a colonel who claimed he was looking for German war criminals."

It was Krupke's turn to speak. "That would definitely be Dimitri Pavel. Can I ask what happened?"

Jawor recapped her encounter with the Russians, including the fact that he had taken the hotel register.

Then Vivian said, "We'll have to leave tonight, *all of us*. That's the only way. We've got to secure the hardware before tomorrow. This was one of the reasons why we scheduled this meeting to coincide with our holiday festivities. The party has given us an unexpected advantage in time."

Just then, there was another knock on the door. Vivian answered and collected a large envelope and returned to the table. She opened the envelope and dumped the photographs of the Russians on the table. She passed them to Franko, who showed them to Krupke.

"That's definitely Pavel," said Krupke. "There is one more asset I have for our escape. I know the Soviet security procedures, especially Pavel's. Do not send any coded messages or make any phone calls from this hotel. Pavel will have a signals intelligence team monitoring any and all emitters coming from this hotel. They'll come back with a whole garrison by tomorrow if you do."

"What do you suggest?" asked Franko, thinking about his own coded messages to Frankfurt.

"If you need to send any message, do so by courier."

Vivian then collected the photographs and placed them back in the envelope. "Gather your belongings. It's going to be a long night for all of us. We have a service vehicle downstairs in the garage. We can all fit, along with the goods. If you gentlemen would be so kind as to help me package the hardware so we can get out of here?"

* * *

THE CHECKMATE TEAM left the Hotel Bristol a few hours after their dinner meeting. It was before dawn. Ranger Battalion supplied a driver. They drove inside Krupke's white utility van to the outskirts of town following Krakowska Boulevard. They made a turn off the main highway onto Zglobice Road and then turned off onto a narrow gravel road. The vehicle stopped. Jawor and Morena climbed out from the back of the van and opened a large door for a storage garage. They motioned the driver to back up into the garage. When the utility van was securely inside the facility, Jawor and Morena closed the door. The ranger driver shut off the engine.

Jawor told everyone, "We stay here until we can secure our caravan vehicles. Unload the goods. The driver needs to get back into town before eight. We only have an hour or so before he needs to leave. Quickly now!"

The facility called Zglobice Mansion was originally an aristocrat's mansion belonging to a wealthy family. During the war, it was a Home Army safe house. Now, in November 1945, it was used as an elementary school for local children. The garage they were now using housed all the landscaping equipment and supplies for the school.

Next to and behind the school was a small villa. That villa had produced hand grenades in the basement for the Home Army during the war. Now the villa served as a safe house along the ratline to the West. This was a Sunday morning. There would be no school in session today, so the team could work without the children seeing what was truly going on. For the time being, the location was safe.

Franko and Poldi helped the three Germans unload the flight hardware from the truck and secured them inside empty wooden fruit boxes. They pushed the boxes off to a corner while Jawor and Morena opened the door for the driver, who then sped off back to the city. The women closed the door, and Jawor addressed Vivian.

"Two Home Army guards disguised as landscape workers will be here shortly to provide perimeter security while we wait for the vehicles. The goods will be safe here while we get some rest. We have quarters set up for you next door at the villa."

Krupke, who spoke Polish fluently overheard Jawor and spoke up. "I can't leave the devices unattended."

Jawor responded, "Yes, I know. That's why you, Hoch, and Mangus will stay here. I'll have blankets, food, and water brought to you. We should only be here for a few hours. The school will be in session on Monday morning. We'll be out of here before then."

Franko said, "I'll stay here with the men."

Vivian looked at Franko. "These men are former Nazis. You are an American officer. I won't let you stay here. You will stay with us in the villa. Our friends will be quite comfortable for the night."

"How do I know they won't do something to the hardware?" asked Franko.

Krupke responded in English, "Let's get something

straight right now, Major. I want the goods in American hands. I have a vested interest in the success of this operation. You have my word, as long as we are moving toward the EXFIL point, the goods will be safe. If, on the other hand, I see that you are stalling or trying to pull a fast one on us, I cannot guarantee the safety of the hardware. Do we have an agreement?"

Franko nodded, but he looked at Vivian for acknowledgment. She nodded too and then said, "All right, but don't forget, I want my money too. So, before we EXFIL, I want to make sure the goods are in working order."

Poldi, also traveling with the team, spoke up. "I'll stay here with them. These conditions are luxury compared to what I've been through. Plus, I want to make sure the goods arrive safely too."

"Agreed," said Krupke. "If I have to, we'll do a power-up before departure to make everyone happy."

Jawor then escorted Vivian, Franko, and Morena to the villa next door. It was only a short walk.

The villa was a small, two-story structure with six windows facing the main school. An elderly couple greeted the team as they walked in. Brief words were exchanged between Jawor and the couple, then individual keys distributed. Each had a single room with private bath. Franko took the room on the upper floor, facing the garage, so he could periodically look out the window and keep an eye on the Germans. As he did so, he saw two rangers take up the security positions outside the garage. Franko only had a small knapsack with personal belongings and COM gear retrieved from the safe house by Home Army rangers. Neither of the team members had had any time to pack a suitcase, especially Franko and Morena. Once inside his room, Franko flung the knapsack on the floor, closed the drapes, then went inside the small bathroom and washed his face. He took his clothes off and climbed into bed. Almost immediately, he fell fast asleep.

Chapter 29

The Polish Home Army Ranger Battalion acted swiftly and promptly, using all their assets. They secured the real Janica Kijowski back into the Hotel Bristol as proprietor overnight. Per Vivian Tate's guidance, Jawor briefed her personally on all the hotel operations for the last five days, especially the part about the piano tuners. It was a sure bet Pavel would return and inquire further on individuals to and from the hotel.

At eight o'clock in the morning, the day after the holiday party, the real Janica Kijowski sat at her desk at the Hotel Bristol. There was nothing extraordinary about the thirty-five-year-old woman, other than the fact that she resembled Vivian Tate. They were both about the same age, height, weight, and build, with short blond hair and blue eyes. The house phone rang on her desk, and she was simply told three Russians from state security were on their way up to see her.

Janica's office door burst open, and the three Russians entered. Pavel and his assistants were not dressed in military uniforms. They wore civilian clothes, much like any other working man would on a busy weekday in the Polish city of Tarnow. Pavel spoke first in excellent Polish as he entered Janica's office.

"Sorry I missed you last night. Let me formally introduce myself." Pavel made all the introductions, then continued. "I represent Soviet, State Security. We're pursuing a former Nazi war criminal believed to have conspired with local resistance units and undermined Soviet intelligence- gathering capabilities during the war. These activities resulted in the death and torture of over one hundred of our intelligence agents. We have reason to believe this individual has re-surfaced in this area and is attempting to make contact with his former network to escape to the West. I have your guest registry in my possession, and I have checked the names of all your guests for the past several days. Every one of them has come out clean, except for you. I have information from highly reliable sources that indicates it is you who is helping this dangerous war criminal."

Janica spoke, "Yes, I know about the registry, my staff informed me first thing this morning. What is it that I can help you with?"

"Where were you last night that was so important you couldn't be disturbed?"

Janica knew this question would come up. She had a prepared answer from Vivian Tate. "I was entertaining my own private guest, if you know what I mean. I gave word to my staff that I not be disturbed."

"I see. And where is this guest now?"

Janica, stalling, took her time answering. "I'm sorry, this guest is another woman. The wife of a high-profile local official whom I invited to the festivities. She has returned to her native country, Romania."

Pavel knew he wasn't going to get anything further

from Kijowski. He decided to pursue a different approach. "The man we're after is extremely clever. He may have several aliases as well as professions." Pavel passed a photograph of Otto Krupke to Kijowski. "This is the man we're looking for. Does he look familiar?"

Janica took the photograph and studied it. She knew all about Krupke from her briefing with Jawor. The key for her was to stay on script and not give the Russians too much information. She had to buy time for the rest of the team to make a clean getaway. In the meantime, Pavel could tell from the expressions on Janica's face that she indeed recognized Krupke.

"Look familiar?" prompted Pavel.

"Why yes, this person came to the hotel just the other day with two other helpers. He claimed he was a piano tuner and wanted to know if we had any pianos in need of tuning."

Pavel interrupted, "Well, then what?"

"Why, I had him tune my pianos, of course. We were having the holiday gathering complete with music, and the pianos hadn't been tuned since well before the war. Since I finally had a little extra cash, I took him up on his offer."

Pavel took out a notepad and began scribbling notes. "Anything unusual about the man you can tell me?"

"Nothing really, other than nice-looking."

"What about his language skills?"

"He spoke perfect Polish. I could not detect the slightest accent."

"What about the other two helpers?"

"They stayed off to the side. Neither of them spoke. Perhaps they are surviving war veterans."

Pavel made a few notes then asked, "You said pianos. How many did he tune?"

"All three of them."

"How long did they stay?"

"They worked till around four thirty. Then I paid them in cash as they requested, and then they left by the lorry they came in."

Pavel turned to his associates and spoke to them in Russian, then they left. Pavel continued his interrogation. "Can you show me the pianos?"

Janica led Pavel downstairs to the main ballroom and showed him the baby grand piano off in the corner. "Open the back lid for me?"

Janica opened the lid to the piano as Pavel looked inside. He took out a small flashlight and inspected the tuning bolts. He could see marks on the nuts, indicating work had recently been done. Also, the strings and strikers were clean and void of any dust or grime. He tapped a few keys with his fingers as he watched the strikers hit the wires. It was nearly impossible to tell whether the piano had been recently tuned or staged to look as if it had been recently tuned. "Show me the others."

Janica showed Pavel the other pianos, and he similarly inspected them as the first. Again, he could not be sure the pianos had been tuned. This was one reason he had his associates find a piano musician who could verify the pianos were tuned.

"Will there be anything else?" asked Janica.

"We wait. My two associates have gone to collect a piano player. He will verify the pianos were recently tuned. If they are out of tune, I will bring you in for further questioning."

A short time later, the two NKVD officers returned with a piano player. Pavel had him play several songs on each piano then asked, "Are the pianos in tune?"

The piano player nodded and replied, "The sound is

excellent. This is the work of an extremely experienced tuning professional."

Pavel turned to his men. "Search this place. Look for anything that would indicate they were harboring someone. Question everyone about the piano tuners and their lorry."

Janica protested, "I have done nothing wrong. You have no right or business to search my property. I must call the local authorities."

Pavel responded, "I must remind you, young lady. This section of Poland is under liberation status. The Red Army controls all administrative districts, including the local police. In fact, you reminded me of something. Our army needs billets. We could just as easily requisition this facility and use it for our forces. You wouldn't want that, would you?"

Janica shook her head.

"Good, I thought so. Now I want everyone from your hotel staff to meet me in the ballroom. I want to question them and corroborate your story about your special guest."

Later that day, after the entire hotel had been searched and the staff questioned, Pavel and his NKGB officers left the hotel Bristol and headed back to their regional head-quarters in Krakow. The drive back was in near silence as Pavel's thoughts were on the woman known as Janica Kijowski.

Finally, one of the NKVD men spoke to his superior, "Why didn't we take her in and seize the hotel?"

"She's not the woman I'm looking for," answered Pavel. "Everything in her story checked out. Five individuals gave depositions that the piano tuners left the hotel around four in the afternoon, driving a white utility van. Three testified Kijowski spent the night with another woman. There is nothing more we could do. She is, in all likelihood, who she said she was, the proprietor of the hotel, lesbian and a Polish national. Besides, there's nothing more she could tell me I don't already know. It would have been a waste of time. Time we can use elsewhere."

"What makes you think so, Comrade Colonel?" asked one of the men.

"Lack of authority and confidence despite her position as proprietor. She was nervous and uneasy as we questioned her. I was told the person we're after has a certain haughtiness about her, very distinct and definitely not a lesbian. No, comrades, this may be more difficult than I originally thought, especially after our incident at the airfield. We will have to take a different, more methodical approach. I'm afraid we're dealing with very thorough professionals.

Pavel took a cigarette from his coat pocket, placed it between his lips, and flicked on his gold-plated lighter. He took a few puffs then, blew the smoke out his window. "Send a team back. Requisition the hotel. Have the hotel proprietor eliminated. It's time we demonstrate to the Polish resistance that *we* are in control."

Chapter 30

What seemed like only a short time later, Franko was awakened by the sound of someone knocking on his door. At first he thought he was only dreaming, but then he heard the noise again. He climbed out of bed wearing only his underwear, grabbed his Colt 45, and approached the door. He heard the knocking again, but this time it was more pronounced. He placed the Colt .45 next to the doorframe and looked for a peephole. There was none. Then he heard the words in Polish, "Room service!"

Franko cracked the door open slightly, keeping the .45 trained on the door, just in case. Then he saw a woman wearing a white hotel utility dress with a scarf over her head, concealing her face. She was holding a tray with food and coffee with both hands. She was not a threat. He presumed it was a hotel staff member delivering his breakfast. Franko opened the door fully as the woman came in. To his surprise, it was Vivian Tate. "I brought you something to eat," she said.

Still holding the tray, Vivian entered Franko's room and kicked a string and paper package on the floor into his room. She placed the tray on the small table, then opened the window curtains.

Franko stood in the middle of his room watching her with only his underwear on, showing off his lean, muscular features. "What time is it?" he asked.

"It's about three in the afternoon. You've been asleep since eight. You can put that ridiculous thing away. You might shoot yourself in the foot. Who did you think I was?"

Franko secured his weapon while Vivian poured him a cup of coffee from the pot. *She's still an enigma*, he thought. He watched her as she took out bread, cheese, fruit, and sliced meat from a platter and placed them on a small plate for him. She looked just like a hotel worker.

Next, Vivian picked up a small pitcher from the tray. "Sugar is still hard to come by in these parts, but they do have excellent fresh cream."

"I'll take just a little cream, then."

Vivian poured the cream into his coffee while she poured a cup of tea from another pot. "Can I take a seat?"

Franko nodded while he slipped on his trousers and sat on the edge of the bed, looking at her intently. Vivian took a seat at the little table and chair. She removed the scarf from her head and shook her blond locks free. Her bright blue eyes were illuminated by the afternoon sunlight coming in from the windows. To Franko, she was getting more and more attractive each day, despite the circumstances.

Vivian continued, "Inside that parcel is a fresh set of clothes. You'll get more at our next courier stop."

Franko picked up the parcel and threw it on the bed. "Hope everything fits."

Vivian ignored his remarks. "Now you know and understand the significance of not having a specific plan in place, Tony. The sudden and unexpected arrival of the Soviets forced us to adapt. We take one step at a time. I need to brief you on the next phase of the operation. For the record, you did good back in Tarnow. In fact, I couldn't have done it any better myself. It appears the Germans fell for the ruse. None-the-less, we must keep on our toes. Krupke is a professional. One can't be too sure of his actual motives. I also cannot divulge the slightest hint that I know more of the operation than absolutely necessary. Remember, I'm the conductor, not an organizer. So, we'll leave most, if not all, of the details to our Polish colleagues."

"Thanks for the compliment. Now what?"

"We were expecting to move from the Hotel Bristol with the caravan vehicles. That plan has been altered. We were to have the two sedans, but they won't join us until our next courier stop. We did secure the large lorry with a painted red star. It should be here tonight. Home Army is well equipped. They got us the forged movement papers from the Allied Control Commission. I have them in my possession. None the less, we'll stick to our plan and move under cover of darkness. We plan on leaving here after midnight."

Vivian took out a cigarette and lit it then took a sip of tea. "There's something else that's come up, so pay attention."

Franko lit a cigarette from Vivian's and then gulped his coffee down. "I'm listening.

"We received a message by courier earlier today. The Russians came back to the Hotel Bristol this morning. It appears it was a local NKVD hit squad. They weren't there to take questions. It was obvious what their mission was. Janica Kijowski had no choice but to take a cyanide capsule. She's dead. Thus far, she was the only fatality. The rest of the Home Army team in Tarnow escaped and is safe. Kijowski gave her life for her colleagues, but the Soviets took control of the hotel. Jawor is quite upset. They've known each other since childhood."

"I'm sorry to hear that. Is there anything I can do?"

"It's personal now for our Polish colleagues. As I told you, we're fighting on two battlefronts on two dimensions. One technical, the other political, the Germans and the Soviets. It will get worse before the mission's over. Here's what I want you to do. First, you and I must keep our relationship separate and professional, even from our Polish colleagues, especially now that my real name has been divulged. That name is an official state secret back in the UK. We can't afford to slip up. To do so will most definitely tip off the Germans possibly the Soviets too. Therefore, from now on, you and I have to meet in private, just like we're doing now."

"Sort of like a cutout then. How will I know when and where to meet?"

"Leave that to me. It will just happen."

"Thanks for the heads up on *that* issue. What else?"

"You and Morena will team up. She's supposed to be your assistant, so we'll have her stick to character. Any time you talk with Krupke and the scientists, she'll be there with you." She reached into her dress and pulled out a folded set of papers. "This is for the first courier leg. You'll get more scripts at each stop. This one basically says that I want you to squeeze the scientists. Get friendly with them. Chummy up to them. The objective is to get more technical information out of them. I want Krupke to know that you and Morena are serious about getting the scientists into American hands, and you're their friend."

Franko took the script and secured it in his knapsack. "What about Krupke? What do I do about him?"

"It's in the script, but see what you can get out of him concerning Soviet intelligence capabilities. As he said, he can be a valuable asset, especially with the latest developments."

Franko got up from the bed and placed his empty coffee cup back on the tray. He stood in front of Vivian, who was still seated on the chair. He noticed she was trembling again, slightly, like she had that night back in the Hotel Bristol, kitchen. Franko responded by placing a hand around the back of her head.

"What's wrong?"

"Nothing," she said.

"Don't tell me *nothing*. You're trembling again. I know something's on your mind."

"Oh, for heaven's sake. Can't you see it, Tony?"

Franko decided to play for a while. "Can't I see what?"

Vivian couldn't stand it any longer. She had to let it out. *Is he really that naive?* she thought. "Remember what I said, back at the Hotel Bristol the night you came by for breakfast? You apologized for your behavior, and I said I was enjoying it. I haven't felt this way about another man in a very long time."

Franko reached out with both hands, grabbed hers, raised her to her feet, and said, "Come here."

Vivian came to her feet. He hugged her gently with both arms. "Let me help you with that." She relaxed and stopped trembling. The two continued to hug each other for a while, then they separated. Then Franko focused on business. "I need to take a bath and then head down to the garage. I'll take Morena with me. I've got work to do. Everything will be all right. Look at the bright side. We've got Krupke, the scientists, and the missile works. We're halfway there."

Despite these early successes, things were not all right.

Little did the couple know, but at this moment, in London and in Poland, events were moving quickly. The two were in grave danger.

* * *

COLONEL ALEXANDER WAS ALMOST positive that the mysterious Russian officer was none other than Miss Vivian Tate. However, before he finalized his report and sent it off to Moscow center, he had to determine the *why*. Why would this former SOE officer want to interview the mistress of a high-ranking Nazi official? The Center would ask for this information anyway, so he coordinated with Colonel Stephens to interview Cordes. He made the trip to Camp 020 and waited for Cordes to appear in the interrogation room. She entered dressed in the same grimy clothes she had had on when Vivian Tate had interviewed her earlier in the month. Not much had changed, and her fate was still undetermined at this time. Calvin was determined to change that status.

Calvin sat in front of Cordes and introduced himself as head of MI-19. Then he began, speaking German. "Miss Cordes, we are in the process of wrapping up our investigation on your case. At the moment, we have enough evidence to proceed with a full arraignment from War Crimes Tribunal. You will stand trial. There are enough discrepancies in your depositions to warrant that."

Calvin could tell Cordes was shaken by the news. He decided the time was right to make his offer. "This is your final interview. The answers will determine your fate. You will either face war crimes, or you will be repatriated.

"A fortnight ago, you were interviewed by a Soviet officer. We have reason to believe that this officer was an imposter. You can help us uncover that imposter if you answer my questions correctly, and I have the authority to set you free. On the other hand, if you choose to remain silent, then your case will proceed to the War Crimes Tribunal. The choice is yours, young lady. Which will it be?" Calvin waited for her answer.

Cordes had no choice. She had to agree. "All right, what is it you want?"

Calvin lit a cigarette and gave it to Cordes. She inhaled a few puffs, then he asked, "Tell me, what did this Soviet officer ask you, specifically?"

Cordes answered promptly, "First of all, I knew there was something about the woman. She seemed very hubristic. She threatened to take me to a prison camp in the Soviet Union if I didn't answer her questions. Just like you're threatening me now."

"I can understand where you're coming from, but you are at the end of the line. It all ends today. So, let's have it."

Cordes finished off her cigarette then put it out in the ashtray. "We insisted all recording devices be turned off, for starters. Once that was accomplished, she began her interview."

"And?"

"She knew I was involved with Krupke's escape, almost every detail. She knew things I'd forgotten or left out. That's what caught me and took me slightly aback. Some of those details were impossible to trace, yet she knew of them. She asked why he fled instead of staying in British custody. She had me boxed in a corner before I knew it. I had to answer her questions. She was a tough nut to crack."

"So, why did Krupke flee?"

"I suppose he knew the gig was up and there was no chance the regime would survive."

Calvin reached into his pocket and pulled out a photograph of Vivian Tate. "Is this the Soviet officer?"

Cordes looked at the photograph and nodded. "That's her, no mistake, same grim face."

"Thank you for that. You'll be happy to know that this woman is a British subject, a civilian who works for the Student Foreign Exchange here in London. She's not a Russian officer. Why would she come to you with forged documents and authorization, disguised as a Soviet officer?"

Cordes shrugged her shoulders.

"Really?"

"I want another officer present who can witness our agreement before I make any more statements to you."

Calvin was impressed. Young Bertha Cordes was indeed a professional, probably trained by the Abwehr. "Very well." Calvin exited the room and came back a short time later with Colonel Stephens. Calvin made all the introductions and assured Cordes that their accord would be honored.

"All right," she said. "The Russian or imposter asked why Krupke fled back to portions of the Third Reich. I knew the answer, so I told her. He fled because he was after advanced Wonder Weapons hidden by RHSA. He knew their whereabouts and the location of the scientist and wanted to recover them so he could cut a deal with the Americans."

Chapter 31

Colonel Vladimir Sivan used his movement orders and took the military train to Warsaw. There, he spent the night and regrouped his notes for the investigative work he'd done thus far. Just as he and NII-9 suspected, the Nazis were indeed working on a more advanced guidance system for their A-4 rockets. It also appeared that the best source of information didn't come from local informants, but rather forest rangers. He would focus his human intelligence on these sources. Also, it appeared the Nazis were hiding key scientists deep in portions of the Third Reich, which was now in Poland. These scientists also didn't have the freedom of movement as did the von Braun team back in Southern Germany and Bavaria. It appeared that many of these gyro experts were forced to continue their research up until the closing days of the war. It was believed by high command that these scientists would somehow come up with a new discovery that would ultimately enable Hitler to turn the tide of the war, especially against the Soviets. It was a futile mistake. The Red Army assured that it would never happen with an assault on Berlin with over two million men.

Sivan now focused his investigation on the Blizna launch complex. He and the NII-9 team were the first to investigate the site back in April 1945, just after the Red Army overran the compound. There, they spent several weeks tuning over every rock and boulder looking for advanced missile components. Almost everything was destroyed or missing. They only found a few rocket engines, fuel tanks, and some crude gyro equipment. They didn't even find operational guidance or flight hardware for actual A-4 launches, nor scientists.

He decided to go back to Blizna and interview the local forest rangers there. Except this time, he would be armed with a 7.26 mm Tokarev submachine gun and its thirty-five round drum magazine. By default, Sivan discovered that these forest rangers had worked closely with the Nazi launch teams, mainly because they told the Nazis where the best spots were for firing the mobile rockets. By the end of the war, the focus of the A-4 research was on mobile launchers, not fixed sites, for obvious reasons; to get away from the Russian Front and Allied bombers.

The next morning, Sivan took a military train to Krakow and from there he switched to a local train and made the trip to Debica, which was the end of the line for rail traffic in Poland. Once in Debica, he found a Red Army detachment and secured a Jeep to make the trip back to Blizna and the Heidelager Concentration camp. It was all straightforward. The Heidelager camp was situated along a narrow-gauge railing that connected to the actual testing site at Blizna, some twenty-five miles away, located in a heavily wooded area. The camp was just as deserted as he had left it back in April. Most of the buildings were destroyed or burnt to the ground for sanitary reasons.

There was, however, a small detention center located adjacent to the former slave labor facility that housed former Nazi SS guards believed to have committed crimes against humanity and were awaiting trial by Polish authorities. Most of these were women. Sivan decided to interview them before the opportunity was lost. He informed the local camp commander of his desires after showing him the orders signed personally by General Kuznetsov himself.

As it turned out, none of the women knew anything about scientists or rocket launches other than the fact they knew they had taken place in the vicinity. After all, they had heard the noise from the rocket engines as they were ignited. However, they all did say that local forest rangers had helped the Nazis extensively, mainly because of their knowledge of the surrounding wilderness. One even went on to say that in March of 1945 she had witnessed a commando work detail that went to a local quarry to bury some equipment. She did not know anything further except to say she saw an SS man lead a prisoner detail from the slave labor camp to the quarry with large wooden boxes. What was unusual about this is that the commando work details typically left in daylight. This detail departed after dinner, in darkness.

Sivan took note of the event, then made the trip up the mountainside to the actual launch complex at Blizna. This too was almost the same as he had left it. However, a little bit of luck came his way. The local forest rangers had taken over the structures that were still standing and used them as their headquarters. Just as in Tuchola, an elderly man was crewing the station. Sivan informed him of his mission and wanted to look around the area but deep into the launch site. Again, he was told that roads were inaccessible, even by Jeep, and that the only way deep into the launch site was by horseback. An hour later, Sivan was on horseback, riding deep into the forest. This time he wasn't looking for abandoned equipment but rather for forest rangers working in the area. A short time later, he heard the sounds of chain-saws in the distance. He followed the noise until he came to a clearing where a crew of forest rangers was busy cutting a fallen tree and making way for a new road.

Carrying his Tokarev machine gun, Sivan dismounted his horse and confronted the men. There were four. Three were in their late thirties and another was younger, a teenager about sixteen. Sivan focused on him in particular because if he asked the older men, they would probably not give him any information because, as he already knew, most of the Polish forest rangers had collaborated with the Nazis in some way. Sivan introduced himself as a military intelligence officer and asked the young man, "I'm looking for any Nazi rocket scientists that may still be hiding in the area."

The young man responded, "I don't know. Most of the Germans left in the spring of last year."

Sivan asked if the men had any water, which they did, and all the men used this opportunity to take a break and have some water. As they were sitting in the shade sipping from a canteen, Sivan again picked up his interview of the young man. "Tell me, young man, what do you know about the concentration camp located at Pustkow?" The young man told Sivan everything he knew but said that the forest rangers were prohibited from entering the camp. He did say, however, that some rangers brought firewood to the officers.

"What else did they bring besides firewood?" asked Sivan.

The older men gave the young man a stern look, then

one of them said, "The boy doesn't know much. He was not working for the rangers at that time."

Sivan changed the topic and moved on. "Well, then what about recently? Have any of you seen anything unusual in the area? Perhaps someone lurking about. Maybe an American who speaks Polish and German fluently?"

Sivan reached into his pocket and pulled out a picture of Major Antonio Franko and showed it to the men. None of the men recognized the person in the photograph, so Sivan placed it back in his pocket. Then he tried a different tactic. He was convinced they knew something, he just had to find out what.

"I have reason to believe that some of your local forest rangers are helping the Home Army, a resistance unit. In particular, they're helping an American team that is working in the area looking for key rocket technology. I must remind you that the Soviet Union now has occupation status over Poland. These resisters are subverting our political ideology. They will be punished for this resistance. We are in control of all administrative jurisdictions, including local police districts. Perhaps some of you know these Home Army resisters?" Sivan asked and waited patiently for a response. There was none.

"Very well, please give me your names and where I can reach you for further questioning," he said as he pulled out a pad. "I will return with a full security detail."

Upon hearing this, the boy was nervous and said, "I do not know the rangers in particular, none of us do, but I can tell you that I did see two rangers, along with one civilian the other day lurking about the abandoned quarry."

Sivan was now very curious given the recent information about the quarry from the female SS guards.

The young man told Sivan that gypsum and gravel were mined at the quarry and the Nazis had used slave labor to bring rock, sand, and gravel up to the hillside in the construction of the camps. Once the camps were finished, the Nazis no longer needed the aggregate, so they abandoned the quarry.

This was something, so Sivan decided to push his luck. He reached into his tunic and pulled out a wad of cash and counted out several bills in Polish denomination and handed it to the boy. It was the equivalent of six months' salary. "It's yours, thank you for the information."

Then Sivan counted out more bills, the equivalent of one year's salary, and looked at the three older men. "What could two rangers and a civilian possibly do at the abandoned quarry?" He held up the cash, waiting for the other rangers to speak.

Finally, one spoke. "As you said, I do know that a group of rangers helped the Home Army during the war. It was a very active group. It was called the AK-22 Ranger Battalion. They even helped the British recover a fully intact V-2 rocket back in 1944. Their activities were largely a myth, since most of us were never involved with that particular group. Word just spread among us. The group disbanded after the war. Their leader was a woman."

"Any idea of where I can find more information about this group, AK-22, and the woman?"

Again, the older man spoke, "You'll have to go to Debica. Try the Roman Catholic cathedral of Saint Jadwiga. The Home Army used the church as a headquarters during the war."

Chapter 32

Colonel Dimitri Pavel sat in his office in Krakow. He had nothing to do now that the elusive Home Army team had slipped through his grasp. He also understood that spying was waiting. Sooner or later, someone would slip up or divulge a minute detail that would enable his Third Department to break the case. He instructed his security detail to be on alert for signals or message traffic coming in from the center that would provide any leads to the where-abouts of the mysterious female British agent. He stood in front of the window, looking down on the streets of Krakow. The inhabitants were still recovering from the war. Many were unemployed. Some were scrounging around the devastated city looking for firewood or food. His thoughts were interrupted by the ring from the secure telephone with a direct connection to Moscow Center. He picked up the receiver and answered, "Colonel Pavel."

The voice on the other end indicated that a secure message was on its way, 'Eyes Only" via teleprinter. Pavel secured the telephone line and proceeded over to the teleprint machine located in his office. He stood over the device and waited. A short time later, the teleprint came to life and printed the message. He waited for the entire message to print out before he read. It was a fairly short report from the center detailing information from their *highest sources* intelligence. The statement read as follows:

TO: PAVEL
FROM: MOSCOW CENTER
RE: HIGHEST SOURCES INTELLIGENCE
SOURCE INDICATES POSITIVE IDENTITY OF
FEMALE BRITISH AGENT SEARCHING FOR
KRUPKE
SOURCE INDICATES AGENT NAME IS VIVIAN
TATE FORMER SOE OFFICER WITH POSSIBLE
TIES TO SIS BEFORE THE WAR
BELIEVED TO BE WORKING WITH POLISH
HOME ARMY RESISTANCE UNITS AK22 RANGER
BATTALION WELL FINANCED POSSIBLY BY AMIS
BELIEVED TO BE LOOKING FOR SECRET
WEAPONS LEFT BEHIND BY RSHA
DOSSIER ON VIVIAN TATE TO FOLLOW
END

This was the break he had been waiting for. However, he had to wait for Tate to make her move. Sooner or later, she or her network would divulge information on their whereabouts. That's when he would make his move.

* * *

AT THE SAME TIME, Colonel Vladimir Sivan was taking matters into his own hands with his investigation on the technical front. It was time to activate the full resources of the GRU. Unlike the NKVD, the GRU did not employ career intelligence support personnel. They took assets from regular Red Army units, many untrained in the tradecraft. On this day, Sivan was allocated four men from other GRU detachments. Two were central Asian conscripts used primarily as muscle men, the other two were non-commissioned officers with very little training. They were more administrative in support than operational. However, as was the case with the GRU, Sivan accepted the assets. He would need all four men to help interrogate the Monsignor at Saint Jadwiga's church.

Sivan used a rusted, dented military truck to make the trip to Debica and Saint Jadwiga's church. There, the five men entered the rectory. Father Florek was a head pastor at Saint Jadwiga. He was in his late fifties, of medium height, with short black hair combed back against his head. He addressed Colonel Sivan as the men entered the rectory holding machine guns.

"What is the meaning of this outrage? Why have you come in this manner?"

Sivan put down his weapon and indicated to the other men to do the same. "My name is Sivan of Soviet military intelligence. I have come to ask you a few questions regarding the Home Army resistance network you assisted during the war."

Father Florek knew that it was foolish to deny knowledge of this. It was an open fact among the local populous that Saint Jadwiga had assisted the resistance during the war. He proceeded with this angle. "There was a war going on. The Nazis were everywhere. Some even took non-Jews away. Naturally, we did everything we could to save the lives of innocent civilians."

Sivan pointed to a chair and indicated he wished to take a seat. Father Florek motioned for him to have a seat on the soft sofa chair. Sivan sat down and spoke. "We are not here to arrest you or seize your church. All we want is information. Specifically, a name. A name of a person you personally helped during the war. She was head of the local resistance unit, AK-22 Ranger Battalion. We are not going to hurt this person or arrest her. All we want to do is ask her a few questions about her war effort. We know you allowed her to use these facilities as their headquarters. So, tell me, Father, what is this person's name?"

Father Florek sat in his chair, contemplating a response.

Finally, Sivan spoke. "We're not leaving here until you tell us her name."

"Very well," said Father Florek. "She goes by the code name Jawor. No one is really sure of her actual name. She went by many."

"Where can I find her, this Jawor?"

"The last I heard she was working as the hotel manager at the Hotel Bristol in Tarnow. You should try there first."

"All right, that will do. What about any Americans? We have information that an American is operating here in the vicinity looking for former Nazi scientists and weapons left behind after the war. Do you know of such a person?"

Father Florek was surprised to hear this piece of information from the Russians because he had heard rumors that an American officer had been ecently seen near Pustkow. "Colonel, I can only tell you what I've heard. I have no direct knowledge and have not seen the person you're referencing, but I can say that there have been rumors of an American officer seen near Pustkow."

"And when would that have been?" asked Sivan.

"Recently, perhaps just a few days ago but less than a week."

The city of Tarnow was only a half-hour drive away

from Saint Jadwiga's church. Sivan and his four GRU agents arrived in the city by early evening. They had no trouble finding the Hotel Bristol. It was located across the street from the train station. As they drove by the hotel, Sivan noticed several Soviet military vehicles parked in front and on the side streets of the hotel. Also, he could see several uniformed Red Army soldiers lingering about. Something was odd about this scene. He decided to park the truck around the corner and investigate further. Sivan and the four men walked into the hotel and saw very quickly that had been taken over by the Red Army. An NCO was sitting at the desk filling out paperwork as Sivan approached. Once the young NCO saw a GRU colonel at the front desk, he dropped everything and asked, "What can I do for you, Comrade Colonel?"

Sivan removed his cap and answered, "I'm looking for the hotel manager."

"I'm sorry, sir, this hotel has been requisitioned by the Red Army. There is no hotel manager. I'm in charge of billeting and room assignments." Just then, three rambunctious Red Army conscripts came down the stairs and exited the hotel. It was probably too late. If a Home Army resistance fighter was the hotel manager, she was, in all likelihood, long gone by now. "I'm looking for a woman who goes by the name Jawor. Does that name sound familiar to you, Sergeant?"

"Afraid not, sir. I can tell you that this establishment was only recently requisitioned by the Red Army after state security personnel interviewed the hotel staff. Evidently, the proprietor committed suicide, and all staff members vanished shortly after that. The hotel was basically abandoned. She must have been hiding something or someone significant."

Sivan was now intrigued about the whole situation. He

then asked the young Red Army NCO where he could find the state security personnel who conducted the interview so he could ask them more information on the situation. The NCO was told that state security personnel never divulge their whereabouts or names of individuals. Sivan knew this but decided to ask anyway. Then Sivan asked to see the office of the proprietor, but again, he was told by the young clerk that state security already gone through the entire office and taken everything away. All that was left was a wastebasket. That room was now being used as a billet for enlisted personnel.

"Do you have quarters?" asked the Red Army clerk. "I can offer you and your staff a room. I have a very nice suite on the top floor. Probably used by the very elite and wealthy. The four other men will have to share a room, however."

Sivan decided he might as well take the clerk up on his offer. The Hotel Bristol would do as a temporary head-quarters until he could find out more about the elusive gyros, and in particular the American officer who might know of their existence. He would wait here until he could get further information. "I'm going to need a telephone in my room, a teleprinter, and a direct, secure connection to the Kremlin."

"That will not be a problem. Do you have luggage?"

Sivan nodded. "I'll have my men bring everything in."

Now it was a game of waiting. Sivan knew he was closing in on the elusive resistance fighters and the American. It was only a matter of time. He would start his waiting game by having all signals intelligence forwarded to the Hotel Bristol. He would have his men begin by analyzing the message traffic, in particular, any information transmitted by the US M-209 decoding device.

Chapter 33

Antoni Franko, along with Morena, made their way down to the garage at Zglobice Mansion. It was after four in the evening. The sun set early this time of year, and with the heavy overcast skies, it was already getting dark when the two arrived at the garage. Morena brought another basket of food and water for the four men resting at the facility. Just as Jawor mentioned, a local Home Army guard was already positioned at the door providing security. He let Franko and Morena in as the four men came to their feet. It was cold in the garage, and the men were covered with extra blankets. Not surprisingly, Krupke spoke up.

"This place is freezing. We had a difficult time getting some sleep. How long will we be here at this godforsaken place?"

Morena dropped the basket of food and water on the floor as Franko addressed the men. "We brought you something to eat; help yourself." All four men reached into the basket and grabbed something.

Morena spoke next, acting on Vivian Tate's instructions. "It's around four in the afternoon. It will be dark soon. Our escape vehicles will be here shortly. We'll leave by midnight. That gives you another six or seven hours here in the garage. I suggest you eat something. I don't know when we'll have the opportunity to get more food."

While the men were eating, Franko found another wooden box and used it as a stool. He sat near the men, who were standing on their feet, eating away. "There's not much we can do except wait for the Home Army to arrive with our vehicles." Franko reached into his pocket and pulled out his notepad. He focused on Hoch and Mangus as per Vivian Tate's request, keeping his distance from Krupke.

"I'd like to go back and talk about the high-altitude tests conducted by the V-2. Specifically, re-entry into the earth's atmosphere. You must have had difficulties in re-entry concerning your larger rockets. You know, the ones capable of hitting New York or Washington. How did you plan on penetrating your warheads through the upper reaches of the atmosphere without burning up the vehicle?"

Dr. Hoch answered while chewing a mouthful of bread and sausage. "We conducted high-altitude tests using smaller sounding rockets launched from Leba. These smaller, sounding rockets reached altitudes over one hundred and fifty thousand feet. We tried a variety of materials, but none were successful given the thrust-to-weight ratio. Then we experimented with lighter-weight, honeycombed material made of ceramic. These proved the most successful for re-entry."

Franko wasn't expecting to hear any answer to the question, let alone the revelation on the honeycomb material. He jotted the points on his notepad and continued.

"When we get to Walbrzych, I'll request the air support for your EXFIL. Naturally, G-2 intelligence staff in Frankfurt may want more information to justify your EXFIL. So, this new bit of information will greatly help your cause."

Both Hoch and Mangus revealed all they knew about ballistic tests as Franko noted everything on his notepad. Even the fact that the Nazis were working on a super rocket called the A-9 and A-10. It was a piloted vehicle ordered by Hitler to attack American cities. The pilot would eject during reentry after he steered the vehicle to its target. Unfortunately, no human would survive a three thousand mile per hour reentry. It was a maniacal, one-way mission. Blue-prints of these rockets were on the micro dots in the sheet music. "You've been a tremendous help. I'll make sure this gets in my report. In the meantime, I'll bring you more blankets and some hot tea. They're forecasting light snow tonight."

Next, Franko turned to Krupke. He wanted to find out more about Soviet abilities to intercept coded messages from the M-209 coding device.

"Earlier, you eluded to the fact that the Soviets could intercept our coded messages. Can you elaborate more on the subject?"

Krupke sat on one of the wooden boxes containing the gyros. "They have machines that can do the work for them. It's a slow, laborious process, but they can intercept and de-code your messages. The M-209 in particular. Usually, within three to seven days is what I was told."

Franko thought about his last transmission using the M-209. If they were lucky, they would just get to the EXFIL point before the Soviets intercepted his communications. "What about the Joan-Eleanor S-phone?"

"As with our services, that is almost impossible to intercept." Krupke noticed Franko seemed visibly worried after the mention of the interception of the M-209 device. He decided to focus his attention on that. "Tell me, Major, have you sent any messages with the coding device? If so, how many, and how often did you transmit?"

Franko was now curious about the Soviet efforts to decode his latest transmission. "I sent one message. It was a progress report. We have a weekly SCHED set up to transmit on the JE, every Monday night at 0300 hours Zulu time. I usually use that. The next JE is set for tomorrow night. If I don't come on the air at the appointed time, we try the following week again. If I still don't make contact after the third and fourth attempt, then Home Station will assume I'm under Soviet control."

"Tell me you didn't transmit our location over the coding device?"

"No, of course not, but I did indicate we were on the move."

"When did you transmit?"

"I composed the message three days ago and sent it off by courier for transmission. I don't know when it was transmitted. Probably no more than a day or two after I couriered the message."

Krupke inched closer to Franko. "It will take them longer than that to decode. Lucky for us, we are on the move. Let me ask you another question. Off topic. The woman, Jankowski, the one you call Agena. Can you trust her?"

This was not part of Vivian's script. So, Franko decided to improvise. "She's been trustworthy in the past. I have no reason to doubt her loyalty."

"Yes, but this is a different kind of mission, am I correct? She's actually going with us all the way. I assume she didn't make the EXFIL with you on your last assignment?"

Franko nodded in agreement.

Krupke went on. "Do you think there is a possibility

she'll divulge our location to the Soviets? After all, she claims to be a capitalist. She could betray us for money."

"No, I have no reason to mistrust her."

"Good, then we will have two or three-days' head start on the Soviets before they close in on us. Get rid of the coding device if you haven't already done so."

Just then, the garage door opened and Jawor and Vivian Tate entered. Vivian had extra blankets and some hot tea. Jawor did all the talking. "The timeline has been stepped up," she said. "The Home Army vehicles will be here by eleven o'clock. We leave then."

* * *

THE FIRST COURIER leg was uneventful. There was little traffic on the roads. Home Army came through and provided the vehicles and a driver for the truck. The first night, at Bielsko-Biala, the team slept during the day in relative comfort at a local safe house provided by the Home Army. The vehicles and gyros were secured in a barn adjacent to the safe house and were protected by Home Army guards. The three women slept in the upstairs bedroom of the safe house, while the men took over the basement. The second leg from Bielsko-Biala to Nysa was more difficult. It snowed all day at the stopover in Bielsko-Biala. When the team assembled for the trip to Nysa, their courier informed them that the primary road was closed due to snowpack and they'd have to take an alternate route, a route closer to the Czech border and mountains. The vehicles would use more petrol going up and down the roads than initially planned. Therefore, a fuel stop would be necessary at Nysa to continue the journey to Walbrzych.

Vivian Tate made the decision to refuel before the team went to the safe house at Nysa for rest. This meant that the team would have to wait for first daylight, around six in the morning, for the petrol crew to arrive at the fueling station, exposing the entire team. She felt the risk was worth taking because if they waited until midnight to refuel, the fueling station might be closed. Thus, they'd have to wait several hours until daylight for the station to reopen. This would put them way behind schedule. At this point in the mission, time was of the essence.

The petrol station was located adjacent to an automotive garage near the rail tracks and manned by former Home Army personnel. Vivian paid cash to refuel all three vehicles. As the team finished refueling and everyone climbed aboard their respective vehicles, Franko came over to Vivian's car, making sure he was not seen or heard by the Germans riding in the truck. He handed Vivian a folded piece of paper. She unfolded the paper and began to read what was on the paper.

"I found this nailed to a wall inside the fueling station. Luckily, the Germans were inside the truck and didn't see it."

What Vivian saw was a 'Wanted' poster with her picture on it. The Soviets were looking for the woman accused of aided and abating former Nazi war criminals. The poster was offering a cash reward for any information, dead or alive, on the woman who was also a British agent. Any information was to be passed on to the local law enforcement agency. They even gave her name, Vivian Tate. She was shocked to see the poster.

Franko leaned inside the cab, closer to Vivian, and placed his hand on her shoulder. "They're closing in on us. They know who you are now. How did they get this information?"

Vivian leaned her head back into the seat and let out a sigh. "Merde, I don't know. I took all the necessary precautions. The facts are the facts. They got the information from someone or somewhere." She handed the wanted poster to Jawor, who was in the driver's seat. She too was surprised to see the sign.

"It's a good thing we dyed your hair blonde. This picture has you as a brunette."

Vivian continued. "It doesn't matter anyway. We'll have to alter our plans slightly. Most importantly, we've got to keep this information from Krupke. If he finds out, he'll most certainly put something together. Especially if he sees the name Vivian Tate. We've been fortunate thus far; let's keep it that way."

Vivian patted Franko's hand, more a sign of reassurance rather than affection. "I'll make contact with you in Nysa to discuss this further."

* * *

THE SOVIETS WERE on firmer footing too. NKVD relied on paid informants for information. There were no shortages of Communist sympathizers who would provide any information for a chance to advance in the Communist hierarchy. They had spies everywhere. Colonel Pavel, now in possession of the identity of the female British operative, had posters made with her picture plastered in all public places. Mostly train, tram, and bus stations as well as local eateries, taverns, and petrol stations. Sooner or later, someone would provide a lead.

Colonel Sivan, on the other hand, relied on signals traffic and decoded messages coming in from Moscow. Most of the signals traffic that came in was from former Home Army officials trying to lead resistance movements against Soviet expansion plans. Thus far, they had not come across any signals traffic indicating an American was operating in the field. On the third day after taking over the Hotel Bristol, Sivan received a coded message from Moscow Center. It indicated that a message transmitted by an American M-209 coding device had been transmitted from the vicinity of Krakow. Sivan read the decoded message. He knew that Giant Killer was the name for US Army G-2 intelligence staff, Frankfurt. Redstone was, in lall ikelihood, the code name for the American operative.

King Six was obviously the name for someone or something, possibly the gyros. He was almost positive the message indicated the team was on the move to the EXFIL point. He had to intercept them. What he could not determine at this point was if the woman known as Jawor was helping the American or if the American was acting alone. He pulled out a map of the local area and began searching for possible escape routes out of Poland. He tried to put himself in the American's position. The railway was out of the question. They would probably use the roads, but which roads? It would probably be close to the Czech border. Next, the message indicated they were headed to a rendezvous point. Most likely a clandestine airfield. He looked at the map closer and saw the town of Nysa, mostly flat terrain. He would start his search there. He would relocate his team to Nysa and search the area.

Colonel Pavel got the break he was looking for. A young man, at a petrol stop in Nysa, informed NKVD that a Soviet motorcade had come by and refueled three vehicles. All three vehicles bore Red Army stars. The interesting fact about this fuel stop was that a woman, who resembled the one on the wanted photograph, had paid for the fuel in US dollars. Pavel immediately called his team and informed them they were re-deploying to Nysa. The noose was tightening up around the Checkmate team.

Chapter 34

The town of Neisse was heavily damaged during the Soviet, Vistula-Oder Offensive in the spring 1945. The Red Army pushed the German Army Group A out of southwest Poland. Many of the historic sites of the town were totally destroyed by Soviet artillery. Most, if not all, the infrastructure was rendered useless.

In November of 1945, Neisse was slowly being rebuilt. One of the first buildings to be restored was the Church of Saint Franciszka on the north bank of the Nysa-Klodzka river. The old tile roof had been heavily damaged but was repaired. It was the perfect location for the Checkmate teams to use as a rest stop and safe house since construction vehicles came on and off the property and left tire tracks gouged into the surrounding grounds. No one would notice their vehicles.

Jawor drove the lead vehicle with their Home Army courier in the front passenger seat. Vivian, as usual, sat in the back seat. As the convoy pulled up to the church, the courier went to the main gate and opened it. He motioned for the vehicles to enter, and then they drove to the back of the compound. They parked the vehicles inside a storage facility that held all three vehicles easily. Once the vehicles were secured, the courier handed the team off to Father Fenci, who was the local Home Army contact. Father Fenci led the group inside the main abby and down to the basement. He told Jawor that they would have a place to sleep inside the abby, but he told them to remain in the basement for the time being until Home Army scouts could determine if the team had been followed. Once it was clear, he would come down and escort them to their quarters.

A short time later, Franko was escorted into his small room on the second floor of the abby. A monk told him that the quarters were used by Franciscan monks, and thus the furnishings were meager. There was a small bed, nightstand, lamp, and chamber pot; nothing more. The shared bathroom was down the hall. A recently replaced small window looked out onto the back cemetery and church grounds, which at the moment were torn up by construction vehicles. The monk told Franko that the team would leave the abby sometime during the night. It was now around noon. The team had been up most of the night, and Franko was extremely exhausted. All he wanted to do was fall into the small bed and sleep. After pulling the thin blanket over his body, he fell fast asleep.

Franko slept most of the day. He awoke and looked at his watch. It was dark outside. He turned on the small lamp and looked closer at his watch. The dial showed it was five-thirty in the evening. He got up and looked around the small room and saw a white envelope had been pushed under the door. He fetched the envelope and opened it. It was a note from Vivian Tate. She told him to use the bathroom down the hall to freshen up and come back to his room when finished. She would make contact with him shortly after that.

Franko did as he was told and came back to his room a short time later. As he unlocked and opened the door, he noticed the lights were out but could tell that someone was there. The room had a layer of cigarette smoke from someone recently. Franko had not smoked a cigarette in two days, so he knew it wasn't from him. That's when he heard her voice.

"Keep the lights off." It was Vivian.

"Where are you?" he asked.

A light flicked on from a lighter as Vivian lit another cigarette. Franko could make out Vivian Tate naked in his bed with the sheets and blanket pulled over her body. He could see Vivian's bare shoulders but her breasts were covered by the thin sheets and blankets. A pile of clothes lay on the floor next to the bed. She had her legs pulled up tight against her body. Not surprisingly, Franko was dumbfounded by the sight. Vivian took a drag from her cigarette, then put it out in the ashtray on the nightstand. Franko moved closer and sat on the edge of the bed, as Vivian switched the light on from the nightstand.

"I'm not going to ask you how you got in here. You know, you should think about quitting. It was a dead giveaway. I haven't had a cigarette in days. Anyway, I thought I had the door closed and locked?"

"I had Father Fenci open the door for me. I didn't sleep a wink. I was up all day, thinking."

"Given the recent discoveries and the wanted posters, I can see why you couldn't sleep."

"I've come up with an alternate plan."

Franko inched closer to Vivian. "Why is it that you keep putting me in a state of utter bewilderment with your behavior?"

"It's because I'm the most experienced member of the team."

Vivian reached under the covers and pulled out a worn, folded map. She turned it around to face Franko. "I received an intelligence update today. The Home Army and their Polish intelligence assets are still extremely capable. For how long, I don't know. The Soviets appear to be moving into Eastern Europe with a vengeance. Taking over one country after another. It seems these war-torn citizens would rather bow down to the Russians instead of the Germans. They're tired of devastation and destruction.

"Anyway, as of yesterday, the clandestine airstrip in Walbrzych has been compromised. Originally, it was usable. Home Army reported the airfield was never used, just an occasional Red Army transport, and most of those landings were daylight operations. Nothing at night. That's all changed. Probably since my identity was leaked. Soviet transports have been reported landing at all times of the day and night. No doubt Soviet intelligence services are relocating. Also, Home Army told me that Motyl has been abandoned. It's no longer under Soviet control."

"That's great news, so why don't we just reverse course and go back to Tarnow?"

"Too risky. The Soviets will cover our retreat options. Possibly even set up an ambush, especially with my picture plastered all over the place. Besides, word travels fast in these parts. Since word got out that we're leading a group of Nazi scientists out of the country, it seems Home Army is inundated with former Nazi scientists coming out of the woodwork, literally, seeking safe passage to the American sector. They've asked me what to do about them. I told them, for the time being, it's too risky to take them out. It could also be a trap set by the Soviets. Plus, you'll have to authenticate their credibility, and that would take way too long. There's too many of them as well. It did, however, give me an idea. It's called a double-sting operation. If there's one thing I've learned in all my years in this business it's this: if done properly, double and triple operations can and will overwhelm the enemy and put us in the advantage."

"What did you have in mind?"

Vivian used the map on the bed to show him. "First, since the airfield at Walbrzych is compromised, and they're expecting us, let's not disappoint them. We'll let them believe we're on the move to that location. We need to get one or both of the Soviet intelligence services to take the bait. That's where you'll come in. Remember, you have blanket movement orders signed by the Allied Control Commission giving you an authorization for movements anywhere in occupied territories. You'll send out a fake message over unsecured telegraph lines, indicating you're moving to the rail station at Gluszyca-Gorna to transport the bodies of missing US airmen found in Poland. You'll even use your own name and authorization. The Soviets, in particular Colonel Sivan of the GRU, will get word of this and surmise that you're not transporting human remains but something, possibly V-2 flight hardware, and will go for the roundup. Of course, the coffins won't have the bodies, and you'll be nowhere near Gluszyca, but it will get the GRU off our tail."

"Okay, assuming Sivan bites, then what? We still have to get out of the country, and we'll still have the NKVD to worry about?"

"Let me show you something on the map. During this trip, as we've moved from one location to another, we've gotten more intelligence. Each courier line that hands us off to the next seems to have a little more vital information I didn't have before. Here it is." Vivian pointed to a small town called Ludwikowice-Klodzkie in the Owl Mountains of Lower Silesia close to the Czech border.

"Home Army couriers informed me today that they are operating a safe house located at regional headquarters for the forestry department." She pointed to the location on the map. "It's practically a fortress castle in itself. We can use that as a temporary base of operations to conduct our EXFIL. It's totally secure, and more importantly, they have all the COM equipment necessary to contact home station and transmit our bluff messages. Home Army also tells me that this area saw no fighting during the war. The Germans and the Soviets bypassed the area completely."

"Why is that so?" asked Franko.

"Let me show you something extraordinary." Vivian pulled out an aerial photograph of the area and showed it to Franko. "Our Home Army contacts gave this to me. It's supposedly the Wenceslaus mines, but during hostilities, the Nazis used this facility as a top-secret research facility. It's called *Der Riese* or Giant in English. When I first heard this information, I didn't put two and two together, but after last night when I couldn't sleep, it all hit me. Didn't you say that Poldi told you about a facility used by the Nazis to conduct experiments on technological devices?"

"Yeah, something about a perpetual motion machine."

"Or, antigravity device! Remember when I told you I interviewed Krupke's mistress and she told me Krupke was going after high-technology, in particular, antigravity devices?"

Franko nodded.

"Well, Home Army tells me that this top-secret research facility was used for the testing of just such a device. They also told me the Wenceslaus mines were the disguise for the facility. Massive amounts of slave labor were used in the construction of this facility. A huge construction and logistical operation existed there. In addition, key SS personnel and equipment were transported into and out of the area using a clandestine airstrip adjacent to the forestry office." She pointed to the airfield on her aerial photo. "You can't see this airfield from any roads in the surrounding area. It's perfect for our EXFIL."

"Are you suggesting we change our plans and use this as the EXFIL point?"

"Precisely. There's also something very intriguing about the Der Riese facility. Toward the end of the war, when the Nazis realized the gig was up and the Soviets would overwhelm their forces, the SS made the decision to destroy the secret research facility. Home Army tells me that all equipment, personnel, and slave labor, were either killed or destroyed to prevent anything and everything from falling into Soviet hands. The place was completely sanitized. The Nazis called it Strategic Evacuation."

Franko rubbed his face, contemplating the information. "Whatever they were doing there was obviously so secret the Nazis didn't want anyone to know, including the Western Allies."

Vivian folded up her map and photograph. "This piece of information gave me the spark to initiate my double-sting operation. Here's what I want you to do. First, we need to find out more about this facility. I think Krupke knows more than what he's leading us to believe about this area. It could also be a double-bluff deception, planned to unmask my identity by Krupke and his mistress. Remember, Cordes told me and me only about the antigravity device. If we mention it to Krupke, it might signal to him that we're under MI-6 control."

"Yes, I see your point. We've got to get Krupke to make the first bark."

"Exactly. Later today, we're going to have a meeting

with all members present on the Checkmate team, including the Germans. We'll have Jawor and Morena take the lead and divulge our current situation to everyone and put out the necessity for an alternate plan. They'll disclose we're moving to the Forest Ranger Battalion Headquarters to sit it out for a few days to assess the security situation and the need to come up with an alternate staging location. We'll even show the Germans our position on the map. Remember, up to this point they've been kept in the dark as to our exact location. This has to get Krupke's attention, to know we're near the Der Riese facility.

"When I'm not around, I want you to squeeze him. Ask him for help. See if he knows of anything that could help us throw the Soviets off our tail. Hopefully, he'll take the bait and divulge more."

"All right, so let's assume he does take the bait. We don't initiate the knowledge of the antigravity device, and he divulges it for our sake. What will that accomplish?"

Vivian smiled. "We use that knowledge to pass on to the Soviets, in addition to your fake movement of Allied airmen. Let's call it sweetening the pot."

"You're ruthless." Franko now asked an essential question that Vivian had failed to mention in her plan. "What about the NKVD? How do you plan on throwing them off our trail?"

"It's the riskiest part of the plan. Let me show you," Vivian said as she once again pulled out her map from under the covers. "The rail station at Gluszyca has a post office adjacent to it. This post office has a telegraph network. Once you coordinate the fake movement of the Allied airmen, I will simultaneously send an urgent distress message to my contacts in London, indicating we're on the run from the Soviets. If the NKVD is smart, they'll have all their emitters on the lookout for just such message traffic. They will then send in all their resources to Gluszyca to intercept us. Of course, Krupke and the gyros will be nowhere near Gluszyca. We'll all be at the forestry office rendezvous location, waiting pickup by transport. So, you and I have to temporarily put ourselves at risk, but it will be enough to throw the enemy off our tail."

"All right, you're the expert. Just tell me what to do, and I'll make it happen concerning sending out my messages and the Wonder Weapons. But this new airfield. I don't know anything about it. I'll have to do an airfield assessment to see if conditions are right for a landing. It will have to support the weight of the transports, not to mention takeoff and landing criteria."

"Yes, I know that. I've already come up with a plan." Vivian once again used her map to show Franko. "Along this road, which borders the north eastern side of the mines, the Ranger Headquarters is a short hike to the airfield. You can cut across the woods to make your daylight and night assessments without being seen."

Franko looked at the location of the airfield and the location of the Ranger Headquarters and agreed that it was doable. "I'll need more photographs and surveys of the site to conduct my assessment of the airfield."

Vivian gave him the aerial photo. "You can have a look at this for starters," she said as she slid under the covers, moved the sheet up over her shoulders, and laid her head on the pillow.

Franko took the map and photograph and began studying the material. He got up from the bed and paced the room, taking in details of Vivian's plan. Her plan seemed to fit, but would it be successful? He'd have to see if the C-47s could takeoff and land at the location, not to mention support the weight of the aircraft. Also, as a technical expert, he wanted to find out more about what the

Nazis had been up to at Die Riese. He was in such deep thought that he actually lost track of time. He placed the map back on the foot of the bed. That's when he noticed Vivian. She was sound asleep in his bed, out like a light. *What am I going to do about her?* he thought. Then he placed his jacket on top of her and sat on the edge of the bed. He did nothing but stare at her beautiful face.

Chapter 35

Home Army rangers woke the Checkmate team up around eleven at night and escorted them to the central kitchen, which was located at the back of the abbey. It was a temporary area set up just for the Checkmate team in a secluded section. They all sat around a large wooden table. There was a pitcher of water and a large platter containing slices of meat and cheese. A basket of brown bread rounded out their meal. Vivian sat on one side of the table across from Franko, Krupke ,and the two scientists. Poldi sat next to Vivian. As soon as the team had plated their meals, Home Army personnel entered and showed Jawor and Morena in. The rangers left and closed the door. Jawor and Morena were holding various maps and drawings, and it looked as if they were getting ready to present a university lecture. Acting on Vivian Tate's instructions, the two women had a look of utter despair in their eyes. Jawor spoke first as she placed her material on the table and began dishing up her servings from the platters.

"I trust that each of you had a good rest because you'll need it after what we're about to tell you."

Morena moved next to Franko and unrolled a map in front of him. Jawor continued her speech. "I want everyone to listen very carefully. Something's come up. Our Home Army escorts have provided us some precious information regarding our passage to the West. I won't sugar-coat this so I'll just tell you like it is. First, we've been informed that the Soviets are on our tail. Some of us on the team have had our identities compromised, and the Russians have relocated to try and round us up. How they got this information is not known to any of us at this time, but it's safe to say it doesn't matter. The Soviets are closing in, both the GRU and NKVD. They even know we're evacuating former Nazi scientists."

Jawor unrolled her map and showed the rest of the team. She pointed to their current location in Nysa and their EXFIL site in Gluszyca. "Our clandestine airfield at Gluszyca has been compromised, and the Soviets are positioning themselves in the area to facilitate a roundup. Therefore, we have to abandon our plans and come up with an alternate. Fortunately, a little bit of luck has come our way, and here it is," she said, and she pointed to Ludwikowice-Klodzkie and the Die Riese complex. She briefed everyone on the Ranger Headquarters and the nearby airfield. She told the team they would have to hold up in this location until Franko could conduct an airfield survey and coordinate an airlift operation for the new site. This would, unfortunately, put the team way behind schedule, but under the circumstances, it was their best plan for avoiding the Russians and their security services. She briefed everyone that they would be leaving for the Die Riese location that night and to make sure they got plenty to eat and drink. They would be leaving the church in a few hours.

Jawor sat down at the table and took her place next to

Morena. She then addressed Vivian. "This was not totally unexpected. As you know, things change, and one can never be totally certain a plan will always go according to plan. We are still secure, and as far as my latest intelligence, the Soviets still do not know our current location. They're just deploying to our original escape airfield to facilitate capture or roundup. We still have time before the extreme winter weather sets in."

Acting on her own script to keep Krupke and the scientists in the dark, Vivian said, "I'm not surprised by the Soviets' move. We've known all along that they were one step behind. I'm going to my room and pack my belongings. Please let me know when it's time to leave," she said, and she got up from the table and proceeded out of the kitchen area.

Franko continued to study the map set in front of him. Then he asked the question posed by Vivian to get Krupke's reaction. "How come Home Army knows so much about this place? Why didn't they divulge the location of the Ranger Headquarters to us before?"

Jawor finished chewing her bread and continued. "First of all, we weren't planning on using this location. We were to bypass the Owl Mountains and use the much safer roads in the low areas. Second, Home Army tells me this place has an extremely dark history concerning Nazi war efforts. It was used by the Nazis to conduct scientific research experiments deep underground in the Wenceslaus mine complexes. Huge amounts of slave labor were used in the project. Toward the closing days of the war, the entire complex was strategically evacuated. Many deaths were reported by locals."

Franko now addressed Krupke. "You were at RHSA Headquarters. Your office would have had direct knowledge as to what was going on there. What can you tell me about this area that can help with our escape plans? More importantly, what do the Soviets know about the complex?"

Franko slowly moved the map and aerial photograph toward Krupke so he could get a good look at the area.

Krupke then studied the material put in front of him. He seemed to have a surprised look on his face and didn't say anything for a while. Then he chose his words carefully. "I must speak to you and only you. If something should happen and the Soviets do succeed in capturing any of us, I don't want the information I'm about to tell you in anyone's mind, understand?"

The room was silent, then Franko looked at Jawor and Morena. "Can you give us thirty minutes, alone?"

Jawor looked at Krupke as if to ask if that was enough time. Krupke nodded. "Very well, I think we could all use a little fresh air. What do you say we all take a little walk outside to the back?" She looked at her watch, then said, "We'll be back at twelve thirty. That should be enough time for you two gentlemen." Then she got up, indicating that everyone except Franko and Krupke would stay in the room.

When the room was cleared, Krupke spoke.

"I know of this area. It fell under the jurisdiction of Hanns Kammler, my boss.

"Yes, I was a collector for Operation Lusty. I know who he is."

"Then you know he was responsible for the development of all Wunderwaffens in the Third Reich. The area which we are relocating to was indeed used to conduct advanced research experiments. There were only a select few, I not being one of them, who knew what exactly was going on at the Die Riese facility. My responsibility was only to issue the orders to have the facility strategically evacuated. As far as how that was done, only Kammler can answer that question. Unfortunately, he's dead. We just wanted to make sure that the facility was evacuated and didn't fall into Soviet hands."

Franko, trying to squeeze Krupke, pushed back. "Come on, Major, can you give me an educated guess? Then what did the Soviets know about what was going on at the facility?"

"I'll need a guarantee. That's why I asked if I could speak to you alone."

"Another one? What sort of guarantee?"

"If I tell you what truly went on at this facility, can you broker a parley on my behalf?"

"That all depends on how important your information is."

"What if I told you it was even more important than anything von Braun could bring to the table? A more advanced propulsion system."

"In what regard?"

"Not until we have a deal?"

Franko, again acting on Vivian's advice, said, "Can it facilitate our escape out of Poland?"

"I would say most definitely."

"All right, same rules apply as with the advanced gyros. When we get to the American sector, I will personally vouch for you. But you've got to give me some tangible proof that you know precisely what was going on at this facility."

"I can share what little I know."

"That might not be enough."

"I was expecting you to say that. What if I told you I can get more information? Solid proof, as you say, but it will involve actually making a trip to the Die Riese and retrieving the information ourselves."

"As in a recovery operation?"

"Precisely, but only you and I must make the trip to Die Riese site, no one else."

"Not even a security detail?"

"Especially not even a security detail. If either of us should be caught by the Russians, it will be all over. This information would be too valuable to Mother Russian, and they'd kill all of us without hesitation. And another thing, you must not speak of any of this to anyone. Not even to your Polish colleagues, especially Fräulein Agena/Jankowski."

Franko thought about Vivian. She had left the room and never heard the conversations from that point on. She was still an enigma. *How did she know?* he thought. "All right, agreed. When we get to Die Rise, I'll coordinate the survey op. You'll go with me."

Krupke looked at his watch. "They'll be back in less than twenty minutes. I'll tell you what I know in that time. Nothing more."

Franko looked at his watch. "Go!"

Krupke then began by telling Franko about a device known as, *Die Glocke* or The Bell in English.

Chapter 36

Officially, the township was called Glowna. It was a small village located in Lower Silesia approximately fifty kilometers away from the nearest major city, Ludwikowice-Klodzkie. Here the Checkmate team safely arrived after leaving Nysa in the early hours of November 1945. As per the operating instructions of Vivian Tate, the team safely moved into the forestry office of Nadlesnctwo-Jugow. All the vehicles were stored in an adjacent area away from any roads, making them virtually invisible from the outside world. The forestry office had a small guesthouse, which the team used as their sleeping quarters. Unfortunately, there was only one useful bedroom, and thus the women took it. The men used the stables next door, which was adequate but cold. After getting some rest, Major Franko awoke around ten o'clock in the morning, washed his face and brushed his teeth, then quietly stepped his way to the guesthouse bedroom. He found the bedroom upstairs and softly knocked on the door. He had to see her. Not surprisingly, Vivian Tate answered.

"How were the stables? Were you able to sleep?" she asked.

Franko took Vivian by the arm, closed the door, and the two stepped into a hallway. Franko reached down and held her hand. Vivian responded and caressed his fingers. He started to move his head and lips closer to hers, but she said, "No, please, Tony, not now."

Franko backed off, then released his grip on her hand. "Let's go downstairs then. They have a fire going in the fireplace, and it will be a lot warmer than in the hallway."

Vivian nodded and followed Franko downstairs, grabbing his hand. There was no one in the facility other than the Checkmate team. The rangers were using the main building next door. Franko looked through the curtains and saw the vehicles outside in the driveway as they left them. "It's snowing outside. Did you get a weather forecast from the rangers? This new plan of ours has set us way behind schedule. The winter season will hit soon and could affect the landings."

"Yes, I know that. Ranger Battalion says this will only be light snow today and tomorrow. Lucky for us, we still have another few weeks before the frigid weather and heavy snowfalls hit."

Franko had already de-briefed Vivian on what Krupke had told him concerning the secret weapons at Die Riese, but he asked, "How did you know Krupke would ask me about the secret weapons without you present?"

"Gut feeling."

"Well, you seem to have a knack for these instincts. Anyway, I want to conduct the airfield survey today. I want Krupke to go with me and then have him lead me to the Die Riese site. How do you want me to go about this?"

"How you go about that is up to you. Remember, you're the technical expert."

"Fair enough. Krupke even mentioned to me that he actually knew of the airfield, though he wasn't sure of the location or its condition. The tasking orders simply came across his desk, and he signed the authorization."

"The only way to get to the airfield and Die Riese without causing suspicion is by horseback. Luckily, Ranger Battalion has enough for you to use. After all, you did sleep in the barn with them. You'll have a ranger to escort you. They claim the individual they're loaning us is well knowledgeable of these areas. Also, I want Morena to go along to provide security. I don't want Krupke to make a move against us, just in case a Soviet patrol comes along, and he decides things aren't going his way."

"Okay, I'll make sure he understands this. Also, I need a camera, preferably two rolls of film to go along."

"Approved, I'll ask the rangers. I'm sure they can come up with one. Now for the double-ruse operation. Leave the details to me. I'll work on that while you're doing the survey. When you get back, I'll have it worked out."

"I do have one last request. I haven't had a real bath in days. Do you think we can get one here?"

Vivian smiled. "You said it yourself. I'm not used to working in the field. I could use one myself. When you get back this afternoon, I'll have something." Then she said something that indicated something more was in store for them when they cleaned up. "Maybe then," she added.

* * *

FRANKO, Morena, Krupke, and their ranger escort left the battalion stables shortly after twelve o'clock. The team munched on a simple breakfast of hard-boiled eggs and cold pork. Like most Poles who had survived the war, the ranger escort was an older man in his late fifties with a scruff of gray hair on his head. Franko, Krupke and the ranger wore the uniforms of Polish forest rangers. Morena stuck to her peasant attire, except she wore a dark green scarf over her head, mostly to keep warm.

The three rode their horses a short distance, sticking to the paved, single-lane road. Within a few minutes they were on an unpaved highway and into a small thicket of pine trees. The ranger indicated they were to dismount here and secure the horses. As they were doing so, Franko realized that, after traveling for days in lowlands and flat-lands, they were now in the wooded foothills of the Sudeten range. The area was surrounded by rolling, heavily forested hills, the perfect place to hide a secret weapons facility. However, the area they were currently in was mostly flat but completely obscured from any farm-houses or roads. The forest ranger then spoke.

"We're standing on the outskirts of the airfield. Just beyond these trees, in that clearing, is where the Nazis landed their airplanes," he said as he pointed. "Come, everyone, take a look."

Franko and Krupke emerged from the clump of trees and saw a large, flat area that upon first sight would appear as an ordinary field for crops. However, this time of year, there was a light dusting of snow on the ground, and it looked as if it could be a cement runway. Franko asked the ranger, "How long is it?"

"I would say about three to four thousand feet. The Nazis used mainly small, utility aircraft. The Junkers 52 was the most commonly sighted aircraft to land at this location."

Franko knew all too well that the Junkers 52 and the C-47 were almost identical in size and characteristics, and if the airfield could support the Junkers, it would certainly support the C-47. Franko came back and got his horse and proceeded to ride up and down the makeshift runway. Once he was satisfied, he came back to the group. He addressed Krupke. "The airfield is in excellent shape, thanks to your fellow Nazis. Get on your horse. We need to take a few photographs and then test the soil.

An hour later, Franko was finished with the airfield survey. He concluded that it could be used to support two C-47s for their EXFIL. The team re-assembled in the wooded area, and Franko moved on to the second phase of his duties. He addressed the ranger.

"What can you tell me about the Wenceslas mines operated nearby?"

Franko could tell that the ranger was not comfortable when asked about the mine. He fidgeted and kicked his boots into the dirt, choosing his words carefully before saying anything.

"This was a place of great secrecy by the Nazis. We were not allowed to go into the compound, which at the time of war was heavily guarded. None-the-less, those of us who have lived here for a long time know that those mines were built a long time ago. Light mining was done before the Nazi occupation. When the Nazis took over, everything changed. The area took on a more sinister appeal. Slave labor was brought in from the camps, and the Nazis built a labyrinth of tunnels and underground highways connecting several of the complexes in Lower Silesia. Even as far away as Ksiaz Castle. Work continued throughout the war. The complex was heavily guarded by the SS. In May of last year, the camp was evacuated. Everything and every human being was wiped off the face of the earth. Nothing was left at the site. The mines were flooded, buildings and equipment destroyed. Then the Russians came. They didn't know what was going on there. The units that overran the complex were not technical. They were mostly infantry conscripts. They knew the Nazis abandoned the camp and could never figure out what took place there. They knew it was some sort of military facility but nothing more. So, they left. I suspect they were hopeful it was gold or a precious mineral mine."

"Can you lead us there?"

The man nodded. "Yes, it is not far. The entrance is just on the other side of the ridge," he said as he pointed to the hills to the west. "We can be there in no time with the horses. I know of a secret entrance."

"Lead the way."

Krupke, for the most part, kept quiet on the ride to Die Riese. Franko suspected he knew more than what he was willing to divulge. Perhaps he was waiting for the right time. He decided to let him continue.

The team rode through mostly wooded hills on dirt or rough trails until they came to a small clearing in the valley. Then it opened up. Right in front of them, they could make out the abandoned structures. The site was completely hidden in the most remote portion of Poland. If the Nazis wanted to hide something this secret, they certainly picked the right place. The forest ranger stopped on a patch of gravel overlooking some level ground. He dismounted his horse and pointed to the valley.

"We came in via the northeast entrance. I wanted to stay off the main road in case a Soviet patrol came by. This section of Lower Silesia was mostly bypassed by Soviet forces and saw no action. To this day, that is still the case. However, we have seen an occasional Red Army vehicle use this pass. Possibly as a shortcut to Upper Silesia. There is where most of the Soviets are encamped. Come take a look."

The rest of the team dismounted and took a look. What they could see was that the ranger had been following the contours of a single lane road, laid long ago. This road disappeared from view behind a large derelict building whose tall arched windows rose into the mist. It was next to this structure that he was pointing to. It was an entrance to a mine shaft. "There are several of these entrances here."

The ranger continued walking until he came to the downed fence that at one time had surrounded the facility. "This fence was torn down by the Red Army as they overran the camp. As you can see, the site was heavily guarded. It was a triple ring of checkpoints and guard houses."

The ranger mounted his horse, and the team rode into a flat area which looked like a marshaling yard. Several mining carts and remnants of the small-gauge track were still visible.

It was at this marshaling yard that Krupke finally opened his mouth. "I told you I would show you the proof. Now here it is. Get your camera ready and take notes as I explain what I know of this facility."

Franko produced his camera and note pad. They all spoke in Polish so everyone could understand. Franko addressed the ranger. "I want you to stay here and wait for us. The girl will come with us."

The ranger responded. "That's fine with me. This place gives me the creeps. A lot of terrible things went on in the camp. Our time is limited. It will be dark soon, possibly snow. We must get back to headquarters soon."

Krupke, Franko, and Morena continued on foot into the valley as Krupke spoke, away from earshot of the ranger. "Everything was disguised to look as if this place was still a mining or light industrial facility. This yard was used as an assembly area and was hidden underground. As you can see, there are wooden planks called, sleepers still scattered about."

Franko could now make out the large wooden planks scattered around.

Krupke continued. "These wooden planks were topped with sod so the area would not be visible from passing aircraft."

"What went on in the yard?" Franko asked, snapping pictures as they walked along.

"I do not know for sure. I can only show you the facility, and you'll have to draw your own conclusions. I only know that this facility was a highly classified site and used to conduct experiments on advanced technology."

They continued down the flat area to the end, and Krupke showed them the facility on the left. It was completely destroyed. In fact, it looked as if it were bombed from the air. Krupke continued. "It was actually built before the war. As far back as 1929. It's a power station capable of burning a thousand tons of coal a day. You saw the remnants of the rail lines earlier used to transport the coal from Ludwikowice-Klodzkie, the nearest rail junction."

Next to the power station and the most prominent feature in the entire valley was a circular, concrete structure fifty-feet across and ten feet high. It looked like a modern-day Stonehenge.

"What was that used for?" Franko asked.

"Again, I'm not sure. I can tell you that this was a finished and completed structure. Take a look for yourselves," Krupke said, as he pointed to the green paint on the structure. "You do not camouflage something that is not completed, and this." Krupke now pointed to a partially exposed underground drain. Its concrete cover had cracked to reveal a ducting about a foot across. "This ducting leads directly to the destroyed power station. Maybe you can explain this?" he asked Franko.

The two men then followed the ducting to the abandoned, destroyed power plant. They talked for a few minutes around the damaged plant then came back to Morena. They pointed to the power plant then Franko asked a question made in the form of a statement. "Do you see any power lines or power poles coming out of the power plant? Or were they also destroyed by the Nazis?"

Krupke shook his head. "I don't understand."

"If this power plant burnt a thousand tons of coal a day, as you say, that would produce a tremendous amount of electricity. Enough to power a small city. No, this facility produced DC electricity, and the ducting provided the conduit leading to this," he said, pointing to the henge. "The power plant was destroyed by explosive charges placed by skilled demolition experts to make it look as if it were bombed from the air." Franko continued to take more pictures, then they walked along the pre-formed concrete pavement to the far side. There they could make out an entrance. It was camouflaged in green and brown paint, but there was no mistake as to the opening of the mine shaft. They all entered the facility and could see that it was used for military purposes. There was an abandoned guard station with an opening to fire machine guns on anyone unauthorized to access the facility. It was lined in concrete and continued deep into the hillside. Unfortunately, there was no power or lights, and they could not see any further than a few feet into the tunnel.

Krupke spoke. "It was destroyed, and the mines were flooded to prevent the Soviets from finding out what was going on in here."

Franko continued to look around the mine tunnel. There was a large, heavy metal door to the left with the

Third Reich insignia stamped on the outside. The words read, 'Dynamite Noble' in German. No one had a flashlight, so they could not go any further into the tunnel or take pictures. Finally, Franko pulled out his .45, shoved Krupke against a wall and pointed the pistol under his chin.

"Why are you showing me this place? What the hell was going on here? Was it atomic weapons research, perhaps?"

Morena unslung her MP-5 submachine gun and also pointed it at Krupke.

Krupke pushed Franko back. "I'll tell you, but you've got to be honest with me about the woman known as Jankowski. Who is she? Really?"

Franko realized Krupke knew more than he was willing to divulge, and he knew there was something amuck concerning Vivian Tate. He relaxed and placed his .45 back in his shoulder, holster. "All right, I'll tell you what I know about her, which isn't much. But you've got to tell me why you showed me this place, and more importantly, what was it used for."

Krupke responded, "First of all, it's imperative I get to the American sector. I know too much. I can't fall into Soviet or British hands. I must get to the Americans. Only the Americans can appreciate the information I have for them. The woman, known as Jankowski, I don't trust her. One moment she acts like a flake, the next, an expert. Sometimes she appears to know nothing, then other times she's commanding the operation. Something tells me she's up to something. I don't know what that something is. She could sell us out to the Soviets. She might even be a British agent, for all I know. Tell me, Major, what do you know about her?"

Franko was taken aback by Krupke's words. He

described Vivian to the teeth. He didn't know how to respond, but he chose his words carefully. "Here's what I know. During Operation Lusty, while we were going after high-tech aerospace technology inside Germany, we came to a dead end. We found everything we could possibly find, but we knew there was more. We had a source. A German officer in the high command."

Krupke interrupted, "Hanns Kammler."

"Yeah, that's right, it appears you know about him."

"Oh, yes, very much indeed, I worked specifically for him."

Franko broke in, "He was the one who provided Team Alsos the locations of all black sites inside Germany. He told Alsos that more secret weapons were hidden inside Poland, but he didn't know the precise locations. Or so he claimed. He gave us the name of a contact here in Poland who could help us. That contact went by the code name of Agena. I was the Lusty collector assigned to the Polish desk, because I speak Polish. My job was to go after any and all remaining Third Reich technology and scientists and bring them back to the U.S. Thus, I made contact with Agena, and she's the one who provided me with safe passage information as well as assistance in getting two aerospace scientists out of the country. She never told me her real name or gave me details of her background. She was simply my contact here in Poland. That is all I know about her, and that is the truth."

Krupke seemed to relax and appeared satisfied with Franko's answer. He nodded, then said, "I have my reasons about the woman. She could be a double, even a triple agent. Remember, I was in charge of all counter-espionage activities inside the Third Reich. All right, I trust you for the moment. Here's what I know. The advance V-2 guidance system is only the tip of the iceberg. There's a lot more the Third Reich had in their arsenal. A lot more! In many cases, a century ahead of anything American technology could even fathom. One of those technology experiments was conducted here. There is something else I must tell you, Major. It has to do with Soviet rocket ambitions. But you must tell no one, especially the Jankowski woman what I'm about to tell you."

"All right, I can do that. But what is it?"

"The Soviets recovered a limited amount of V-2 technology after the war, but they also have scientists developing their rocket program to compete with the German V-2. The Soviets also have a rocket man. His name is Sergei Korolev and was believed by many in the Third Reich, to be von Braun's counterpart in the Soviet Union. Currently, he's working with captured V-2 scientists who have gone to the Soviets instead of the Americans, either voluntary or involuntary, perfecting the V-2. Time is running out for the Americans because it's only a matter of *when*, not *if*, the Russians get the atomic bomb. Korolev is so important, the Soviets have kept his name an official state secret in fear the Americans will try and go after him. I have complete knowledge of his activities and research in my head, but I will not divulge this information to any US intelligence officials until you get me safely to the American sector. How's that for sweetening the pot?"

Krupke spent the remaining time showing Franko and Morena around, explaining what he knew about the facility. It was all bordering along complete science fiction but in Franko's view, all too probable. They came back to the forest ranger who was still waiting by the henge. Snow started to fall, and the temperature was dropping. They had to get back to the ranger station before nightfall.

Chapter 37

The four galloped into the courtyard of the ranger station just as the sun was setting over the surrounding hillsides. The skies were overcast, and snow fell gently to the ground. Jawor and Vivian were waiting out in front of the stables as the survey team came to a halt. A ranger appeared out of nowhere and secured the animals to the barn. Franko brushed snowflakes from his clothes as the others did the same. It was wet snow, and the three riders were wet from the short ride from the Die Riese facility.

Jawor spoke.

"We got a lot done today while you were gone. First things first, let's get you out of those wet clothes." She pointed to Krupke. "You'll move into the cottage for our remaining time here. The weather will get worse over the next few days. Temperatures will fall during the nights. It's too cold in the stables."

As Krupke moved toward the cottage, Jawor grabbed Franko by the arm. "You'll stay in the forestry office. You're needed there to operate the communication equipment." She then escorted Krupke to the cottage. Vivian Tate, Franko, and Morena remained outside.

Vivian finally addressed Morena. "You and Jawor will stay in the forestry office. We just said what we said so Krupke doesn't know where we'll be going next. They're waiting for you." Then she pointed in the direction of the forestry office as Morena took her cue that it was time to go their separate ways. Vivian then addressed Franko. "You, come with me."

The couple walked around the corner of the cottage, and down the long driveway to the main parking lot of the forestry office. There was a small, utility truck used by the forest rangers, complete with forestry markings, parked. The engine was still running. No one was in the driver's seat. "Your bags are already in the back. The rangers have loaned us the vehicle. Get in the driver's seat. I'll tell you where to go, move!"

The couple left the ranger station and drove a short distance on the little used, single-lane road leading to a small hamlet called Jugow. Franko drove the truck. Vivian sat next to him in the front seat. She motioned for him to pull off the road into a driveway just before a Catholic church on the right. There, in the middle of a small field, was what could best be described as a sizeable three-story country estate, complete with a barn. This time of year, little or no farming was conducted due to the weather, so the owners rented out rooms to travelers. It was effectively a guesthouse. Franko stopped the car.

"You and I will be staying here," said Vivian. "We'll stage our operations from this facility instead of the forestry office. If we're going to play a double-ruse operation, we can't give the Germans the foggiest idea of what we're doing. When we get inside, tell me how everything went today."

"Not before a well-deserved bath. After all, you did promise me that."

"Yes, I know. That's why we're here. Grab your stuff and follow me. My belongings are already inside."

A few minutes later, Franko was soaking in the bottom of a nice warm tub in the bathroom. He scrubbed his body and washed his hair and was now just relaxing in the warm water. It felt good to finally wash away the grime, not to mention to warm his body from the cold horseback ride into the woods. Then to his surprise, the bathroom door opened and Vivian Tate walked in, holding a stack of large white towels.

"This is becoming all too frequent. I had the door locked, you know."

Vivian placed the towels on the bathroom counter and then lifted herself onto it. There wasn't a lot of room since the sink and towels took up most of the space. She looked down on him in the tub.

"Relax, after all, it's not the first time I've seen a man naked."

Franko debriefed Vivian then and there. He told her everything, and the notion that Krupke believed her to be a possible British agent was working against them. He went into detail about the suitability of the airfield and the strange and mysterious place known as Die Riese. He informed Vivian that he would make detailed sketches and drawings of the facility. He told Vivian that he believed Krupke still had no choice but to trust her and the team getting him and the other Germans to the American sector. Franko finished up with one question.

"What's our plan for the double-sting operation?"

"As I've said before, leave that to me. This latest bit of information you provided on Die Riese can help us. I'll incorporate that into my plans. Now, before we go any further, I want you to do something for me. Close your eyes."

Franko did as he was told and slipped deeper into the tub, closing his eyes. That's when he felt Vivian's hands on his shoulders, rubbing his aching muscles. He could smell the sweet aroma of Vivian's body. She had obviously freshened up and taken a bath. She continued to massage his neck and shoulders as Franko unexpectedly reached behind and placed his hands around both of her arms. "That feels so good, thank you. I needed this."

He continued to move his hands up and down Vivian's arms, rubbing them as he lay in the tub.

"I already took my bath in the downstairs bathroom. They have a room upstairs already made up for us. Just the two of us."

Chapter 38

The master guest bedroom in the farmhouse was exquisite. The room had a tall ceiling with large cathedral windows facing the hills to the west. The bed was a large feather bed complete with canopy and posts. The bedding was soft and luxurious, complete with fluffy down comforters. Vivian and Franko slept in the bed together, but both were extremely tired, and after taking the long, warm baths, the two fell asleep almost the instant their heads hit the pillows.

Vivian was the first to wake up, at first daylight, which was around seven in the morning. Vivian had slept so soundly that at first, she wasn't quite sure where she was. Then she came to her senses. The room, though daylight outside, was still darkened, especially with the heavy curtains pulled tight over the large windows. She sat upright in the bed, naked. It was then she saw Tony Franko sleeping on his side facing away from her. He too was naked. She couldn't believe that the two of them had slept together, but neither had made a romantic move. She wondered if there could ever be a future between them.

She brushed the thought out of her head, then reached

over to the nightstand for a cigarette. She lit one and smoked it, still looking at Tony sleeping peacefully beside her. She had to savor the moment because it was the first time she had slept with a man in a very long time. Vivian took the oversized comforter and pulled it over his shoulders. As she did so, she leaned over and gently kissed him on his shoulder. She didn't want to wake him, so she sat upright in the bed, keeping the blankets up tight against her breast, mostly to keep herself warm. Then she reached back over to the nightstand, picked up her maps, drawings, and paperwork, which she had worked on the night before. She took out a plain sheet of paper and began jotting down simple notes to herself.

After a few minutes, she decided to get out of bed and try to get some coffee or tea without waking Franko. She slipped her bare body out of bed and went to the closet, where she put on a robe, which was supplied by the guesthouse. She stepped into her large overboots and proceeded to leave the bedroom.

Franko must have heard the door close behind her because he woke just as soon as Vivian left. He was so tired and mentally exhausted that he realized he must have fallen asleep as soon as he hit the bed. He turned over so he could face Vivian, but he realized she wasn't in bed next to him. *Maybe I was snoring too loudly*, he thought.

He climbed out of bed and looked for his clothes. That's when he remembered he'd left them in the bathroom down the hall. Vivian told him she would have them laundered. He looked around the room for something to wear. That's when he saw a robe hanging over a chair next to the windows. He placed the robe on, then peeked through the curtains to get a look at the weather outside. It was still overcast, but it had stopped snowing. There was a light covering of snow on the ground. Then he heard the bedroom door open. Vivian entered, carrying a tray with a pot of coffee and two cups. She placed it down on the small table beside Franko.

"I didn't want to wake you. You looked as if you hadn't slept in weeks, so I got up and got us some coffee. By the way, you've got me hooked on coffee instead of tea in the mornings. The owners will have a full breakfast for us downstairs when we're ready. This will do for now."

Franko saw that Vivian was wearing a robe similar to the one he was wearing. He didn't know what to say, so he grabbed his coffee and took a few sips. "What happened last night?" referring to them sleeping together.

"I assume you mean between *us*? Well, nothing actually. You fell asleep. You were very tired."

"Sorry about that. I hope you're not disappointed."

"Of course not. You were quite the gentleman."

Franko placed his cup down on the tray. "Where do we go from here?"

"I assume you mean, what's next in our escape plan?"

Franko nodded.

Vivian took a sip of her coffee. "I took the liberty while you were gone yesterday and sent off your urgent message about the MIAs you supposedly recovered. The messages were sent out over clear airways. That should get the Soviet's attention."

"Then what?"

"Tonight, you, me, Jawor and Morena move out to Walbrzych. We have a safe house not far from the railway station. It's actually an automotive garage. We'll take the forestry van. The garage provides maintenance on the vehicles, so this will help our cover. We'll stay the night there. The next morning, you'll go to the station and meet with the stationmaster. You'll tell him you're expecting a rail shipment from the East, and that it's vitally important for him to arrange connections through Czechoslovakia to Bavaria. You won't tell him they're bodies, but by showing him your authorization from the Allied Control Commission, he'll get the idea what you're doing. That shipment, which will be three large wooden boxes, the size of coffins, will be shipped by rail to Walbrzych from Krakow, thanks to our Home Army colleagues. It's important that the stationmaster sees you. It's part of the plan.

"When you're finished at the station, make your way back to the garage. I'll make my move once you're safely back. I'll send my urgent distress message from the post office located next to the station. We'll all meet up at the garage and proceed back here in the van. This should set the stage for the double-sting operation. Once we get a notification that the Russians have taken the bait, that should buy us enough time to coordinate the EXFIL flight from here. You said two days at the most right?"

Franko nodded. "Assuming the weather holds out."

"I've already taken care of that. I got the forecast. So far, the weather should hold out for another week. We should be gone well before then."

"And if it doesn't?"

"You should know me better by now. We make an alternate plan, simple."

Franko looked at her affectionately. That's when he realized they were speaking in English. And, to Franko's surprise, Vivian didn't have her stuffy, British accent. It was definitely more Slavic. Almost peasantlike. "You're amazing, you know that?"

"Yes, I know," she said, giving off one of her seductive looks.

* * *

FRANKO ACCOMPANIED by Morena walked down the street leading to the Walbrzych train station. Jawor and Vivian stayed at the automotive garage safe house. The snow was beginning to fall steadily now. The couple trudged through the thin snow layer as they made their way to the rail station. Franko had a heavy wool overcoat with wool cap. Morena was dressed in pants, a long coat, and heavy wool scarf over her head. She carried a small shopping bag. Inside the bag was an MP-3 submachine gun, complete with extra rounds of ammunition. Franko had his Colt .45 hidden in his shoulder holster under his heavy garments. The couple would split up before they reached the station while Franko proceeded on his own. Morena would stay outside as if waiting for her train. Her assignment was to cover all the entrances to the station to make sure no Soviet intelligence forces made an appearance.

The couple took up their positions as Franko entered the stationmaster's office. The stationmaster was an older man in his late sixties. He obviously had survived the Nazi occupation and was probably quite busy during the war handling all the various rail movements to and from portions of the Third Reich. He was bundled next to a potbelly stove. Large chunks of coal glowed inside the chamber, giving off considerable heat in the small room. Franko entered and removed his cap. He spoke in Polish.

"Good morning. My name is Major Antoni Franko, United States Army." He produced his military identification card along with the authorization letter from the Allied Control Commission and handed them to the stationmaster. While the elderly man read, Franko continued, "I'm here on behalf of the victorious Allied forces." Franko took out a wad of bills in US currency and placed them before the man as he gave him an overview of why he was there (the shipment of Allied airmen remains).

The stationmaster fully cooperated after taking roughly one thousand US dollars and scheduled the transfer of the coffins on the next train, which was scheduled to come through in two days. When all the coordination was complete, and the purchase had been made, the station-master said, "You must have had a long and difficult journey. How did you get from Tarnow to Walbrzych?"

Franko told him the truth, again acting on the script provided by Vivian Tate. He told him how he had used a series of courier lines, which had handed him off from one sector to another. The man then got up from his stool and disappeared to the next room. Franko moved his hand inside his coat just in case he had to pull out his weapon. A few minutes later, the stationmaster reappeared with a tray of bread and sausage. "Come, have something to eat before you go."

The two men ate and talked for several minutes. Franko asked if any Soviet intelligence forces had come to the city. The man replied only a few. Most of the Red Army was garrisoned north. Franko realized he had spent more time than he had originally planned and told the old man that he must go. Franko placed on his cap and coat, then exited the stationmaster's office. As he came outside, he saw the snow had come down more substantially, and the temperature had dropped several degrees. He proceeded to the right, toward the passenger terminal, and looked for Morena. She was nowhere to be seen. He searched inside and out of the facility but couldn't find any trace of her. He walked across to the platforms, but still there was no sign of her on either side of the tracks. Then he went outside and looked around the depot. He retraced the steps they had taken to reach the station in hopes

Morena had simply gone for a walk to keep warm. That's when he noticed her huddled up next to a brick wall under the railroad overpass. He came over to her and noticed she was shaking. She was freezing, and her body was covered with snowflakes.

Franko wrapped his arm around her to give her warmth. "Why did you wait out here? You should have gone inside."

"There were Red Army soldiers everywhere. Didn't you see them? They were coming and going from the station. One patrol came by driving in an American Jeep. Two men dressed in civilian clothes. They passed by close enough for me to hear them speak. The two made a pass in the turnabout as if looking for something or someone. I decided to keep my distance and wait under the bridge."

Franko remembered the comments from the station-master that he'd seen no Soviets in the area. "You must be freezing. Let's get you back to the safe house."

The couple returned to the automotive garage, where Vivian and Jawor were waiting. Thankfully, they had a large pot of borscht heating on the stove inside the kitchen. Franko and Morena took off their coats and jackets while Jawor dished out large portions of the hot soup for the two. Vivian glanced out the windows, checking to see if the couple had been followed.

Vivian came back to the kitchen and took a seat next to Franko. "How'd it go?"

Franko sipped the hot borscht from his spoon. "All coordinated with the station. He'll transfer the boxes on the next train headed to Prague, then on to Germany."

"Tell me about the stationmaster?"

Franko gave her a detailed report. Then Vivian said, "No doubt, he's probably already called his Red Army contacts and informed them of this recent discovery, just like I suspected. Everything is going according to plan."

Franko knew by now not to question Vivian's intuitions. He simply nodded. "Now what?"

"You three stay here. I need to make my move on the post office by myself. The Home Army guards stay with you. One downstairs, the other will take a position here in the flat to overlook the streets. I should be back within an hour. Two at the most."

"I'd feel a lot more comfortable if I went with you."

"Too risky."

"Okay, what about taking one of them?" he said, as he motioned toward Jawor and Morena.

"A good idea, but this is part of my plan. I have to act on my own. I'll be okay. The Home Army scouts tell me there's a pathway to the tracks in the open space next to the liquor store. I'll take that to and from the station."

Vivian then started to place her coat and overboots on. Next, she grabbed a cloth shopping bag. Inside she had a large Polish sausage, some cheese, and a towel—no weapons. Then, she left the flat.

Franko got up from the kitchen table and looked out the window just as Vivian crossed the street and disappeared toward the open space. He turned around and faced Jawor and Morena. "Go after her. Give her ten minutes. Establish perimeter security around the post office."

"Agreed," said Morena. "Too many Russians in the area."

"Get ready. Take your weapons, all of them. I don't want her walking into an ambush."

Chapter 39

Vivian used the post office telegraph and sent off her emergency distress message to the fake address Mr. Bor had set up for her. Next, she called the number Mr. Bor had provided and left the message for the duty officer. All messages were transmitted in clear, unsecure methods. Together with Franko's request and the disloyal stationmaster, she felt comfortable that the Soviets would take the bait. She paid the postal worker in cash for his services and then exited the post office.

Vivian used the open space adjacent to a liquor store on Niepodleglosci street. There was plenty of cover from trees, shrubs, and bushes so that she had no trouble working her way to the railroad tracks and the post office. Vivian used the same route to head back to the safe house. As she was following the tracks, using the large trees alongside the tracks for cover, she thought she heard voices nearby. It was nearly three o'clock in the afternoon, and she suspected it was probably from the residence on nearby Niepodleglosci street. She stopped and listened again, but heard nothing, so she continued.

They appeared out of nowhere, but it was their cigarette smoke that gave them away. But it was too late for Vivian to scurry off in a different direction. She practically walked right into them. The two men were large, powerful figures dressed in civilian attire. Both wore Russian fur caps and overcoats. There was no mistake to Vivian. They were Russians, probably GRU. The three made eye contact, and Vivian continued along the tracks as if nothing was out of the ordinary. That's when one of the men made his move. He spoke in very poor Russian, probably not his native language.

"Stop right there, young lady."

Vivian ignored his commands, pretending to not understand and continued. Then the other man made a move toward Vivian and blocked her path. Vivian stopped but not before she got a glimpse of the pistol held in the Russian's hand. He spoke in Russian again, this time asking where she was going and where had she come from.

Vivian again ignored his questions and replied in Polish that she was heading home from the station. The other Russian came up to Vivian from behind, and the two could tell that Vivian didn't understand the men. Then one of the men pointed to her shopping bag and repeated something in Russian. Vivian, who speaks Russian fluently, understood what the men were trying to do. They were asking what was in her bag.

Vivian looked down to her bag and replied in Polish. "It's my bag of food. I just came from the station. I'm on my way to the bakery to buy more bread to eat with my sausage." She opened the bag and showed it to the two men. Both men then started laughing, continuing to speak in poor Russian. Vivian, on the other hand, was not amused. She knew instantly that the two Russians were

Soviet military intelligence officers, most likely GRU. They were not skilled in field craft. Vivian knew she would be no match for them. She could easily make a move and kill both. But to do so would most likely signal the rest of the intelligence detail and her plan would unravel. No, she decided to play along. She acted as if she were a local woman coming back from the train station using the short-cut. She spoke again in Polish to try and give her adversaries the idea by pointing toward the opening in the shrubs. The two Russians then finally got the idea but not before the two decided to play the bully role. One of the Russians asked for the shopping bag. Vivian refused and pulled it tighter to her body. The Russians were not amused. One made a move and tried to grab it. That's when Vivian tried to run. One Russian blocked her way while the other snatched the bag from Vivian's hand, breaking the handles in the process. He looked into the bag and pulled out the sausage. The two spoke to each other in Russian, then started to laugh. Again, Vivian tried to run, but the Russians were too big. Then they started to pull the other contents out from the bag, namely the cheese. Then they bit into the sausage, handing each other the cheese and sausage to nibble on. Vivian started to cry. It was all a ruse, but she had to make it look convincing. Vivian then made a run for it as the two Russians were busy nibbling away. They tried to go after her, but they were too large and clumsy. Vivian ran toward the open space to get away from the Russians, but as she did so, she lost her footing on the steep slope. She slid down a few feet in the snow and rolled over. That's when she felt someone grab her from behind and cover her mouth. She was flipped over by the figure, only to see Antoni Franko holding her.

He placed a finger to his lips and spoke softly. "Don't

be afraid, it's me." Then he pointed. "There's another one just a few feet ahead. I don't think he's seen us." That's when he heard the two distinct sounds of a weapon with a silencer, *Pop-Pop*. Then two distinct sounds of dead weight hitting the dirt.

"That would be Jawor and Morena taking care of business. Quickly, get back to the safe house. We'll handle it from here." He got Vivian to her feet and gently pushed her from behind. "Off you go."

In the meantime, Franko ran into the direction of where the other Russian was. It was obvious that some sort of perimeter security had been set up by the Soviets around the train station. He tried to use the brush for cover, but in this direction the foliage was too thin, not to mention he was too late.

A Soviet officer dressed in uniform made eye contact with Franko. It was Colonel Vladimir Sivan of the GRU. The Russian was startled for just a second as he seemed to recognize Franko. Then he spoke, in English, "You!" and tried to pull out his Makarov pistol.

Franko made a sudden move and kicked the gun out from the Russian's hands. The two were now looking at each other face-to-face, enemy and foe. The Russian swung back and hit Franko on the side of the head, flinging him backward. Franko regained composure and counter-attacked, punching Sivan in the chin. The two men fell to the ground, each hitting the other in the process.

The Russian spoke in English. "I've got you surrounded. My men are everywhere. It's useless. Just hand over the hardware, and I'll spare your life."

Franko ignored Sivan, and the two continued to wrestle on the ground. Franko got to his feet and pulled Sivan up from the ground, then swung him toward a tree. Sivan hit the tree and fell to the ground, rolling down the steep drop-off toward Niepodleglosci Ave. That's when Franko saw the Jeep parked on the curb. Sivan got to his feet and headed for the Jeep. Franko would never reach him in time to stop him. Sivan would probably return with reinforcements and surround the area. Franko then heard noise and movement in the surrounding bushes. It was Jawor and Morena.

They saw Sivan climb into the Jeep and start it up. Jawor then shouted to Franko, "We can't let him get away! We've got to stop him."

Franko pulled out his .45 and emptied the magazine but missed Sivan.

That's when Morena stood up, pulled a pin from a hand grenade, and rolled it down the hill toward the fleeing Russian. The grenade exploded under the Jeep just as Sivan was about to hit the accelerator. The Jeep flipped on its side in a ball of fire.

"Quickly, let's get out of here," shouted Franko.

AT THIS SAME TIME, just a short distance away, Colonel Dimitri Pavel had established a headquarters near the other Walbrzych train station. This station was called Koplania and was used primarily for freight. Acting on all his latest intelligence information coming in from Poland and Moscow Center, he determined that Jankowski's team would eventually make their way closer to this station. This station was also closer to the clandestine airfield secured by Red Army forces.

Pavel positioned his forces to surround the airfield and look for any aircraft trying to make an approach to the field. If so, they would be shot from the sky. Pavel took over the mining museum as his headquarters. It was here, as he was sitting down for his evening meal, when he received an urgent phone call from Polish law enforcement officials sympathetic to the Communists about an ambush of a Soviet intelligence team operating near Podgorze (the other Walbrzych train station). Two men had been killed and another seriously injured. The survivor claimed to be an officer working for Soviet military intelligence.

"Where is he?" shouted Pavel to the police officer on the other end of the phone.

The policeman replied, "He's been taken to a local Red Army field hospital, not far from your location, in a military compound. He was seriously injured from a grenade explosion. They want to evacuate him to a larger facility to care for his wounds. I thought you should know before he's evacuated in case you want to question him about his encounter."

"Give me the location of the field hospital!"

A short time later, Pavel was standing in front of his rival intelligence officer at the local field hospital. Sivan was wrapped in bandages. His face was swollen with bruises and cuts. Sivan was asleep from a sedative given by Red Army doctors. Pavel placed a hand on his shoulder and gently gave him a shake. Sivan came to and saw a man about his age, dressed in civilian attire, looking down on him.

"Comrade Sivan, my name is Dimitri Pavel, State Security, Third Department. I'm truly sorry for what happened to you. Is there anything you can tell me?"

Sivan spoke with difficulty. "You and I are acting on the same intelligence information. Each of us has separate tasks. I was following my lead. I tried to set up a surveillance team around the Glowy train station. We were expecting an American military officer to show up. This officer is a technical collector from Wright Field, Ohio, looking for former Nazi secret weapons. We believe he has recovered some devices and is trying to make an escape out of the country. I know this officer. His name is Major Antoni Franko, US Army Air Corps. He was there. He and I made contact. He recognized me too. He went straight for my weapon. A fight broke out before I could reach for my pistol. He flung me down an embankment. I was trying to make a getaway with my Jeep. That's when someone threw the grenade at me. It hit the rear end of the Jeep. Luckily, it was not thrown under the Jeep, but a meter behind and exploded. If it had been another half meter closer, I wouldn't be here now."

"They want to evacuate you to Moscow. You have a shattered arm with second and third degree burns over your body. Tell me about your mission, so I can continue."

Sivan shook his head. "I can't do that, Comrade. I cannot fail. I must proceed with my mission. I have to recover those devices. It is a matter of national survival for the Motherland. You can understand my position."

Pavel sat on the edge of Sivan's bed and told him about the political mission he was on and the necessity of capturing the Nazi war criminal Otto Krupke. The two then compared the similarities of their respective missions. It appeared that both men had separate pieces of the puzzle. Pavel was acting on information about a British agent known as Irina Jankowski, who also went by the name of Vivian Tate. Sivan was acting on information on the American and a female Polish Home Army officer known as Jawor. Both enemy teams were probably trying to make their way to the same egress airfield in Walbrzych, thinking it was secure. Pavel also knew that at least some of that hostile team was still in Walbrzych since Sivan had made visual contact with Major Franko. For the time being, he would hold his forces in check. The enemy teams would probably go into hiding somewhere in the city and wait for their EXFIL flight. But unbeknown to either Pavel or Sivan, Vivian Tate's double-sting operation had accomplished its objective. Both Soviet teams would stay put in Walbrzych.

Chapter 40

The ride back to Ranger Headquarters was conducted in near silence as soon as the grenade exploded under Sivan's Jeep. The team immediately went back to the auto garage, retrieved Vivian Tate, and then all members left in the utility van. Jawor drove the vehicle with Morena in the front seat. Franko and Vivian sat in the back. It was around seven at night when they reached Jugow.

Jawor stopped at the farmhouse first to drop off Vivian and Franko, then would continue on to Ranger Headquarters. As Franko and Vivian exited the back seat, Vivian said to Jawor, "Get some rest. I'll meet you at base headquarters tomorrow noon. We'll debrief at that time. No doubt, with the deaths and attacks on the GRU men this has, in fact, thrown the Soviets off our tail. We'll know more by tomorrow. Good night, ladies. Nice work."

Franko and Vivian entered the guesthouse and went straight up to their room on the top floor. As they entered, Franko dropped his bags on the floor, and Vivian did the same. There was a fire burning in the fireplace, and Vivian came closer and warmed her hands. The weather was changing, and she knew time was running out. They had to get out before the harsh winter set in. She rubbed her hands slightly, then turned to Franko.

"Why don't you freshen up and use the bath downstairs. I'll do the same using the one up here. When you're finished, meet me here. I'll have something brought up to eat."

Franko didn't say anything, keeping unusually quiet since the trip from Walbrzych. He agreed by nodding, then left the room.

Franko took a long hot bath. Sitting in the tub, he couldn't stop thinking about Vivian. They'd come close to losing her to the Russians. It was by chance and his persistence and insistence that she wasn't. After all, she did tell the entire team to wait at the safe house for her return. If they hadn't ignored her words, she would be in Russian hands by now, probably tortured as well. The thought of losing her on this mission was something he just could not accept. It was with this thought, that he finished his bath, put on the white bathrobe, and returned to his and Vivian's room on the top floor.

The door was unlocked, so he pushed it open and entered, carrying his dirty clothes. There, inside the bedroom, standing in front of the fireplace, was Vivian Tate. She was holding a small glass of sherry with both hands. She had an unemotional look on her face, but the most interesting fact about her was that she was dressed in an elegant evening gown. In fact, it looked to Franko as if it were the same evening gown she had worn in Frankfurt the night they left on their mission. Franko was again bewildered by her actions. Her blonde hair was slightly wet, and she had on a fresh fragrance, which Franko could smell when he entered the room. He thought, *It's time*.

Franko came closer to Vivian. She motioned to a small

table with her eyeballs. On the table was an open bottle of Polish beer. "I ordered you one. They just brought it up. I think it's still cold."

Franko reached for the beer at the same time he noticed that Vivian had nothing on under her gown. He could see her hard, firm nipples protruding. He was instantly aroused as he gulped down the beer. "I swear, that's the same gray dress you had on in Frankfurt the night we left."

"You do pay attention, some of the time. I had it packed in my personal belongings since we left. But you were told to wait at the safe house. You deliberately disobeyed my orders."

"Yes, I know."

Vivian could see Franko's anatomy since he had nothing on under his robe. Then, to his surprise, Vivian reached for his hard shaft with one hand and pulled it, and him, closer to her body. She trembled slightly, and the Sherry glass shook in her other hand. Vivian placed the glass on the small table. The couple did not need to say anything further. It was all emotional at this point. Franko placed his now empty beer bottle on the floor and grabbed Vivian and hugged her. He placed his arms around her back and shoulders, feeling the scar tissue beneath her gown. Vivian did not object. The couple embraced and kissed. Franko then raised Vivian's gown up over her head as he knew she had nothing on under the garment. They shuffled to the bed, where Franko placed Vivian down on the soft down comforter. Franko did not waste any time, took off his robe, and immediately straddled her. Vivian moaned with passion. Franko entered her easily. It wasn't long before they both climaxed, and Vivian felt his warmth, flow inside her. Her breathing was deep. She had obviously not had this much physical excitement in a very long time. When it was all over, and both were spent, Franko rolled off her. Vivian lay still on the bed, then she wept slightly. Franko grabbed her once more and pulled her over his chest. They were now bare breast to breast; Vivian still panted slightly. Then tears began to flow down her cheeks. Next came uncontrollable sobbing. The once high and mighty Vivian Tate crumbled.

Franko stroked her blonde hair. "You're not so tough, you know. There *is* a soft spot. When I saw you in the hands of the Russians, I thought it was all over. I couldn't stand the thought of losing you and you going through another ordeal like you did in Berlin. Plus, I almost lost you once, in that frigid water, and I wasn't going to let that happen again, ever. Irina, when we get back to Frankfurt, I'm not going back to the States. I'm going to London . . . with you, because I love you."

Vivian dropped her stuffy British accent. "Tony, you're crazy. Do you realize what you're saying?"

"Yes, I do. I want to be with you. You're the one! I've loved you since the day I met you in the Annex canteen. Irina, I want to spend the rest of my life with you. I know it isn't very romantic. I've never been that type anyway. I'm asking you to marry me."

Vivian was speechless. All she did was sob. "Tony, I . . . can't marry you. You don't even know me."

"Don't give me that crap. I know enough. I know you're a beautiful, intelligent woman who I can't live without. There's a church across the street. Let's do it now. I'm Catholic, we can get it done tomorrow. Then we'll go to London—together. You as my spouse with legal travel orders. No more sneaking around the Continent. I can get a job anywhere in England. I'm a trained engineer. The UK is going to need all the help they can get with the war over."

"Tony, I still can't marry you."

"And why not? If you need more time, I'll settle for a, 'I'll think about it.'"

"Oh, Tony, it's not that, it's Morena. She's the problem. She's attracted to you. Haven't you noticed? Remember, you've spent more time with her than you have with me. If she finds out, she'll be very upset. She could even put the mission at risk and do something crazy or stupid."

"That's no excuse, Irina. She'll never know about it. I'll have the church mail the marriage certificate to my postal address in Frankfurt. I'll buy you a ring later."

"Even then, I still can't marry you."

"You're still not giving me a legitimate reason. Why?"

"Because there *is* something you still don't know about me."

"And . . . what could that possibly be that I don't already know? You're running out of excuses."

Vivian pulled herself up from Franko's chest. She got on top of him just as Franko's anatomy came to life again. She stroked his hair, then placed her arms around his head.

"Oh, Tony, I do love you. I thought I could never say that again to another man." She kissed him on the lips. The same time, Franko penetrated her once again. She stopped, took a breath, and paused, "Because . . . I can't marry you in the Catholic church. I was raised Jewish not Christian."

"You really are full of secrets."

"More than you can imagine. I've given enough for my King and country. All I want is my life and identity back. That's not too much to ask."

"No, it's not."

"All right, I'm marry you, Tony. Once we get back to the American sector. We'll have a civil ceramony."

* * *

THE NEXT DAY the weather cleared up, but the temperature was still cold. Franko and Vivian returned to Ranger Headquarters around noon. Franko drove the small utility van while Vivian sat in the passenger seat. She clutched his arm ever so gently during the short ride. The two were practically speechless after their previous, love-making the night before. This was as far as the couple dared to go with their affection.

They were slightly late for their twelve o'clock meeting, something Vivian rarely did. The couple entered Ranger Headquarters and were escorted to the briefing room on the first floor by Home Army rangers. There, all members of the Checkmate team were assembled except for the Germans and Poldi. This was to be a closed meeting for the time being. They took seats at the conference table. Franko took the empty place next to Morena. Vivian took the one across from Franko. Jawor was standing in front of a large forestry map of Lower Silesia. This was to be a confidential meeting to discuss the latest Soviet intelligence moves and to finalize plans for EXFIL.

Vivian kept her gaze down, looking at the table, making sure she was not making any eye contact with Franko. Morena, on the other hand, did just the opposite. She couldn't take her eyes *off* Franko. Vivian then produced her maps and notes from her magician's briefcase. As she did so, she finally looked up at Jawor, then Morena. She noticed Morena gazing upon Franko but brushed the thought off to avoid any more confusion, something they couldn't afford at this stage of the mission. Then she addressed Jawor. "All right, let's have it?"

"First of all, our guests are getting extremely anxious. Krupke, in particular but not surprising. It appears they have too much time on their hands. They know that something's come up, but thus far, we've kept them in the dark concerning the Soviet activities. They keep asking for more information. Today I finally told them we'd have more information about our escape plans today. They, along with Poldi and our Home Army guards, will be invited to the meeting once this closed-door session is complete."

"Tell me about the latest Soviet moves." asked Vivian.

Jawor used the map on the wall to conduct the brief. "Our plan seems to have had success in that it has thrown the Russians off our tail. Our latest intelligence suggests the Soviets took the bait but at a hefty price. With the deaths of the two GRU agents, NKVD has retaliated with a vengeance. They've called in more reinforcements and took control of all GRU assets in the area. It's now a state security matter, not an intelligence matter. They're conducting house-to-house searches, looking for anyone who can give them information on our whereabouts, often paying huge bribes for any information. The automotive garage was also hit. The two mechanics were arrested before they could escape and presumably are being interrogated as we speak. I don't know how much longer they can hold out before one of them cracks, but it must be assumed we've got no more than forty-eight hours." She now turned her attention to Franko. "If there is ever a time to coordinate the rescue flight, the time is now. Preferably within the next thirty-six hours." Jawor indicated she wanted Franko to speak.

Franko got up and came closer to the map to brief everyone. "I agree. We've got a break in the weather, and the runway surface condition is excellent. The ground is hard and firm from the cold temperatures. It can easily support airlift operations. If this would have been late fall or spring, we'd be fucked. I need to contact Frankfurt and give them the time and coordinates for the pickup. Normally, I'd cable them. But in this particular case, since the Russians will be aggressively monitoring the airways, we can't take the chance. The safest way is to send a message by courier using the cutout in Krakow. I can't make this trip. Too risky, though I'd prefer to go myself. Our only option is to send someone else."

Vivian knew immediately whom to turn to, plus it would eliminate one potential problem, given her current situation. She now looked at Morena. "You'll do it."

"I agree," said Jawor, answering before Morena could speak. "It's the only option, even though it means back-tracking. We can have the rangers drive her there and back."

Franko looked at his watch, noting the time and day. "It's roughly twelve-forty-five in the afternoon on Tuesday, November fifteenth. The best time of day for clandestine landings is at dawn. We'll make it at dawn, on November seventeenth."

Vivian looked at her notes, "Sunrise is at 0700 Zulu."

Franko responded, "That's final then. 0700 Zulu, day after tomorrow. Morena should be back well before then. We're going to need everyone back by then for the rendezvous. Security is most important."

"Speaking of security, here's what we're up against," interrupted Jawor. "Ranger Battalion has the resources to provide perimeter security of the airfield for the landing and takeoffs. However, they will be armed with small caliber pistols, nothing more. If Soviet combat forces show up, it will be no match. I've been told if that's the case, they can't accept the consequences. They'll have no choice but to break off the engagement and retreat. We'll be left to fend for ourselves. We'll have to make up the difference. We'll take everything we've got, which are several MP-5 submachine guns, several hundred rounds of ammunition, and hand grenades. This should hold off the Soviets should they arrive."

Franko looked at Vivian to get her approval. Vivian nodded in agreement. Franko took out his notepad and started scribbling. When he was finished, he handed it to Morena. "Details of the EXFIL. Pass this on to the cutout in Krakow. I want you to memorize this, word for word, then destroy it."

Now that the closed-door portion of the meeting was over, Vivian indicated it was time to bring in their guests so they could brief them on the EXFIL procedures.

Chapter 41

A few minutes later, the Germans, Poldi, and two Home Army rangers entered the briefing room. The Germans looked terrible. Their faces were unshaven, and all three had lost weight. Their clothes hung from their bodies like drapes. Franko took charge of the meeting while Jawor sat next to Vivian. Morena left to get ready for the trip to Krakow. This left Krupke, Hoch, Mangus, Vivian, Jawor, Poldi, and the two Home Army rangers facing Franko. Franko pushed the map aside and used the chalkboard. He drew a sketch of the airfield with chalk as he began in German for everyone's sake.

"We've come to the final phase of the mission, EXFIL. You will be happy to know that our rescue has been set for the day after tomorrow at sunrise. As you know, the weather has not cooperated with us for the past few days. There is a break, however, and the forecast is favorable for air operations. I must brief you on the rescue procedure because the maneuver is based on promptness. Here's how it will go down."

Franko used chalk to detail the operation. "The EXFIL

flight is scheduled as a double-operation. Two C-47s will make the landing at the airfield, one at a time. The lead aircraft will land first, followed by the wingman. The risk is far greater with a two-ship formation as opposed to a single ship, but we felt the added aircraft will give us greater safety and flexibility should something go wrong with one or both of the aircraft." Franko used the eraser to simulate the aircraft. "The prevailing winds are from the west. The lead aircraft will circle overhead and wait for my signal that the field is secure. This will be accomplished by light signals. We don't want any emitters in case the Russians are monitoring several frequencies and can compromise our position. The plane will then maneuver for a landing to the west, land, turnaround, and taxi back to the takeoff point, then reposition and wait for the second aircraft to make the same maneuver. This will be an engine running on load to facilitate a rapid departure."

Franko then drew a simple sketch on the blackboard. "I'll be the only one exposed on the runway until every aircraft is safely parked. I'll then signal the rest of the team to make their way out from these trees," he said as he drew a circle. "The advanced gyros will be on wooden carts provided by Home Army. We'll move the carts to the aircraft here." Then he looked at Krupke to emphasize the point. "One cart will have the advance gyros and three batteries. The other will have the older gyro plus the remaining three batteries. Hoch and Mangus will proceed to the first aircraft ready for departure. They'll board first, followed by the new, advanced gyros. Once safely on board, you and I'll go toward the second aircraft along with the older gyros and Poldi. We'll load-up, board, then depart after the first aircraft."

"Why can't I go first?" asked Krupke.

Vivian answered, "It's because you and I have a little

business to settle, remember. Which will eat up a certain about amount of time. Before you get on that plane, I need your account number and authorization to transfer money to my numbered account."

"She's right," replied Franko. "While Hoch, Mangus, and the gyros are being loaded onto the first aircraft, you two will work on the transfer. I'm sorry, but that was the condition you demanded. If it were up to me, I'd leave immediately and make the transfer later. But you insisted."

Vivian came back. "The normal way of making such transfers is by wireless telegraph. We just happen to have that equipment we can use in the field. We'll have it all set up. When the time's right, we'll establish the connection and make the wire transfer."

Krupke sat in silence for a while, contemplating the situation. "How much time do we have? To make the transfer that is?"

"Should be no more than five minutes after we connect," answered Vivian. "Don't forget, we'll be loading the other gyros and Poldi during this time frame. When the transfer is complete, Franko will escort you onto the aircraft. You'll depart then."

"Krupke came back. "Not so fast. How do I know you'll let me get airborne after the wire transfer? Worse yet, what if the plane makes a turn to the east and the Soviet sector? No, I want a ten-minute delay in the transfer. That should leave enough time to board the aircraft and head west."

Vivian came back. "Fair enough."

"Good, that's settled then. Now, let's move on to the security of the airfield," said Franko.

After the meeting was over and the team dispersed, Franko and Vivian drove back to their quarters at the guesthouse. As the couple was driving on the road, heading south, Vivian spoke.

"I need you to do me a favor."

"Sure, anything, love."

"I want you to take me to the nearest three-star hotel. I've got to send a telegram to my contact in London and advise him of the EXFIL time and date."

"What about the Soviets monitoring the airways?"

"That's why I need a three-star hotel. It will appear as a normal routine transmission to another three-star hotel . . . in Wales."

* * *

A SHORT TIME LATER, back in London, General Cameron was in his office, sifting through the mountains of paperwork on his desk. It was four-twenty-five in the afternoon. He was about to wrap things up and head home for the day when his internal office telephone rang. He picked up the white telephone receiver, "General Cameron."

A female voice on the other end of the line spoke, "Sorry to bother you this late in the day, sir but I've got an urgent call, priority one, holding on line two from our switchboard in Wales."

Cameron picked up the black, office phone and pushed line two. The transmission was scratchy but audible. A female voice spoke on the other end with a faint sound. "Authentication Victor-Tango Seven-Kilo-Foxtrot-Zulu. I say again, authentication Victor-Tango Seven-Kilo-Foxtrot-Zulu."

Cameron replied, "Authentication, Sierra-Charlie-Alpha-Alpha, going secure," then pressed the red secure button on the side of the telephone. "Go ahead, Miss Tate, we're on the secure scrambler."

Vivian didn't wait for pleasantries. She gave Cameron an abbreviated de-brief on the status of Operation Checkmate and the necessity of immediate EXFIL transport with packages secure. She informed him that Franko had already contacted Frankfurt and requested two C-47s and coordinates for the flight.

Cameron came back. "Excellent, now I want you to listen to me very carefully because it's vitally important we proceed with this next phase of the operation with extreme caution and detail. I'll get a copy of Major Franko's airlift-tasking orders. I'll arrange that one of those aircraft is flown by RAF crews. Obviously, you won't know which one that is, so you'll have to make that decision once the planes arrive. Make sure Krupke gets on that aircraft. If, for some reason, only one aircraft makes it and that aircraft is flown by American crews, we'll put everyone on that aircraft, and we'll worry about extradition later. Do you understand?"

"Perfectly."

"All right, Miss Tate, see you back in England."

* * *

BACK IN WALBRZYCH, Pavel and his Third Department knew that time was running out. The Western intelligence team had escaped his net once again. Colonel Sivan's investigation could have actually helped close the net, but due to inter-agency rivalry, that advantage was lost. Pavel now used any extraction method at his disposal. He concentrated on Polish Home Army resistance fighters, many of whom were employed by the forestry department. This proved difficult since many of the resistance fighters were extremely loyal and tight-lipped. So, he focused on a technique used in occupied Germany. The Soviets would simply bribe the local populous for information. Since many were hungry and homeless, the monetary reward was lifesaving.

Pavel rounded up a group of civilians every day at twelve noon. He opened his briefcase and pulled out a bundle of Polish currency. He told them the money was theirs if they could provide any information on a Polish Home Army unit working with Western intelligence agencies. The second day after the attack on Sivan, the strategy provided results. A lone worker at a petrol station confessed that a Polish forest ranger truck had stopped for fuel a couple of days earlier. What was different about this ranger truck was that it was from the local battalion headquarters located in Jugow. Pavel looked at the location on the map and made a startling revelation. The Ranger Headquarters was located near a former Nazi secret weapons facility. Pavel next channeled all his resources into mobilizing to Jugow. Then he contacted Sivan, who was still at the hospital waiting for transport back to Moscow.

"Comrade Sivan, what can you tell me about the secret Nazi weapons facility in Jugow?"

Sivan, still in pain from his injuries, replied, "It was called Die Riese by the Germans. All I know is that GRU assets combed the area in May of last year. Military intelligence discovered that the SS destroyed all sites and flooded the tunnels. The scope of the recovery operations would take decades, not to mention hundreds of millions of rubbles, something we can't afford at this time."

Pavel continued, "What if I told you a Western intelligence team is working in the area with the help of Home Army Ranger Battalion?"

"That makes sense. The team that attacked me had

weapons and organization. They could not have pulled it off working alone."

"I'm moving the entire Third Department out to Jugow."

"Let me go with you."

"Out of the question in your condition. You need to be seen by doctors back in Moscow."

"I don't need to go into the field. Just take me with you. I'll set up someplace nearby. That way, if you need my assistance, I can easily provide it to you. It could save precious time."

Pavel thought for a moment, then agreed. "Your point is well-taken. We have a safe house in Ludwikowice-Klodzkie. You'll stay there until I call you."

Chapter 42

It was still dark on the morning of the EXFIL on November 17, 1945. As per Franko's instructions, two wooden horse-drawn carts were waiting in the shadows of the thick foliage, along with Vivian Tate, Poldi, and the three Germans. Jawor stood lookout, holding an MP-5 submachine gun. Nearby, Franko and Morena were pacing off distances, marking the improvised landing strip for the aircrews. The ground was hard and frozen, and the aircraft would have no difficulties with a landing or takeoff. Also, the Nazis had gone through great efforts to hide the airfield from the surrounding areas. The makeshift airport was perfect in the sense that it was concealed from the ground. There were no official roads leading to or from the airfield. The only way to access the airfield was to cut through the farm fields. Also, the airfield was surrounded by rows of trees planted parallel north and south to the east-west runway. A thickly wooded area protected the east end, and a small outcrop of trees shielded the west end. The rangers would only provide a light detail to protect and watch over the north end of the runway, which had the only road nearby. If any Soviets or Communist sympathizers approached, the rangers would hold them up or re-route them away from the landing strip. This was not expected because this early in the morning there was little or no traffic on the roads. If any vehicles approached, the rangers would simply stop them and detour them around. On the other hand, if a well-armed force approached, they would not deter them as previously agreed. The Checkmate team would have to fend for themselves.

This was the primary reason why the two Polish agents were heavily armed. Both Jawor and Morena had four each MP-5 machine guns, four hand grenades and several hundred rounds of 9 mm ammunition. Hopefully, this would hold off a Soviet detail long enough for the team to escape.

Franko and Morena came back to the rest of the group, satisfied with the airfield, and reported to Vivian that they were ready to receive the airplanes. It was almost daybreak. The first aircraft was scheduled to arrive at sunrise. The second would follow minutes later. Franko took out his JE equipment and prepared the receiver. Vivian, set up a Marconi Mark III transmitter to send her fake message to her Swiss bank. Everything was set. All they had to do now was wait.

Five minutes out, the lead C-47, flown by an American crew prepared for landing at the clandestine airstrip. On board, the JE radio operator was manned by Sergeant Sanchez from Frankfurt G-2. He tuned his transmitter to the correct frequency and attempted to contact Franko. "Giant Killer to Checkmate, how do you read?"

Franko came back on his end of the JE, "Giant Killer, this is Redstone, I read you five-by-five. Surface winds are two-seven-zero at five knots. Ceiling and visibility are okay. Proceed with a left, downwind arrival for runway two-seven. I'll turn the beacon on now. Expect landing clearance."

Sanchez relayed this information to the pilot while he simultaneously descended the aircraft in preparation for landing.

Franko took his headset off and addressed the team. "They're inbound, five minutes away." Franko raised a pair of binoculars and scanned the horizon looking for the aircraft. The sun was just breaking over the ridgeline from behind when Franko saw the C-47. He put on the headset of his JE and contacted the aircraft. "Giant Killer, this is Redstone. I've got you visually. Proceed to my homing beacon. I'll flash the high-intensity light to signal your approach for landing. Good to see you."

This first C-47 touched down on the snow-covered field. Then the plane slowed to taxi speed. It made a one-hundred-degree turn and proceeded to the east end of the runway, where Franko was standing holding the homing beacon. He waved to the pilot and indicated the direction he wanted the plane to maneuver so the second aircraft would have room to turn around and depart. As the plane came closer to the team, Franko made the signal for the aircraft to make another one-hundred-eighty-degree turn, then stop. Franko went to the pilot's side of the aircraft and shouted to the pilot. "Don't switch off your engines! Keep them running!"

The back troop door opened and Sergeant Sanchez jumped down and motioned to Franko. Franko ran to the back of the aircraft and greeted his colleague. "Boy, I'm glad to see you. How far behind is the second aircraft?" he shouted over the noise of the engines.

"They're ten minutes late! Sorry, sir. They had some trouble along the way that put them five minutes behind schedule."

"We'll have to wait. Get back and tell the pilot to switch off his engines. We don't want all that noise. He'll have to start up as soon as the second plane lands."

"Right!" and Sanchez returned back to the aircraft to brief the pilot. A short time later, the C-47 engines came to a stop.

Franko came back to address the rest of the team.

"What's wrong, why did they shut down the engines?" asked Vivian.

"No problems, the other aircraft is running ten minutes late, that's all. I didn't want all that engine noise, possibly alerting someone of our presence. Quickly! Set up your wireless to make your transaction."

Vivian nodded in agreement. She came back and address Krupke and the other Germans. "The second airplane is ten-minutes late. They've shut their engines off to keep the noise down. Now, you and I need to finish our business before you leave."

The two made their transactions. Krupke gave his account number to transfer funds to Vivian's. The process was complete except for the ten-minute delay after departure. Vivian would send that request supposedly as soon as the aircraft was airborne, she told Krupke. He appeared satisfied.

"Much to my surprise, Miss Jankowski, you have held your end of the bargain. My apologies for mistrusting you in the beginning, but I had to have some guarantee you were who you said you were."

Vivian said or did nothing. She simply closed the suitcase radio transmitter and looked into the distance. Finally, she spoke, "We're still not out of the woods. That second aircraft hasn't arrived. Anything could happen. Don't forget, I have my guarantees too. You're going on that *second* aircraft." Vivian now motioned to Jawor. "Start the loading process. Get the scientists and the gyros on that aircraft. They depart as soon as the second aircraft touches down and turns around. Go!"

Jawor gave a signal to Franko that they needed to move. Franko, on prearranged instructions, indicated it was time to move the wagon so they could load the aircraft. All the men, Franko, Krupke, Hoch, Mangus, and Poldi, pushed the wagon out from the wooded area toward the aircraft. Luckily, it was not heavy, just cumbersome. The ground was still hard from the cold temperatures the past several days, and in no time the wagon was alongside the aircraft. Two crew members jumped down from the transport and gave instructions on how the gyro containers were to be loaded.

A short time later, the precious cargo, the advanced triple-mix V-2 guidance system known as the Inertial Guidance System, was onboard the C-47 ready for shipment to the United States. The men pushed the empty wagon back to the cover. Franko then instructed Krupke to wait by Vivian's side. Then he came to Hoch and Mangus. "You two men can now board the aircraft. Stay with the gyros until you land in Frankfurt. I'll be on the second aircraft, right behind you. If something should happen to me, at least the gyros will be in the hands of the Americans." Franko extended his hand out to the Germans. "I thought I'd never say this, but thank you for all your help."

Krupke said his farewells to the scientists, then Hoch and Mangus boarded the C-47. The American crew showed them their seats and briefed them on safety procedures. Shortly after this, the second C-47 was in radio contact with Franko. Jawor and Morena took up defensive positions to guard the airstrip. Each woman had her MP-5 machine guns ready. They could spray protective cover, giving the team enough time to escape if needed.

GREGORY M. ACUÑA

As soon as the second C-47 was in visual contact, Franko gave the signal for the first C-47 pilot to start engines. The engines started with no problems, and the crew hatch was closed. Franko motioned the pilot that he wanted him to taxi forward and slightly to the right, so the second C-47 could turnaround and depart. A short time later, Franko, using his JE, contacted the second aircraft and gave them landing clearance. The airplane touched down and maneuvered in the same manner as the first. As soon as the second C-47 turned around and faced to the west, Franko gave the first C-47 the signal to take off. There was some question about the obstacle terrain at the west end of the runway, but the C-47 had no problems taking off, and after a short takeoff roll, the C-47 with the Inertial Guidance System, Hoch and Mangus was airborne.

* * *

UNKNOWN TO THE Checkmate team at this time was that the first C-47 that landed had set up a holding pattern almost directly over Ludwikowice-Klodzkie at an extremely low altitude while they attempted to contact Franko. This maneuver woke up Colonel Pavel. He leaped out of bed just as the C-47 departed its holding pattern and flew to the east. He sent two teams in pairs. One on the northeast route the other on the southeast highway. The two teams would meet up at Jugow.

Sivan also awakened with the commotion. He called Pavel from his room telephone and asked what was going on. Pavel told him a C-47 was maneuvering overhead. They would investigate the matter, and Pavel emphasized that he wanted Sivan to stay at the safe house and wait for his orders. Pavel then left with the rest of the group. This time Pavel would not be caught by surprise. He knew that the Western team was led by competent individuals. They would almost certainly recognize the Soviet uniforms and the Russian language and would make another escape. He had an ace up his sleeve. He and his entire Third Department would dress in Polish Army uniforms and use American equipment left behind by Red Army units.

Chapter 43

It was too late for Pavel to do anything as he watched a C-47 fly by at low altitude. They could not even get a shot off. The plane had, however, just taken off from an airstrip nearby. The reception committee would almost certainly still be there. He ordered his three-vehicle Jeep formation to go off the main road and cut through the fields. As they did so, they came across an opening in a nearby area. It was amazing how this airfield was wholly hidden from the surrounding roads. The players were professionals, and he knew this was the team he was looking for. He only hoped he was not too late.

Franko heard the noise first as he came to Vivian and Krupke ,who were getting ready to board the second C-47. "Someone's coming."

It was too late. Pavel, dressed in a Polish Army uniform and riding in a Jeep mounted with a fifty caliber machine gun, came into view at full speed. They stopped just a few feet from the team. Pavel exited the Jeep, gave a signal for the rest of his team to surround the unit and then spoke in

Polish to Vivian. "What's going on here? We saw an airplane depart a few minutes ago."

Vivian was remarkably calm, but the rest of the team was in an utter state of terror upon seeing Polish Army soldiers. Vivian stepped forward and spoke in Polish. "What you saw was a Soviet transport taking a secret cargo back to Moscow."

Pavel now showed signs of disbelief upon hearing those words. Vivian told Pavel about the secret weapons recovered from the Die Riese site.

It was enough time for Jawor and Morena to come closer and get a good look at the Polish soldiers. Jawor recognized Pavel immediately. He was the same man who had shown up at the Hotel Bristol on the night of their holiday celebration. He was the same man who had worn the rank of colonel in the NKVD. He was not Polish but Russian, and he was probably the same man who had executed her long-time friend, Janica Kijowski. She did not allow Vivian to query further. Jawor slowly and methodically raised her pistol and shot Pavel point-bank between the eyes. Pavel didn't even have time to recognize Krupke. He crumpled to the ground in a heap of flesh. "They're Russians, not Polish!" she shouted.

Before anyone could move further, Jawor and Morena began to fire their MP-5 submachine guns in full, thirty round, automatic bursts, hitting the Soviets. Most of the team dropped to the ground for cover as bullets flew overhead. Then Morena shouted, "Get to the aircraft, we'll provide cover. Move!" she said as she emptied her thirty round magazine, then slapped in another. The two women moved to the cover of the second wagon with the older V-2 gyros.

The rest of the Soviets were caught off guard. Most were non-combat personnel and were quickly neutralized by the overwhelming and violent firepower from the two Polish women. Jawor not only took out Pavel but his driver and machine gunner on the Jeep. The NKVD men from the two other Jeeps quickly dropped for cover and tried to return fire with bolt-action rifles, a considerable disadvantage. Crewmembers from the C-47 were shouting for the rest of the team to hurry as Jawor and Morena continued to mow down their adversaries.

Franko recognized what was happening. He took out his Colt .45 and emptied the entire magazine out on the Russians. Then he grabbed Vivian and Krupke by the arms. "Let's go! It's our only way out!"

Franko led Vivian and Krupke to the waiting C-47, all the while crouching down, avoiding bullets flying everywhere. As they came to the aircraft, a crew member reached down to assist them. Franko hoisted Vivian up first, followed by Krupke. As soon as the two were on board, Franko leaped onto the C-47 floor. At this time Vivian turned to business. She made a signal to two more crew members, who were off to the side, and pointed to Krupke. The two men came forward and placed handcuffs on Krupke. The men spoke with a British accent. One of them said, "On behalf of His Majesty's service, you are now our prisoner, once again."

Krupke shouted obscenities to Vivian. "I should have known it was you!"

Vivian spoke over his harsh words. "Yes, I am a British agent. It's useless. You trusted us. Your greed got the better end of you, and you and I had a little debt to settle ourselves. Did you actually think I would forget about what you did to me? Checkmate."

Krupke continued to shout obscenities.

Franko was about to shut the crew hatch when he saw the carnage outside. Jawor and Morena were taking turns firing their weapons. One would fire a full thirty rounds, then the other would spring up and fire another, followed by grenades. Both women used several weapons as they quickly overheated from the repeated use. The C-47 was starting its taxi run for takeoff when Franko made a decision. He saw the Jeep with the fifty caliber machine gun unoccupied, dead Russians all around it. If he could get to it and return fire, it would give Jawor and Morena enough time to board the aircraft. If not, they would both perish. He shouted to Vivian.

"I can't leave them! I'm going after Jawor and Morena!"

Vivian came to Franko. "No, please! You'll be cut to pieces."

"I'm going to make a run for the fifty cal."

Vivian continued to shout, "They knew what the risks were, leave them!"

"Hey, I'm going to be your husband, remember? I'll be right back before you know it!"

Then he jumped down from the C-47 and ran for the machine gun. Vivian shouted to the crew. "Don't take off. Give him three minutes, then leave!"

Krupke saw and overheard the commotion. "Looks like you've got your own troubles on the chessboard. Check!"

Jawor and Morena were in the fight for their lives. Each weapon they were firing was overheating quickly, but it appeared the strategy was working as Morena saw Franko, Vivian, and Krupke board the C-47. Unfortunately, the Russians outnumbered them. Sooner or later, they would outflank them and take them out. They had no choice but to keep engaging. Then Jawor saw something she couldn't believe. Franko was running away from the C-47 toward the unoccupied Jeep. She motioned to Morena to what Franko was doing. Morena took out a grenade, pulled the pin, and threw it toward the Russians. The explosion flipped one of their Jeeps over.

* * *

SIVAN WAS NOT GOING to fail. As soon as Pavel left, he hoisted himself out of bed, got dressed, and took a Jeep that was remaining at the safe house. He turned on to the main road and headed toward Jugow. He took the quickest route, through the secret Nazi facility at Molke. As he came around the corner, heading to the Ranger Head-quarters, he saw the second C-47 fly overhead to the east. He followed the aircraft as it disappeared below the tree level. He continued to the East, hoping to find access to the landing site. It was at this time he heard the gunshots. He sped the Jeep up faster and cut across the fields. He finally saw the tail of a C-47 sticking out from the trees. He drove to that location, and then he saw the carnage. Bullets were flying everywhere. Dead bodies slung about. A C-47 with the engines running, waiting amid the gunshots.

Then he heard the explosion. A Jeep flipped over in flames. Sivan's Jeep came to a stop just before the battle zone. He could see Russian soldiers dressed in Polish uniforms frantically shouting at each other. A non-commis-sioned officer was giving instructions for an outflanking maneuver. That's when he could make out the figure of the familiar face. It was Major Antoni Franko pulling back the cocking mechanism on the Jeep-mounted fifty caliber machine gun. Bullets now began hitting the Russians and tearing men to pieces. Franko moved the machine gun from side to side, hitting everything in a twenty-meter arch; nothing survived. Most of the men didn't know what hit them. Then he could see Franko shouting at two women crouched down in a low spot. The two women stopped firing and ran to the C-47. It appeared that Franko's heroics were giving the women enough time to make an escape. He had to try and stop them, but Franko was still firing in his direction, and Sivan had no weapon.

Franko laid down cover fire with the fifty caliber and gave Jawor and Morena just enough time to make a run toward the C-47. He emptied the entire 250-round box magazine. As the dust and dirt settled, he could see no more movement from the Russians. He jumped down from the Jeep and ran back toward the C-47, leaving the older V-2 gyros abandoned on the wagon.

Sivan realized he was all alone and the lone survivor. He got up from his hiding place saw a rifle next to a dead soldier. He checked the gun and saw there was only one round left. Franko and the team were about to escape, and he would be left empty-handed. He struggled with his shattered arm, now in a cast, and took aim at the C-47 just as the two women were hoisted aboard. It was only Franko left on the ground, waiting his turn to board. Sivan looked carefully into the sight, took a deep breath, and fired. The round hit Major Antoni Franko in the abdomen, severing his spine.

Vivian was reaching down to grab Franko's arm when she realized he'd been hit. "Someone help me, please! He's been hit!" To her amazement, the one closest was Krupke. His hands were cuffed so he couldn't physically help her. Finally, one of the crew members jumped down and grabbed Franko and hoisted him aboard. Franko rolled over in excruciating pain. Blood was pouring from his side. The crewman closed the hatch, and the C-47 began its takeoff roll.

Vivian clutched Franko's face and shouted, "Tony, can you hear me? Please hang on. We're almost home."

Vivian could tell by his wounds that he was in serious

trouble. He was losing a lot of blood, and his body was motionless.

The two military policemen tried to give first aid, but they had nothing to combat the seriousness of Major Franko's wounds. One of the MPs looked at Vivian. "I'm afraid it doesn't look good, ma'am. He's probably not going to make it. Hell of an act he pulled off back there. He saved all of us."

Vivian couldn't believe what she was seeing. Franko coughed twice; each time, blood came up from his mouth. Then there was nothing. The remaining Checkmate team sat and could do nothing. Morena started to cry. Then Franko's heart stopped beating.

Krupke sat in disbelief as he witnessed, heard, and saw the entire event. "He was a brave man Miss Jankowski. Checkmate to you."

Colonel Sivan watched as the second C-47 broke ground and turned to the west. He was all alone on the snow-capped field. Then he saw something that caught his attention. A wooden cart with a sturdy wooden box resting on its side in the bed. It had never made it onboard the aircraft. He smiled ever so slightly.

Epilogue

Dame Irina Jankowski (aka Vivian Tate), OBE, emerged from her small, modest flat at number Sixteen Lexham Gardens. The war years and post-war years had taken their toll on the forty-seven-year-old knight. Except on this day, she had a car and driver to take her to work at Broadway Street. She locked her front door, then walked down the steps to her car waiting at the curb. Her MI-6 driver opened the rear passenger door for her.

"Good morning, ma'am. In the back. He's waiting. It's rather important business, I'm told."

Irina didn't respond or acknowledge. She simply stepped into the back seat. As she moved into the car, the driver quickly closed the door and then drove off. Seated in the back was none other than General Stanley Cameron, her personal assistant.

He didn't beat around the bush with pleasantries this time. All he said was, "The Soviets just launched a satellite into Earth's orbit, Sputnik I. The question is, *how come?* We had all the best scientists and the Inertial Guidance System."

Irina placed a Silver Service cigarette between her lips, "General, I paid dearly for this one. We'll have to find out, won't we?"

"Yes we will. He was my colleague too. Looks like you've got a busy schedule today, C."

Author's Conlcusion

On April 16, 1946, after months of testing and research, the first "captured" German V-2 rocket was launched from White Sands, New Mexico, by the von Braun team. Shortly thereafter, every major aerospace company in the US was bidding for a government contract to develop and build a guided missile for the military. This was the beginning of the space race.

By 1957, the Gyro/Flight Guidance Genie was out of the bottle. The Redstone/Jupiter rocket used an improved, domestic guidance system developed in conjunction with MIT and the Chrysler Corporation, called the Ford ST-80, Inertial Guidance System. There is a high probability that scientists at MIT and Chrysler back-engineered advanced German V-2 guidance systems designed for the A-9 and A-10 Amerika rockets with the help from 'captured' German scientists.

In June 1958, the PGM-11 Redstone ballistic missile entered service with the US Army in West Germany. It was the first US missile to carry a live nuclear warhead. The Redstone was a direct descendant of the German V-2 rocket developed by a team of predominantly German rocket scientists brought to the United States after World War II, part of a ratline initially known as Operation Overcast.

The Redstone design (Jupiter Class) used an upgraded, gimbaled engine that allowed the missile to carry a 3.8 megaton nuclear warhead with incredible accuracy for that time. A significant effort by the von Braun team improved the Redstone's reliability and produced one of the most capable rockets of the era. This included several milestones, notably the first US unmanned satellite (*Explorer One*) and the first US astronaut (Alan Shepard in a Mercury *Freedom 7* capsule) on top of a Redstone rocket.

On July 16, 1969, almost twenty years after the first V-2 test launch at White Sands, Apollo 11 lifted off on top of the Saturn V launch vehicle. The Saturn V, developed by Wernher von Braun, was nothing more than a gigantic version of the original German V-2 rocket using an enhanced triple-mix, inertial guidance system.

Finally, up until the end of the Cold War, the Soviet Union could never fully develop an accurate and reliable guidance system for their ballistic missiles. Despite the best efforts by Sergei Korolev, and his rocket team the Soviets could only back-engineer so much. They relied on home-grown versions far inferior and less accurate than the US systems. They also never fully-developed accurate and reliable Multiple Independently Targeted Reentry Vehicles (MIRVs), though they supposedly possessed them in their arsenal. The Soviets did, however, make up for this shortfall by developing larger and more powerful nuclear warheads. To put things in perspective, the Tsar Bomba was a fifty megaton warhead 3,800 times more powerful than the plutonium device dropped on Nagasaki, Japan.

Today, modern jetliners use Air Data Inertial Reference Units (ADIRU) or systems for attitude stabilization and guidance along with global positioning satellites for navigation. The ADIRU is nothing more than an enhanced and modernized V-2 guidance system developed during World War II.

To this day, the Die Glocke (The Bell) and the activity at the Die Riese (The Giant) site are the greatest unsolved mysteries of World War II.

About the Author

This is Gregory M. Acuña's fourth book. He is currently writing his fifth book, another Cold War Thriller about a U.S. Army officer who tries to sell Pershing II Missile deployment information to the Soviets. However, his beautiful East German contact is also a double agent working for the Americans and East German intelligence.

Gregory M. Acuña is a former USAF pilot and current B-777 Captain for a major U.S. air carrier.

f

As a way of saying thank you, for purchasing this book, I am offering a free copy of my second book, The *Balkan Network* when you join my Reader's Group at:

WWW.GMACUNA.COM

More books by Gregory M. Acuña

Available in ebook, print and audio formats at all online stores.

Credible Dagger

The Balkan Network

Nimble Dodger

author@gmacuna.com